My name is Jara

She came up behind him, quiet as a cat, and plunged the knife into his heart. His eyes bulged with horror and pain, stricken not only by the act itself but by the look in her eyes.

"My name is Jara," she hissed, "daughter of Benjamin, born on the Masada. Daughter of Rachel, whom your men raped and sold." He made a small gurgling sound as she withdrew the dagger only to plunge it into his chest.

"Jara!" she said again, her voice low, throbbing, yet barely more than a whisper, "Sister of Sharona, whose life you destroyed!" She saw his mouth twitch and watched the light go out of his eyes, then placed one hand on his throat and pulled the knife out of his body.

Berkley books by Brenda Lesley Segal

IF I FORGET THEE
THE TENTH MEASURE

BRENDA LESLEY SEGAL

If I Forget Thee

BERKLEY BOOKS, NEW YORK

This Berkley book contains the complete
text of the original hardcover edition.
It has been completely reset in a typeface
designed for easy reading, and was printed
from new film.

IF I FORGET THEE

A Berkley Book / published by arrangement with
St. Martin's Press

PRINTING HISTORY
St. Martin's edition published 1983
Berkley edition / November 1985

ISBN: 0-425-08384-5

A BERKLEY BOOK® TM 757,375
Berkley Books are published by The Berkley Publishing Group,
200 Madison Avenue, New York, New York 10016.
The name "BERKLEY" and the stylized "B" with design
are trademarks belonging to Berkley Publishing Corporation
PRINTED IN THE UNITED STATES OF AMERICA

Contents

If I forget thee, O Jerusalem,
    let my right hand lose its cunning;

Let my tongue cleave to the roof of my mouth,

If I do not set Jerusalem above
    my highest joy.

—PSALMS

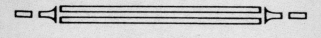

BOOK I

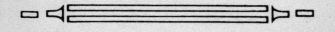

1

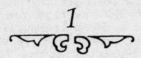

IT IS WRITTEN that for want of an axle the city of Betar was destroyed, and for want of Betar all Israel was lost. But on the day the Lady Livia's carriage broke down, the inhabitants of Betar, many miles south of Tiberias, where the Roman *matrona* sought the healing hot springs, were hardly aware of their place in history. And Israel was only a province called Judea, a poor piece of Roman property tucked away in the larger Syrian domain, a rough and ragged bit of land still struggling to recover from its disastrous bid for freedom in the last days of Nero.

Nearly sixty years had passed since the fall of Masada, where the last rebels against Rome had chosen finally to take their own lives rather than surrender. Their demise had prompted the emperor Vespasian to breathe a private sigh of relief and to say, notwithstanding his public declaration of victory some three years earlier, "Now, at last, it is over."

But is it over? mused Marcellus Quintus, the centurion accompanying the Lady Livia, as he absently studied the road ahead. *Is it?*

"The thing you've got to remember is that the Jews don't give up," Plinius, an ancient veteran of the Tenth Legion, had said only the night before. "They fight past hope or reason. And for what? A God no one can see and a patch of land not worth a half denarius. If it was up to me I'd leave them to themselves. A few months without us and they'll be killing each other off, that's how crazy they are. And don't make the mistake of thinking kindness will change them," he'd added.

3

"Look what happened when Trajan tried to be a good fellow. Promised they might rebuild their holy Temple, didn't he? And the minute the emperor turns his back, the Jews in Cyprus up and start another bloody war. And now, Hadrian. He keeps saying all he wants is peace. Goes and gets rid of Quietus because that long-legged rabbi, whatsisname, Akiva, complains the governor's too rough. And meanwhile that skinny crane is just waiting for the chance to start something. Oh, I see it coming, centurion! I tell you, it's still not over. The way that rabbi's been cozying up to the new governor, Tinneus Rufus. . . . Mark my words, Akiva's got something up his long sleeves. And I'll bet my bloody pension it's the short sword."

"But Hadrian has given the Jews every promise of friendship," Quintus had broken in. "As you say, he has recalled Quietus, appointed a new governor, and let it be known he desires to rebuild Jerusalem. It makes no sense for this rabbi of yours—this Akiva—to be planning another rebellion."

"He's no rabbi of mine," Plinius had growled. "And nothing the Jews do makes sense anyway. You're new to the country, centurion, but you'll soon find out all I say is true. To the Jews a kind Roman master is as bad as a wicked one. Nothing will do but they must have no master at all, except their God, who's never done them any good far as I can tell."

"Hadrian can help these people. He can improve their lives—"

"Beg pardon, centurion, but that's not what they think," he'd tried to explain. "Their lives are ruled by their own Law. Torah, they call it. They say the Torah is everlasting, that it was given to them by their God. They say that so long as they have their Torah, why, no matter what anyone does to them or how many of them may be killed, they can never be destroyed."

"Well, a war now would be madness," Quintus had replied, still thinking of Hadrian's promises and the reforms being instituted throughout the Empire. "And though I have been in Judea only a short time, I see no signs of one in the making," he'd added. "It seems to me the people are fully occupied in rebuilding the country, which, from all accounts, suffered grievously under Titus' assault. As for the rabbis—and this Akiva appears to be no exception—they are cooperating fully with our officials. The governor himself declares they are the first to bring forth any evidence of mischief, so anxious are they to keep the peace."

"Maybe so, centurion, maybe so. But I've been here a long, long time. And I know this: The Jews may want peace, but they also want us *out*. They talk about a man to come, a leader who will restore their Kingdom of Israel. They call him *messiah*. All I'm saying is, keep your eye sharp and your hand close to your sword. There is no love in this land for men like us."

Men like us, Quintus thought, amused at the comparison between the old foot soldier and himself. But Plinius was right about one thing: A soldier of Rome should always keep his eye sharp and his hand close to his sword, no matter how pleasant the way ahead appeared.

It was late winter, and the hills of the Galilee were a lush green. The air was still fragrant with rain that had fallen during the night. Flowers were beginning to appear by the side of the road, and the young almond trees were flecked with pale blossoms. The sun felt kind on his shoulders, and Marcellus Quintus knew he was happier than he had been for a long time. His friends thought he was mad to return to the legions, but after the death of his wife, he was determined to get away from Rome and all that reminded him of that lovely woman. There were no children, no ties. He might have requested a higher position, but he liked the office of centurion and the intimacy with the rank and file that accompanied it. In any case, he answered only to the emperor, although on the surface he would appear of ordinary station.

The road, he reflected, was a fine piece of Roman work; as he surveyed it, he could not help thinking with satisfaction of the race to which he belonged and which he now represented. Rome had founded an empire that included nearly all the civilized world. Moreover, the Empire had not only conquered the world, it had unified it, connected it by means of laws common to all the provinces, by a kind of universal language (Greek for cultural, Aramaic for commercial exchange), and, in the most practical sense, by splendid highways that stretched from country to country. The Galilee alone was covered with roads like this one, not only to and from points within Judea, but from Egypt to Assyria, from the sea to the desert, from the Phoenician coast to Samaria, Gilead, and Damascus.

And everywhere, the centurion thought, *there is peace. Even, finally, in Rome.* The excesses of rulers like Nero were a thing of the past, a matter now of anecdote and history, best forgotten, although the writer Suetonius, Hadrian's curator of archives, was preparing a large work on the twelve Caesars. But certainly that was in keeping with the emperor's intellectual pursuits and reflected no desire to emulate even a Domitian, who'd had his streak of cruelty, let alone a Caligula. No, those days were gone. Hadrian was "the Good Emperor"; he had ushered in what was already being called a golden age, for surely there had never been a time so filled with prosperity and contentment.

The earth daily becomes more civilized, the centurion thought. *Everything is accessible, known. Hadrian has done what no ruler before him had been able to accomplish: he has made the Empire whole.*

"Rome and its provinces must come together," the emperor had said to Quintus. "We must be one."

And we shall be, the man pledged silently.

"How fierce you look, centurion."

The woman's voice startled him, brought him out of his reverie no less for having broken the rhythmic rumble of carriage wheel and horse's hoof than for its own quality.

Rufina Livia, the wife of Judea's military governor, was a pretty woman, pale and petite, with soft, fair hair and blue eyes that seemed always to appear startled or apprehensive. She was thin, too thin even to be called slender, and she seemed to drift through the halls of the palace in Caesarea like an apparition, hardly more substantial than the gauzy fabric of her gown. Quintus always felt as if he should plant himself before her with drawn sword, to defend her not only from human assassins but from moths, birds, butterflies; she seemed so slight, so vulnerable. He was always amazed when she spoke, for her voice was low and throaty, a voluptuous instrument sending forth the startling information that inside this childlike, fragile figure a woman really lived.

He cleared his throat. "I was thinking of Rome, lady."

"Ah. And duty, I suppose. That would explain the determined thrust of your jaw."

"I see you've been studying me."

"And hoping you might talk to me. Do you realize, Marcellus Quintus, how many miles have gone by without a word between us?"

"Your pardon, mistress, I did not mean to be discourteous. I am charged with getting you to Tiberias safely. The road is new to me. I must keep my mind on the way ahead."

"From the look in your eyes I would say you have in fact been far away."

"On the contrary. My thoughts are all on Judea."

"Do you find the province interesting, then?"

"I do not yet know it. This is my first real journey outside Caesarea."

"That's right, I'd forgotten. You have only been with us a few weeks. Tell me, what are your impressions thus far?"

"Too soon to say. On the surface I see only a small, sleepy land more poor than rich, more countrified than city-bred. There appears to be no distinguishing art or architecture, and notwithstanding legends of ferocious warriors like the Maccabee or the Zealot Sicarii of the last war, the Judeans are unimposing in look or attitude. I've known Jews in Rome whose cultural refinement and knowledge earned them deserved praise, but these people seem hardly capable of art or war."

"Don't be misled by appearances, centurion. For all we've done to them, their spirit is not broken."

Startled, he regarded her quizzically. Was that pride in her voice? And if it was, why would the wife of Tinneus Rufus harbor such a sentiment for a subject race so universally despised?

She sensed the question behind his stare. With new gaiety she asked, "Do you miss Rome?"

He was still disturbed. He'd already accepted her as the quiet, shy creature she'd presented in Caesarea. And there was something in her eyes now, as though she were seeking something from him. "Do you?" he asked bluntly.

The blue eyes took on their familiar, startled expression. She stared at him a moment. Then, quite simply, she said, "No."

It was his turn to be startled, but she offered no explanation. Instead, she remarked formally in a voice from which all music had fled, "You are quite right, of course, to occupy yourself with duty. The roads are never safe."

"Rebels, I suppose."

"Bandits. The Samaritans seem to have made a virtual profession of thievery. And there are any number of renegade soldiers—bands of legionaries who have settled in Judea and no doubt find life hard."

He frowned. "Legionaries riding with highwaymen?"

She laughed. "What a noble product of Rome you are! Does that seem so incredible? But surely a man who has learned to live by the sword must find it difficult to take up the plow." She tilted her head a bit, studying him with a small smile. "I can't imagine you as a farmer."

"Perhaps not. But neither can I see myself a thief. Nor any of my men," he added.

"Oh, you are noble indeed," she murmured. "But then, you are of an old aristocratic family, are you not? Your father was a senator, and you are, my husband has said, friend to Hadrian."

"I have been honored on occasion by the emperor's company," he admitted stiffly.

"But he is truly your friend?"

"Caesar is friend to all citizens of the Empire."

"Well," she said mischievously, "if he really cares for you, you may find yourself wondering one day why he has sent you to Judea."

"I am here, lady, not because of the emperor's affection for me but because of my love for him and for Rome." With that and a brief nod he urged his horse forward, thereby ending what he considered a strange conversation. But her remarks made him wonder and set him to thinking again of old Plinius' warnings. It was in the midst of these thoughts that he found himself staring at a figure still as a statue on a hill ahead. Instinctively his hand went to his sword, but as his horse carried him nearer, he relaxed his grip.

It was only a girl. A child. She did not move from the great gnarled oak against which she was poised, her back slightly arched—like some nymph of the wood. Her hair, a heavy, sunlit mass of curls suddenly lifted by the breeze bending the branches above her head, blew wildly about, strands licking her neck like tongues of chestnut flame. Quintus stared at her, charmed by the image she presented, which reminded him of a poet's fable or tale of the gods.

The road veered sharply to the right. As Quintus rode below

the promontory on which the girl stood, he deliberately looked up at her, about to offer a benevolent greeting, but the smile died on his lips.

Her eyes were very large and very light, her face curiously catlike. All this would have been beguiling but for the fact that she was staring back at the centurion with a look of hatred so pure it was chilling.

There is no love in Judea for men like us, the old legionary had said.

If the emperor cares for you, why has he sent you here? the wife of Judea's governor had wanted to know.

Marcellus Quintus turned his horse around and rode back to the carriage lumbering slowly down the muddy road, suddenly awakened to the necessity of guarding the fragile lady in his care.

THE CHILD on the hill watched the carriage with its escort of soldiers and servants disappear from view. She considered throwing some rocks in its direction but dismissed the action as inconsequential. What were a few stones? What she really needed was a sword. With a grin and a sudden, quick gesture, she snatched up a branch lying nearby and proceeded to attack the tree from which it had fallen with vicious enthusiasm.

"Take that!" she cried. "And that! Think we are cowards, do you? Little better than dogs, you say. Well, by the Almighty, you shall learn what a liar you are, mighty Caesar, Lord of Pigs!" She began to dance around the oak now, in high spirits, whacking away at the great, gnarled trunk until the branch in her hand finally splintered and broke. Then, laughing, she threw herself down on the damp grass and, seeing now the small cat which had watched her antics with some curiosity, laughed again.

"You think I'm mad, don't you, Jezebel? Well, I'm not. And I'm no coward either!" She made a face. "Not like everyone else around here. It was different once," she went on dreamily. "The Galilee was the home of warriors. Men like John of Gischala, who defended Jerusalem. And Judah of Gamala, who fought wicked King Herod. And Eleazar ben Ya'ir, who led the people of Masada," she added, going back and forth in time, wonderfully indifferent to chronology. "Once, the people of Judea stood proud. All the young men were warriors—good as any legionary. They didn't sit all day with their noses pressed to books, with soft faces and soft hands," she said, stroking the cat, which had climbed into her lap. "You know, Jezebel, when Father was alive, I met a scholar from Jabneh, where the rabbis have their Council and great house of study. Why, I could have toppled him over with one breath! *Poof!* Like that!"

The cat responded to the sudden gust of air on its fur by leaping out of the girl's lap. Again the child laughed and, getting to her feet in a movement as quick and fluid as the animal's, started down the hill. She was tall for her twelve years, long-limbed but fine-boned, her features an intriguing blend of sensitivity and budding sexuality. She had already forgotten the Roman, but as she drew closer to home her high spirits noticeably ebbed. The joyous run down the hill turned into a leisurely skip on the road and soon became an even slower walk. By the time the girl entered the village, her step was sullen; her expression had become inscrutable, contained.

Kefar Katan was an old settlement, older than most, though not large enough to boast a wall or ten men rich enough to hire laborers, which were the marks of a real town. Clustered together, nestled among the hills of the Galilee, the small houses were built over those destroyed by Vespasian in his march across the North. Those in turn had been erected atop structures razed by Antiochus the Greek, in the time of the Maccabee, which had gone up over Amorite dwellings sitting on the ruins of Caananite huts. A piece of broken pottery lying on the ground in Kefar Katan might have been there a day or a year or a century; whole ages had settled over the village like the seasons of a single year.

The girl stopped to pet one of the goats which had gotten loose. For twenty years following the war, the rabbis had forbidden the people to breed these animals, as they were prone to destroy the saplings newly planted in the devastated land.

Her next stop was at a small cottage. Sheaves of barley over the door and windows signified its recent construction.

"Look, Jezebel," the girl told the cat, which was now rubbing its back against the doorpost. "This is where Sharona will live after her wedding tomorrow. Isn't it lovely? Of course, it's not so fine as the house my grandmother lived in, nor any of her family, but I wouldn't mind it for myself." She sighed. "Anything would be better than staying with Arnon and Batya. Except maybe living with Nathan. Poor Sharona. I don't envy her that. Nathan may be a scholar, but I think he's stupid."

The cat meowed.

The girl laughed. "I knew you'd agree. Come on, we'd best go home. Batya will no doubt have a hundred chores waiting."

Jezebel seemed not to think much of this and ambled away, leaving the girl to enter the home of her half brother and his wife alone.

Batya was suckling the newborn. Another child, a boy of two, sat on the floor, tugging at his mother's skirt. The woman looked up, saw the girl, and frowned. "Where have you been? There is work, you know. I can't do it all myself. You're supposed to help."

The girl said nothing. Her face was expressionless; its blank stare served only to irritate Batya further. "Don't look at me like that," the woman said angrily. "I can't help it if your brother is too poor to hire servants. The Almighty knows your father left us nothing but the care of you. Avram! Stop pulling at me! You will drive me mad! I cannot feed you until I finish with the baby!"

The girl went over to a small cupboard and took out a piece of bread, which she gave the child. "Here, Avi, eat this. Come, we'll wash your face, yes? Would you like that?"

"His hands are filthy. The Almighty knows what he has found to play with. If you'd been here where you belong . . ."

"Where is Sharona?"

The woman was busy with the infant and did not answer.

"Where is my sister?"

Batya looked up. "Sister? She's not your sister. The Almighty alone knows how you are related, what with the number of wives your father had. Judging from your character," she added spitefully, "I would say you are no kin at all. There never was a sweeter soul than Sharona, nor a kinder heart, nor—"

"A more willing slave for you and everyone else to command," the girl finished.

"Oh, you are cheeky! It's a wonder Sharona puts up with you at all! I daresay she's the only friend you have. No one in the village likes you, any more than they cared for your mother when she was alive. Well, we'll see how close you and

Sharona remain after tomorrow. When a girl weds she must think only of her husband, and it isn't likely Nathan will want you around, filling his bride's head with all your nonsense.''

"It isn't nonsense! Sharona must not forget! We are descended from a great house—"

"With the Messiah himself likely to drop out from between your legs, I suppose." Batya laughed. "Listen to me, you little wretch. No one around here cares a fig for what happened long ago. The war with Rome is over. It was over when my own parents were born. It's done with. There is peace now, and that is all that matters. Let the rabbis worry about Jerusalem and the Temple. As for me, I'd like a new robe. Now get this room swept before your brother returns. He hates a dirty house.''

Her face once more a mask, the girl started for the broom.

"I almost forgot," Batya said suddenly. "The Old One wants to see you. She's dying," she added with some satisfaction.

The girl smiled slightly. "The Old One will never die."

"God forbid! Just what I need! The two of you here forever! She living on and on, and you with no chance of marrying until your flow commences. Well, have there been any signs?"

The girl shook her head.

"And so tall you are. . . . It's a mark of evil, I daresay. Well, there you are, my fine princess! For all your glorious past! Any farmer's daughter your age would be betrothed by now. And you not yet a woman. You will have a hard time making babies, you'll see. When the flow comes late, a woman has difficulty bearing children, if indeed she can have them at all. You know," she added with some satisfaction, "it is a curse from God to be childless. Avram! Stop pulling at me!" She smoothed her skirt and smiled. "Now I, on the other hand, am not descended from princes and priests, but I—Where are you going? Come back! The room is not swept!"

But the girl was already out the door.

THE HOUSE OF Arnon the physician was the typical "four space" dwelling of the Israelite: a number of rooms grouped along three sides of an open courtyard. An upper story would have been a mark of affluence, but Arnon was not a wealthy man or even a very good doctor. If he was, he might have lived in nearby Tiberias, where Herod had built a palace and where now the Roman commander of the Galilee made his headquarters. Certainly the hot springs of Ammatha, outside Tiberias but considered part of the city, would have drawn a steadier stream of patients. But something—politics, perhaps, or his own vagaries of character, or a combination of events and personality—had conspired to see him settled in this small, undistinguished village.

What was more curious to some was the fact that his father, also a doctor, had chosen to live in Kefar Katan rather than Caesarea or Lydda or Jericho or, if he were a truly pious man, in Jabneh, seat of the great Academy of Learning. Benjamin—Arnon's father—had been a curious man in many ways, not least of which was the matter of his three wives. The first was a childhood sweetheart unable to bear children, as was proved by the fact that his second wife, taken after the death of the first, bore him two daughters and two sons. The younger boy was killed by bandits. The second wife and both daughters died during an epidemic in the early days of Trajan's reign, leaving Arnon and several grandchildren, one of whom was Sharona, the bride-to-be. Soon after the death of his second wife and children, the physician went on a journey to Caesarea, disappearing for some months. When he returned he had a new bride: a silent, aloof young woman hardly older than his grandchildren. A year later she died in childbirth, leaving a girl-child who had not grown to look much like Arnon or Sharona or any of the physician's other issue—nor even much like the woman who had borne her. Still, no one could doubt she was Benjamin's daughter; there was something of him in her eyes, in the set of her chin and the length of her long legs, even in the way she held her head with its mane of brown curls streaked with gold. Nor was there any doubt that he doted upon her; it was as if he had found something in this child which he had long sought. She seemed generally unkempt, however, a wild little thing whose robe was always too short, whose hair sorely needed combing. At first the Old One had cared for her, even as she had once been the father's nurse. But time finally turned that ancient female feeble, and there was no one to look after the household but the child herself. She did not seem to mind this; from the beginning she exhibited a strong, independent spirit. And if she was lonely, kept from the other children by parents who had not liked her mother or found the aging doctor, his old nurse, and his waiflike daughter too eccentric to associate with, she did not seem to mind this either.

Soon after the girl turned ten, the physician was killed in a flash flood similar to those which had wreaked havoc upon the Roman camp the winter that Silva besieged Masada. Curiously, it was in that very vicinity that the doctor died, it being his habit to ride periodically into the desert where the great cliff fortress stood. The child was taken in by her half brother, who alone would receive her, and by his wife, who was openly reluctant about the matter. Nor was Batya thrilled to inherit the caretaking of the Old One, who, it was said, was more than a hundred years old. It was the girl now who saw to the Old One's needs. But for the crone, the kind-hearted Sharona, and a stray cat she'd named Jezebel, the child was truly alone.

THE OLD ONE rarely left her quarters now. Sometimes, in that moment when the sun plunged behind the hills, the girl would help her outside and turn her toward the sea and listen as she murmured to the racing orb and the pale moon that took its place. At such times, the Old One did not speak Aramaic, the language of Judea, or Hebrew, the tongue of Torah and common bond of Jews all over the world. It was a kind of Greek the woman spoke, and though the girl often asked her the meaning of her prayers and incantations, the Old One would not answer. "You must learn the ways of your own people," was all she would say. But she did teach the girl what she knew of roots and herbs and the power natural things had to heal and help the puny creatures who believed themselves lords of the earth.

Slowly the girl entered the room which had become the old woman's entire world. The place was dark and quiet. In such dim light the bundle on the mat in the corner might have been a storage jar or pile of rags; it might have been only a shadow rather than the huddled figure of a woman crouched there.

The girl hesitated, taking in the odor of the room, the scent she had learned to associate as the woman's from earliest days. It was a stale, bittersweet perfume: the incense of brown, fallen leaves, of dust and wind mixed with the smell of herbs and roots in the little bags tied to a rope around the Old One's waist. For a moment, the girl wanted to leave, to run outside again, where the sun was bright and the air filled with the scent of fresh, familiar life. But the woman had already sensed her presence.

"Eh? Who is it? Who's there?"

She took a step forward. "It is I. You called for me."

"Eh? Who?" The black eyes—eyes that seemed to see everything while revealing nothing—were like dark jewels glittering among the shadows. "Come closer. Let me look at you."

The girl moved forward again; again, hesitated. The odor in the room was different today; something new was present, a scent she could not define. Perhaps the Old One was dying after all.

"You ought to lie down," the girl said. "You must rest on something soft, with a warm blanket. Let me fetch one for you. The room is damp."

"Stay, stay . . ." Blanket and bed were waved away. "There is no need of anything between me and the earth. We are one. Or will be soon enough." There was a sound that might have been a laugh.

The girl was silent.

"But it is kind of you to offer. My daughter . . . my little owl . . ." Her voice trailed off, her eyes closed.

The girl waited.

"Come closer," the woman said once more, opening her eyes again. "Closer." She studied the girl intently, then sighed. "For a moment, I thought . . . but you are not my little owl. You are the one with the eyes of the cat. Eyes like my mistress had. . . ." Again her voice trailed away.

The girl remained silent. She was used to this. The Old One often mistook her for someone she called Little Owl, and another whom she called Mistress. Often the Old One spoke of things and people of which the girl had no knowledge.

"How are you called, Cat-Eyes? I have forgotten. . . ."

"I am Jara."

"Jara." She nodded. "For the one the Romans call Ben Jarius. Eleazar, who led the people of Masada. Your grandfather." She chuckled. "Your own father was a grandfather himself when he took your mother to wife. Yes? Is it not so?"

"Yes."

"From where did she come? I have forgotten. . . ."

"I don't know. She died at my birth."

The woman nodded again. "She was too small in the hip. A fool could see she was too small. Stand up. Let me look at you. You are tall. Proud and tall, like the one for whom you are named. How old are you now?"

"Nearly thirteen, I think."

"To whom are you promised?"

"No one. None of the families wants me." She shrugged. "Anyway, my flow has not begun."

"No?" The woman was surprised. "Never mind. It is for the best. Soon enough they will buzz around you like bees to honey."

It was the girl's turn to be surprised. "Buzz around . . . me?"

"As they did my mistress. But there is no one worthy here. They are sheep. They know nothing but to pray to their God and rub their noses on the boots of the soldiers." She spat. "Sheep. And the droppings of sheep."

"Not my father," the girl protested, her chin coming up.

"He was a good man," the Old One acknowledged grudgingly. "He chose the way of the healer. I remember now . . ."

"He was a wonderful physician."

"Good enough. But too gentle for this world. He let that woman, that piece of Galilean rubbish, make his life a misery."

"Who? Arnon's mother? Was she like Batya?" The girl frowned. "I thought everyone loved Father."

"Until he took your mother to wife."

"Why?" She knelt beside the Old One again. "Was she so terrible?"

"Who knew what she was or would be? She was not around very long. When she was alive she kept to herself, even with me. The people of Katan did not like this. Nothing is private in a place like this. Whoever withholds anything is thought sullen, proud. The people did not like your mother's silence, or that your father took a stranger to wife, one younger even than his own sons and daughters. That is why they do not treat you well. But listen. Listen to me." She leaned forward. "The others, they are dirt. They treat you like dirt, but it is they who are nothing. Your grandfather was Eleazar ben Ya'ir, whom the Romans call Ben Jarius, commander of the Masada. Your grandmother was—'' Her voice seemed to break here, to catch in a kind of sob. "Your grandmother was the woman Alexandra,'' she continued finally, "daughter of the great House of Harsom, and of the line of David. Your father was born on the Masada. Born free. With the blood in him of kings and priests.''

The girl nodded. She had heard all this many times over from the Old One.

"Do not forget who you are. Do not forget the blood from which you come. The others will say it is nothing. But it is everything. It is what you are. Let no one take this from you.'' Exhausted, the woman sank back against the wall. But she was not finished. "Soon your flow will come,'' she said softly. "You will be a woman. I will not be here to help you or in the time ahead. You must take your strength from yourself, little cat. The earth, too, will make you strong and comfort you.''

"The rabbis say the Lord is our strength.''

"Then let the rabbis look to the Lord.''

The girl grinned.

"No,'' the Old One quickly amended, a look of fear or uncertainty crossing her features. "No, I do not mean the God of Israel is without power. It may be only that I cannot comprehend His plan. In any case, the time is near when I shall know the things I have long wished to understand. Last night I dreamed I died and was laid to rest. I could feel the weight of the earth on my breast. It was a good weight. Heavy, like a man. Trees grew from my palms, I could feel them growing out of my hands. And I could feel the rain on my face, washing me away, carrying me to the sea. . . .'' Her voice drifted off.

After some moments Jara decided the Old One had fallen asleep and rose to leave. The woman's voice stopped her at the door.

"Do not forget, little cat. Do not forget who you are.''

THE SUN made her blink. Entering and emerging from the Old One's room was like going back and forth in time or between worlds. Jara had no real conception of any Deity, but she could well imagine the Old One talking to God—much more so, in fact, than the rabbi of Katan.

Catching sight of a pretty young girl with long dark hair,

Jara's face lit up. She broke into a run, legs, arms, and curly mane flying. "Sharona! Wait! Wait for me!"

The dark-haired girl turned and smiled.

"Where have you been all morning?" Jara wanted to know, falling into step beside her.

"At the *mikveh*. The ritual bath is prescribed for all brides."

"Ah, I'd forgotten." Her lips turned up impishly. "Did the rabbi see you without your clothes?"

"Jara!"

"Nathan will see you without your clothes," she went on. "Tomorrow night."

Sharona blushed.

"Are you scared?"

The girl did not answer.

"I've seen a naked man," Jara offered casually.

Sharona stared in disbelief.

"It's true. When father was alive. We came upon a fellow the soldiers had beaten and left for dead. There was a great deal of blood, and he moaned so. They had done terrible things to him, I guess."

"And grandfather let you stay?"

"I helped. I really did, Sharona. I put my fingers on the places father told me to press, so as to stop the spill of blood. It was wonderful. I mean, the way the bleeding stopped. Father said I was a good aide. He said I would make a good physician because I didn't flinch from the sight of opened flesh. It's true," she said thoughtfully. "It didn't bother me at all."

Sharona shuddered. "I would have fainted."

"I know." She shrugged. "I don't think I'll ever faint."

"You would if you saw something really horrible. Or if someone was about to hurt you terribly."

"No, I wouldn't. I don't know why, but I wouldn't." She grinned. "Will you faint tomorrow night? With Nathan?"

Sharona blushed again, then drew herself up in serious fashion. "You ought not talk so," she reprimanded gently. "It is not seemly."

"Pooh to that!"

Despite herself, Sharona broke out laughing. "Oh, Jara," she cried, hugging the girl, who, although two years younger, was the same height as herself. "You always make me laugh! I don't know what I'd do without you!"

"Then we will still be friends when you are wed?"

"Friends? How silly you are!" She smiled and put out her hand to smooth the other's hair. "We must see if you can come and live with Nathan and me. After all, you are my little sister, are you not?"

"No, I'm your aunt, I think. Or half aunt. It's really crazy, isn't it?" But she was content.

"We're sisters," Sharona said firmly. "That's what we decided, and that's what we are."

Jara was about to ask her if she thought Nathan would really allow her to live with them, when she became aware of a sudden commotion nearby. "Listen!"

"What?"

"I don't know. Something's happened. Come on!"

"Jara! You mustn't run like that!"

But she was already gone.

"YOU MUST LEAVE at once," Samson, the smith, was saying. "They'll be back, looking for you. There's no time to lose."

"Are you mad?" Jara could make out the angry voice of Enosh ben Jacob. She pushed her way through the crowd. There were Samson and Enosh, all right, and, in a tight little group, Dov, Eli, Baruch, and Assaf, all friends of Nathan's. The four boys stood with lowered heads, but they appeared more angry than ashamed, Jara thought. They had obviously gotten into some kind of trouble—bad enough, it seemed, to make the whole village turn out.

"What will happen to the rest of us," Enosh continued, "if these mischief makers don't answer up for their actions? Must I pay for their folly? And my wife? And my children?"

"No one need answer for what I've done but I myself," Assaf said now. "And I'll do that with more of the same!"

"Crazy. He's crazy," Enosh said. "Boaz, what kind of son have you raised? I always thought he was a smart boy. Now he wants to die and get the rest of us killed as well!"

"We might as well be dead for the way we live," Dov retorted. "You ought to be proud of us! We beat them! We made them run! When did any of you ever send a Roman soldier scurrying down the road, slipping and sliding in the mud like the pig he is? And don't tell me you wouldn't like to!"

"Why, you—"

"Enough! Enough!" The smith came between the boy and the man.

"What is it?" Jara asked the woman next to her. "What's happened?"

The woman did not answer. She only sighed and shook her head.

"Why didn't you just give them what they wanted?" Assaf's father asked the boys now. He was obviously bewildered. "To fight . . . over nothing. Nothing."

"It isn't nothing," his son replied. "It's everything. Don't you see? It's *everything*. Every day of our lives. We're like animals to them. Less. They value a horse more."

"You think I don't know that?" Enosh said angrily. "You think none of us knows? But what do you want? A governor like Quietus? Have you forgotten what he was like? Now you must rouse Rufus against us as well?"

"Quietus or another, they're all the same. . . ."

The argument would have continued but for the sudden, rather dramatic appearance of Rabbi Kawzbeel, who silenced all parties simply by raising his hands. Called away from the synagogue by the noise outside, he had been standing quietly during the debate, head cocked to one side, listening intently while one of the men present informed him of what had occurred. Now he spoke: "There is no value in discussing what prompted the boys to behave as they did. The deed is done, and the fact is they have defied the authorities. Now they—or we—will be made to pay for it. How, I cannot say."

"The boys must leave here," Samson urged. "They can lose themselves in the hills, as our people have always done. Or they can ride south, to Tur Malka, the King's Mountain. Bar Daroma leads the people there. They say he harbors rebels—"

"Stop! I want no talk of rebels! We have enough on our hands." The rabbi turned away from the man. "I did not hear that, Samson," he said pointedly. "None of us heard." He turned to Enosh. "Someone must inform the commander at Tiberias that we have the offenders and await his judgment."

"Wouldn't it be better to bring them in ourselves?"

"You will not lead my son to the Roman!" Boaz stepped forward, fists clenched. He appealed to Kawzbeel. "Samson is right. The boys must ride away. If the soldiers come, we say nothing. We know nothing."

"Do you think they would believe us?" The rabbi shook his head sadly.

"Then let them remain here. Send a messenger to Tiberias if you must, but do not send the boys."

"It would be better to do as Boaz says." Jara recognized the voice of her brother Arnon. "The soldiers could return before we speak with the commander. If they don't see the lads, they will think we helped them to escape. We will be right in the middle again."

There was more talk, but Jara, seeing the smith emerge from the crowd, ran to him. "Samson! Wait! Tell me what happened!"

The man merely shook his head in disgust and continued walking away.

"Samson, please! You must tell me! What happened?"

He looked at the girl a moment. "Trouble," he said. "Trouble."

SHE WATCHED HIM stoke the fire, mesmerized by the flames and the shadows they cast.

"You don't remember," Samson said. "You don't know. They've left Katan alone these last few years. It's been quiet, peaceful. And now, this. . . ."

"I hate them," Jara said. "I hate the Romans. You're wrong, Samson. I know all about them and the Great War. My father was born on the Masada, son of a great *bacchur*. My grandmother's family were all killed. Her brother died in the arena. All their wealth was stolen by Vespasian."

"That was long ago, even before I was born. I am thinking of the time after and not so far in the past, when Quietus was sent by Rome to govern Judea. Those were hard days. It was like another war. The War of Quietus, the rabbis called it. His hatred for Jews was fierce. They say it grew out of the battles he saw as Trajan's general against our brothers in Egypt and Cyprus when they tried to throw off the Roman yoke." Samson thrust the metal piece he had been wiping back into the fire and watched it glow red and bright. "He was a black man. A Moor. A man of much violence."

"All the procurators—that's what they used to call the governors before the Great War—all of them were horrible. The Old One says there are no abominations they did not love."

"Then Quietus was their brother. If he were still in Judea, there would be no marriage celebration tomorrow. It was Quietus who permitted his soldiers to seize new brides. 'The right of the first night,' he called it."

"What's that?" She leaned forward, eyes big and golden in the firelight.

He withdrew the metal piece, inspected it briefly, and thrust it back into the flames. "It is better not to talk of such things."

"But I want to know! What did you call it? The first night?"

He looked at her, then back at the fire. "I know how Enosh feels," he said. "I know what the rabbi fears. Quietus is gone, but we are Jews, and anything can happen. And yet, to go ourselves to Tiberias . . ." He shook his head, mouth set in a grim line.

"I still don't know what's caused all this fuss."

"A carriage on the road—"

"Yes! I saw it!"

"The road is full of holes after the winter. This carriage threw a wheel. The axle shaft broke. The boys were carrying the poles for the bridal canopy. They'd cut the wood themselves from Nathan's tree, the one planted at his birth. The soldiers ordered the boys to repair the axle, using the poles, and to fit the wheel on again. One of them got pushed in the mud. Dov said that as they wanted the poles so much, they might have them, and forthwith swung his around, felling the bastard neat as you like."

"Hurrah!"

The smith grinned. "From there on it was a sweet fight, with the boys routing the soldiers. They came back singing, arms about one another, full of mud and happy as larks." He grew serious again. "Now the piper must be paid."

"We can't let the soldiers take them! They'll be killed!"

"Yes. But when Rome wants her due, she gets it, one way or another. If not the lads, perhaps the whole village. That's what Enosh and the others fear. Still . . ." He withdrew the metal piece from the fire. Jara could see now that it was a sword blade, slightly misshapen. The smith stared at it thoughtfully. "Handing the lads over just about seals it for them. But if they're gone from here when the soldiers come, why, then whatever happens is up to the Almighty, I guess." He put the blade down.

"How can you make their weapons?" Jara asked suddenly. "You hate the Romans, yet you repair their arms and take orders for things like that."

"I make lots of things, little girl," he replied calmly. "A man has to live."

"Well, that one's crooked. I daresay the soldiers will not want it."

She could not be sure—he was standing in the shadows—but it seemed to her he smiled.

THE MEN stood watch during the night, but no soldiers rode into the village. Somehow, sometime before dawn, the four boys managed to slip away. In the morning it was discovered that they were gone.

The women refused to have their day spoiled. Let the men worry over what might or might not occur; meanwhile, great quantities of food had been prepared, wine had been set forth, hair freshly braided and oiled. New veils, earrings, and brooches suddenly appeared, and there was a delicate tinkling sound of tiny bells and filigree as the women bustled about.

Even Jara looked presentable, Batya thought, surveying the child with a critical eye. Her robe was worn but clean, and there had been an attempt to braid the mass of curls. Still, that head did not look neat and, Batya thought, no doubt never would. The girl had stuck flowers in her hair as well, which only served to emphasize a quality that Batya found disturbing, although she could not say why.

But even this annoyance was forgotten as the bride was brought forth, her dark hair loose and flowing, crowned with a wreath of myrtle. The women fussed over Sharona, touching her hair, straightening the wreath, smoothing her robe, telling her how beautiful she looked, which indeed she did with her flushed cheeks and bright eyes. And if her lips trembled a bit, was that not all the more appealing? Only Jara worried at this sign, until Sharona, seeing her, stretched out her hand and squeezed the child's fingers reassuringly. Then it was time to bring the bride, borne aloft in a litter, to her bridegroom, attended by a merry group, some of whom chanted hymns while the children danced alongside.

Nathan had already set forth from home accompanied by family and friends. He was a serious lad of twenty, the proper age, according to the rabbis, for a young man to wed, and he walked now with head high, stiffly, perhaps, as though impressed by the solemnity of the occasion, which was solemn to him but certainly not to everyone else. People were singing now; others oohed and ahed over the young couple, trying to outdo one another in flowery praise of the bride.

Sharona was a queen today, and it was rabbinic injunction that she be accorded all the attention and respect due her station, that she be honored, praised, and in all ways made happy. If she had been orphaned or poor, her dowry, trousseau, and everything she needed to be wed would have been provided by the village under the auspices of the charity committee that was an integral part of each and every Jewish community. It was considered a great *mitzvah*, or good deed, to provide *hakhnasat kallah*, the bridal throne and all accouterments, for a poor girl. The rabbis at Jabneh had declared a community might sell a synagogue item, even a scroll of Torah, in order to raise money for an orphaned bride.

The retinues of bride and groom filled the village square. Children left the schoolroom of the synagogue, running out to join the festivities, for it was also permitted to sacrifice time from the study of Torah in order to help lead the bride to the canopy.

The two parties caught sight of each other now. Nathan and his attendants halted. The litter was put down, and he approached it, coming before the bride's throne, veil in hand. Gently he placed the veil on Sharona's head, covering her face. Sharona's mother, who had removed the myrtle wreath, now replaced it, and Rabbi Kawzbeel stepped forth to recite the blessing given to the biblical Rebekah before her marriage to Isaac: "Our sister, be thou the mother of thousands of ten thousands." The veiling ceremony concluded, all proceeded to the *huppah*, or bridal canopy, whose four sturdy poles—and the absence of those who should have been holding them—served as a sudden reminder that all was not as it should be.

*   *   *

THEY WERE man and wife. Dancing had broken out, the young men circling Sharona, chanting her praises. Food was being brought forth, mothers pushing away the hands of children eager for a sweetmeat or, laughing, putting a little something into their mouths. Wine was poured; in a sudden gesture of affection Arnon pulled Jara to him and, to Batya's annoyance, gave her a sip from his cup. He smiled happily at his frowning wife. Arnon was always happy when there was wine. The festivities could well last several days. He would be happy for quite some time.

"Soldiers! Soldiers! They're riding into the village!"

Everyone froze. Arnon and Kawzbeel exchanged glances. Nathan and Sharona, on their way to the banquet table that had been set outside, halted. Jara saw Samson, the smith, tighten his grip on the staff he held.

About a dozen legionaries were galloping up, led by two officers in plumed helmets and red cloaks that spread out like fans over the backs of their horses. One of these was Florus Valerens, commander of the garrison in Tiberias, charged with the administration as well as the security of the entire Galilee. Kawzbeel recognized him at once.

"We are honored by your presence," he said, quickly stepping forward to greet the Roman, who did not bother to dismount. "May I assume you have spoken to the messenger we sent to Tiberias?"

"I have spoken to no such person, Jew. But a party led by my colleague, the centurion Marcellus Quintus, did indeed meet some of your people on the road yesterday. That is why I am here, as you no doubt are aware."

"Commander, honored sir, you must realize that what happened was without the knowledge or approval of anyone here. As soon as the boys told us what they did, they were placed under lock and key. We sent someone to notify you."

"All right, where are they? Bring them here."

"Gone. Gone, commander. Somehow, they escaped during the night."

The Roman smiled crookedly. "Somehow . . . ?" He looked around, frowning. "Is that cause to rejoice? I seem to have interrupted a celebration."

"A wedding," the rabbi hastened to explain. "It has

nothing to do with what occurred on the road.''

"Still, here you are, merry as can be. While two good and decent men—soldiers of Rome—are back in Tiberias, one with a broken arm and the other with his head nearly split open. Fortunately, my colleague Marcellus Quintus had ridden ahead with the Lady Livia, and so the governor's wife was spared whatever indignities and violence might have befallen her had she remained in her carriage.''

"The governor's wife!''

"She is safe in Tiberias''—he cast a quick glance at the Roman beside him—"under my protection.''

"Commander—you must believe—we are loyal citizens of Rome. We do not condone what occurred. We want no trouble.''

"I'm sure you don't. But something must come of all this. A lesson must be learned. Nor can you expect me to ride all this way for nothing, as you say the boys I want are not here. In any case, my men will search the village to be sure.''

"What names have you?'' Samson asked now, stepping forth.

"I don't need names, Jew. I need four males, between the ages of seventeen and twenty-two. As I look around, I see a half-dozen or so fitting that description.''

"They are all innocent,'' the smith said. "You know that as well as I.''

"What I know is this: Four Jews from the village of Katan disobeyed a direct command from a Roman officer. They committed violence against persons of Rome. Their actions insulted and endangered the wife of the governor of Judea. That is treason, Jew. I could level this entire village—now—and be justified.'' He shook his head. "And all for a broken axle and thrown wheel! Rabbi, rabbi . . . what do you teach your people? Would it not have been a kindness to help those on the road? Or are your good deeds only for your own?''

"The boys asked to be allowed to fetch new wood. The poles they were carrying were not theirs to give—''

"Theirs? Caesar's! *Caesar's!* When will you people understand that *all is Caesar's?*''

The rabbi tried again. "Commander, please. It is tradition. When a child is born the parents plant a tree. When he is grown and to be wed, the tree is felled to provide wood for his house and to make the poles for the bridal canopy. The wood was from Nathan's tree. It is tradition," he said again, lamely.

"Tradition. Yes. That you understand. Very well. There are Roman traditions too, rabbi. I know of one in particular that concerns itself with weddings. My old friend Lusius Quietus found it very useful in reminding you people that you are, whatever else you may think yourselves to be, the subjects and property of Imperial Rome."

"What . . . what do you mean?"

"*Ius primae noctis.* The right of the first night. As representative of Rome, I command you to bring forth the bride that Caesar may receive his due."

The centurion beside Valerens appeared startled at this. "Surely you do not mean . . ."

"They must learn their lesson, Quintus. Acts of rebellion cannot be tolerated."

"But it was a misunderstanding. If I had known about the wood—"

"Let us not debate before these people," Valerens murmured.

"Yes, of course," the Roman agreed quickly. He cleared his throat. "However, the emperor advocates a policy of reconciliation. Surely—"

"Reconciliation? With whom, centurion? With what? This scum?"

He cleared his throat again. "We are perhaps too harsh. . . ."

"We are not too harsh. You are too soft. That is what life on an estate in the Imperial City has done for you. Do not question me further. Be content. You are new to Judea. You do not understand. That is why I came here with you today, to show you what we must deal with and how we must do so. I know you are the emperor's eye, Marcellus Quintus. I, on the other hand, must be his arm, else the eye lose its sight on the point of a sword."

Quintus sighed. "All right." He nodded in the direction of the four young men the soldiers had brought forward. "These are not the ones. I gave the order before I rode off with the Lady Livia. These are not the men."

"Look around, then. Take your time."

"They are not here. There's no sense searching. They must have run off, just as the rabbi said."

The crooked smile returned. "Very well." He turned to one

of the soldiers who had dismounted earlier in response to a
gesture from the officer. "Have you got the girl?"

"They're bringing her now, sir."

The sound of wailing filled the air as the soldiers dragged
Sharona forward. The girl herself was silent, her face white as
her robe, her pupils dilated in fear.

"Shut those women up!" Valerens ordered. "Quiet! I want
quiet!"

A hush fell over the place. There was only the sound of
some weeping child, confused and frightened, and the muffled
sobs of the bride's mother, who, half-swooning, had to be
supported by those near at hand.

Florus Valerens looked around him in disgust. "Idiots. You
ought to be glad I demand such little payment for your mis-
deeds. I could have twenty boys crucified with or without the
centurion's acknowledgment. I could burn this whole miserable village to the ground. I might still, if it pleases me to do
so. No doubt the world would be better off without you." He
glanced briefly at the officer beside him, who was staring
stonily ahead. "Certainly Rome would." He nodded at the
legionary who now mounted his horse, pulling Sharona up
with him. At that moment several things happened.

Samson sprang forward, fury overpowering his reason and
rage in turn giving the smith the strength of his namesake. It
took four men finally to bring him to the ground, a sword at
his throat.

Valerens turned to Quintus. "You see?" he asked wearily.
"You see what they are like?"

The centurion did not reply. He was staring at a girl, a child
really, who, at the same moment that the Jew leaped to attack,
uttered a single cry. The man beside her had immediately put
his hand over her mouth, but not before the sound caught
Quintus' attention. Once more he found himself staring into
those large, light eyes that had so chillingly reminded him the
previous day just what his position in Judea was and what her
response—the response, he no longer doubted, of all the
people in this land—to him must ever be.

"Scourge and crucify the man," Valerens instructed the
soldiers holding Samson.

"I am a smith, with contract to deliver weapons to your garrison," Samson growled. "Kill me and you will be more short
of arms than you are now."

"If we are short of arms, it is because you people are the most inferior craftsmen the world has ever known." He turned to Quintus. "It's true. We are in constant demand because everything these beggars make breaks off at the hilt or is lacking in some respect. I ought to kill you for that alone," he told the man on the ground. "Well, you are having your little feast day. I shall be kind." He nodded at the soldier whose sword was still pointed at Samson's throat. "Only scourge him."

Jara, who had shaken free of Arnon, looked around, hardly believing what she saw. Samson had been bound; he was being whipped. The officers were riding out of the village, followed by the soldier carrying Sharona on his horse. No one else appeared to move or speak, not Nathan, not Arnon, not even Rabbi Kawzbeel.

"Stop them!" she cried. "Why won't you stop them?"

"Be quiet!" Arnon slapped one hand over her mouth again, grabbing her shoulder with the other, his fingers digging hard into her flesh.

She let out a muffled cry of pain and wrenched herself free. Before anyone could stop her, she was running after the departing soldiers, barely avoiding being trampled by the men who, having finished with the smith, had remounted. The horses' hooves crushed the gray cat that appeared suddenly, scampering after the girl.

"No!" Jara cried. "No!"

She ran after them, out the village, down the road, running in the dust kicked up by the horses until her breath, mingling with sobs, stabbed, and she stumbled and fell in the pock-marked road.

She pulled herself up, the flowers gone from her hair, and resolutely began to climb the hill from which she had sighted the Roman carriage the previous day. All she could see now was a ball of dust on the horizon. She waited, watching until even the ball of dust disappeared, consumed by the afternoon sky. Exhausted, she caught hold of the trunk of the old oak and pulled herself to it, hugging the tree, wrapping her arms around it as far as they might go, pressing her body against the ancient wood, as if some warmth of sap within might stop the trembling that now engulfed her.

She had wept before: when she learned of her father's death, and sometimes, at night, those first months without him, when Batya or another had been unkind. But for a very long time she had not wept for herself; she had learned not to. And certainly for no one else. Now tears flowed, not from sorrow but from fear and anger. What would happen to Sharona? Would she be returned?

And no one but Samson had even tried to stop the soldiers.

Still sobbing, Jara began to slap her hand against the tree, pounding the bark until her own palm became raw and red.

No one had done anything to stop them.

No one.

IT WAS DARK when Jara returned. She paused at the smith's door, then knocked softly. "Samson? Are you all right?"

There was a sound that might have been either a sigh or a groan.

She pushed the door open. The place was dark, the fire nearly out. She could make out the figure of the smith lying face down on the straw mattress in the corner. She took a tallow candle from a niche in the wall, lit it, then went over to him.

"Samson? It's Jara. Are you all right?"

He did not answer.

She brought the candle closer and saw now the crisscross web of welts and open wounds on his back. The skin was streaked with dried blood and dirt. "Has no one attended you?"

"Go away, little girl. I'll be all right."

She put the candle in a holder on the table. "I'll be back," she promised.

She ran quickly home and was gathering up the things she needed when Arnon emerged from his room. "Jara? Are you all right? I was afraid—"

"I'm fine."

"Did they—" He swallowed, suddenly frightened. "Your dress is torn."

"I fell."

"What are you doing with that salve?"

"I'm taking it to Samson."

He sighed. "He wouldn't let anyone near him. I thought it best to leave him be. In the morning—"

"The wounds must be cleansed now. Poison could enter his blood."

"Well, in the morning . . ."

"Never mind. I'll take care of him."

He nodded.

"What is it? What's going on?" Batya came out now, swathed in a blanket. "Oh, it's you," she said, seeing Jara. "I thought you'd run off for good."

"Shut up, Batya," Arnon said evenly. He looked at Jara, who returned the stare a moment, then disappeared out the door. Arnon turned back to his wife, who was still standing there and, in direct opposition to his admonition, was openmouthed. "You'll wake the children," he murmured with a sigh.

SAMSON HAD not moved.

"It's me," she whispered.

He opened his eyes.

"I'm going to wash your back. Then I will put something on it to heal the wounds. I'll try not to hurt you. See, see how softly I touch you."

He sighed. "Little girl's hands. For a moment I thought . . ." He closed his eyes again. "I've been dreaming."

"Sleep is good. Sleep heals."

He tried to smile. "How is it you know so much, little girl?"

"I don't know anything, Samson. I thought I did, but . . ." she shook her head. "What will they do to Sharona? Will they bring her back?"

"Yes. They will bring her back. It is to be a lesson, you see."

"But she did nothing! Why must she suffer?"

His eyes opened, closed. "Why . . . ?" He sighed.

"I hate them," she said. "And I hate this village. You were the only one who tried to do something. You were the only one who fought back."

"Too late . . ."

"What are you saying?"

"Seven years ago . . . another village . . . I stood with my hands at my side, like Nathan. . . ." He drew in his breath so that it was almost a sob. "They brought her back, but she was hurt . . . inside. I brought her here, to your father. There was nothing he could do. She died. I stayed here. I could not go back. . . ."

"Samson. My poor Samson. . . ."

Grimacing with pain, he pulled himself up. "I'm getting out of here. Come morning I'll be gone."

"To Tur Malka? The King's Mountain?"

He nodded grimly. "I'm tired of this game. Making bad weapons so's they send them back. I want the feel of a real sword in my hands now, not to stick in the fires of my forge but in the bellies of a thousand legionaries!"

"Take me with you!"

He shook his head. "No, little girl. It's best you stay. Besides, Sharona will need you." He reached for a garment but fell back on the mattress before he could slip it over his head.

"I'm going to give you something to drink, Samson. It will make you sleep and lessen the pain. You cannot travel now. Wait a day or so. Please."

He sighed. "All right." He quickly downed the potion, then rolled over on his stomach and closed his eyes.

"Samson. . . ." She touched his arm gently. "Assaf and the others . . . they're in Tur Malka, aren't they? You helped them to escape."

"Please, God, they are safe. That's all that counts."

She watched him a moment, then, sure he was asleep, rose to leave. At the door she stopped and, turning back, said softly, solemnly, "You are a great *bacchur*, Samson. My grandfather, Eleazar ben Ya'ir, would have been proud to know you."

He was not sleeping after all. Eyes still closed, he smiled.

SHE SLEPT FITFULLY. A little before dawn she bolted upright like one coming out of a bad dream. There was the sound of a horse galloping into the village. She was out of the house in an instant, and saw the soldier let Sharona fall to the ground and then, with a laugh, ride away.

She ran to the girl, embraced her. "Sharona! You're alive! I thought we'd never see you again. . . . Don't cry, don't cry. . . . I'll help you. Put your arm around me. . . . Yes, like that. I'm strong. I can hold you up. There, you see, you can walk. It's all right. It's all right. You're home. You're home."

Doors were opening. People stared at the two girls as they made their way across the square. Jara stopped, expecting the others to help or comfort the dazed, disheveled Sharona. But no one moved. They just stood in their doorways and stared. And as on the day before, Jara felt something grow hard and bitter inside her. She stared back at the people with whom she had lived all her years and knew they would always be strangers to her and she a stranger among them, and the hatred in her eyes was no less than it had been for the Roman on the road.

"Come," she said softly to Sharona, who was weeping uncontrollably now. "Come, I will take you home."

The girl nodded, and Jara began to lead her away. For an instant her step faltered. She had started instinctively for the house of Sharona's mother. Now she realized Sharona's place was with Nathan. Turning, she trod resolutely in the direction of the new cottage still decorated with sheaves of barley. Jara knocked at the door. It opened slowly. Nathan appeared. He seemed startled. Then, stiffly, he drew Sharona inside and closed the door. Jara remained outside, staring thoughtfully at the house. Then she turned away.

People still stood in their doorways, watching silently as she made her way home, her arms hugging her body. She did not want anyone to see her shiver, but the morning air was cool, and she had no cloak. She suddenly realized she was sweating. She felt strange, uneasy; there was a new, drawing sensation in her legs. No doubt she was simply tired, feeling the effects of all that had occurred. But when she reached her room she discovered there was more to it than that.

Her flow had begun.

2

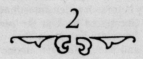

THE SUN WAS SHINING. Another winter had passed, without further visits to Kefar Katan by Judea's military occupiers. There was a visitor in the village this day, however, a rather notable one. Rabbi Tarfon, a most eminent scholar and a member of the Council in Jabneh, had come to see that the community was in accordance with the Law. Besides the presence of a House of Assembly or Worship, there must also be a school with a proper teacher where all males above the age of six might receive an education; a *mikveh;* a charity committee, and, depending upon the size of the community, a physician in residence. Rabbi Tarfon had stopped now to see Arnon, whose father he had known.

"Not only your father but your grandfather as well," the rabbi noted. "Solomon ben Ya'ish was a great and good physician. Even more to be blessed, he was a man of wisdom and foresight. Who can say what this world would be like if he had not helped Rabbi ben Zakkai escape Jerusalem? Bad enough to lose the Temple, may the Almighty grant its restoration. But to have lost the knowledge inside the head of Johanan ben Zakkai would have been an equal tragedy."

"Surely another would have taken the lead," Arnon said with a smile. "Obviously God meant for Torah to survive, if not through the efforts of ben Zakkai, then with the help of another."

"If not the Messiah, then another Messiah, eh? No, no. All is appointed, my friend. All is appointed."

"The deed or the man?"

"An interesting thought. Would that I had time to discuss it with you."

"At dinner, perhaps."

"No, no, I cannot. Many thanks. I must be on my way. I am expected in Ammatha this evening. What a day!" he exclaimed as he stepped outside. "What a sky! What a beautiful girl," he added without thinking. Gesturing toward the young female who had caught his attention, the rabbi asked, "Who is that creature with her hair flowing so?"

"My sister. Half sister, actually. Her name is Jara."

"How is it that her head is uncovered?"

"She is unmarried."

"Can it be so? A beautiful girl like that?"

"She does not wish to be wed. Several families have come forward, but she is unwilling. I am her guardian, but I wouldn't force her to a match that would make her unhappy. The rabbis agree, do they not? Past the age of twelve a maiden may not be made to marry one she does not wish to wed."

"What does a woman know at any age?"

"Still . . . I would not force her."

Something in the man's voice made Tarfon study him a moment. Arnon was unaware of the rabbi's penetrating gaze; he was himself staring at Jara, who was bent over the well in the village square. Tarfon looked back at the girl. "A comely female," he said softly. "She is young. But not so young as not to stir the Evil Impulse in men."

"She was always like that. Even when she was a little girl. There was always something about her. . . ."

Tarfon turned back to Arnon and studied him again, this time warily. Then, with an understanding look, he patted his shoulder. "Get her married," he declared. "Do not waste another moment. Meanwhile, see that her hair is covered. For her own good as well as the souls of the men of Katan."

Arnon appeared startled. Then he sighed. "Yes. Yes . . . you are right."

Tarfon patted his shoulder again. "There is something I wanted to discuss with Rabbi Kawzbeel. Perhaps I shall tell him now of your intention that the girl be wed. I know he will be of help."

"Yes. Yes, all right. I'll walk over with you."

Tarfon smiled. "Good."

"You were called, you know, to meet her mother," Arnon remarked as they strolled toward the rabbi's house.

"I was? I do not remember this."

"My father sent word to you. He thought you might have some knowledge of the woman's family. She was a bit of a mystery."

"Yes? I am sorry, I do not recall."

"You were in Antioch. With Akiva. By the time you returned, the woman had died in childbirth."

"Ah. I'm sorry."

"Well, perhaps it was for the best," Arnon said with a slight shrug.

"You are like the sage Nahum of Gimso," Rabbi Tarfon said now with another smile. "Whatever happens to him— illness, the loss of family, catastrophe unequaled—he is like Job, poor fellow. Still he replies, '*Ish gam zo*.' 'This too is for the best.' At Jabneh we used to call him Gamso-Gimso, may God forgive us. A man of unshakable faith. Please God he shall not forever be tested."

"Nor the rest of us. It is a hard thing to be a Jew these days."

"When was it not? Was Pharaoh kind to us? Nebuchadnezzar? The Greeks? And now, Rome." He sighed. "When I was born the Temple still sat upon the Mount Moriah. Every Jew the whole world over paid a half shekel yearly to sustain it. No matter how poor the man might be, the humblest Israelite, he paid this and with honor and delight. Now the Temple is no more. Jerusalem is destroyed. Slowly we try to rebuild our lives atop the ravages of war. And we must pay our half shekel now to the Temple of Jupiter in Rome. Every Jew in the world must pay to sustain that pagan monument. Well, let them have their insidious joke. God laughs last. Meanwhile, we, His people, are alive. They destroyed the Temple, not Torah. Like Gamso-Gimso I say, 'This too is for the best.' " He cast another look at the girl, who was walking toward them now, one arm raised to steady the water jar balanced on her head. "Could it be I knew the mother's family?" Rabbi Tarfon mused. "Maybe. Maybe not. She is certainly tall. . . ."

"My father was tall."

"Yes, he was. Strange, because I remember Solomon ben Ya'ish was not a very imposing figure but a man of average height. Well . . ." He looked at Jara again, puzzling over her identity, then looked away. "She is too comely. Cover her hair, my friend. You must cover her hair."

HAVING BROUGHT the water to Batya, who was pregnant again, Jara sought out Sharona. More than a year had passed since the soldiers had come to Katan. Samson had left the village as soon as he was well enough to ride, joining the four boys who had escaped to Tur Malka and whose rebellion precipitated Sharona's abduction. The Old One was dead at last. Even Jezebel was no more. Jara had interred the cat's remains the morning she became a woman.

The physical change was subtle. She was still thin, more arms and legs than anything else, but there was something about her that caught men's eyes. There had always been something about her, as Arnon said, from the time she was a child; now, when she was little more than that, the effect was more pronounced. It was not in the shape of her breasts or hips so much as in the way she walked, the way she moved, with an unconscious grace more feline than simply feminine. How the young men of Katan itched to embrace that long, supple waist. But more than that, perhaps even more than her body, it was the girl's spirit, which seemed to them wild and free, like that of an animal, alluring because it was dangerous, that they longed to possess.

"She belongs to no one, that one," it was said of her, referring to the absence of father, mother, and husband; yet what a true expression of Jara's condition this was. Behind her back and certainly not when Arnon was present they called her *ha-Toole*, "the Cat," and sometimes Witch's Child, because of the Old One who had raised her and the strange, silent woman who had given birth to her. It was said her eyes held demon fire; they were cold and gold and green, shaped like a cat's and with a cat's inscrutable stare. One of the men swore he'd seen her walking in the dark when all good people slept, her eyes gleaming like an animal's.

Lilith came in the night, the people reminded one another. From the time of Adam she had crept into men's dreams, awakening the Evil Impulse, making poor boys without wives toss and turn and spill their seed.

And yet, for all this—the talk of witches and demons; the gossip surrounding Jara's mother who, it was whispered, might not have been a Jewess; the growing disregard for what family the girl had, Arnon being often too full of wine to attend to his duties, and Sharona a broken, pitiful creature since her defilement; and last but not least the fear of the girl's inherent sexuality—for all this, still young men came to their fathers and asked for a betrothal, and fathers themselves, widowed, hinted they would be willing to assume a husband's responsibility for the doctor's ward.

To all, Jara said no. She despised the men of Katan, and perhaps none more than Sharona's husband, Nathan.

Sharona's suffering had not ended when the soldiers returned her. She was a marked creature, at best the object of pity, and always a reminder of the shame of being a subject people. Perhaps no one felt this shame more than Nathan. After a reasonable period of time to allow the "uncleanliness" of Sharona's defilement to depart, he had attempted to consummate their marriage, only to meet with such fear and revulsion as to turn him away from her. Each time thereafter that he tried to come close to her, she shrank away. Finally, frustrated beyond his ability to cope with the situation, he took to using her simply to gratify himself, which only reawakened and reinforced the memories of her night in Tiberias.

Jara found her huddled in the corner of the small cottage. "Why are you sitting here all alone?" she asked gaily. "Come outside! It's lovely and warm, the sun is bright. . . . Sharona, what is it?" She went to the girl, turned her face away from the wall. "How did you get that mark on your cheek? Did you fall?"

Sharona shook her head, bit her lip.

"Was it Nathan?" Jara asked suddenly. "Did Nathan hit you?"

Tears spilling from her eyes, Sharona threw herself into Jara's arms, sobbing.

"He mustn't! He mustn't!" Jara cried angrily, at the same time trying to soothe Sharona by patting her on the back.

"He doesn't mean to." Sharona sighed and wiped her eyes. "But I anger him so. He says I make him feel as if he were the Roman. And it's true, Jara. The commander, Nathan . . . they're the same to me. I can't bear it when he touches me. I don't want him to touch me!" she cried with sudden hysteria.

"Sshh, sshh . . ." Jara frowned. "Something must be done about this."

"What? What? You're clever, Jara. Tell me what to do. I can't go on. Everyone looks at me as if I'd done something wrong! Batya says I must have committed a sin for which God has now punished me. She says God chose me because I was evil."

"Batya is an idiot. I've always said that, haven't I?"

"What did I do that I must suffer so?" Sharona was pacing back and forth now, wringing her hands. "I try and try to think. . . . Once, when I was little, I opened the door and a gust of wind blew out the Sabbath candles, and they had to be relit. My mother said it was a bad sign. But I did not know the wind would come and blow out the candles. Was that a sin? And now . . . every night I lie awake and I remember . . . the soldier who rode with me . . . the things he said . . . the way he put his hands on . . . ." She closed her eyes, opened them. "The commander made me take off all my clothes and stand before him. He said . . . he said he could do anything he pleased with me because I was nothing. I was the property of Rome. He took his goblet of wine and spilled it on my breasts. When he was done with me, he gave me to a soldier and said, 'Take her back.' But the soldier led me outside . . . someplace . . . his friends were waiting. . . ."

"Don't think of it," Jara urged softly.

"I can't help thinking of it, Jara. It's no use. Batya's right. There must be something evil in me and I'm being punished for it over and over. . . ."

"You are not evil! I shall kill Batya, I swear it! Don't you see, Sharona? The only thing evil is allowing those pigs—those Roman pigs!—to do as they like with us!"

"Nobody wants another war. . . ."

"Is this better? He said you were nothing. The property of Rome. Do you think God wants that?"

"He must—"

"No! He's just disgusted with us, that's all. Because we do nothing and we let them do everything to us!"

Sharona put her face in her hands and shook her head. "Nathan says—"

"Nathan! A fine one to talk! Where is he now?"

"He is in the House of Assembly."

"He beats you and then goes to pray!"

"That is why he is praying, I think. He knows it is wrong."
She sighed. "I think he will divorce me."

"Maybe that's best."

"Then what shall become of me, Jara?"

"I don't know," she answered truthfully.

"Sometimes I think it would be better if I were dead."

"Don't say that, please. . . . We could run away," she said,
brightening at the thought. "Together. We could go to Tur
Malka."

"No, it would be too dangerous. There are men on the
road. . . ." The girl shuddered.

"Pooh to that! I'm not afraid."

Sharona smiled wanly. "You would be, if you knew. . . ."
She stopped, tears coming to her eyes again. She shook her
head. "No. No, I will not leave Katan."

"Then I will take care of you," Jara said.

Sharona shook her head again. "You will be wed yourself
soon."

"Not I!"

"Nathan says Assur talks of you constantly. He told
Nathan the way you walk drives him mad."

"The way I walk?" She was puzzled. "What do I do when I
walk but move my feet like everyone else?" She wrinkled her
nose. "Those scholars are crazy!"

"Assur wants to marry you. It would be a good thing. He is
the nephew of Rabbi Kawzbeel."

"I will not marry a scholar and certainly not the nephew of
Kawzbeel." She studied Sharona thoughtfully. "But if I did
marry—and if Nathan divorced you—why, you could come
and stay with me. Then no one would ever hurt you again."

Sharona smiled. "When we were little I was always asking
my mother if you could live with us." Her face grew sad.
"Now she is ill all the time. Ever since . . . and it's all because
of me."

Jara hugged her. "Everything will be all right."

But soon after their talk, Assur left to continue his studies at
the academy in Jabneh. There was no word from any member
of his family regarding a betrothal to Jara. Nathan did not
divorce Sharona, but increasingly visited physical abuse upon
her. Meanwhile, a widowed merchant from Jericho, passing
through, caught sight of Jara and began negotiations for her

hand. Joseph ben Hanina was well over fifty, with small, narrow eyes, and the corpulent body thought befitting a man of means. His spice orchards had been untouched by war, balsam and such being as prized by Romans as by Judeans. Moreover, he was of a priestly family and benefited from the tithes that the rabbis insisted upon continuing in anticipation of the Day of the Messiah, when the Temple would be restored. Jara found him odious, but Batya was ecstatic at the thought of a merger. A rich man! A priestly family! Better still, ugly as a toad. Quite the best thing for all concerned.

"No," Jara said.

"He's rich!" Batya exclaimed.

"No."

But Batya had made up her mind.

One morning some weeks later, Jara awoke to find Batya hard at work cleaning the house. Even more astonishing, the woman was actually humming. Jara watched her a moment, wondering what was up.

"Good morning." Batya sounded uncommonly cheerful. "Now that you are awake, sleepy-head, be so kind as to fetch some water from the well. Then you shall have a nice breakfast. And some dates, yes? It is always good to start the day with something sweet."

Jara did not answer. She regarded Batya quizzically, then, with a slight shrug, picked up the water jug and left. When she returned, she saw that Batya had set out some food. Without a word, she set down the pitcher and began to devour all that was before her.

"What an appetite you have," Batya murmured.

Jara did not bother to reply. There was no need to remind the woman that her dinner consisted of whatever was left in the pot after the others had taken their fill. Each morning the girl awoke ravenous with hunger, but breakfast was not much more than a bit of bread and cheese snatched while helping to care for the children.

"Today you shall pick flowers for the house," Batya was saying. "You have an eye for arranging them prettily. And tonight is *Shabbat*."

Shabbat. So that was it. But the Sabbath arrived every week, and never before had Batya risen with the dawn to clean house. She left that to Jara.

"We are having company tonight."

All right, but why this solicitous manner? Why such happy anticipation? Batya did not like guests. She did not like the burden of preparing for them, which, in any event, would be left to Jara.

"Joseph ben Hanina is coming."

Jara sighed. "Again?"

"No, not again. Tonight is different. Tonight, arrangements will be made." Her voice was shrill with forced gaiety. "You are going to be betrothed, my girl!"

The milk cup came down sharply on the table. Jara rose to her feet. "I told you, no!"

"It is not for you to tell anyone anything," Batya snapped. "Your brother has decided you must be wed."

"Arnon would never make me marry one I hate."

"Hate? What is it you hate? A fine, prosperous man who will look after you and care for you in a better manner than you deserve! Why he wants you I shall never know. He is kind, that's why," she went on before Jara could say anything. "He has pity on a poor, orphaned girl. You ought to give thanks for such a man. You ought to pray with all your heart to be worthy of this blessing."

"He is old! And fat! And ugly!"

"He is the descendant of priests. Priests! Isn't that what you want? You, with your fine line!"

Jara clenched her fists. "I won't marry him."

"Don't you threaten me," Batya said, taking a step back. "I am with child. It is a sin to upset a pregnant woman, and you are making me quite ill. It is you who should be getting things ready for tonight, not I. You ought to bring me breakfast, not the other way round. I feel faint. It is a sin, I tell you. A sin."

Disgusted, Jara let her hands drop to her side and turned away. "Where is Arnon? I want to talk to him."

"No! No, you shall not! It shall be as I say! Arnon has already decided. I will not have you talking behind my back," the woman said fiercely. "The two of you are always together, whispering, talking behind my back while I must look after the children. I won't have it anymore! I want you out of here. I want you out of this house!"

"I . . . I must talk to Arnon." The woman's vehemence confused her.

"Stay away from him! Stay away from my husband!"

Jara stared at her, astonished.

Batya's fists were clenched now. "From this moment you will do as you are told. You will marry Joseph ben Hanina. And you will stay away from Arnon." She sucked in her breath. "Now. Fetch some water and be quick about it."

"I just did." Jara gestured toward the water jug, her eyes still on Batya. As always that cold, catlike stare unnerved the woman.

"I don't care!" The shrill scream woke the baby, set him crying. "I want water! Fetch more!"

Jara decided Batya needed calming. She shrugged. "All right. But I must empty this first." Picking up the jug, she flung its contents full in Batya's face and walked out the door.

JARA CROSSED the village square, not quite sure where she was headed but determined to get away from Batya and Joseph ben Hanina. Catching sight of Sharona, she stopped and waved for the girl to join her. Sharona did not see her; her head was down, her eyes focused on the ground as always now, when she ventured outside. Two of Rabbi Kawzbeel's students were also crossing the square at this time, so engrossed in conversation they failed to take notice of Sharona until they almost fell over her. Startled, Sharona looked up, and for a brief moment the eyes of the young men and the young woman met. The scholars quickly averted their heads and made way for the female to pass, less a show of courtesy than an act of deliberate ostracism. Sharona's head fell forward again, cheeks flaming. In her haste to depart she stumbled and fell; the pitcher in her hand rolled on the ground, shattering against a rock. Immediately Jara was at her side, but instead of allowing herself to be helped up, Sharona kept crawling around on all fours, vainly attempting to gather together the pieces of the broken pitcher. She began to mumble strange, incomprehensible words. Her hands shook. She seemed unaware of those around her.

"Her veil has fallen off," one of the scholars whispered. "Nathan can divorce her for being bareheaded in public. We are witness to it."

Jara heard this. She gave up trying to help Sharona and planted herself in front of the young men. "Divorce? Better she should divorce him!"

"Do not speak to her," the other warned. "It is not becoming for a scholar to speak to a female on the street."

"It is not becoming for anyone to stand like a stick while another has fallen," Jara retorted.

"Do not look at her," the young man urged his companion.

"You shall look at me!" She was furious. "You shall not turn away!"

But they had hurried off.

"Cowards!" she cried, shaking her fist at them. She spun around, aware now of the others watching her. "Cowards, all of you! And you," she called after the retreating scholars, "you who do nothing but sit before books all day, you are the worst of all!"

"What is it?" Enosh ben Jacob asked, coming up to her with a frown. "What's going on here?"

"Look at her." Jara pointed to Sharona, who was sitting on the ground, head in her hands, moaning softly now. "Look what you've done to her!"

"I?" He was genuinely astonished. He looked around. "Not any of us. This is the work of those accursed Romans."

"It is your work!"

He sighed. "Listen, what happened, happened. No one could stop it. It's over, done with. What do you want? Revenge?"

"Protection! And failing that, comfort!" She regarded the other villagers who had joined Enosh, making a kind of ring around them. "You act as if what happened was a thing between men. The Roman pleasure. Your shame. What of Sharona? What of her? It is she who was abused, not any of you. I saw the marks they left on her body. Look at her! There is a mark inside her that will never go away! Yet whom have you consoled? Nathan! And to her you speak not a word. Is this the teaching of Torah? Is this lovingkindness?" She was choking on her own tears now. "You let them take her! You let them have her! You would fight over sticks of wood—Nathan's tree!—but not for her! And now—you are worse. You all are worse than—" She could not go on, and with a last look of anguish and contempt, ran from the place.

KAWZBEEL STUDIED THE GIRL. She irritated him; she always had, but never more so than now, with her insolent, in-

scrutable stare and sullen lower lip. The light from the oil
lamps cast a halo around her hair, which fell loose, a mass of
curls nearly to her waist. The rabbi turned away, fiddled with
a piece of rolled parchment, angry and embarrassed by the
sight of her bare head. "Why are you not veiled?" he asked.

"I am unmarried."

"But not a child. No longer a child, Jara, daughter of Benjamin. It is not proper. You must see that your hair is covered
or at least tied back in more modest fashion. This is the look
of a *zonah*, a harlot. It is but one of the complaints against
you."

Her chin came up. "I am not sorry for the things I said.
And I'm not sorry about Batya. She was hysterical. My father
always told me—"

"Your father is dead. Arnon is your guardian, and Batya has
been like a mother to you these past years. And you bring
nothing but shame and unhappiness to them both."

"What shame? What have I done?"

"You run about immodestly, like a child, when you are not
a child. You refuse all who would wed you. You speak against
me—yes, I am aware of it. And now you belittle those who
study the Word of God, whose prayers and piety are our only
hope of being forgiven our sins and brought to the Day of the
Messiah."

"I belittle those who have forgotten what it is to stand up
and fight for the Word of God, who are more concerned, it
seems, with defending His house against women than against
Rome."

He stared at her, astonished. "Where did you learn to talk
like this? Never have I heard a woman—a child—speak so."

"You just said I wasn't a child."

"You are a witch." He turned away again, shaken. "I will
not listen to you. The Evil One has many guises. He shall not
enter this house or invade my thoughts."

She shrugged and turned to leave, but his voice stopped her
at the door.

"You can no longer live in Kefar Katan."

She turned around.

"There is no place for you here. You draw apart from the
community. You refuse to wed, yet your beauty, may the Lord
protect us, brings forth the Evil Impulse. If you will not be
given to a husband and take your place as a good wife and

daughter of Israel, then you must leave this village. You are a distraction and a disturbance."

"Leave. . . ." For a moment she was about to agree when a new thought struck her. "If I go, Sharona will have no one."

"What nonsense is this? Sharona has Nathan. Soon, please God, she will have children."

"She is alone but for me. You know how everyone treats her. Don't send me away. She needs me."

He shook his head. "You cause trouble. Nathan has told me how you make Sharona cry."

"I don't! It is he—" She stopped. What was the use? "All right," she said with a suddenness that startled the rabbi. "I'll marry."

He was so surprised he could think of nothing to say.

"Is that all right?" she asked anxiously. "I mean, if I consent to a husband and . . . and try to be . . . to be kinder to everyone?"

He nodded slowly, trying to digest this sudden turn. "Yes . . . yes, that puts things in quite another light."

"But not Joseph ben Hanina. Please. . . . Not him."

"He is a fine man. He is of a priestly family and wealthy besides. You would have many servants, fine clothes, jewelry . . . all the things women love."

"But he is—" She stopped, bit her lip. "Rabbi," she pleaded softly, kneeling beside the man's chair. "He is old, so old. I would not mind if he were your age," she said shyly, knowing full well Kawzbeel was quite the elder of the two. "Or a man of God, like yourself."

"I thought you hated men like myself."

She lowered her head penitently. "I have acted so only because I realize no scholar would want me . . . an orphan without dowry but for what the community would provide. . . ."

Hesitantly his hand went out to pat her bent, shining head, then quickly withdrew.

"I am unkind and wicked," she whispered. "I know I cause Batya nothing but sorrow. But there has been no one to teach me the ways of goodness. My father was always busy with his patients, just as Arnon is now—and besides, Arnon has his own family to care for. Batya has the children. . . . I want to be a good daughter of Israel, rabbi! I do! If you would teach me . . . someone like you . . ." She looked up, her eyes bright with tears. "Only do not make me marry Joseph ben Hanina."

"Well . . ." How frail and soft she looked, not at all like the wild little creature he'd always thought her to be. She was hardly more than a child and obviously had never received proper guidance. Joseph ben Hanina was a man of means, but to give him this girl was like placing a flower in a bear's paw. What if he were of the priestly line? What good had that blood-sucking class ever done, God forgive him for such thoughts. Even now, with no Temple to serve and no useful function but a reminder of the past, even now with the people taxed and driven by Rome, unable to reap in full whatever fruits remained of the torn land, even now they demanded their God-given tithes.

Rabbi Kawzbeel cleared his throat, looked away, then back again at the girl's plaintive, upturned face. "My nephew Assur . . ." He sighed. "I sent him to Jabneh, hoping . . . But he does not pay attention to his teachers. His mind is . . . elsewhere." He nodded to himself. "He needs a wife, no doubt of it. He is eighteen. He should be wed. Maybe then he will . . ." He broke off, stared at her as though seeing her for the first time. "He wants you. I have been against it. But perhaps . . ."

She grabbed his hand. "I will be a good wife to Assur! I promise you I will!"

He withdrew his hand as if stung by fire. "Well . . ." He rose from his chair, troubled, and began to pace thoughtfully back and forth. "Very well," he said at last. "I shall send word to Assur and inform Batya and Arnon of my consent to this match." He nodded, more sure now. "It seems to me this is the best solution to two problems, Assur's and your own."

"Yes! Yes!"

"I shall go now to the House of Assembly. I must pray for guidance in this matter. You too must pray."

"I will! I will!" But her mind was busy with plans as to how Sharona would live with Assur and herself after their marriage.

"A SCANDAL," Leah, the wife of Enosh ben Jacob, declared.

"That's what it is. A scandal."

Batya sighed. "What can I do? Does anyone listen to me? The girl is trouble, I tell you."

Leah clucked sympathetically. "How you must suffer."

"My main fear has always been for the children. She has bewitched them. They love her, I think, more than they love me."

"Agh!" Again a cluck of the tongue. "She is a witch. No child turns from his mother unless under a spell. You ought to talk to the rabbi."

"Kawzbeel?" Batya snorted. "He is the greatest fool of all. Consenting to a marriage between Assur and that little baggage!"

"But what could he do? The boy would not eat, could not sleep. . . . Such a promising young scholar. Better he should wed some rich man's daughter, so he would not have to worry about life but could devote himself solely to learning."

Batya's mouth became a thin line. She was remembering Joseph ben Hanina. No more Sabbath guests came to her house now with lovely pieces of embroidered silk, ivory combs, or vials of rose oil as gifts for the hostess. She looked longingly at the small copper urn that still occupied a place of honor on the wall shelf, then shook her head angrily. "No good will come of this," she said. "For myself I shall be happy merely to have her out of the house. But I pity Kawzbeel."

"He seems as bewitched as his nephew," Leah murmured. "But perhaps it is because of her line. Arnon's father was of some renown, was he not? There was talk of priests. . . ."

"The line of David. Yes, yes, my little Avi is of the line of David. But that is all on the side of Arnon's father. And Arnon's mother was a good, respectable woman. The girl's, on the other hand . . ."

"You don't have to tell me. That woman was so strange. No family. No friends. Hardly a word out of her to anyone. I will tell you something. I don't think she was a Jew. Never, not once, did she go to the House of Assembly. And I heard that once, at the start of the Sabbath, someone saw the physician lighting the candles himself!"

Batya nodded. "I have heard this. Can you believe it? The nephew of Rabbi Kawzbeel marrying a girl whose mother was

not a daughter of Israel! You know what that makes Jara—"
The sudden arch of Leah's eyebrows together with the
woman's alarmed expression seemed to be a signal to halt this
conversation. Turning, Batya saw Jara come into the room.
"There you are!" she said brightly.

Jara did not reply.

Enosh's wife cleared her throat. "I'd best be going. I have
so much to do. . . ." Chattering nervously with no care as to
whether anyone was listening to her or not, she swept past the
girl and out the door.

Batya brushed the crumbs from the table. "Well," she said
without looking up. "Your wedding day draws near. Leah and
I were just saying how unusual it is for a betrothal to be so
short. It is only a matter of months since everything was
agreed upon. I suppose, however, the rabbi has his reasons."

"And you are anxious for me to leave this house."

The woman straightened. She took a deep breath. "Yes. I
am."

"Why do you hate me?"

"What are you talking about? I don't hate you. I simply
think it best for you to have your own place, a husband,
children. . . . Believe me, my girl, if I did not care for you I
could well wish you to remain homeless forever, without a
man to protect you."

"Protect . . ." Jara murmured, thinking of the pale boy
whose hands had trembled so during their official meeting as
prospective bride and groom.

"Personally, I should think you would prefer Joseph ben
Hanina. You would be mistress of a fine, grand estate, with
many servants and all sorts of lovely things. You would lack
for nothing. And with his children practically grown . . . Why,
the man has a son nearly as old as Assur."

"That is why Rabbi Kawzbeel did not wish me finally to
enter the house of ben Hanina. You never told him about the
son. He said," Jara reminded her, "it would be an unhealthy
situation."

Batya did not reply.

"So you are happy for me," the girl went on thoughtfully.
"That is why you speak of me with such fondness and recall
my dead mother with such respect and affection."

"You keep away from me! Witch! Devil's child! I say

nothing no one else has not already said a hundred times! Your mother was a Gentile! And the Lord alone knows what you are!''

The girl bit her lip, struggling to keep back the tears. "Why do you say those things?" she whispered. "What have I done to you that you hate me so?''

Batya stared at her a moment, then hung her head, ashamed. Finally, slowly, she said, "No woman will ever love you, Jara. No woman can.''

WHEN ARNON entered the house, the first thing he saw was the girl sitting by the fire, her profile illuminated, the one eye visible to him shining eerily like a cat's reflecting light. He paused, then slowly closed the door, walked over to the table, and set down his physician's pouch.

She looked up. "You are late returning from the house of Manasseh. Batya has gone to sleep. Are you hungry?''

"Manasseh's wife gave me some food. Anyway, I don't want anything. Some wine, perhaps.'' He watched her rise and bring him the pitcher and cup. "How is it you are not abed?''

"I could not sleep. Is Manasseh all right?''

"Yes, nothing serious. Something he ate, no doubt, judging from the garbage his wife put before me. I showed her how to wrap hot ashes from the fire to hold against his belly. She kept moaning that the idol pot was broken, Manasseh having flung it away in a fit of anger. I tried to explain that it wasn't the idol that soothed the pain but the warm ashes inside the vessel. I doubt if she believed me. They never do.'' He downed the cup of wine, filled it again. "Why can't you sleep? Are you excited about becoming a bride? Two more days, isn't it?'' He drank the contents of the cup and filled it once more.

"I can't marry Assur. I can't marry anyone until I know who I am.''

"You don't know who you are? Let me tell you then. You are my sister. All right, half sister. The rest you know pretty well unless the Old One was talking into the wind all those years.''

"That is on father's side. You know as well as I—Arnon, will you put that cup down? You know true lineage rests with the mother. One is not a Jew unless one's mother was a daughter of Israel.''

"So?"

"Who was she, Arnon? What was she? I've never really known. . . ."

"And now you want me to tell you."

"Yes. You must."

"What makes you think I know anything?"

"Because you are more clever than you pretend to be. You know many things. And you keep it all locked up inside you. That's why you drink so much wine. Only I can never decide if you are drinking to keep your secrets locked up or in the hope that despite yourself they will fly free."

"A wise little puss, aren't you? You're another, sweet Jara, proud Jara, who's smarter than folks give you credit for being. The way you've turned Kawzbeel about . . ." He smiled. "Want some wine?"

"I want the truth! Tell me, Arnon. Tell me about my mother."

"Later perhaps. Right now I want to rest. I want to drink wine and look at you. I like to look at you, Jara. You shine in the dust of this miserable existence like a gold coin. I look at you and I believe the stories of the Old One. Maybe that's what our father felt. Maybe that's what he saw. He loved you. You were the only one he really loved. He would look at the rest of us and it was as if he saw us but did not see us. As if he were always looking for something, only to find it gone, missing, maybe never there at all. I don't know. I know I wanted him to love me. He did, I suppose, but not the way he loved you. He was always . . . alone. In the midst of everyone . . . alone. I wanted him to know he didn't have to be alone, that I was there. But he couldn't see that. He couldn't see it with any of us, except you perhaps."

"Because of my mother?"

"No." He gave a sudden laugh. "Because of his." He poured the wine again, then stared dreamily at the cup, smiling a little. "I remember, once, when I was a boy, the Old One told me about her. It was like a dream, a wonderful dream filled with great houses and servants and platters of gold and silver. . . . And a young woman who left all that for the life on the Masada. I confess, though, I was more interested in the stories of our grandfather, Eleazar ben Ya'ir. My brother Joshua and I would play at being Sicarii—until my mother forbade it. She quarreled with father and said it would only mean trouble, bringing attention to ourselves as being of the family of ben Ya'ir. After Masada, father had been adopted by the physician Solomon ben Ya'ish, and mother refused to admit or recognize any tie other than that. We were forbidden to mention the Sicarii or Masada. She made sure we kept away from the Old One."

"Did father agree to this?"

"He accepted it. Half the time he seemed to be in his own world. He would just take off somewhere. Oh, he'd mumble something about having to see someone here or there, or pick up a new supply of balsam—and then he'd disappear for a week or a month. . . . He never returned with what he'd gone out to procure and generally looked surprised when anyone mentioned it. I followed him once. I told myself it was for his protection, but I really wanted to see where he went. It was always the same. Three times I followed him, and always it was the same. He went to the Masada."

"That's where he died."

"The old fool." Arnon shrugged. "He was probably happy it ended there." He paused. "The moment he approached the wilderness he came alive. You could see it in the way he urged his horse forward. That miserable wasteland! And he loved it. Loved it the way he could never love anyplace else. The way he loved you."

"And my mother? Did he love her?"

"He looked at her the way he looked at all of us. Love her? No, I think he felt sorry for her."

"Why?"

He started to reply, then stopped. He looked down into his wine cup and shrugged.

"You know the answer. Why won't you tell me?" Angry at his silence, she reached out to take away the cup, but his hand caught her by the wrist.

"Don't do that, Jara," he said softly. "Mind your business. With me and everything else."

"But it is my business! You're all I've got, Arnon. You and Sharona. Look what's become of her. And now you. . . . Why do you do this to yourself? You never used to be like this."

"Why?" He deliberately poured more wine, sipping it slowly until the cup was drained. He wiped his mouth with the back of his hand. "I was always like this. You just never saw it. And I never knew it, until . . ." He turned away. "The rabbis would say that the Evil One has taken possession of me. They would say a woman—yes, a woman, always women are the cause. When the Evil One enters it is because a woman has unlocked the door." He turned back, took a step toward her, touched her hair. "They will say you are evil because . . . because . . ." He let his hand drop, shook his head, and sat down heavily. "It is not you. It is not you," he said again.

"Was my mother evil?"

"No! No! Don't you see? Anything they can't comprehend is 'bad,' 'evil.' The only evil is stupidity, Jara." He started to laugh. "Oh Lord," he recited, throwing back his head, "I thank Thee for not having made me a Gentile! I thank Thee for not having made me a woman! I thank Thee for not having made me an ignoramus!" He was laughing uncontrollably now, and suddenly there were tears in his eyes and he began weeping softly.

Jara was about to go to him when Batya appeared. "What is it?" the woman asked, frightened. "What's going on? You!" She took a step toward the girl. "What have you done to him?"

"Go to bed!" Arnon thundered. "Go to bed!"

"She's bewitched you," Batya declared. "I shall go for the rabbi."

"You shall go to bed before I kill you!" Arnon cried, rising from his seat at the same time lifting his hand as though to strike her.

Shocked, Batya retreated. With another look at Jara and one at her husband, she let out a small whimper and disappeared into the bedroom.

"Slut!" He sank down again, passed his hand before his eyes. Finally he looked up at Jara, who had not moved. "I don't know everything," Arnon said at last, his voice tired but calm. "I mean, about your mother. One thing I can tell you: You are a Jew. She was a Jew, and you are a Jew. Take it as you will, curse or blessing. As for the rest . . ." He sighed. "Let it be, Jara. Let it be."

"I cannot," she replied. "I must know. I'm not afraid," she said suddenly. "But I must know."

He yawned. "I'm tired. I must be getting old. I get so tired. All right. I told you, I don't know everything. But there is a woman in Tiberias . . ."

"Where? Where in Tiberias? Where does she live? What is her name?"

"She used to live in the street behind the perfumers, but she may have moved. She may no longer be in Tiberias. If she still resides there, all one need do is ask the way to Ziva's. Generally speaking, some fellow will know where to find her."

"I will go there tomorrow."

"No—"

"I must! I will be wed—"

"I mean, you can't go alone. I need some things in the city," he went on before she could protest. "Perhaps I'll ride there myself. You may come if you like."

"Arnon!" She threw her arms around his neck. "Thank you!"

He started to return her embrace, then drew back and gently displaced her hands. "Do not be so quick with your thanks, little sister. This may not prove to be the best of all possible wedding gifts."

IT WAS little more than an hour's ride to Tiberias, but for Jara it was like entering a different world. First there had been the startling, dramatic change of scene as she and Arnon made the descent from the hills to the western shore of the Sea of Galilee. The air grew warmer; they began to see palm trees instead of oak and sycamore. In the distance ahead, below the wall and city whose houses looked like children's blocks tumbled down a hill, lay a stretch of blue-green water dotted with fishing boats, its shore lined with white columns and graceful palms.

They entered the city gates, traditionally a place of assembly as well as station for beggars, peddlers, and self-appointed prophets. Here was a group of scholars hotly debating a point of Law, next to them a mixed lot of citizens and soldiers arguing with equal intensity the merits of the latest group of charioteers. Further on some local sage held forth to an admiring crowd, while still ahead a wild-eyed creature, his beard flecked with saliva and straw, cried out against the demon Beelzebub, who he claimed had possessed his wife in the form of a corporal from the First Thracian Cohorts. An Egyptian in a long robe embroidered with stars and strange signs thrust a stick beneath the red cloak of a smiling legionary only to bring it out miraculously changed into a snake. The mat-weaver sitting cross-legged on the ground nearby appeared unimpressed, much less aware of the tumult around him as housewives called after lost children, vendors shouted their wares, and beggars stretched forth bony fingers or poked at passers-by with their staffs.

"Don't be afraid," Arnon said. "Just keep your hood up and your eyes down. Do not return the look of any man."

But there was no way she could keep her eyes fixed to the ground, and she was soon pulling excitedly at Arnon's cloak. "Look! Look there, Arnon! That stall is filled with idol pots! Look at that one, Arnon! Is it supposed to be a pregnant woman? And that statue!" She stared, astonished, at the phallic idol. "Why, the man has—I mean, surely it is impossible—"

"Do not look. Such things are not for you to see."

"Well, they're there, aren't they? Oh! What's that?"

He followed her to the wall where several tablets made of thin sheets of lead had been posted. Various inscriptions in Latin had been scratched on the plaques. " 'To the god Pluto,' " he read. " 'Bind Niamus, son of'—I can't make out the name here—'for stealing the cloak and boots of R. son of N.' They're cursing tablets," he said, turning to her. "*Tabellae defixionum,* the Romans call them. It is a way they have of asking their gods to destroy their enemies."

"Enemies like us?"

"More likely a charioteer whose loss cost some poor soul his wages. Where are you going now?"

"I smell something wonderful!" Before he could stop her she ran around the corner. "What is he cooking?" she asked Arnon as he hurried up to her.

"I don't know. Nor do I want to know. Whatever, this food is forbidden to us."

She sighed. "It smells delicious."

"It is unclean, Jara. Even were it not pig, meat must surely spoil kept outside in this heat and with no covering. Just look how the flies buzz about."

The vendor, hearing this, let out a stream of curses and, brandishing a stick topped with a piece of roasted meat, called for them to be gone from his sight before he had them arrested.

Jara was still laughing as they rounded another corner.

"Now listen to me," Arnon said sternly, taking her by the shoulders. "We must be careful. We are strangers. We are Jews. And you—well, you attract attention, Jara. I have seen how the men look at you. Even bundled up as you are."

"I'm awfully hot, Arnon."

"Better hot than—" He broke off, looked around. "There is always danger."

"Because of the soldiers? There are so many! I've never seen so many!"

"Tiberias is their northern outpost. That great white building you were so interested in a while back is the palace of Florus Valerens, commander of the Galilee."

"The man who took Sharona?"

"Yes."

She fell silent now.

"Come now, let us attend to our business and leave. I don't want to spend the night here."

She nodded and followed him down the maze of streets until they came upon a man grilling fish over an open fire.

"*Shalom*, Pappas."

The man looked up. "Ah, the doctor. How are you, my friend? You were right, you know. It was a bad tooth. I had it pulled. Look. See. . . ."

The two men spoke while Jara nibbled at the small fish Arnon bought for her. It had been brushed with oil and the juice of the citron, then fried until it was hot and crisp. It seemed the most delicious thing Jara had ever tasted. And as she stood on the shore of the lake, eating her fish and watching the boats glide across the blue-green water, with the noise of the market behind her and the scent of sand and sea and fire and fish, it suddenly struck her how much more there was than Kefar Katan, or a house of her own—even one with a court-yard. For a moment the reason she had for being in Tiberias slipped away, and all she knew was a deep and sudden hunger not just to learn who she was but to discover what the world was. Then Arnon touched her shoulder, and the moment was gone.

"Come," he said. "Let's be on our way. The woman we seek may yet be found."

Another labyrinth of streets and alleys and they were standing before the door of a small, shabby dwelling. Arnon knocked; after some time the door opened and a woman ap-

peared. "Well," she said with a smile, appearing to recognize
Arnon. "Well, well, well." She caught sight of Jara now. An
eyebrow went up. "What's this?"

Arnon pushed Jara forward. "I will be back within the
hour," he said hurriedly. He nodded at the woman, who was
still standing in the doorway, one hand on her hip, her mouth
open in surprise. "Ziva will tell you what you need to know."
And with that he was gone.

"Wait! Where do you think you are going? Come back!"
The woman let out her breath, muttered something, then
turned to the girl and stared at her, a frown on her face.
"What's going on? Is this a trick of some kind? You may as
well know I don't like tricks."

Jara had been staring intently at the woman, as though by
studying the face before her she might find some clue as to the
female who had been her mother. Now, startled, she said,
"No. I mean, there is no trick. I've come to ask your help."

It was the woman's turn to be surprised. "My help?" She
looked the girl over, then shrugged finally. "Come in," she
said, nodding for Jara to follow. The girl did so immediately,
only to halt a few steps inside the door, eyes wide at the sight
that greeted her.

Niches in the walls displayed an assortment of idols, some
of which Jara recognized from the market. A rug of alizarin
red with woven stripes of saffron-yellow and indigo was
thrown across a wide pallet. Next to this a table held an array
of small pots and jars, cosmetic tools, perfume flasks, and a
mirror of polished brass with a wooden handle. A yellow box
with painted red dots and domed lid lay open on the bed, near
it a heap of colorful beads: carnelian, agate, blue glass, sar-
donyx—and a single silver earring. Ziva scooped up these
treasures, dumped them in the box and closed it quickly,
sliding the lid onto the flat base. "Well, are you just going to
stand there?" she asked. "What do you want?"

"I'm sorry. . . . It's just that I've never seen such fine
things."

"Fine? You call all this fine?" The woman laughed.
"Where do you come from anyway?"

"Kefar Katan."

"Katan . . ." The woman frowned as though remembering
something. "What do you want?" she asked again, brusquely,
a look of fear coming to her eyes. She jerked her head toward

the door. "Why did he bring you here? Look, I'm in business for myself, understand? I work alone. I don't work for anyone, and no one works for me."

"Oh, I don't need employment! Thank you just the same. I'm to be married day after next. To a scholar."

"Congratulations" was the dry reply.

"But I need your help."

An eyebrow went up.

"Arnon—my brother—you seemed to know him—he said you could tell me about my mother."

Silence filled the room. Then, "Your mother? How would I know your mother? I don't even know who you are."

"My name is Jara. I am the daughter of the physician Benjamin. My mother—"

"You must be hot, wrapped up like that," the woman said suddenly, blinking. "Why don't you take off that heavy cloak."

Surprised but grateful, Jara complied.

"Your hair . . . it's very beautiful."

"My mother—did my mother have beautiful hair?"

"Yes. Not so light as yours, though. No, it was dark, very dark. . . ." She stopped, shrugged. "Perhaps."

"Tell me about her. Please!"

"Why come to me? She was your mother, not mine. Surely you know what there is to know, and whatever that is should be enough for you."

"I know nothing. She died at my birth."

"Your father, then."

"He never spoke of her to me. Only to say that she was kind and good and beautiful."

"She was." Softly. "She was very beautiful. And good. She was a good girl. A good girl," she repeated firmly.

"Then why did people hate her? Why do they say she was strange and silent, that she was not a Jew?"

"She was! She was a Jew!" The woman sat down. "Not that it did her any good," she muttered. "Not that it—" She broke off, shook her head, and did not go on.

"Tell me about her. Arnon said you are the only one who can."

The woman sighed. "I know nothing. Nothing."

"But you knew her. Please, say that you knew her. . . ."

The woman looked up and through a mist of memories finally saw the young girl who stood before her, hands clenched together, lips trembling. "How old are you?" she asked softly.

"Fourteen."

"You are tall. . . ."

"Like my mother?"

The woman smiled. "No. She was about your age, though, when we first met."

"Did you know her family? Did you know my father?"

"Whoa! Hold on there. If I am to do any talking, it must be in my own way. And I still don't know if I—" She broke off as the forlorn expression returned to the girl's face. "Well, you are a grown woman as far as the world cares. About to be wed, you say. That should be enough for you," she declared suddenly, putting her hands on her hips. "What does it matter who or what your mother was? You are getting married!"

Jara shook her head. "If my mother was a Gentile, then I am one as well. I couldn't marry Assur. It wouldn't be fair."

"You love this man?"

"He isn't a man. He's a boy. No, I don't love him, but— oh, it isn't just Assur! It's me. Who I am. All my life they've called me Witch's Child and Demon Daughter. And sometimes I wonder, I wonder . . . because I have all these feelings inside me, and I don't know what they are or where they come from. In the village, at night, nothing moves, nothing stirs. The people huddle inside, they hurry to close their eyes and sleep before the fire dies away. Only when the sun appears will they go out again. If something should happen during the night, if they are forced to leave bed and house, then they whisper prayers as they enter the darkness, and carry charms and amulets to protect themselves from Asmodeus. While I stand by my window and see the moon and all the stars and wish I had wings to fly from my room . . . high above the trees . . . away from Katan . . . away from the Galilee. . . .

"And I'm not afraid of God, the way the others are. Nor of devils and demons, nor Caesar and Rome. There is only one thing that frightens me, and that is . . ." She stopped and looked about, as though startled by having said so much.

"Let us have something to drink," Ziva said, patting Jara's hand. "And a sweet cake, perhaps. Are you hungry?"

"No," she said slowly, still caught up in the thoughts she had shared. In her mind's eye she was seeing again the boats that glided across the Sea of Galilee. "Arnon bought me a fish."

"Then for sure you must be thirsty. Here is some wine. Not too strong and not too sour. The *posca* those legionaries swill is pure vinegar. Still, I must keep it on hand. But this . . . yes, it's good, isn't it? There. . . . Brought a bit of color to your face. And now you shall have a honey patty. Those are pistachios inside. And here is another made with walnuts. Whenever I fancy the world has gone too hard for me, I go out and buy some cakes and maybe a bracelet if the money's there, and all's right again. That's all there is to it, my darling. That's what it's all about. Something sweet in your tummy and something glittering on your arm. Why, your mother and I had many a party like this." She sighed. "I tried so to cheer her."

"Were you children together?"

The woman looked up, startled.

Jara tried again. "Do you know how she met my father?"

The woman said nothing. Then, suddenly, the words tumbled out. "Know. Of course I know. He found her in a brothel."

There was a silence, and then Jara said politely, "Excuse me?"

Ziva stared at her a moment, then burst out laughing. "Sweet Aphrodite! The child doesn't know what I'm saying! A whorehouse, girl! A place where—"

"Enough." Jara made a small gesture. "You need not explain further." Her voice was calm but barely more than a whisper. "I understand."

"No. You don't. Forgive me, I did not mean to be cruel. Sometimes, without meaning to—or wanting to—people become like those they most despise. I spoke too suddenly. Cruelly. I spoke from my own wounds."

Jara shook her head. Her body was numb, but her brain was racing. "How did my father—?"

"He was called to the house because he was a physician, and she, poor thing, was near to dying. She had been taken—kidnapped—by a gang of soldiers who'd had their way with her and then sold her to a house in Caesarea. The master beat her all the time, for she did not give herself willingly. It was the one thing of which she was proud, that always they had to take her. Always she fought.''

The girl's head, which had dropped as the woman began her story, lifted now, her stricken look replaced by one of fierce pride.

"Yes . . ." Ziva nodded. "That same look was in her eyes. She fought them. How she fought them! But to what avail? Her body was covered with scars. Red lines crossing here and there like the roads her tormentors have built across this land. Roads across flesh." She nodded again to herself and sighed. "Finally, unwilling or perhaps unable to bear the pain, she managed to grab hold of a blade and stabbed herself. The proprietor of the establishment was willing enough to throw her out for dead, but I . . . that is . . . one of the girls took pity and hid her. This . . . girl . . . had a friend who'd spent some time on the road with a physician newly come to the city. He managed to find the man and brought him to your mother. Perhaps it was only pity that moved the doctor. I have a foolish heart and like to believe he fell in love at first glance of that sweet face. In any event, we got her out of the house, and he took her to his own quarters and healed her—of all wounds, I cannot say. The fact is, she lived. When he left Caesarea, he took her with him.

"Some years later, I myself left Caesarea and settled here. I was married, you might say, to a sergeant of the Tenth. Got himself killed in a brawl, but his friends have been kind enough to me. I chanced to see your father one day in the marketplace. He told me your mother had died and left a baby girl. And now, here you are. . . ." The woman made a passing gesture at her face, as though to brush away a fleck of dust or dirt. But her eyes were suspiciously bright.

Jara said nothing for a time. Then, with a sigh, "I still don't know who she was."

"Did she never speak of her family to your father? Did she never say whose daughter she was?"

"No. I don't think he ever knew."

The woman nodded. "Nor would she tell any of us." She shrugged. "Not that anyone in Caesarea cared. She was a Jew," she said suddenly. "I can tell you that."

"How do you know?"

"The way she kept herself. So clean, she was. And very particular when it was her time of month. The master never allowed for more than a few days at such times—and if a customer did not mind or liked a bit of blood, why, that was all right too. But your mother . . . she cried so, saying she could not. . . . It seemed to be the worst thing they could do to her. Why do I say such things?" She let out her breath. "I should not be telling you this."

"No, I want to know everything. Everything."

"Why?" Ziva asked, her eyes full of pity.

"Because it's what I am." *As much as the other*, she thought, remembering the Old One's stories. "Do not forget who you are," the Old One had said. "Do not forget the blood from which you come." This, too, was her blood; and she knew she must accept it as fully as she had the other part of her: the shame as well as the glory.

"She would not eat all that was given to her," Ziva was saying, "even if it meant she must go hungry. Once, they forced food down her throat, meat forbidden to your people. She threw up, and the master beat her something fierce." The woman shook her head. "The more she resisted, the more terrible were the things done to her, yet she would not cease. We tried to tell her—the other girls and I—but she would not listen. 'You people are supposed to be clever,' I told her. 'Where are your brains? Close your eyes, think of something else. Eat what they give you. Do what they want. It's a matter of moments, and then it is done. The main thing is to survive. To not get hurt.' But she was like a trapped animal without thought or reason but to fight, to escape, or to die."

"She must have had family. Did she never say their name or try to get word to them?"

"She said they were dead. I supposed they had been killed when she was taken. I remember your father asking her name, who her own father might be. She would not answer, even close to death as she was then. She just kept shaking her head from side to side, saying, 'Dead. They are dead. I to them and they to me.' But once—I remember now—she spoke to me of the place where she was born. It was a farm of some kind—no —wait—it was an orchard. Yes, that was the very word she used. 'The orchard.' She said there was a great school there, and that her father was one of the teachers. A rabbi. He must have been important. She told me he had hundreds of students, that people came from far and near to hear him.''

"Did she say his name?"

"No, she would not even say her own name. The master called her Ariane.''

"Her name was Rachel.''

"Perhaps.''

Jara nodded. She was about to ask the woman something when the door flew open and a rather grimy legionary burst into the room.

"Ziva! I'm back! Bring some wine, woman! Come and show me how you've missed me!'' Striding forward to embrace her, the man unbuckled his sword belt and let it drop to the floor. Another step and the chestplate was off as well, leaving him clad only in hobnailed sandals and a soiled tunic. "What are you waiting for, woman? Give us a kiss!'' Arms outstretched, he stopped, suddenly aware of another presence. He turned now and saw Jara. "Well. Hello. What have we here? Ziva, my pet, have you brought your love a bit of chicken for supper? A mite skinny, but tasty, I warrant. Yes . . .'' His eyes traveled the length of the girl's body and then returned to her face. "Yes, very nice indeed.'' Suddenly he threw back his head and laughed. "A party! We shall have a party, the three of us! Ziva, you're wonderful!'' But it was to Jara he moved.

"Leave her alone," Ziva snapped. "She's not what you think.''

"No? And what do I think? What is she doing here anyway? Who the hell is she?''

"A friend, that's all. The daughter of a friend.''

"Daughter of a friend, eh? What's she doing here? You setting her up in business?'' He winked. "Or keeping her for yourself?''

"Shut your filthy mouth.''

"Shut your own mouth, whore. Or I'll do it for you. Now, then . . .'' He took another step toward Jara, who was standing quite still in a cold, contained manner. "Let's see what we have here. Skinny, like I said. But promising. Definitely promising. Aye, there's a wild look to that face that's the mark of a pure animal heart.'' His arm went out. "Come here, girl," he said huskily. "Let's see how you taste.''

She moved back, evading his grasp. Suddenly Ziva was between them. "Leave her alone," she said, laughing. "What do

you want with a skinny chicken like that anyway?'' She put
her mouth to the man's ear and began to whisper things that
soon had him laughing with her. The two sank back on the
bed. ''You're a lot of woman, Ziva,'' the soldier said, running
his hands over her body. ''But don't try and turn me away
from what I want.''

''She's a baby.'' Ziva pouted. ''Soon to be a bride. Leave
her be, my darling. Leave her be.''

''A bride, eh? I had a bride myself once. Not my own, mind
you.'' He laughed. ''Nice all the same. Where's that wine?''

''What are you talking about?''

''Some little village. We took the girl to teach the Jews a
lesson. Whew! What is this sweet stuff? Get me some real
wine.''

''Katan.''

He looked at the girl, surprised to hear her speak. She had
been standing still as a statue. ''Eh? What?''

''It was the village of Katan. The girl was my sister,
Sharona.''

He set down the cup and stared at her. ''Your sister?'' He
grinned. ''Well, well. Think of that!'' He started to laugh.
''Did you hear, Ziva? It was her sister! The bride I had was her
sister!''

''You pig,'' Jara spat.

He stopped laughing.

''Foul, ugly pig.''

He rose from the bed, started to go to her, then stopped,
halted by the look in the girl's eyes, by that green-gold glare
raking his flesh. His face turned red. Then he laughed again.
''No need to fight, you and I. More than likely we'll soon be
good friends, you being a bride and all. I mean, Rome must
have her due. It's only fair, seeing how much work we put into
taking care of you. The village of Katan, eh? Yes, I remember
it now. Seems to me your people were willing enough to pay
such small tribute to Caesar.''

''Not any more!'' She moved closer to him now, fists
clenched. ''You try it! You just try it, and see what happens!''

His eyes narrowed. ''And what will happen? Tell me, Cat-
Eyes. What will happen?''

''See for yourself!''

''Enough! Enough!'' Ziva was pushing her toward the
door. ''Get out! Go! I want no troublemakers!'' She pushed

Jara's cloak into her hands. "Leave now," she whispered. "Say no more. Just get out."

The door opened, closed, and Jara was in the street. She looked about, confused and uncertain, and saw Arnon coming toward her. She smiled weakly.

He started to say something then stopped and simply put his arm around her. "Are you all right?" he asked softly. "You look pale."

She nodded. She was trembling.

He studied her a moment, then said, "Come. We had best go home now."

She nodded again and let him lead her down the street.

After a while he said, "Tomorrow you will become Assur's wife. All that matters is what you are, Jara, not what went before. Look at me. I am no ben Ya'ir. I'm not even a very good doctor. As for your mother . . ." He shook his head. "What can I say? These are the times we live in. Only . . . don't let her pain become your pain."

She wanted to tell him that while he was right, he was also wrong, but she did not know how to say this without sounding argumentative and perhaps foolish, and so she said nothing. Meanwhile her head was filled with images that swirled behind her eyes like dolls riding a whirlwind, and Arnon's words echoed in her mind and mingled with the things Ziva had told her, all of it fading finally as she saw once more the Old One and in the end could hear only the Old One's voice:

Do not forget who you are. The others will say it is nothing. But it is everything. It is what you are.

Arnon had stopped. He was staring at her, his face concerned. "You are too quiet," he murmured. "If you want to talk . . . if you want to cry . . ."

Her chin came up. "No," she said. "I don't want to cry. I want to fight."

THE MORNING of her wedding the wind blew from the east: a desert wind, warm and wild. It was all the young men could do to keep the bridal canopy secure; the carrying of the curtained litter that would bear Jara to her groom was put off again and yet again in hopes the wind would die down. At last, late in the afternoon, impatient to proceed, Jara prevailed upon the company to let her walk rather than ride, and while this deviation was considered an omen, it was not agreed whether it signaled something good or evil, many present being pleased to see the proud girl "humbled."

Her long hair, whipped about by the wind, encircled her torso like a coil of silken snakes; her white robe fluttered and flapped as she walked across the village square, one hand firmly holding on to the myrtle wreath. The songs of the children were lost in the wind; at times Assur, moving toward her, seemed obliterated by the clouds of rising dust. But even without the wind she hardly saw him, any more than she'd seen or heard the people who had gathered in her brother's house all morning. Her thoughts were in Tiberias and what she had learned there. None but a very few sworn to secrecy knew where and in what circumstances her father had found his third wife.

"He confided only in those he thought might aid in seeking out your mother's family and true identity," Arnon had said.

"Would she never say who they were?"

"No. She wanted them to believe that she was dead."

Assur was coming closer. She could see her bridal veil fluttering in his hands, like a bird trying to fly free. And suddenly a gust of wind tore it from his fingers, and the white fabric sailed above their heads and glided across the sky like the boats she'd watched move across the Sea of Galilee. She could hear the onlookers gasp (or was it only the wind?). Another omen. Surely this one bode no good. Still, she smiled.

The whole thing was like a dream. Was this really her wedding day, or was she only dreaming? Everywhere there was dust and wind and an unnatural heat. The very air was alive, while the people around her seemed dead, like statues or sticks.

The veil had blown away; no one could catch it. For a moment it seemed to hang in the sky like a shroud or ghost.

Then through the wind came the sound of hoofbeats, and the ground seemed to tremble underfoot. Jara watched the veil fly away and, turning back, saw the fright on Assur's face. She looked around and saw they were surrounded by soldiers.

And still as if in a dream, she saw the face of the Roman commander, those pale, dead eyes, the small cruel smile, the scar alongside his mouth.

"It is a mistake," Rabbi Kawzbeel was saying. "A misunderstanding or, worse, a terrible joke. No one here plans war. We have no insurrectionists among us. Look for yourself. There are no rebels hidden, no store of arms. It is a mistake."

She never took her eyes from the Roman's face, and she knew, though he barely glanced at her, that he had seen her and wanted her.

She sensed Assur moving to her side and realized with some surprise that despite his fear he meant to protect her. She touched his hand gently, for that one moment his wife. Then she turned to the Roman and raised her arms so that he might lift her up onto his horse.

Nothing more was said. As they rode away she caught a last glimpse of Arnon and had the certain feeling she would never see him or anyone else in Katan again.

3

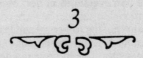

FLORUS VALERENS let the document he had been studying fall from his hand and proceeded to stroke his beard, thumb and forefinger bringing the hair to a point, hardly aware of the gesture as he turned his gaze toward the girl in his bed.

He was forty-five, a lean, well-built man who prided himself on his appearance. No matter where the campaign or assignment, his tunic was spotless, his chestplate unmarred and polished so as to catch the slightest ray of sun. It had always bothered him that despite every attention a dark shadow remained constant on his jaw, and so he had finally adopted the short "philosopher's beard" which Hadrian had made fashionable, even though he despised the Greek culture it represented and resented what he considered to be paltry recognition of his years of service by the emperor. After all, he had fought beside Lusius Quietus in Mesopotamia, and it was no small task to keep Judea quiet. The Jews were a queer, crazy lot; there was always trouble brewing. Here was a report before him now, naming specific towns that were centers of insurgence. According to his informant (whom Valerens had no cause to doubt and every reason to believe) great numbers of rebels were gathering for a conclave or council of war. All this while Tinneus Rufus conducted long philosophical discussions with the rabbi Akiva.

Idiot.

Didn't the fool realize his own wife was becoming a Jew in the process?

Well, that was Rufus' problem. There would be greater ones to deal with if the governor did not crack down soon—and

hard—on these people. The trouble was, Rufus was not a true
military man, as Quietus had been. Hadrian had gone back to
the old system of appointing *legati* who had comparatively
little military experience, usually senators of praetorian rank
who would hold the appointment for no more than a few
years. It was supposed to signal a new era of relations between
Rome and Judea. Well, the tribunes were just as bad, Valerens
thought with a sigh. Most of them young puppies putting in
six months' service in order to return to the political *cursus
honorum* of senators. Certainly, he mused with bitter humor,
the greatness of the Roman army did not lie in its method of
appointing commanders. Whatever success the Empire enjoyed was due to legion organization itself, to the discipline
and obedience of the common soldier, and most of all to the
efficiency of the centurions.

He was himself of that extraordinary breed, reaching now
the rank of *praefectus legionus*. It was the highest post he
would hold and in fact the end of his military career. Perhaps
that was why Hadrian had not expelled him along with
Quietus, who had been executed, not for his treatment of the
Jews, but for failing to support the new emperor's accession.
Perhaps Hadrian had simply decided it was more prudent to
make use of Valerens' experience than to dismiss him. After
all, the prefect thought, again with a certain wryness, that experience could hardly be less than an asset to an occupying
army commanded by amateurs.

Marcellus Quintus was no amateur. What a man with his
distinguished record was doing in Judea was still a bit of a
mystery, unless Hadrian was not so blind to events as he,
Valerens, thought. In any event Quintus would be privy to this
new information concerning rebel activity. Perhaps he could
get Rufus to use a little more muscle.

His eyes still on the girl, Valerens tapped absently on the
rolled parchment. The sound caught her attention, and he
found himself looking into those large, light eyes whose stare,
he had discovered earlier, could be rather unsettling.

She was sitting up now, eating an apple, the fur coverlet
held tight under her arms. From the moment he'd left her side
she had been totally absorbed by the tray of food beside the
bed. Slices of cold fowl, cheese, olives, fruit had disappeared
down her young throat with unselfconscious enthusiasm. He
found himself amused by her appetite. In fact he was wholly

intrigued and wondered what fascinated him most: her beauty, her composure during their interview, or her seeming indifference now not only to his presence but to that which she had just experienced. All in all, a strange little bitch.

But then, everything about the day had been odd. That wind rising out of nowhere, his mood upon awakening, the sense of anticipation as on the morning of a battle. For a moment, he'd thought he was back in Cyprus. And the feeling, that gut instinct of imminent danger, had persisted.

He'd been restless, uneasy. When the report came in from that drunken sergeant, he'd leaped at the opportunity to take action, any kind of action, and ridden off to investigate the matter. After all, the village was not without incident. There had been a fight on the road only the year before. There had been a wedding then. Another girl . . .

It was as if something unseen had propelled him back to that place. And always the sense of danger . . .

But there proved to be nothing to fear from that pathetic little settlement, just as he'd known in his heart there would be. (And still, the sense of catastrophe.) Nor was there trouble on the road either going or coming: no ambush, no tree falling across his horse, no sudden opening of the ground to swallow him up, no strange wind turned into thunder and fire. Yet all of it was odd. And strangest of all, the girl.

She had the look of someone waiting, expecting nothing, ready for anything. She had not wept or pleaded or railed against Rome. She had made no attempt to kill herself, nor had she cowered in the corner upon reaching his chamber. In fact, she behaved with admirable composure while he deliberately ignored her, issuing a number of orders to his aides. Then they were alone, and still she showed no fear. She had walked about the room looking at his belongings, touching various objects, taking in the width and breadth of the place—*like an animal*, he thought suddenly, *staking out its territory*. Finally, brusquely, he'd asked her what she wanted. "I am not a fool," he'd told her. "Things do not happen twice in the same place. And young girls in a situation such as the one you are in do not stand about calmly fingering an incense shovel like someone browsing in a shop. They cry or plead or faint."

She had appeared almost to smile. "Do you want me to cry or plead or faint?"

"I want to know what this is about. You came willingly. Too willingly. Why?"

"I did not want you to whip anyone."

"What if I whip you?"

That had startled her. For a moment he'd had the satisfaction of seeing something like fright in her eyes. Or was it anger? Even now he wasn't sure. She had remained silent after that, saying finally, thoughtfully, "I do not think I would like being hurt."

"Few do" was the dry comment. "And yet," he had found himself continuing, "there are some who take pleasure in pain, their own as well as others'. You don't know what I'm talking about, do you? Not many in this miserable little country do. Oh, there are enough lovely creatures, but never any surprises. They fight, or they faint, or they are willing but stupid. You . . . you are a bit of a surprise. So far. I imagine I will be disappointed soon enough." This speech had been met with silence; but a sudden spark or gleam in those catlike eyes had driven him to say next, "All right. Get on with it. Bargain!"

"For what?"

"Your life. Your body. I intend to have the latter in any case. The condition in which it is returned depends on what you say now."

"Then I will say nothing. But if, later, you agree that I have pleased you," she went on quickly, "then I will ask a favor."

Another surprise. He had stared at her a moment, his body growing warm, suspicion turning to amusement and then excitement. "Please me? Aren't you a virgin?"

"Yes. I am."

"Then how will you know what pleases me?"

She had shrugged. A small and, to his eye, exquisite shrug. "You will teach me."

It was then he had summoned the servant and told him to bring food and wine. All things considered, he had reasoned, it was going to be a long evening.

THE HOUR was late now. He watched as her teeth tore into the apple, and smiled slightly. He pushed away the informant's scroll, got up, and went to her, sitting down on the edge of the bed. He put his hand on her shoulder.

She looked up briefly, then placed the apple core on the tray beside the bed, licked her fingers, and calmly meeting his gaze once more, said simply, "Again?"

He nodded. His mouth was dry. He brushed the heavy mass of hair back from her shoulder and traced the curve of flesh with his finger. "It will go better for you this time," he murmured and bent forward that his lips might better follow the path his hands would take.

HE AWOKE to find her standing by the bed. For a moment the feeling he'd had upon awakening that morning returned. Then he relaxed and smiled.

She gave a slight nod.

He frowned. "Why are you dressed?"

"It will be morning soon."

"Never mind that." He smiled again. "What matters is that you must pay Caesar's tithe in full before I return you to your husband."

"I have no husband. The ceremony of consecration did not take place."

"No? Well, that alters things a bit, doesn't it? Hmmmm. You were supposed to be a bride. And now I find you are not."

She shrugged, as if to say, did it really matter to him?

He laughed, and motioned for her to sit beside him. "I feel wonderful," he told her. "And the fact is, you look none the worse for wear. Better perhaps," he mused, twirling a lock of her hair around his finger. "You are quite lovely, you know. I daresay another year . . ." He smiled again. "As the apple ripens . . . you will be extraordinary. And with the proper guidance . . ." His voice trailed off, but he continued to play with her hair. "I think I'm going to keep you," he said suddenly. "They'll make your life a misery back in that idiot village of yours, now, won't they? Your young man won't touch you now."

"You think little of my people."

"All people, my dear. All people."

She did not reply.

"That's it, then. You are staying here, with me."

"You cannot make me your slave."

"I seriously doubt you could be any man's slave. Let us say, I would like an arrangement whereby I offer my protection in exchange for your company and, shall we say, continued diligence as my pupil."

"What happens when you tire of me? Will you give me to your soldiers, or sell me to a house of women?"

"Probably. Therefore I would say it is in your best interest to continue to please me. Yes, I said it. I have not forgotten," he went on before she could speak. "You have pleased me. You do please me. Tell me now what you want."

She went over to the table that served as his desk. It was covered with various documents and bits of parchment. "You have a paper—"

"That's it! I should have known! Why didn't I guess?" He was out of bed in a single bound, the fur coverlet pulled around him like a cloak. One bare arm snatched up a scroll and waved it before her face. "You've got a brother—cousin —someone on my list of rebels! You want him spared—"

"No, I have no one—I don't know what you mean."

"You know no one in Ein Gedi? Tekoa? The villages of Kobi and Kosiba?"

She shook her head. "I have never traveled from the Galilee. The places you speak of are to the south."

He frowned. "Then what is all this about a paper?"

"I would like to have a paper," she explained, "saying I may travel wherever I like and that no soldier may harm me."

He blinked. "A writ of safe conduct? Why would you want that?"

"I thought—before—that I would like to come now and again to Tiberias. I like the city. It is very wonderful to me. But I am afraid of the soldiers. If I had a paper with your name signed to it they would leave me alone, and I could come and go as I pleased. Now, since you want me to stay with you, I think it would be very good to have such a thing."

He laughed. "You won't need it, but all right, if that's what you want." He sat down at the table and shook his head. "I can't believe that's all you desire. But I suppose, to a Jew, it would be important."

"It is," she said softly. "To walk in freedom . . . without fear, is . . . important."

"All right, then. Let me find something to write on. Here.

Here we are." His back was to her now. His hand moved quickly over a piece of parchment. Suddenly he paused. "What is your name?" he asked. "I don't know how you are called."

"Jara."

"Jara. No family name, of course. Jews have no surnames. We'll just say 'the female known as Jara.' There, that should do it. Well, there you are, my dear. This will keep you safe. In fact," he continued, turning around—but he said no more, nor ever would. For she had come behind him, quiet as a cat, and with the swiftness of the striking animal plunged into his heart the knife that had lain on the tray of fruit beside the bed. His eyes bulged with horror and pain, stricken not only by the act itself but by the look in her eyes.

"In fact," she hissed, "my name is Jara, daughter of Benjamin, born on the Masada. Sister of the female known as Sharona, whose life you destroyed!"

He made a small, gurgling sound as she withdrew the dagger only to plunge it again into his chest.

"Jara!" Her voice was the sound of steaming vapors rising from the hot depths of Hades. "Daughter of the woman Rachel, whom your men raped and sold and . . ." She swallowed. "My name is Jara," she said yet again, her voice low, throbbing, yet barely more than a whisper. "And I am the granddaughter of Eleazar ben Ya'ir and Alexandra of the house of Harsom." She saw his mouth twitch and watched the light go out of his eyes, then placed one hand on his throat and pulled the knife out of his body.

Valerens' corpse remained upright in the chair. Jara stood there a moment, breathing heavily, watching for some sign of life. There was none. The dagger fell from her hand. She jumped at the sound, but the noise had brought her back to action.

She tipped the chair back and dragged it over to the bed like a wagon or lorry, then tipped it forward so that the prefect fell into bed. His legs dangled over the edge; she lifted them up and swung them onto the bed, then arranged the fur throw in a natural fashion. He was lying face down; his blood would soak into the pallet; there were no visible stains on the coverlet. She turned the man's face sideways, away from the door, and closed his eyes. Then she brought the chair back to the table, went over to the water basin and washed her hands, which had become stained with the Roman's blood. It was only as she lifted the water pitcher that she realized how markedly she was trembling.

She dried her hands, then forced herself to stand quite still and breathe deeply for a moment, fighting the stronger instinct to bolt. It was the same technique she had used in the ride to Tiberias, when she realized her body was rigid with apprehension, her discomfort made even more acute by the jarring gallop of the horse. She had forced herself to relax, to seek out and find the animal's rhythm and then sink into it, at the same time feeling the man's viselike grip become less constricting. And so she had been able to think, not actually to plan, but to think of what awaited her, what she knew had awaited others, and of how she might emerge from the situation. And later, in bed with Valerens, she had again willed herself to remain calm, to allow the experience to occur, and to seek and ride the rhythm of the man so that she would not be harmed. It was not pain she feared so much as the possibility of becoming incapacitated, helpless, at the mercy of those who she knew had no mercy. Withal, she was unprepared for the searing flame that tore through her body when he entered her, and though the moment was brief it was one she would remember all her life. After that he had allowed her to rest, and when he took her again it was, as he had said, better, not unpleasant, even interesting. But never for one moment did she not know who he was and what she intended to do. The paper of safe conduct would get her to Tur Malka. It was the name she'd heard over and over in the galloping hooves of the horses. *Tur Malka. Tur Malka.*

She would be safe there.

MARCELLUS QUINTUS strode up the steps of the administrative palace in Tiberias, startling the guard, who was unprepared for so important a visitor at this hour.

"You are alone, sir?" the soldier asked, wondering at the wild look in the centurion's eyes. "Did your men meet with trouble on the road? It is not good to ride at night—"

"I am alone. The way was peaceful enough. Get someone to take care of the horse, will you? No doubt he's more tired than I."

"Yes, sir. Right away, sir."

"Don't disturb your commander. I will see him in the morning."

The doors to the palace swung open, and the Roman strode impatiently inside. He was tired now. The ride had done him in. If only his brain might fall asleep. Still the images persisted. Just thinking of Livia in Rufus' arms was enough to drive him mad.

"He hasn't wanted you for months," he'd wondered. "Why now?"

"I don't know," she had replied. "Amusement, I suppose. Perhaps he is in the mood for stoic consent."

"Don't go." His hands had gripped her arms. "Don't go to him."

"How can I refuse? Quintus, he is my husband."

"And I? What am I to you?"

She had touched a finger to his lips. "You," she had said, "are my love."

And so he'd ridden off. Florus Valerens had requested a meeting; very well. No doubt the prefect would like to conspire against Rufus, but if he thought Marcellus Quintus would join in any of his plans, he was mistaken. Whatever he felt for Livia, however much he disliked Rufus, the centurion was convinced Hadrian had picked the right person to govern Judea. So long as the military was kept to the background and the rabbis allowed to officiate in civic disputes among the Jews, Quintus was convinced the Judeans would accept their place as Caesar's subjects. There would always be young hotheads, and a certain hostility which he had learned to recognize as being directed not against Rome per se or against Hadrian, who was viewed with great hope for his promise to rebuild Jerusalem, but against the army, the legions with their cohorts and auxiliaries of Samaritans, Syrians, and men from Arabia, all of whom indulged their hatred of the Jews as much as power permitted. Moreover, commanders like Florus Valerens did not bother to check this condition; instead they fed it, allowed it to grow. Quintus had heard more than one tale of the "games" the prefect liked to play, and the amusements of which he had partaken in the company of the late Lusius Quietus. He had himself witnessed that incident in the village soon after his arrival in Judea. It was the kind of thing that made corporals grin, but bred revolt.

The trouble was, he mused, the system had to be revised again. Hadrian had allowed the difference in status between the legions and their *auxilia* virtually to disappear. Moreover, he'd done away with the statute whereby only Roman citizens were eligible for service in the legions, so that vacancies in the ranks might be filled from local sources. Expedient as the practice was, it had resulted in an occupying force without the discipline and character that Quintus would have liked to see. Too many of the men serving in Judea were born *castris*, meaning they were the sons of men who had "contracted" marriage alliances contrary to Roman law while in military service. Bastards. With a built-in hostility toward the Jews inherited from their Greek or Samaritan mothers.

Quintus had just about decided to communicate these thoughts to Hadrian when a sudden commotion down the hall caught his attention. One of the guards was attempting to lead away a young female. The man was grinning, the girl protesting.

"All right, what's going on?"

The soldier let go of the girl. "Nothing, sir. Nothing at all."

Quintus had caught up to the pair now. The girl turned, and he felt a shock as he recognized those strange green-gold eyes.

"Please," she implored, "I have a paper. You must let me go. I have a paper."

She was breathing hard. Her pupils kept changing, receding, then growing large. It was strange, hypnotic. He took the piece of parchment from her hand, read it, then said to the guard, "She is free to leave."

The man cleared his throat. "I know, sir. It's a bit strange, though, the commander saying nothing about this."

"He's sleeping," the girl said. "He does not want to be disturbed. He said he would flog anyone who bothered him." She looked at Quintus. "He drank much wine."

He was still staring at her. She had grown since he last saw her, and the wild beauty that had first captivated him was even more provocative now. More than ever he sensed a strange mix of something strong and earthly with something else, something elusive. . . .

"What are you doing here?" he asked quietly.

She seemed surprised by the question.

The guard answered. "The commander took her, centurion.

From some little village up in the hills. There were rumors of rebels hiding there. Didn't find none. The commander, though, he took her with him."

"For what cause?"

It was the soldier's turn to be surprised. "Cause? Why, she's just a Jew, centurion. Anyway, I guess it will teach them a lesson."

"Another lesson," Quintus murmured, thinking of the scene he'd witnessed a year ago. He studied the girl again. She appeared agitated, somewhat breathless, her eyes darting here and there as though seeking some avenue of escape. That was not difficult to understand. What "lessons" had she learned this night? He passed a hand before his eyes. "It's all right," he said tiredly. "Go. Go home."

"I want a horse," she said quickly. "He said I could have a horse."

"Well, all right, then," the guard said now, smiling broadly. "Like I told you, girl, you come with me and we'll see you get a fine ride." He winked at Quintus and tried to take Jara's arm again.

"No! Bring it here. To the front of the palace. In plain sight."

"Now, I can't do that, girl. You just come with me—"

"Please . . ." She turned to Quintus. "I don't want to go with him."

The guard was grinning. Quintus looked at him a moment, then nodded grimly. "Bring a horse to the front," he told the soldier. "We will wait for you there."

The man's mouth fell open. Then, cursing silently, he went off.

Quintus took hold of Jara's elbow and led her out the palace. She was trembling; could he expect less? He took a deep breath, letting the cold night fill his lungs with sweet pain. For a moment he could see Livia's face in the darkness, not as she was now but as she must have been at fourteen, given in marriage to a man more than twice her age, a man she did not love nor ever would. . . .

He closed his eyes, opened them. "I'm sorry," he said.

She studied him a moment; he could not be sure what she was thinking, and then the horse was brought forth. He helped her mount. There was a bundle of some sort under her cloak. He wondered what she'd stolen from Valerens.

She held out her hand. "My paper."

He gave the writ to her. "Will you be able to find your way?"

She nodded. "Please. I want to go now." She sucked in her breath. "I cannot . . . I cannot stay here any longer."

He nodded, and watched as she turned the horse, riding away, out the city gates and into the darkness.

It was only when Jara heard the gates of Tiberias close behind her that she loosened her grip on the dagger hidden beneath her cloak and stuck it into the cord around her waist. A pouch was also fastened there, one she'd found in the prefect's chamber. It held an apple, some bread, a few dates, a piece of cheese, and the document Florus Valerens had waved in her face. The Roman had thought it was important. Samson, in Tur Malka, would know what to do with it.

SHE RODE through dawn, far beyond Kefar Katan. At Scythopolis she was stopped by two soldiers. Upon seeing the paper Valerens had given her, they allowed her to proceed.

She continued another hour's distance, then turned off the road, looking for a brook or well to water the horse. In this way she came upon a shepherd bathing in a pool fed by the Jordan. His clothes were spread out on a rock, newly washed and still damp. She took the boy's tunic and short mantle and quickly changed into them, fatigue dissipated by their cool touch. Then some miles away and hidden from the road, she took the knife from the cord tied around her waist and began to hack away at her hair until the ground was littered with curls. Then she buried her hair, finished the apple, counted the dates left in the pouch, and took a swig from the waterskin that she'd also stolen from the shepherd.

The sun was high in the sky now. They'd be looking for her. Despite the lack of incident thus far, she made up her mind to stay off the highway and to avoid the towns alongside the road. The way was straight and sure, but it led through Samaria, which was as dangerous as further encounters with the legionaries might prove to be. There was great enmity between the Samaritans and the Jews. Although the people of Mount Gerizim professed to worship the One God, there had been much intermarriage with foreigners like the Romans, and they were more pagan than not. Moreover, the Samaritans had a well-earned reputation for thievery, murder, and generally brutish behavior. Not for nothing had pilgrims in the days of the Temple forded the Jordan to avoid passage through Samaria on their way to Jerusalem. The situation remained unchanged, especially since Rome had set up colonies in the area after the war for her retired legionaries.

Jara studied the sky, watching the sun move from east to west. There was another road, alongside the Great Sea: the famed Via Maris. But there, too, she would find many soldiers. Besides, she would have to cut across the mountains to reach it, or return to Scythopolis where the road branched off.

There was another way. She could follow the Jordan. The river ran south to the Dead Sea, where, the legend went, it spilled into the mouth of the great beast behemoth, whose flesh could feed the world.

The road she had been on ran parallel to the river, but looking down all one could see was a veritable jungle or forest, a serpentine green ribbon of trees and tangled bush.

She hesitated.

The rugged banks of the meandering river were known to shelter all kinds of animals. At evening one might find lions, foxes, roes, stags, or leopards and wild boars drinking there. But if an animal could hide in those thickets, so too could a man. Or a runaway girl. "Let the Jordan be thy border" was the saying when someone had to take flight and hide.

Leading the horse, she made her way on foot down to the river bank, feeling the heat and humidity rise about her: flowers, grass, and herbage coming up past her knees until she thought she would sink into broom and thistle, the brakes of cane, the oleander.

Another look at the sky. She must follow the river now, checking direction by always crossing the path of the sun. On her right shoulder the mountains of Galilee and Samaria. To her left, on the other side of the Jordan, the hills of Gilead. And somewhere ahead, Tur Malka.

4

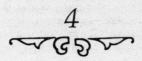

THE TWO MEN on the road appeared to be in no hurry. One was
dark-skinned: a Nabatean, of indeterminate age. The other
man was about thirty-five, with reddish-brown hair and a
deeply bronzed complexion. He was a big man, almost too
large for the horse he sat, with big hands, and a strong, open
face. His eyes were blue, not the startling aquamarine of the
Galileans, who were said thus to carry a bit of their lake forever with them, but gray-blue, flecked with sparks of topaz,
and characterized by a direct, steady gaze and the slight squint
that came from a life spent under a harsh sun. He could well
have been a farmer on his way to or from some rabbi, seeking
a verdict on a land dispute or dowry question; certainly he was
no artisan, scholar, or merchant. But to say this man was
merely one of that great mass called disparagingly *am
ha-aretz*, "people of the land," would have been a disservice;
there was something in his gaze that reached beyond the normal, short-sighted concerns of a simple peasant. A fire burned
behind those deep-set, speckled eyes, glimpses of it surfacing
in the flecks of gold that danced around the dark pupils.

He nodded at the Nabatean. "Just ahead." His voice was
rough, strong.

The black man checked to see if they had been followed or
were being watched. They were alone, on a seemingly deserted
path where the Judean hills met the mountains of Samaria.
Badlands. Home of thieves, outlaws, fugitives. Even the
legionaries kept their distance; it was too easy for a man to
disappear here, to wind up with his throat cut and body
stripped.

The Nabatean nodded assent and followed his companion

off the road. "How many to meet us?"

"As many as Joshua manages to round up."

"Too many will bring the soldiers. Rufus has spies everywhere. They will report who has left this city, that village, who comes from the South, who journeys from the North. . . ."

"So long as they don't know where we're meeting. What if they do?" he declared. "The hell with it. Let them come."

The Nabatean smiled slightly. "You are anxious for it to begin."

"Now that I've made up my mind to it, yes."

"It would be foolish to die before the real fight, Simeon."

"Don't worry, Obodas. I have no intention of getting killed." He grinned. "You're the one always saying I'm under heaven's protection. What happened? Have you lost faith in your stars? Anyway, I don't believe the legions are waiting for us. Spies, maybe. Fine. Let them take our message back to Rufus. Let him eat it."

"Simeon . . ." The Nabatean shook his head, but he was smiling. "You give no quarter."

"I give as good as I get. When the day comes, my friend, that the emperor says to me, 'Simeon ben Kosiba, me and my army are taking leave of your land, seeing as how we have no business there in the first place and appear to be causing you people no end of misery'—why, then, I'll shake the bastard's hand and say, 'Goodbye, God bless.' Until then . . .'" His face grew grim.

The Nabatean was about to say something when the sound of a nearby struggle caught the attention of both men. As they broke through the bush, they saw in a clearing ahead a man throwing what appeared to be a young lad face down on the ground. The boy struggled to get up, only to have a second man force him down again. Leaning against a tree, a third fellow watched, laughing coarsely.

The first man had already loosened his underclothing and now he raised up the youngster's buttocks. Pulling down the boy's undergarment, he looked up, startled, and said with a laugh, "Here's a surprise—"

"Here's a better one!" Simeon grabbed the boy's attacker, swung him around, and with one hand dealt him a cutting blow across the throat. The Nabatean meanwhile had pounced on the man by the tree and rendered him unconscious. He now turned his attention to the fellow who'd been holding the boy's arms and was now advancing toward Simeon with drawn dagger. Before he or the Judean could move, an arrow caught this assailant between the shoulders, and a group of men emerged from the surrounding trees.

Simeon ran a hand through his thick mop of hair and laughed. "Now that's what I call good work! Who shot that arrow? Joshua?"

The man so identified looked around, concerned. "I thought no one knew we were meeting here. Who are they?"

"Well, the one you took care of isn't going to say anything. See to the others. I'll talk to the boy."

During all this Jara had managed to roll aside and quickly cover herself, after which she lay panting on the ground, exhausted from the struggle with her attackers. Now she pushed herself up on her elbows and, looking up, saw a tall man with broad shoulders standing before her, his legs spread wide, one hand extended. Her mouth fell open. The sun had slid between the trees behind him so that his head and shoulders appeared outlined in flame. His face, shadowed, was too dark for her to make out the features. But surely he was the largest man she'd ever seen. Was it possible he was human?

"Goliath," she gasped.

There was laughter at this.

"Hear that, Simeon? The lad thinks you're a Philistine!"

More laughter.

The big man crouched beside her. She could make out his face now. It was rather a nice face. In any event, he did not look as if he would hurt her. Still . . .

She inched backward, her fingers groping for a stick or rock. Suddenly her hand closed around the dagger the dead man had let fall. She raised the knife. . . .

The big man appeared surprised. Then, with a swiftness that took her by surprise, knocked the blade away.

"Watch out, Simeon!" One of the men called out, laughing. "Even mosquitoes sting!"

"The lad's frightened, that's all." He got up and, with the same suddenness which he had used to disarm her, pulled her to her feet. As his hand closed around her wrist, a startled look came into his eyes. He said nothing, however, but continued to stare at her, taking in the curve of her legs, the narrow ankles, the small waist caught with cord above which the folds of the shepherd's tunic hid any discernible shape. "You have nothing to fear," he said at last, in a gentle tone. "Who are you?"

Before she could answer, one of the men came over with the pouch she'd stolen from Valerens' chamber. He'd removed the documents which he now handed to the man called Simeon. "Those two are Samaritans," the man remarked. "Wonder where they got these. The bag's got Roman markings."

"It's mine!" Jara cried now. "The papers too! Give them to me!"

Simeon was reading the scrolls. He looked up at her, then back at the papers in his hands. "Leave us alone," he said to his startled comrade. "Let me talk to . . . the youngster."

The man withdrew. Jara allowed Simeon to lead her aside. He crouched down, sitting back on his heels in the manner of desert men, poking at the grass with the knife he'd knocked from her hand. Without looking up, he motioned for her to come close. As she complied, kneeling before him, a faint smile crossed his face.

Jara put her hands in her lap and waited.

"All right, girl," he said in a low voice. "Who are you? Where did you get those papers? Why do you put on the appearance of a male in defiance of God's Law?"

"I thought I would be safe dressed as a boy."

"Safe? Do you think the soldiers care who they abuse? Or animals like the ones we pulled off you? They would lie with sheep. . . ."

"I wasn't thinking . . . of that."

A quick look. "You're running away. . . ."

She nodded.

"Why?"

She was silent.

"Are you a slave?"

"I am no slave!"

"Have you been accused of some crime, then? Where did you get those papers? By the Almighty, female or no, if you serve Rome—"

"I do not!" She took a deep breath. "My name is Jara—"

"The name on the paper."

"Yes."

"Why did the commander of the garrison at Tiberias give you safe conduct? What are you to him?"

"I—he—"

"I want the truth, girl. Before, I said you have nothing to fear from me. That may change."

She nodded.

"Well?"

"My name is Jara," she said again. "I come from the village called Katan, in the Galilee. Two days ago—no, three, I think—I was to be wed to Assur, the nephew of our rabbi. But the Roman came and took me as he had my sister before. . . ." She swallowed. "I can't go back," she said finally. "I saw how they treated Sharona . . . after. . . ." She sighed, shook her head. "I can't go back."

He did not say anything for a moment. Then, softly: "What about your husband?"

"They took me away before the ceremony of consecration. I have no husband. Besides—"

"What? Go on."

"I killed the Roman."

The knife stopped scratching at the dirt. "You—what?"

"I killed him. I'm sure of it." She pointed to the dagger. "With that."

He turned it over in his hands. "The *sica*. Where did you get this?"

"It was in the commander's chamber. He used it to cut fruit."

He raised an eyebrow at this, then let out a short, dry laugh. Turning the dagger in his hands again he said, "It is a Judean knife. Look. Here, carved in the handle . . . three letters. Do you know what they stand for? *Death. Freedom. God.*" He looked at her. "*Death is nothing. Freedom is everything. Only God shall be our King.*"

She felt a chill cross the back of her neck. "The words of the Sicarii. . . ."

He nodded. "The knife must have been a souvenir from the war. It's very old."

"Perhaps—" She hardly dared say it. "Perhaps—from the Masada!"

"Perhaps." He looked quizzically at her. "How do you know about the Masada and the Sicarii? Not many dare speak those names these days. Who are you?"

"Give it to me," she said, ignoring his question and snatching back the dagger. "It's mine! It belongs to me." Her eyes were shining. "Show me again the letters."

"Here." He studied the curly head bent so intently over the knife.

"Which is for 'freedom'?"

He put her finger on the letter. "Can't you read?"

She flushed. "Of course! It is just difficult to see, that's all. It's getting dark."

He looked up. "Yes, it is. We may as well camp here for the night. Don't worry, you'll be safe. No one will hurt you. Just don't get lost in the dark. I have a few more questions I want to ask, such as, what you intended doing with this list of names. Also, we'd better figure out what to do with you."

"I'm not going back to Katan!"

"No, you're not," he agreed. "If you really did kill a Roman, then the legion in the North is out looking for you right now. You're an outlaw, girl."

She smiled.

"That doesn't bother you?"

How could she tell him? She'd lost her maidenhood, killed a man, cut her hair; Rome had a price on her head, and she could never go home again. For the first time in her life she felt truly free.

IN THE MORNING they set out again. The two Samaritans were absent, having been disposed of during the night.

Jara had slept well, wrapped in the cocoon of Simeon's great cloak, the smell of him in the wool somehow comforting. He made her talk long into the night, going over every detail of her encounter with Valerens and escape from Tiberias. He also questioned her on anything she might have overheard when the prefect spoke to his men, and if any in her village seemed disposed to fight. Jara told him all she knew. She felt safe with Simeon, not only because he seemed so big and strong, but because she sensed commitments similar to her own. She'd wondered if he were in fact Bar Daroma, the "Son of the South," but when she asked Joshua if he were, he smiled and shook his head, adding she would see Bar Daroma soon enough. So she was safe indeed, and in a spirit of kinship revealed to Simeon her own heritage. He was surprised but not impressed.

"So you are the granddaughter of Ben Ya'ir," he'd drawled. "Better the man had fought to the end than kill his own."

She was so shocked at this remark she could do no more than stammer, "What . . . what would you have done?"

"Fight," he said succinctly. "To the last man. To the last child."

"Because you are ordinary," she'd come back angrily. "You are *am ha-aretz*."

He'd grinned at that but said nothing more.

Now the Nabatean, who was riding alongside her, said, "You are fortunate to be found by Simeon ben Kosiba. He is no ordinary man. The stars protect him. Your own God, too. I know Simeon many years," he went on. "I have seen him slip away from Death a hundred times."

"Is his name on the Roman's list?" Jara asked suddenly.

The Nabatean nodded.

"He is a warrior for Judea." Jara sighed happily. "I knew it!"

"He is more than a warrior." Obodas gestured toward the man who had ridden ahead. "He is a king. Your king."

"My—what?"

"Simeon ben Kosiba is of the line of David, king of your people."

Jara laughed now. "He and a thousand others! Why, I myself—"

"Thousands are not called before Caesar, as Simeon's father was. It was in the time of Domitian," the Nabatean confided. "Word went across the sea that David's son would destroy Rome and rule Israel again."

"That is a very old prophecy. Long before Domitian—"

"Yes," Obodas agreed. "In the days of Herod. But while later kings cared nothing for a messiah of the Jews, Domitian was plagued with fear. He called for an accounting of all men of the house of David and had them brought to Rome. Simeon's father was among them. But when the Jews stood before Caesar—men of the soil, shepherds, workers of wood —the Roman saw he had nothing to fear and said they could go home. Yet none returned alive."

"Domitian had them killed?"

"Simeon's mother thought so. She left Birat Malka, where Simeon was born, and returned with her child to Kosiba, the place where her own family dwelled. She would no more speak the name of her husband for fear the Romans would take Simeon and kill him as she believed they'd killed his father. Much later it was learned that the ship, returning to Judea, had been attacked by pirates from Cyrene, and all on it killed or drowned. Still, the woman believed this was the work of Rome. Simeon, too, blames Caesar, saying his father would never have been at sea otherwise."

Jara stared thoughtfully at the man descended from Israel's greatest hero. Simeon was poised with his horse on a ridge ahead, surveying the distance before them. The sun reddened his hair; it seemed aflame, like David's: "touched by the finger of God."

His back and shoulders were very broad, tapering to a narrow waist, behind which lay a rolled bundle Jara recognized as the cloak in which she'd slept. She remembered the smell of it, that not unpleasant odor of grass and sweat and wool, and she thought suddenly of Florus Valerens and the way the Roman had touched her with his hands and his mouth and his body. And she found herself wondering what it would be like to know Simeon's hands, to kiss his mouth, to feel his body on hers.

She twisted slightly on the horse, restless now, wishing Simeon would turn around and at the same time afraid that he would. When at last he turned back however, he took no notice of her, saying to the Nabatean, "There's someone on the road ahead. Asleep, I think. Or dead. We'll soon see which."

THE YOUNG MAN was neither sleeping nor dead, but simply lost in thought, dreaming with his eyes open, legs stretched out before him, back propped against the stone "mile marker" some Roman engineer had placed alongside the road. His tunic was so worn the fabric shone, and the thongs of his sandals were precariously frayed. Still, his expression was cheerful, and while his complexion was pale, he seemed healthy and of a sturdy build.

"*Shalom*," he said pleasantly, not the least concerned at being surrounded by a group of mounted men.

"*Shalom*," Simeon said, returning the traditional Judean greeting. "Peace unto you. Tell me, do you usually sleep beside the road?"

"Only when the sun is very warm and my legs are very tired."

"You would find shade beneath a tree."

"Unfortunately the birds seem to think this is a nest," the young man replied, pointing to the mop of wiry black curls

that covered his head. "And as we are forbidden to turn away
the homeless, it's possible I could find myself sitting under
yon tree permanently."

"Have you come a long distance?"

"It feels as if I have."

"Where are you headed?"

"Where are you going?"

Simeon grinned. He did not take long to judge people and
he had already decided he liked this poor scholar. (What else
could the fellow be with that pale face and those smooth, un-
marked hands?) "Rimmon."

"The town of Rimmon?"

Simeon paused, squinting slightly as he studied the young
man. "The Valley of Rimmon," he said at last.

The young man looked steadily back at Simeon, then at
each of the men with him. "Rimmon," he said firmly, as
though having come to a decision. He got to his feet. "So be
it."

Simeon grinned again. He pointed to a bundle on the
ground. "Don't forget your books, scholar."

It was the young man's turn to smile. "Writing materials. I
earn my bread, such as it is, as a scribe."

"Well, I didn't think you worked in the fields." Simeon
eyed the fellow's stocky build, his strong shoulders and arms.
"Although you seem capable of turning a rock or two," he
added. "In times like these it might go better to hold a sword
than a writing tool."

"Yesterday I might have answered thusly," the young man
returned, not at all perturbed. " 'Let each serve in his own
way.' Today I say, 'Perhaps.' " He shrugged and smiled.
"Perhaps. Why not?"

Simeon's grin returned. "Come along, then."

"I have no horse. Shall I ride with the lad?"

Simeon looked back at Jara, who was staring at the newcomer with undisguised hostility. Simeon took note of the
girl's animosity and wondered briefly what caused it. "No,"
he told the young man. "We've steeds to spare. Take your
pick."

The scribe raised an eyebrow at this plethora of riding
animals, but obligingly took hold of one of the horses brought
forward. He mounted clumsily, placing his pack before him.
They had not gone far, however, before he remarked ruefully,
"I used to wonder why people found it difficult to adjust to

sudden wealth. Yet now that I myself am the recipient of good fortune,'' he said, indicating the horse beneath him, with whose gait he was clearly at odds, "I know what is meant." He rubbed his backside. "When I walked, I merely grew tired."

Simeon laughed. "You'll get used to it." Then, in a more serious voice, "The place we are going could be dangerous."

"To the body or the soul?"

"Enough wit. I speak plainly now. Listen to what I say, and if you want to keep my respect don't answer in parables or scripture. Now . . . you know how our people suffer at the hands of Rome. There isn't a city, town, or village that hasn't had its share of misery and paid out in blood. That lad you thought to ride with, that's a girl, hiding from the legions. They took her on her wedding day."

"Sounds like the work of Quietus."

"Quietus is dead, but what makes Rufus any different? Because he invites Akiva to his palace in Caesarea? Underneath this governor's smile, underneath his spotless white robe are the same fangs and bloodstained sword of Quietus and all the rest."

"But Hadrian—"

"Hadrian is no different either. He has just announced that the rite of circumcision is prohibited. The sign of the covenant—our covenant with God."

"It is an old decree," the scribe replied, uncertain. "It was meant to halt a certain mutilation the Egyptians practice—"

"Hadrian has revised it. And it is directed not against the Egyptians, but against us, the men of Israel."

The young man was silent, absorbed in thought. At last he murmured, "Impossible. It is impossible to obey such an order. What has Jabneh declared?"

"Jabneh debates. Which doesn't do much for those with newborn males."

The young man looked up, alarmed.

Simeon held up his hand. "Don't worry. The Law—our Law—will be kept. What remains to be known is how—or if—Rome intends to enforce this edict."

"Impossible," he said again. He shook his head. "It would mean war. Even the rabbis would have no choice but to agree."

Simeon smiled. "Exactly. Finally, an issue no one can dispute."

"You want . . . war?"

Simeon was silent a moment. Then he said, "Only a fool wants war, scholar. But I want to be free. To live according to the laws of my people, not Caesar's. To see my brothers standing tall and proud, as they were meant, not servants and slaves to pagan masters. To worship my God in His Holy City and in every corner of this sacred land."

A hush fell over the group on the road. There was only the sound of the horses' hooves as they trod along the highway, and the voice of a solitary bird calling to its mate. Although Simeon had spoken softly, his every word had pierced the heart of those behind him, and Jara, listening, felt a chill cross her neck as when she had realized her dagger was a Sicarii blade. At the same time she felt enveloped in a wondrous warmth.

Finally, the scholar spoke. "You have opened your heart to me, and now I will tell you what I am thinking. When I saw you back there on the road, it was as if we'd met before. I suspect many people feel this when they see you. I don't know why. But it is a pleasant feeling. For me, you appeared at a most providential moment. You see, back there at the road marker, I was—am—at a kind of crossroads in my own life. For a number of years I have studied with a very learned man, one who was once part of the innermost circle at Jabneh. My teacher immersed himself not only in the writings of our people but also in those of the Greeks and other ancients, of the sectarians, the *minim*, or heretics, as our rabbis call the followers of Jesus—and even those whom the Christians themselves call heretics."

"Elisha ben Abuyah," Simeon said. "The one called Aher."

"Yes. Aher. The 'Other.' "

"You share his beliefs?"

The scholar laughed softly. "If I only knew what they were! All my life I have sought only to serve God. I wanted, I thought, to be a rabbi. Ben Abuyah took me in, taught me what I must know in order to present myself to Jabneh, or at the school of one of our great rabbis. His house is filled with books in every tongue, but none was ever forced on me. And it was he, finally, who told me to leave, saying it was time for me to go to one who could effect my ordination as a teacher of the Law. He said in any event he could guide me no more, unless I wished to follow the path he had taken.

"So?"

"So I set out. All along the way I have seen the remains of villages destroyed by Vespasian and Titus and now, so many decades later, still in ruins. I have seen soldiers swaggering about, kicking aside man or woman as they might a dog on a dusty day. I have seen hunger, fear. . . ." He shook his head as though to clear it. "All those years reading, studying . . . I accepted my own poverty because it didn't matter to me. But to see a child without food . . ." He looked up at the sky. "The sun is bright enough to blind a man. But in those dark rooms filled with books, we also go blind. Blind to life . . ."

"What about serving God?"

"That is still my wish. The thing is, I am no longer sure how best to do that." He smiled. "When you came along, it seemed the answer. I'll go where the wind blows me, I thought, lying there in the sun. And there it was. Rimmon."

"Like I said, scholar, it could be dangerous."

"Perhaps. But with Simeon ben Kosiba—"

"You know my name?"

He gave a startled look, then laughed. "I didn't. But I should have. Yes, yes it all fits. It must be you. Wherever I stopped," he explained excitedly, "there was talk of Simeon ben Kosiba. They say you can uproot a tree with one hand. They say you once caught a Roman lance in midair and halted the charging soldier by overthrowing rider and horse. They say you stopped a falling boulder by bouncing it off your knee."

Simeon laughed heartily at this, as did everyone else except Jara, who was shivering with excitement, her eyes bright and big.

"They said," the scribe recalled now, "you were meeting with ten thousand men in the Valley of Rimmon. Bar Daroma was bringing another ten thousand."

"Ten thousand, eh?"

"And one." The scholar pointed to his own chest.

"Called?"

"Mesha. My name is Mesha."

"Well, Mesha, have you decided then to serve God by joining us?"

"I don't know," he answered honestly. "I've never held a sword. I don't know if I could kill a man, or would want to even if he is my enemy. But I'll ride with you to Rimmon. Let me see the faces of the men there. Let me hear what they say."

Simeon nodded, not the least put off but admiring this honest and sensible answer. From the corner of his eye he caught sight of Jara, however. Observing the contemptuous curl of lip and the sullen stare that she directed toward the newcomer, he wondered again what could have transpired in her life to cause such obvious disdain for one who not only seemed perfectly likable but whose profession and aspirations would have evoked the highest respect from most Israelites.

THE PLACE might have been one of the devastated ruins of which Mesha had spoken, but the signs of destruction were recent. Smoke curled upward from a burned house; the smell of charred timber hung in the air. The ground was littered with broken pots and other refuse, and there was the sound of weeping as their party rode up.

Simeon dismounted quickly—almost before the horse came to a stop—with an agility surprising for so large a man. "Shem!" he called. "Tirza!"

A young woman came running up. "Simeon! Here, quick!"

He followed her into one of the houses. A man was lying on a pallet, holding a bloody rag to his shoulder. "Judah . . . What happened?"

"Soldiers. Looking for you, I think." He grimaced, pressed the cloth harder. "They're running crazy. One of their commanders was killed up north. They say a rebel did it. One of the 'new Sicarii.' Then they burned Shem's house as a warning—and Mordecai's because his wife is pregnant. That was to let us know the rite of the *brit* is forbidden. They might at least have waited," he added wryly. "Mordecai's wife might have a girl."

Simeon did not smile.

Judah bar Menashe jerked his chin toward the door. "What's that?"

Simeon turned to see Jara enter the room. "That," he said, "is your 'new Sicarii.' "

"What?"

"I can halt the bleeding," Jara said, stepping forward quickly. "I know how to do it. Truly." Before anyone could stop her, she was beside the wounded man. "Hold up his arm," she commanded. Then, fingers exploring the crevice behind his collarbone, she found Shem's pulse and pressed hard. When she was satisfied the flow of blood had ceased, she had Tirza bring her a clean cloth, which she wrapped tightly around the wound.

"Funny boys you have with you, Simeon," Judah said. "This one works magic. And damn me if he doesn't move, smell, and feel like a woman."

Simeon grinned. "Well, I see the Romans haven't damaged your brains any. It's a girl, all right. I'll explain later. Get some rest. I don't expect you'll be riding with us now."

He pushed himself to a sitting position. "Damn if I don't!"

"We'll see. Rest."

"Simeon—"

"I know you're with me, Judah. You don't have to prove anything. When the time comes, I'll need you well and strong."

The man nodded and fell back.

"Obodas and I will look around, see if we can be of some help to the others."

"Don't stay too long, Simeon. The hills are crawling with pigs. Like I said, they're crazier than usual."

Simeon nodded.

HE FOUND Jara outside, her cheeks flushed with excitement. Her face and arms were covered with scratches, gift of the thorny banks of the Jordan, and there was an ugly bruise below her left eye where one of the Samaritans had hit her. Still, she was a bit cleaner than when Simeon first met her, and he found her piquant, catlike features not altogether unappealing. He ruffled the cap of curls. "Where did you learn to work such good medicine?"

Her cheeks grew even pinker, but before she could reply, Obodas said, "Simeon, look . . ."

They watched the figure coming down the road: an old man on a mule, his clothes dusty and rent, his head fallen forward so low on his chest that his beard came nearly to his waist. He looked up slowly as he neared them, seeing the burned houses and other signs of recent catastrophe. He passed a hand before his eyes. His shoulders began to shake.

"He weeps," Obodas murmured.

"He is a stranger here," Simeon said. "At least I've never seen him before. Someone's given him a bad time."

He had forgotten the girl who stood beside him, but Jara

saw the concern in Simeon's eyes, and she wondered that he could feel so deeply for someone he didn't know. Turning back to the old man, she realized with no small shock that the stranger was not unfamiliar to her.

"Here, even here. . . . Everywhere . . ." The traveler stretched forth his arms as though to embrace the burned huts or perhaps to implore some unseen Grace. Simeon helped him dismount. "Who are you, old man?" he asked gently. "What has happened that your clothes are torn and your beard full of dirt? Who has done this to you?"

The old man did not answer. He stumbled forward, looking around like one dazed, then finally sat down on a tree stump and put his head in his hands. "No more, Lord," he mumbled. "Take pity. Pity us, Almighty God. Turn evil away. Thy wrath . . . Thy wrath, Lord . . ."

"You know him?" Simeon asked Tirza.

She shook her head, puzzled.

"I am a rabbi," the old man said with a sigh. "A teacher of Torah, in the North. The soldiers came. They destroyed everything . . . everything. . . ."

"What is he saying?" Jara pushed through the crowd that had gathered around the man. "Rabbi . . . Rabbi Kawzbeel . . ." She knelt at his side. "It is I, Jara."

He let his hands fall. Slowly he looked up and saw now the slim figure in the shepherd's tunic, her cropped hair, and in the midst of the scratched, sunburned face the green-gold eyes of a cat. He let out a cry of fear, recoiling from the startled girl. "Witch," he uttered hoarsely. "Demon!" Saliva bubbled from his lips. "Murderess!"

Simeon started forward angrily, but Kawzbeel had already risen and was pointing a shaking finger at Jara. "Murderess," he said again. "Murderess!"

Her eyes flashed. "Yes! I killed the Roman!" She got to her feet, fists clenched. "I killed him, and I'm glad! He raped Sharona! He—"

"You killed Arnon! Batya! Assur!" Each name was like the slash of a sword. He started to cry. "Assur . . ."

"Wha-What are you saying? What do you mean?"

"They came. The soldiers came back to Katan. Your brother is dead. Dead. Everyone . . . everyone . . ."

"No . . . no . . . It cannot be. . . ." She shook her head. "Why?"

"For you! For you!" He raised a trembling fist, but his

emotion was too great, and he slumped down again, burying his head in his hands once more.

Simeon reached down to take the man's arm, but Kawzbeel waved him away, at the same time lifting his head to stare at Jara. He let out a great sigh. "When you did not return, your brother and I went to Tiberias," he said in a calmer but tired voice. "There was a great commotion in the city . . . many soldiers riding about, in and out the gates. . . . When Arnon identified himself at the palace they dragged him inside. I had no chance to say a word. The door was shut in my face. Then I learned from one of the people that the prefect had been slain. 'The girl?' I asked. 'What of the girl?' " He shook his head. "No one knew of you. It was the work of rebels, they said. And now all Judea would pay. I hastened home, but the soldiers had already been there. The houses, fields, everything had been set afire. Bodies lay everywhere. Assur . . ." He swallowed. "Assur had been nailed to the cross. Batya was dead, her stomach split open. I can still see before my eyes . . . on the ground . . . the babe that was inside her. . . ."

"What about Sharona?" she whispered.

"So many killed, injured. . . . I don't know. I don't know." He closed his eyes. "All day and far into the night I helped bury the dead, said the prayers. . . ." He opened his eyes. "They came back the next morning. With Arnon. In a sack. They opened the bag and threw the pieces of your brother's body to the dogs."

Simeon looked quickly at Jara. She was rigid, all color drained from her face. She made no sound; her eyes were like glass, her whole expression inscrutable, contained. He did not wonder at the strangeness of this seemingly controlled reaction; he had been through too much in his own life not to recognize the signs of shock. He moved toward her, but the rabbi was not done.

"You killed them," Kawzbeel said again. "Your betrothed, your own brother, the others—innocent—all dead, because of you."

"Be still, old man," Mesha, the scribe, urged gently. "This is unwise. And unkind. The child did not raise her hand against her own, but to protect herself, I'm sure. Your sorrow blinds you."

"It is you who are blind! All of you! The Lord is our only protection. Only He may stretch out His hand. As for the girl, she is evil—a curse upon those who take her in!"

"Enough," Simeon said angrily. His face was livid. In a low, tight voice he said, "The only curse upon us is the cowardice of those who wait for God to perform what they themselves must do. All these years, you and men like you have been silent, accepting every evil pressed upon you. And those of us who fought back, you denounced. The smallest animal in the field would not fail to defend its life and freedom. Even the jackal stands by its own." He nodded grimly. "The soldiers who destroyed your home will answer for it. They and they alone are the cause of your misery." He paused. "Maybe it is the work of a Higher Power. Maybe God has seen fit to punish men like you for your generations of silence. For all the children of Israel whom you and not the legions have cast to the dogs." He turned to Jara, but the rabbi's voice stopped him.

"Truly," Kawzbeel said bitterly, looking at the man and then at the girl, "truly it is said: 'A woman is a pitcher of filth. Her mouth runneth over with blood. Yet see, see how all run after her!'"

There was silence. Then Simeon nodded at Obodas. "Let's go," he said. "We're getting out of here." He looked again at Jara, who had taken a step back and was staring, wide-eyed, at the rabbi. Simeon picked her up and put her on her horse. She blinked. "Are you all right?" he asked. She nodded. He gave her another look, then gestured to his men, and they all rode out of the village.

THE ROAD dipped and turned, rising suddenly, then descending, falling away on one side into a chasm of stone with here and there a protruding bush. Obodas stayed close to Jara. She was pale and silent but otherwise alert. Several times Simeon looked her way, but she stared ahead, appearing to take no notice of him. He wondered what to do with her. It had been his intention to leave her with Tirza, but after the old rabbi's denouncement, that did not seem wise. Better for the girl to be someplace where no one knew her history. Safer, certainly. Still, he ought to have let Tirza outfit her more appropriately. Mesha seemed to know his thoughts.

"I took from one of the women a garment which I have given the girl," he told Simeon when they had camped for the night. "It is no longer necessary for her to dress as a male."

"She did it to escape the attention of the soldiers."

"Yes, such a transgression would be permitted in order to save a life. But that is no longer necessary," he said again. "I believe you will keep her safe."

"I can't keep her at all." He sighed. "I was going to leave her back there. But with a rabbi's curse . . ." He sighed again. "Even those who have no fear of Rome are afraid of demons and evil spirits."

"It is an abominable pagan belief that, unfortunately, has become as common among our people as among the Gentiles."

Simeon looked at him. "What happened to you? You speak like a rabbi now."

Mesha smiled sheepishly and rubbed his wiry beard. "I guess part of me is—or wants to be one, at any rate."

"Like the old man back there?"

"He didn't know what he was saying. He spoke from the depths of sorrow and horror. Just as you spoke out of anger."

"Wrong."

"There is anger in you, Simeon ben Kosiba. Can you deny it?"

"No. But I know what I'm saying. There's the difference."

"You are so certain. . . ."

"Yes! Yes. This is our land. Our Promised Land. The land of Israel. For too long it's been nothing but a Roman garbage pit. Caesar's private holdings. That's right. Judea is not even considered a member of the Roman Empire. It is, since Vespasian accorded it so, the personal property of the emperor and his family. Caesar's own warehouse of flesh. His vineyard, orchard, arena. His urinal." He looked away. "Yes, I'm certain what must be done. And I think—I know—I can do it!"

"Many have tried before," Mesha reminded him. "Even after the great war. During Trajan's reign—"

"But never together. Never united. I'm convinced that's why we've always failed. In Jerusalem, bar Gioras fought John of Gischala, and when they finally got together it was too late. And Ben Ya'ir, on the Masada . . . If he had marshaled his men . . . Even before, it was always Galilean against those of the south, the priests and the rabbis at odds. . . . And our people across the sea—the Jews in Alexandria, in Rome— they did nothing to help us, and when it was their turn, we did nothing to help them. When the uprisings in Cyprus began, we ought to have joined our brothers. The rabbis held us back.

They were afraid. . . . And what of Parthia?'' he asked suddenly. ''There is a power even Rome cannot subdue. Jews enjoy a strong and favored position in Mesopotamia. If they were with us . . .'' His eyes were shining, his voice had taken on a rich timbre.

''You have a vision,'' Mesha said, studying the man, thinking how forcefully he spoke. ''Now I see why so many look to you.''

''A vision? Perhaps. I dream of a new Kingdom of Israel. Free, united, every man with his vineyard and field . . . living in peace according to the commandments of Eternal God.''

'' 'And it shall be in that day that we shall be as a light unto all the nations,' '' Mesha recited softly.

''A light for all the nations . . .'' Simeon smiled. ''Well, the Almighty knows Rome has laid her yoke on more than us. But we can't help anyone until we free ourselves. That's why we must come together. All of us. This time, the rabbis must give their support. With men like Akiva behind us . . . Well, we shall see. Tomorrow. At Rimmon.''

''Akiva . . . at the Valley of Rimmon?''

''Now you know why this meeting is so important. The people love Akiva as they love no one else. Why do you laugh? What's so funny?''

''Forgive me. Not at you, believe me.'' The scribe took a deep breath. ''So Akiva ben Joseph will be at Rimmon. Thus doth the wind blow. In my pouch,'' he explained, ''there is a letter from my teacher Elisha ben Abuyah asking Akiva to take over my training. I was on my way to B'nei Berak, the rabbi's home, when you found me. I have been wondering if my indecision was not simply fear,'' he confessed. ''Fear of meeting such a great man, of being rejected by him, of perhaps discovering my own unworthiness to sit at his feet. And now it seems I will see Akiva after all, not at B'nei Berak, but in the Valley of Rimmon.'' Mesha shook his head, smiling. ''Truly, truly the Lord works in His own way.''

HE FOUND her sitting with her back to a carob tree, her knees drawn up and hugged to her chest. She was shivering slightly.

''Come closer to the fire. The nights are still cool.''

She did not answer but continued to stare at the flames.

Simeon sat down beside her. She had exchanged the shepherd's tunic for the robe Mesha had found. Too wide, too short, it gave her the appearance of having been dumped into a coarse sack tied around the middle. Her neck, rising from the straight and plain-cut borrowed garment, without benefit of veil or flowing locks, seemed particularly vulnerable to him. The small head with its boyish cap of curls was more like that of an innocent child, he thought, than of a young female so intimately acquainted with violence.

"Tomorrow," Simeon said softly, watching her eyes, "we will reach the place we have been seeking. Some of the men you will see—perhaps those who cry loudest against Rome—may be in Caesar's pay. I want you to stay close to Obodas. Speak to no one. Do you understand?"

Jara nodded.

"I have been trying to think what to do with you. I know you want to go to Tur Malka, but I think it's better to give you to Akiva."

Her head shot up, the pupils of her eyes dilated.

"There's nothing to fear. Akiva has the best heart in the world. He may seem to enjoy a close relationship with Tinneus Rufus, but he would never turn you over to the man. And"—he grinned—"I doubt the governor would think to look for you in B'nei Berak."

"Akiva . . ."

"Yes, Rabbi Akiva. Even in the Galilee, you must have heard of him."

"He is a rabbi. . . ."

"Yes, a very great one."

"No! No rabbis! No rabbis!"

"Sshh . . . Don't be alarmed. There's nothing to fear, I tell you."

"No rabbis!" She jumped up, backed away. Her eyes had become dark, all pupil.

"Jara . . ." Simeon went after her, moving slowly, his voice low, gentle.

"You heard what he said back there! He called me a witch! A murderess!"

"The man was near crazed with grief. What do you expect after what he's seen?"

"Then you also think I—"

"No!" He shook his head. "No . . . you did what you had to do. It took courage, strength. . . . I still don't know how you managed to get out of there alive and make your way down here. Maybe, as Obodas would say, your stars are good." He smiled. "Maybe God is with you."

She drew in her breath, fixed him with a cold stare. Then in a calm, clear voice she said, "There is no God."

He did not reply.

"The man I killed was the enemy of our people. The enemy of God. Why, then, was my brother murdered, his body cut up like an animal's? Why was Assur crucified? And Batya, her unborn child . . ." She looked away, back into the fire. "For my deed?" She shook her head violently. "No . . . I will not live among rabbis and scholars. I don't want to hear their prayers and their praise of an Eternal Being whose children we are. We're nobody's children. We're all orphans, every one of us."

"You will not think so with Akiva."

"No! I'm not going!"

"There is no choice—"

"There is! Let me stay with you," she said eagerly. "I can help. You saw what I did for your friend. And I can fight! I've already killed one man."

"No. It is not possible."

"Please! Oh, please, Simeon, let me stay! I know you haven't a real home—I don't care! I don't mind sleeping on the grass, living in the open. And I can be useful. I know how to keep house. I'll cook for you, mend your cloak—see, it's ripped, there. Anything—"

"No!"

"Please . . ." She took a step toward him, her voice breathless. "I'll be your woman. I can please you. . . ." She wound her arms around his neck. "I know how. . . ."

"Stop . . . Stop it!" He pulled her arms off and held her hands hard before him.

She blinked, confused. He was glaring at her, angry. She looked at her hands imprisoned in his, then into his eyes again. She began to cry.

He felt her slip to the ground, and put his arms around her, kneeling with her as he drew her close to him, pulling her finally onto his lap, cradling her as he would any lost and frightened child.

She was sobbing now, the full horror of all she had experienced finally breaking upon her. She could see Valerens' face, the way it had come so close to hers, his tongue jutting into her mouth. . . . She saw the knife plunging into his chest, again and yet again. . . . And the journey along the banks of the Jordan . . . the snakes and the sound of animals in the night . . . the men who'd beaten her . . . Kawzbeel . . . Arnon . . .

The sobs, the half-screams subsided at last to a whimper and quiet weeping, and finally with a shudder and a sniffle she was asleep in Simeon's arms. And still he held her, rocking back and forth with her, clumsily stroking her hair. His eyes were far away, lost in private images the girl had reawakened. Every now and then anger surfaced, then faded into sadness, only to emerge once more as a kind of cold and deadly fury dancing in the darkly opalescent eyes.

Simeon looked up at the star-strewn sky, then down at the girl asleep in his arms. She was wrong. There was a God. Cruel and kind. And no matter how hard men fought to establish His justice, no matter how piously they prayed, still terrible deeds were done and the innocent fell victim. He had no answer to this, only a terrible rage that it should be so. Yes, Simeon ben Kosiba believed there was a God. But he did not love Him.

The girl let out a little sigh, pressing closer, and rubbed her nose against his chest, leaving a drop of moisture on his tunic. He wiped it away, smiling slightly. She was so young. And yet, his Ruth had not been much older when . . .

He pushed the memory aside. His arms tightened around the girl. "No one will hurt you again," he promised in a rough whisper. "Not so long as I draw breath in this world!"

5

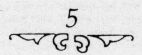

THE HILLS, rising steeply on all sides, provided a natural amphitheater. On the fringes of this opening, groups of men huddled together talking, sometimes angrily. Others strode about clasping this hand or that in welcome, or simply lounging against the pomegranate trees, waiting. Watching from a ridge above the valley, Jara felt a thrill at the scene below. Surely this was how it had been when the twelve tribes of Israel had gathered to make war. She could almost see the tents of those early Hebrews with their clusters of women and children, their banners fluttering in the breeze, the world's first coats of arms: the red standard of the House of Reuben, with its emblem of mandrakes; the black banner of Issachar, embroidered with the sun and the moon; Zebulun's white flag on which a ship rode; the sapphire standard of Dan, its emblem a serpent; the bullock and wild ox of Ephraim and Manasseh; the banners of Simeon, Levi, Gad, Naphtali, Asher, Benjamin —and the standard that was perhaps the most familiar of all: the azure banner of the tribe of Judah, on which a lion blazed.

She watched for Simeon and noted with vicarious satisfaction how warmly he was greeted. He seemed to tower above the rest, not only because of his height and broad shoulders but because of a kind of energy he exuded even in those moments when he was still. The sun on his hair highlighted its red cast, so that his Davidic inheritance seemed unquestionable. Forgotten now was Bar Daroma, whom Jara had for so long imagined Judea's champion. Simeon was the man to lead the people; she could feel it in every muscle and nerve of her body. Her eyes never left him, watching, always watching as he moved about with easy grace. "There is the Lion of Judah," she breathed, unaware she had spoken aloud.

"No." Obodas shook his head. "Not the lion, but the bull. Taurus."

She turned to the Nabatean. "Taurus?"

"Ben Kosiba was born under the sign of the bull. It is a good sign for a man. Very strong. Very powerful."

Jara returned her attention to the scene below. She could no longer see Simeon. "Can't we move closer?" she asked impatiently.

"We must keep out of sight," Obodas replied. "This is no place for a female."

"But I see a woman. Look." She pointed to a slim figure crossing the area.

Mesha had also spotted her. "Who is she?" he asked Simeon, who had come up behind them.

"Who?"

"The young woman down there. Big, dark eyes . . ."

"You must mean Beruria. She is the daughter of Rabbi Teradyon."

"How is it she walks so freely in this company?"

Simeon smiled. "Beruria's not like other women. If she were a man, she would have been a rabbi long ago. As it is, the sages of Jabneh don't hesitate to ask her opinion. Anyway, Teradyon can't do without her. He's not in the best of health. He must be near as old as Methuselah."

"Then Rabbi Teradyon is also here. . . ."

"Along with some others who may surprise you. It would appear Jabneh is taking us seriously, as well they should." He nodded at Jara. "How are you, girl?"

"Can I come with you?"

"Stay where you are. There's a friend of yours will be coming by shortly. A smith by the name of Samson."

Her face lit up.

He smiled. "And you'll soon get a look at your hero, Bar Daroma. Don't be disappointed. He has no wings."

She looked down shyly. How could she tell him? It no longer mattered about Bar Daroma. When she looked up again, Simeon was gone.

Men began to speak now. One by one they took their place in the middle of the circle in the valley. They had come from every part of the land: blue-eyed Galileans, with their rough country accents; men with deep tans from Tekoa and Ein Gedi near the Dead Sea; the seemingly more sophisticated Judeans from the coastal Plain of Sharon, which abounded with scholarly academies, and men like Simeon ben Kosiba and Aaron ben Levi, known as Bar Daroma, from the towns and villages perched like scattered jewels atop the mountains surrounding Jerusalem. Whatever their individual experience, one common concern had driven them together now. The ban prohibiting circumcision struck at the very heart of Judaism. Blows to the flesh could be endured, the ravishing of field and flower withstood, for bone and muscle healed, and the soil could be planted again. Even the destruction of Jerusalem and the Temple that had stood like a wonder upon Mount Moriah, even this ultimate tragedy to the nation could be absorbed; cities and temples were made of stone and could rise where they had fallen. Even the strangers in their midst, those colonies of discharged legionaries and foreign landowners, the *matziqim*, on whose great estates they were forced to toil or else starve, this too could be tolerated however much it scraped their wounds; in their hearts they knew that whatever the name on the deed, the land of Israel was always, only, theirs.

One thing, however, this stubborn people could and would not abide. It was the essence of the rallying cry of the biblical tribes, of Moses, of the Maccabees, wherever and whenever the Jew took up the sword: "Do not stand between me and my God!"

As the sun traveled across the sky, its golden light becoming tinged with red like a blood omen, again and yet again the vote was cast and the shout went up for war.

Bar Daroma voiced the opinion of most. He was, as Simeon had hinted, an ordinary-looking man, but with a gift for fiery oration. "For many years our smiths and craftsmen have been deliberately meeting the Roman quota with poorly made weapons," he declared at the end of a long, impassioned speech. "As these were cast off we returned them to good condition and hid them away. We will soon be able to outfit every man in Judea. And I say we have the arms and the men to take our country back!"

A great, prolonged cheer went up at this, followed by hushed silence as a group of men made their way forward. Each was old, very old; but with the exception of Rabbi Teradyon, who had to be helped by his daughter, they walked erect and sure. To Jara they seemed to float, unreal specters, though she knew they were flesh and blood. Their long robes of gray and brown interspersed with blue or vermilion stripes flowed from their shoulders to the ground. Their heads were covered with the mantle called *tallit*, with its fringes, or *tzitzit*, as ordained by Moses, dangling at the corners. On each forehead a black leather box called a *tefillah* had been fastened by a black leather thong; a second *tefillah*, which contained passages from Exodus and Deuteronomy, was bound by another leather thong which intertwined among the fingers of the left hand and up the arm. Thus was the Jew required to place the words of the Law for "a sign upon thy hand and a frontlet between thy eyes." The wearing of these *tefillin*, erroneously translated by the Greeks into the peculiarly inappropriate name *phylacteries*, signifying "amulet," was generally accomplished during morning prayers—although it was said that Rabbi Johanan ben Zakkai had "never walked four cubits" without them. The fact that these sages had chosen to appear so adorned was a signal that the occasion demanded the greatest seriousness and piety.

The first to come forward was an extremely tall, thin man. He spoke in a conversational tone, as if he were in a room with only one other, yet each person in the audience leaned forward intently as if he and he alone were the recipient of the rabbi's words. Jara, on the other hand, soon found her attention wandering. Many hours had passed since she'd taken her place on the hillside. Her elation at seeing Samson again had faded. She was hungry and tired, and Obodas would not let her out of his sight even to relieve herself. It had also become exceedingly warm. For the first time in her life she wished a veil covered her head. Life on the road was fine, but it would be good to sit in a proper chair, or curl up on a pallet with a cup of herbal tea to soothe her headache. But as she thought of her bed in Arnon's house she remembered there was no house anymore. No Arnon, no Batya . . .

She swallowed. The pounding in her temples grew worse, and her stomach felt as if it were full of sharp, broken things. Meanwhile the rabbi's voice droned on.

"He is a wonder," Mesha breathed. "He takes a pack of angry, snarling beasts and turns them into creatures of reason.

He is a wonder," he said again.

"Who?" Jara asked wearily.

"Akiva, of course."

Headache and hunger forgotten, Jara turned her attention back to the forum below, studying the speaker with new intensity. So this was Rabbi Akiva, with whom Simeon wanted her to live. "What is he saying?" she asked Mesha.

"Akiva believes the edict regarding the *brith* is a misunderstanding. It is an old law, prohibiting self-mutilation. Akiva does not think the emperor intended for it to be applied to the men of Israel. He says Hadrian is planning to visit Judea. He is in the area already. Akiva has gotten Tinneus Rufus to agree neither to enforce the order nor to prosecute on the basis of it until the rabbis can speak personally with Hadrian. Furthermore, it makes no sense for the emperor, who is universally esteemed for his intelligence and tolerance, to instigate a crisis on the eve of his arrival here. In any case, such a policy would not be in line with his promise to rebuild Jerusalem."

"They always promise Jerusalem," she said, stifling a yawn.

"But Akiva has seen the letter. Moreover, Aquila of Pontus, a proselyte to our faith, has been entrusted with the reconstruction. Look, there is the man now! See, he is passing around the document with the emperor's seal on it!"

There was a great murmur from the assembly as a scroll was handed round. Alarmed, Jara saw that the temper of the crowd was vacillating. Suddenly Simeon came forward, making his way to stand beside Akiva, who appeared to welcome him. Simeon was quite as tall, but even with his broad shoulders and vigorous appearance, he did not overshadow the rabbi. Still, Jara was pleased with the figure he presented and the accompanying expectant air from the men gathered around. To her disappointment, however, Simeon addressed the rabbi in a calm, respectful voice.

"With your permission, rabban, I speak to you now not as one who would disagree with his master, but as one who wishes to supplement his words. We all know you are a man of peace. Many times you have said, 'He who spills another's blood diminishes God's image.' I have my own thoughts on this, but I won't debate the issue now. Nor will I list the crimes committed by Rome, not only against our people but against

God. We have already spent a long day listening to such accounts. Only give me now the benefit of your wisdom. Answer these questions.

"First: You say Rufus has told you he will not enforce the emperor's edict against the sign of the covenant until there is further clarification from Hadrian. But I have just come from a place where houses were burned as a show of the governor's will. I ask: Is the word of Rufus reliable?

"As to Jerusalem. Rabban, they hold out the promise of our city like a sweet to a child, or a carrot dangling from a stick before the donkey's nose, only to be withdrawn time and time again. Trajan also said he would give back Jerusalem and allow us to rebuild the Temple. And always it was postponed. So I ask: Is the word of Rome to be taken in good faith?"

Akiva nodded. "You show good sense, Simeon ben Kosiba. I am glad the time we have spent together has not been without fruit. What happened in the village of which you speak may well have occurred before the soldiers received Rufus' orders. I myself have come straight from the governor. I believe he would not lie to me. Besides, it would be foolish for him to start disturbances on the eve of the emperor's visit. He knows as well as you and I this ban could not be accepted quietly. Now, as bad as rebellion would make us appear, it would make him look even worse.

"As to Jerusalem. I believe this time it is different. Hadrian is not Trajan. He travels across the world not as a conqueror but as a redeemer. Wherever he goes, he calls for magnificent buildings and monuments to be constructed, cities rebuilt. He is hailed everywhere as Benefactor, Rebuilder, *Restitutor*. Why should he not be as kind to Judea as he has been to Achaea, Libya, Bithynia, and many others? That is why it is so important that we do nothing to incur his displeasure now. Look, here you see the imperial rescript." He opened the scroll and read aloud, " 'It is to the interest of the Empire that Jerusalem be reestablished.' What could be plainer than that?"

Simeon nodded. " 'To the interest of the Empire.' But, rabban, what makes you think that is also to our interest?"

Akiva was clearly startled.

"Perhaps Hadrian does mean to allow Jerusalem to rise again," Simeon went on. "But as what? As our Holy City? Or does the emperor, with his Greek and Roman ideas, intend for it to become a pagan center, with idols and shrines, circuses and theaters? Will we be allowed to reside there? Or will this new Jerusalem be another colony for Rome's discharged soldiers?''

"Never," Akiva said with certainty, his voice rising above the growing murmur. "God would never allow it."

"Forgive me, rabban," Simeon replied with a small sigh. "God has already allowed Jerusalem to be destroyed. While we speak, the City of David houses soldiers' camps and brothels. The standard of the Tenth Legion with the emblem of a wild boar—a pig!—even now flies from the Temple Mount."

"I know, Simeon. I know."

"Will you tell me this is in accordance with God's design?" The anger he had managed to control thus far began to surface in Simeon's eyes. His fists became clenched, and the newly resonant timbre to his voice sent shivers of excitement down Jara's body. "Will you tell me this is to be endured another fifty years? Another hundred? Will you tell me that you of all people can endure it?"

"I have endured it," Akiva replied calmly. "Because I know it will end. Listen to me—all of you—I have seen the desolation of Jerusalem. I have walked among the heaps of rubble, watched the soldiers play their games of chance on our most sacred site. I remember I saw a jackal running among the ruins of the Temple. I did not weep as those with me did. Instead my heart was filled with joy. Do you know why? Because I realized that as the prophecies foretelling the destruction of our city have proven so completely true, so too will the prophecies of a rebirth greater than what went before."

"Let us make that last prophecy come true, rabban."

"It will come true, Simeon. Through Hadrian."

"And if not?"

Akiva paused. "If we are denied the rite of circumcision, we shall have to break the Roman law." He nodded. "I will support this."

"And Jerusalem?"

"Wait and see. I have hope, great hope. Give me your support now. If I am wrong, then I will give you mine."

Simeon gave a short nod. "Done."

A great noise arose now from the valley as those present

began to discuss what had just occurred. Some appeared to accept Akiva's proposal; many seemed relieved to hear it. But a number raised their voices angrily. It was then that another of the sages present that day came forward. He was an ungainly figure, a man whose features, though not misshapen, combined to give him the most plain and homely appearance imaginable.

"What an ugly man," Jara murmured without thinking.

"That is Joshua ben Hananiah," Mesha whispered to her. "You are not the first to make that observation. Once, in Rome, one of the emperor's family said so to his face. In reply, Ben Hananiah merely asked the lady why she kept her wine in earthenware vessels rather than jars of silver and gold. 'Because the wine would spoil,' she answered. 'So it is with the good in man,' the sage is reported to have said. 'Moreover, one ought not to judge the contents by the container.'" Noting with satisfaction that the girl had the grace to blush at this, Mesha turned back to the scene below.

Joshua ben Hananiah, one of the five disciples of Johanan ben Zakkai, who had in fact helped carry the rabbi out of Jerusalem in a coffin in order to escape not only Titus' legions but the fury of the city's Zealot defenders as well, began to speak. His voice, which was as beautiful as his mien was plain, was not the least diminished by his greatly advanced age. In fact, Joshua ben Hananiah had been a Temple singer, and as no Levite might commence service before the age of thirty, Mesha reckoned that the man was now well into his nineties. The young scholar leaned forward intently, his interest and affection for Ben Hananiah mirrored in the faces of those encircling the man.

Unlike Gamaliel and Eliezer ben Hyrcanus, titular heads of the Sanhedrin, Joshua ben Hananiah was not an aristocrat. After the fall of Jerusalem he had settled in Peki'in, a small town between Jabneh and Lydda, where he earned his living as a needlemaker. Despite his poverty (he took no pay from his students), he was noted in academic circles for the logical acumen of his legal interpretations as well as for his worldly wisdom. Not only was his knowledge of Scripture and Law extensive, but he had mastered on his own Greek, mathematics, and astronomy, with great proficiency.

"My brethren of Israel," the elderly rabbi began. "Hear me! This day has been a long one, and tempers are short. We grow tired in body as indeed our souls are weary of all we have endured these many years. Yet let me tell you a story. Once it was that the mighty lion, while devouring his prey, began to choke on a bone. He sent out a call to all the other animals, offering a reward to anyone who would take the bone from his throat. But none would come forward. Finally, a crane came along, shoved his long beak into the lion's maw, and took out the bone. But when he demanded the reward the lion had promised, the king of beasts waved him off, saying mockingly, 'Go away, foolish bird, and be glad you got your head out of the lion's mouth!' " The rabbi nodded at the appreciative laughter that followed. "So, too, my brethren, we must be glad that, having fallen into the clutches of this nation Rome, we are still, thank God, intact."

THE VARIOUS GROUPS were dispersing. As Simeon made his way back to where he'd left Jara with Obodas and Mesha, he caught sight of her trying to slip away down the hill. He managed to stop her by grabbing hold of her arm.

"Where are you going?"

"To find Samson and return with him to Tur Malka."

"You're going with Akiva. I've already spoken to him—"

"I don't have to listen to you! I'll go where I want to go. And that's Tur Malka. You go live with your precious rabbi. Go on, sit at his feet and pray for the Messiah to come and deliver Israel."

Simeon frowned. "What is this?"

She turned on him, tears welling up in her eyes. "You gave in! You gave up! You're just like all the rest," she accused him bitterly. "I thought you were different—"

"Now, hold on—"

"You're afraid. You're nothing but a coward. One word from Akiva and you lie down like a dog!"

"You don't understand—"

"Words, nothing but words, that's all there ever is! And that ugly old man—I'd like to stick his head in a lion's mouth! Let him see how it feels!"

"Have you no respect—"

"No! None! Not for them"—she jerked her head toward the circle of rabbis—"and not for you!"

He was about to reply when a man came up to them and put

his hand on Simeon's shoulder. It was Bar Daroma.

"Simeon . . . You spoke well."

"But did not turn him, Aaron."

"It doesn't matter. You struck a bargain. Besides, some good has come out of all this. You and I, the brothers of Kefar Haruba—we're all together now. Soon enough Akiva will see the truth with his own eyes. He will have to support us or give up being a Jew."

"Why do you care?" Jara broke in. "What does it matter what some rabbi says?"

Bar Daroma looked at her in surprise. "What's this?" he asked Simeon.

"A piece of trouble" was the grim reply.

Bar Daroma looked Jara over, taking in the short hair, the awkward-fitting robe, and the stiff, defiant stance. "Boy or girl?" he asked, puzzled.

"Well," Simeon drawled, "what would you call an uncircumcised Israelite?"

The man's eyebrows went up.

"A girl, Aaron. A girl. Look, I'll meet with you later. We've got a lot of work to do. More arms need to be stored. We've got to prepare the underground passageways and outfit the caves properly. Now that we know who's with us we can't waste any more time." He sighed. "Truth is, I wanted it to begin. I'm tired of waiting. . . ."

"We all are. But if we don't give Akiva the chance to be proven wrong, we'll have half the country against us. Bad enough we must take on the legions, the Greeks and Samaritans in our midst, and in all probability the followers of Jesus."

"The *minim*?" Simeon asked in surprise. "Christians? What makes you say that? They are a people of peace."

"But they want Jerusalem for themselves. They may think to abet Rome in return for certain promises."

"I doubt it. If anything, they'll just stay out of the action, as they did in the Great War, when they left Jerusalem to settle in Pella."

"Simeon, I know for a fact that Valerens, the Roman commander in the North, had as his best informants two sectarians from Capernaum."

"Well, Valerens is dead. Speaking of which, let me get this female settled away. Then I'll get back to you."

"Ah! This must be the one Samson told me about!" He peered curiously at Jara. "Did you really kill him, girl?"

"Yes."

Bar Daroma grinned. "It's a good sign. 'And the day shall come when all the children of Israel will take up their swords and smite their enemies,' " he recited.

"If this one had her way, I think she'd like to take up a sword against me," Simeon muttered. He nodded a farewell at Bar Daroma and gave Jara a little push. "Let's go."

"Where?"

"Go! Move!"

When they had walked a short distance and were hidden from the others in a grove of pomegranate trees, he gave her another little push indicating she should sit. "I haven't much time to give you, girl, and I don't know why I even bother. I guess I feel sorry for you." He cocked an eyebrow at the tousled head, beat-up face, and ill-fitting gown. "Lord knows you're the sorriest-looking thing I've ever laid eyes on. With a big mouth and a sharp tongue, to boot. But you have courage. It wouldn't hurt to follow that up with some sense as well. You think I don't know what's inside you? You killed a man. An enemy. He deserved to die. But it doesn't end there, does it? And every time you think of the others—your brother, for instance—you don't know whether to weep or throw up. Making war isn't a child's game. If you go in, you go in to win. Revenge isn't enough. Revenge alone isn't worth it. Not when so many will die, the good as well as the bad, your friends as well as your foes. Once begun, there's no pulling out, no going back. Now . . ." He took a deep breath. "If we're going to beat the so-called Masters of the World, there must be no division among ourselves. Otherwise we're done. Finished."

"All right," she agreed. "I understand that. But Akiva—"

"Akiva is essential to the cause. He has traveled to every Jewish community in the world. They know and respect him in Parthia, Rome, everywhere. With his support, not only can we count on every man in Judea, but there's a good chance we can get our brothers across the sea to join us. Look . . ." He held up his hand, fingers spread wide. Slowly his fingers curled into a fist. "From many, one." He slammed his fist into his open palm. "And that's how we'll hit them! Hard!"

She smiled.

He smiled too.

"Then you haven't given up," she said softly.

"Not for Akiva or anyone else. This is our land. God gave it to us. And I intend to take it back from Rome, with or without the Almighty's help."

Her eyes widened. For a man so keen on rabbinical support, this was as close to blasphemy as one might come. Then she smiled again.

"I want you to stay with Akiva," Simeon said. "I know you'll be safe with him. Besides, you can be of some help to me," he added, thinking to soften the blow.

"How?"

"See which way the wind blows. You may even get the chance to meet Hadrian."

"I could poison him," she said excitedly.

"No, nothing like that," Simeon answered hastily. "Just keep your eyes and ears open." He smiled. "Will you do that for me?"

She nodded vigorously.

"Good girl." He put out his hand to help her up. "Come on, they're waiting for you."

She rose, hesitated. "You will come to see me, won't you?"

"Of course. How else will I learn what news you have?"

She nodded again, smiling now.

"Let's go, then. We have much to do, you and I."

MESHA HAD MADE his way to the rabbis' encampment, where he saw again the young woman Beruria. She was carrying a waterskin, which she proceeded to fasten to the harness of one of the mules tethered to the trees. She passed no more than a few feet from the scribe, who did not take long to decide she was the most beautiful thing he'd ever seen. Her hair was pulled chastely back under her veil, and her dark eyes shone forth large and luminous from a pale, oval face. Her skin was exceedingly fine, a lush cream tinged with rose. She had a long, slender neck, and her fingers were also long, the nails perfect ovals, like her face. She was like a pearl, Mesha thought. A pale, pink pearl.

She sensed his gaze and, looking round, blushed to see the intensity with which the young man stared at her. Color spread from her face down to her throat. Mesha could not take his eyes away; he watched, fascinated by the crimson stain.

Unsure, torn between the desire to put this stranger in his place and something else which she could not name, Beruria lowered her head, confused. Her fingers fumbled with the harness, and the waterskin fell to the ground.

Mesha was beside her instantly, retrieving the skin and holding it out to her. "With your permission I will fasten it," he said.

Again she blushed. "My fingers seem to have lost their skill."

"The animal moved," he apologized for her. "He appears skittish. See, it is difficult for me as well. But there . . . that ought to hold."

She lowered her eyes again, giving a little nod that appeared to be both thanks and dismissal.

Respectfully, Mesha took a few steps back. Then, remembering he sought Akiva, he raised his hand, saying, "A moment—"

"Yes?" The voice behind him was male. "You are looking for something? Someone?"

Mesha spun around. "I was about to ask where I might find Rabbi Akiva."

"So? You go up to a female? With five hundred fellows around?" He wagged a finger at Mesha. "Not nice, young man. Not nice."

"You don't understand. I am a scholar—"

"So? Even worse. Six things there are unbecoming a scholar. One is to converse with a woman in the street."

"I wasn't conversing. I mean I—"

" 'He that talketh much with womankind bringeth evil upon himself.' True, true. 'Therefore, do not converse much with women.' Good advice, good advice."

Mesha caught Beruria's eye. The sudden spark there as well as her uplifted chin revealed distinct contempt for these words. But she said nothing.

"I am Rabbi Yossi. Yossi the Galilean, they call me. So. You seek Akiva. So tell me. Why Akiva?"

"I hope to become his student."

"A worthy ambition. Then you are not just another of these Zealots, eh?" Before Mesha could reply, he turned to the young woman, who was about to depart. "Beruria, if you please, don't go just yet."

She stopped.

"I must journey to Lod. A matter of no small importance. On the other hand, it is of no great importance either. I am told you and your father have just now come from the very place to which I must go. So tell me, how far is it from here to there?"

The spark returned to Beruria's eyes. She pursed her pink mouth just a trifle and shook her head sorrowfully. "Not nice, Rabbi Yossi. Not nice."

"Eh? What is not nice?"

"So many words to a woman! Quite unbecoming."

The rabbi's mouth fell open.

"You ought to have posed your question like so: 'Beruria. Lod. So? How far?' "

Rabbi Yossi was about to say something in his own defense when he realized further conversation would only affirm Beruria's acid observation. He let out a sigh and nodded. The young woman nodded in return and turned gracefully to depart. Rabbi Yossi could stand it no longer. "Beruria," he blurted. "So? How far?"

But she was already out of sight.

The man sighed again, and turned back to Mesha, who immediately stopped grinning and assumed a solemn expression. "Do you believe that one?" the rabbi asked. "No wonder her brother ran away and turned to banditry. He was killed by his own gang," he added, waving good riddance to that poor creature. Another sigh. "Still, she's right. She's always right. One thing I can tell you, don't argue with Beruria. Especially concerning *halakhah*. She knows every law there is. Why, once she learned three hundred laws in a single day."

"How does her husband keep up?"

"Are you crazy? Who could be wed to such a one? Her father's students are always falling in love with her, but she only laughs at them. Says she'll never marry until she meets someone who can teach her something she has not already learned."

"Three hundred laws in one day . . . She must be clever indeed."

"It's all Teradyon's fault. He has always treated her as his best pupil. Which, no doubt she is. It was nothing for her to accomplish the three years of study necessary to become a rabbi. But of course she will never receive *semikhah*."

"*Semikhah*," Mesha repeated softly. "Ordination." He had almost forgotten that was his purpose for being here. "Can you tell me, Rabbi Yossi, where shall I find Akiva?"

"I shall present you to him. How are you called?"

"Mesha."

"Son of . . . ?"

The scribe reddened slightly. "Just Mesha," he said.

AKIVA READ the letter slowly, then folded it carefully and looked up. "Your teacher speaks well of you, young scribe."

"So who is it?" Rabbi Yossi could not resist inquiring. "With whom has he studied? Ishmael? Tarfon?"

"Neither." Akiva seemed to smile slightly. "Another."

"I am—have been—the student of Elisha ben Abuyah," Mesha told the curious rabbi. "I will not deny this, nor," he added, turning back to Akiva, "hide it."

"Loyalty is always commendable. As far as I am concerned, there is nothing to hide. Elisha ben Abuyah was my friend."

"Was, rabban?"

"It was he who chose to turn away, Mesha, not only from the road of a *tanna*, preferring to immerse himself in personal, philosophical speculation rather than the duties of a teacher —but also from those who loved him."

"It grieves me even to think on it." Rabbi Yossi sighed. "But it was inevitable. He was always humming Greek airs. Whenever he attended the academy," he told Mesha, "books of the *minim* would fall from his pockets." He shook his head.

"Yossi," Akiva said gently, "enough. We must not intimidate this young man. I have already done him a disservice by not conducting this interview in a more private fashion. After all, my friend, he has not come all this way to hear judgment on his teacher, but to seek a place as my student. Therefore what is said must be between him and me."

"Perhaps nothing more need be said," Mesha said stiffly.

"Come," Akiva told him, disregarding this. "Walk with me. Do not think too hard of Rabbi Yossi," he said when they were alone. "He has the curiosity of a child—and the innocent heart of one as well."

"He seemed quite upset to see me with the daughter of Rabbi Teradyon."

Akiva laughed. "That is because his own wife was such a shrew and made his life such a misery that he was finally persuaded to divorce her. Even so, after the divorce he treated her generously. He still supports her and her second husband, who, unfortunately, has become blind."

Mesha was silent.

"So you have studied with Elisha ben Abuyah. . . . Tell me now, Mesha, were you Aher's student or his disciple?"

"The one you call Aher seeks no disciples. He seeks only to learn the Truth."

"Some would say that what is apparent need not be sought."

"Apparent to you, rabban. But, sadly, not to him."

"And what is apparent to you, Mesha?"

"That we are creatures of an Eternal Being. That this world in all its beauty is His gift to us, and that we alone make of it a heaven or a hell. That God is everywhere, rabban. In us and about us. And that the way we may come to know Him is not through mathematical formulae or magical incantations or philosophic speculation based on 'reason'—for even science, I believe, ultimately rests on faith—but by performing His commandments to us, and by opening our hearts to Him."

There was silence for several moments, and then Akiva said with a sigh, "Would that you had been Ben Abuyah's teacher and not the other way around."

"But it was he who bade me come to you. He told me a story. He said once there were four young men who entered an orchard together. It was no ordinary place, but a garden such as might be found in Paradise, abounding with marvelous fruits and flowers, each path leading to something yet more glorious than the eye had already seen. And the taste of the fruit was sweeter than apples dipped in honey, yet one never felt surfeited, no matter how much he ate. And the light that shone on this place was a pure golden light. And the four young men entered together. But one looked at all that was around him and it was too much, and he died."

"Ben Azzai," Akiva murmured.

"And the second looked into the eye of the golden light and went mad."

"Ben Zoma," Akiva said, his voice breaking.

"And the one called Elisha ben Abuyah became Another, and forthwith wanted to destroy the plants and trees of the garden."

Akiva was silent.

"Only one, Akiva ben Joseph, emerged unscathed, smiling, serene."

Again there was silence. Finally, Akiva said softly, "You realize, of course, that your past association has exposed you to many things which the council at Jabneh would term 'heretical.' How do you answer such an accusation?"

Mesha picked up a fruit that had fallen from one of the trees and held it out to Akiva. "I was hungry, rabban. I found a pomegranate. So I ate the fruit and threw away the husk."

Akiva was clearly satisfied. "I shall be very pleased," he said, "if you would return with us to B'nei Berak."

As he spoke, Mesha caught a glimpse through the trees of a young woman mounted on a gray mule. "I would like that," he said. "I would like that very much."

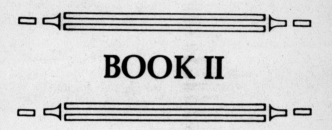

BOOK II

1

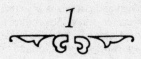

JUDEA'S WESTERN BORDER was the sea. It was not only a border, it was a barrier; never, as it might be for other nations, a highway. Unlike the Greek Odysseus, tempted by the sight of distant islands, whose broken and embayed coastlines were an invitation to voyage, the Israelite saw only a stiff and often stormy line down whose length was little to tempt men in and nothing to tempt them out. For that reason, perhaps, the Hebrew word for "sea" (*yam*) was the same as that for "west," signifying no more than the horizon.

But east of the sea was a land of milk and honey. Also, one of the world's great warpaths.

Along the level, open coastland of Judea's Maritime Plain, rising ever eastward by dim slopes to that range of hills culminating in the mountains of Jerusalem, the embassies and armies of Asia and Africa had long passed to and fro. Here, Amenhotep II and Thothmes III traveled north to the Hittite frontier. So came Seti, and the Ramses, and Sargon, sweeping south to the cities of the Philistines. So Sennacherib marched his men to the borders of Pharaoh. So Necho went up to Assyria, and Nebuchadnezzar came down to Egypt. Here Alexander passed, entering Samaria to punish the inhabitants of Shechem. So Antiochus from Syria and the Ptolemies from Egypt surged up and down in alternate tides of blood and rapine. And when the Maccabees burned the Greek ships at Jamnia, the light from the fires could be seen as far as Jerusalem, "three hundred stadia off."

For the last hundred years or so, the legions of Rome had marched and counter-marched along the Via Maris, from the northern stretch called the Plain of Sharon, for its lush oak forests, to the southern Lowland, or Shephelah, where the sycamore took root. The various Caesars were hardly unaware of history's trek across this natural bridge between continents. More than the taxes that could be collected, the land that would be confiscated and colonized by retiring legionaries, the loot dug up from sacked cities, the produce and human muscle to be shipped where needed, more than this, the value of the tiny province of Judea was as the overland link to Egypt's vital grain supply. Strategically, it was a shield against Parthia, Rome's one serious rival.

But on a warm and golden spring day it was hard to think of any army marching through the coastal plain. Beyond the beaches and the strips of sand and grass, a profusion of poppies, pimpernels, anemones, narcissus, and blue iris—"roses of Sharon and lilies of the valley"—were thickly scattered. The shimmering air was filled with bees and butterflies and birds. In the distance a shepherd boy whistled to his flock.

Jara lay contented in the grass, watching a lizard make its way up the sunny bank. She liked being so close to the earth, liked the smell of it, the sweet spicelike odor surrounding B'nei Berak that was a mixture of field and flower and food continually cooking in the great kitchen to feed Rabbi Akiva's students. The house itself was large, as befitting an academy of learning, and surrounded by several dozen smaller houses. Withal, Akiva preferred to teach outdoors, seated beneath the spreading branches of a fig tree.

The dining hall was grand. Dinners often lasted hours while the rabbi and his colleagues conducted discussions that, it seemed, no one wished to end. At such times Jara did not sit at the long table but remained in the kitchen with the other women, so as not to be a distraction to the young scholars. The presence of women was not forbidden; Beruria, daughter of Rabbi Teradyon, was often present, and the wives of other rabbinical figures also sat at supper. Even Tobita, the servant woman who literally ran both house and kitchen, was often called in to the dining hall, where she would be praised for her fine soup and offered a glass of wine.

But Akiva had quickly taken note of the effect Jara had on the young men studying at B'nei Berak, and while he in no way limited her freedom, he took care that she should not become a disturbing element. He was an astute observer of human nature, this man who began life as an impoverished shepherd and who still reckoned the instincts of animals and humans as the most accurate barometer of events. And while he saw that Jara did not try to entice men, that, in fact, she appeared oblivious to the looks and sighs cast her way, he also saw that plainly dressed, her hair hidden beneath a veil or caught in a net of fine wool, her face devoid of paint, her skin unscented with oils or essence of perfume, her ears, throat, arms, fingers bare of beads or bands of gold or filigree, even so she was more alluring than a queen in all her finery. The scent of her flesh was as tantalizing as the jasmine that bloomed in the night. Her green-gold eyes, fringed with dark lashes, set below fine, arched eyebrows, also dark, and above the high, feline cheekbones, seemed to hold the promise of delicious mysteries conducted in secret, sun-dappled glades. Her mouth, with its sullen lower lip, invited bites as well as kisses. And beyond all this there was the nubile body, the way she walked. She not only looked like a cat, she moved like one.

"She ought to be married, that one," Tobita said one day when the rabbi stopped by the kitchen for some broth to take to one of his students who had fallen ill. "If I did not know better, Akiva ben Joseph, I would say you'd like to have this girl for yourself. I see how you sit and talk with her, how you look at her."

"A young body to warm these old bones, eh? Never mind, Tobita, I am not King David. Besides, I am warm enough. I have the memory of my Rachel."

The woman sighed. "Never was one more beautiful than she."

"In every way, Tobita. In every way. All that I am today I am because of her."

"And yet I see you look at this girl almost the way you looked at your wife."

"There is something about her that reminds me of Rachel," Akiva admitted. "I don't know what it can be," he mused. "Everything about her is as the night compared to day. Or perhaps it is the other way around, for Rachel was dark." His eyes took on a faraway look. " 'Though I am dark I am comely, o ye maidens. . . .' "

"Now don't start that, rabban," Tobita snapped, turning away so Akiva would not see the tears that had come to her eyes, for she had dearly loved the rabbi's wife. "Or that poor boy will never get his broth. No, no, I'll take it myself. What should a man like you be doing with such fetching and carrying when the very world is falling apart and in need of your prayers?'' She paused at the door. "I will tell you one thing, and that is you must get this girl a husband. It is not your young scholar's stomach which pains him, but his heart. And if you do not take action, a plague of lovesickness will sweep from one corner of this house to the next.''

Akiva smiled delightedly. "Is it so? Are they all in love with her?''

"In love? Or full of the Evil Impulse?''

"Do not speak so,'' Akiva reprimanded the woman gently. "That is an ugly phrase. It maligns the most sacred of acts, the most beautiful thing that may occur between a man and a woman. I will not have those words said in my house,'' declared the man who had vigorously fought for the inclusion of the Song of Songs in Scripture, declaring the work to be the holiest book of the Bible.

"Even so,'' she grumbled.

"Good Tobita, it is spring. Now is the time of singing . . . the voice of the turtledove is heard throughout the land.'' He patted her shoulder. "A little love is good for the soul. As for Jara, we must look after her, you and I. She has suffered, Tobita, suffered much for one so young. A husband now is not the answer, but to feel safe and loved, like a child in the bosom of family. In time, when her heart is healed of this anger caused by sorrow, she will take her place as a good daughter of Israel and bring forth sons and daughters of valor and grace.''

Unaware of Akiva's prophecy, Jara lay dreaming in the grass. Months had passed since she'd been delivered to Akiva's care. Winter had come and gone, drenching the land with rain, yet never had Simeon ben Kosiba come to see her as he'd promised, or even sent word. It was as if he'd disappeared from the world. No one seemed to know his whereabouts. Meanwhile, all Judea buzzed with preparations for Hadrian's visit. Soldiers were everywhere, paving roads, clearing long-neglected areas of debris, checking various vicinities for "security" purposes. Akiva was often absent from B'nei Berak, conferring with the Council of Rabbis in Jabneh as to how their concerns might best be presented to the emperor. He also served one day each week on the Judicial Court there, for while Rome's governor alone held the power of life and death, disputes among the Jews were left to the Sanhedrin. (If a Jew disagreed with a rabbinical decision, he was free to bring the matter before the authorities in Caesarea, but such action would have resulted in excommunication by the Jewish community.)

Akiva was absent from B'nei Berak this day, gone not to Jabneh but to Caesarea, to welcome the emperor. He had been in the provincial capital nearly a week. To her surprise, Jara was discovering that she missed the long-legged rabbi. Like everyone else who knew him, and despite her prejudice, she had come to love him. It was impossible not to, for the affection he exuded made a far greater circle than the wall with which she had surrounded herself. Bit by bit, day by day, the stones of that wall were crumbling. Now she looked forward to their little talks, which were never of Law or Scripture—that would only have put her on her guard—but revolved around commonplace occurrences. Except, Jara thought with a smile, Akiva never found anything commonplace. He was like a child, delighting in the first red anemone sighted by the road or the song of a sparrow overhead. And if he probed, he did so gently, kindly, quickly, so that later, when Jara realized she'd said more than she wanted to say, she felt no more harmed by the experience than if a butterfly had brushed her hand.

He was a fastidious man and interested in all matters of health. When Jara expressed the opinion that the customary passing of wine cup from mouth to mouth was the reason Rabbi Yossi's cough had spread from one person to another, Akiva's eyes lit up in wonder. Henceforth, as later Talmudists would record, he was never to be seen touching his lips to a communal cup and strongly opposed the practice.

But it was not Akiva who occupied Jara's thoughts now. The clouds above her seemed to take on the shape of a man with a sword; the golden sun reminded her of a burnished head and beard, and the sky made her think of eyes that were a funny, speckled shade of blue.

She put her hand above her own eyes, shielding them from the sun. The cloud warrior was dissolving, floating away. A hawk flew across the puff of white, seeming to explode in a shot of light as he crossed the sun; then all the birds went quiet. In this silence Jara felt something moving across the field. She got to her feet, body tensed, watching, listening for whatever it was that approached. Then she saw them: two men, their legs nearly hidden by grass and flower, their figures seeming to melt in the quivering air. They carried the long staffs of travelers, and their heads were covered as protection against the sun. Again Jara's hand went up, a frail shield against the blinding glare, then shot out in a gesture of happy greeting. "Simeon," she called waving frantically. "Simeon!"

The two men stopped, waiting as the girl ran toward them.

"It is you," she said breathlessly, coming to a halt before the startled ben Kosiba. "And Obodas!" she cried, giving the Nabatean a quick hug. "What's wrong?" She took a step back, looking from one to the other. "Don't you know me?"

It was Obodas who spoke first. "Little Cat," he said, his eyes sparkling with recognition.

"Yes! It's me, Jara!" She turned again to Simeon. "Don't you remember me?"

He cleared his throat. "Remember, yes. Recognize . . ." He shook his head, obviously stunned by the lissome figure before him. "You're all grown up!"

"Well, it's months since you last saw me," she retorted, hands on hips. "Why did you take so long? I thought you wanted my help."

"I . . . ah . . . that is . . ."

"Never mind," she said happily. "You're here now. That's all that matters. But Akiva's gone. He's in Caesarea."

"I know. He will be back tomorrow. With Hadrian and all the rest."

"Hadrian? Here? In B'nei Berak?"

He grinned now. "I've come to tell Tobita to have all ready." He gave a slight bow. "As any faithful servant would do."

She clapped her hands delightedly. "That's why you're dressed so! And without a horse! Well, come on, then. Let's tell her the news."

But he didn't move.

"What is it? What's wrong?"

He shook his head once more. "Nothing. It's just that . . . you look so different." He touched her cheek. "This was all black and blue. That eye was nearly swollen shut. Your hair . . ."

"It grows fast," she said, wishing he wouldn't take his hand away.

"There isn't a mark on you," he said, wondering. "Your skin is like cream. And your—I mean, you—" He made a vague gesture in the direction of the upper part of her body. "Well, you're . . . ah . . . fuller." He cleared his throat. "What am I saying?" he muttered to no one in particular. "Come on," he said somewhat brusquely, annoyed at Obodas' grin, "let's find Tobita."

"THE EMPEROR? Here?" Tobita's hand went up, slapping the side of her face. "*Oy-va-voy!* What shall I prepare?"

"No more than a good *Shabbat* meal, Akiva says." Simeon grinned. "Maybe a little hemlock on the side," he added facetiously, recalling Jara's original proposition.

"Hemlock's too good for that murderer, may his head grow like an onion straight into the ground."

"A little respect, woman. You're talking about the king of the world."

"What world? Whose world? Not my world." Her thumb jabbed the air. "Up above. There's my King."

Simeon gave her a hug. "Ah, Tobita, if you were a man, I'd make you a general!"

"Get your hands off me, you great hulk. If I were a man! You mean, lose what brains I have? There isn't one of you half as smart as any woman living. Right?" she asked, nodding at Jara. "Hey! Girl! You're supposed to be snapping those beans, not eating them!" She sighed. "What an appetite. She puts away enough for ten, and not an inch of fat on her."

Simeon cast an appreciative glance at the slim-waisted figure. "She's young. You were the same at her age."

"At her age I had two babies. She's not so young, that one."

" 'She.' 'That one.' I have a name," Jara protested good-naturedly.

"Excuse me, Princess Salome. Would your royal highness be so kind as to see if any figs have ripened on the tree?"

Jara rolled her eyes in mock exasperation and left.

Tobita's eyes were on Simeon as he watched the girl depart. "There's the one you should be putting your arms around," she told him.

He looked back at the woman, startled.

"I know how you found her, brought her to Akiva. I know all about it. Every day she waited for you to come. Now I see you together, and it is all clear to me.''

He reddened. "She's only a child.''

"She's not a child. You and Akiva . . . you think she wants to be cuddled like a babe. That's not what she wants or needs. She needs strong arms around her, to hold her in the night when the bad dreams come, to drive away the fear—not as a parent comforts a child, but as a husband covers his wife's body with his own, blotting out the past, the shadows, the dreams.''

Simeon looked away. "B'nei Berak is full of young men—''

"Yes, I thought as you. But I was wrong. I see that now. She would gobble up any boy fool enough to take her on. Her fire would consume him. She needs a man. A strong man.'' She put her hands on her ample hips. "Or maybe you're afraid. All these years without a wife . . .''

"Don't talk foolishness, woman. What kind of husband can I be? What can I offer? I own no land, no house. My name is on every Roman officer's list.''

"Simeon. She's a good girl. You men look at her and see only one thing. But I have come to know her, and I tell you, she has a good nature. She is used to work. She does not shirk it. It breaks my heart sometimes to see what she thinks is expected of her. She has been used badly. Yet she will say nary a word against those she lived with.''

"She has spirit,'' he agreed.

"And beauty.''

He got up, clearly uncomfortable with this conversation. "Where's Obodas?''

"Gone to see about getting you some horses. Simeon—''

He kissed her on the cheek. "I'm already wed, Tobita.''

"What? To whom?''

"To Israel.''

She snorted derisively. "Coward. Coward!'' she called after him. "That is a coward's reply!''

HE FOUND HER gathering fruit by "Akiva's tree.'' Without a word he reached above her head, picking the figs from the branches and dropping them into the willow basket set on the ground. They worked in silence for some time until finally Simeon said, "I still can't believe it. You look like a woman.''

"I am a woman,'' she replied with a smile.

"I mean," he amended, "you don't look like a lad. Not that you ever really did. That is, I guessed right away . . . back there . . . in the hills."

"Did you? How did you know?"

"Your wrists. No boy has wrists that small and fine. Not even Hadrian's pet."

"The emperor has a pet boy?"

"Antinous. About your age. Hadrian dotes on him. What is it? What are you thinking?"

"I'd almost forgotten . . . how strange they are. Since I've been here, it's as if the rest of the world doesn't exist."

"It exists, all right," he said grimly. "And it gets worse. For every man Akiva manages to save by interceding with Rufus, ten others are imprisoned."

"But so many come to him. He does what he can, Simeon."

"It isn't enough. And it isn't the way. Why should any of us have to beg for mercy? And I don't give a damn for clever stratagems either. That game we're forced to play of outwitting the devil. You should see them in Caesarea. Well, you'll see it soon enough. Long, endless, philosophical talk and oh-so-clever debates on this 'Hebrew practice' and that. And all of it cat-and-mouse. Because if Akiva wins, he loses. And if he loses, he still loses. The *goyim* will never understand us. They don't want to. They don't care. And they'd just as soon be rid of us." He shrugged. "The hell with them. Let them think as they like. Just so they clear off our land and leave us alone."

She was silent.

"Isn't that what you want?"

"Yes . . . yes . . ."

His eyes narrowed. "But perhaps you have forgotten. What it's like being in their hands. What they can do." His eyes took in the surrounding countryside over which the late afternoon was settling like honey. "B'nei Berak is an island in the midst of a stormy sea. A safe, peaceful harbor. I suppose that's why I put you here." He looked back at her. "And you have been happy, haven't you?"

"Akiva is very kind. He calls me 'daughter.' He's taught me to read and write. Beruria is teaching me Greek. I was ashamed because I was so ignorant. . . . And do you know what Akiva told me? He was forty years old before he had any schooling at all! He went and sat with the children, beside his own son, slate in hand. Just imagine, a grown man . . ."

Simeon smiled, thinking how the ripe sun had turned her hair to gold. "Yes, the story is often told."

"But it's true! Akiva said so himself. And Tobita told me about his wife, Rachel—did you know, that was my mother's name? Akiva's Rachel was the daughter of Kalba Sabua, one of Judea's richest men. And Akiva was a shepherd on her father's estate. And they fell in love, and she gave up everything to marry him and made him go to school and study, because she saw what a great man he could be."

He was still smiling. Her face and gestures were animated; he'd never seen her look this happy. He reached out, touched a tendril of her hair. "It's good to see you like this," he said softly. "Perhaps this is best after all," he murmured, more to himself than to her, "that you forget. . . ." He tucked the curl behind her ear, realizing that he suddenly felt a sense of loss. Still he forced himself to say, "You must stay here, where you are safe . . . marry a young scholar . . ."

Even as he spoke, he was aware that the expression on her face had changed; it was as if a cloud or veil had settled over her features. Her eyes became a flat, pale color, giving back to him only the reflection of his own uncertain self.

"What's wrong?" he asked. "What have I said to disturb you?"

She did not reply.

"I thought . . . you admire Akiva so . . ."

"Don't you know anything?" she blurted. "Don't you know anything at all?"

He stared at her, silent, confused.

With a sigh she picked up the basket of figs and started toward the house. Suddenly she turned back. "Tobita was right," she called to him. "You're all fools!"

LATER THAT NIGHT he found an opportunity to come to her room. He stood in the doorway, clumsily apologizing for whatever confusion he'd caused her.

"First I berate you for being ignorant of what passes in Judea, and then I tell you that is exactly how you must be." He frowned. "I don't know why I said all those things to you. You're only a child."

"I'm not. You're the only one who . . . You always treat me like a child. And the strange part is, when I'm with you I feel like a child. And I know I must act like one."

"No . . ." He put his hands on her shoulders. "What I meant is, you're very young. Your life is all before you. You must forget what's happened. You must go on—"

"I forget nothing! Nothing!" She stepped back, went to a small woven trunk and took from it a dagger that he well remembered. "This *sica* might have been my grandfather's. He died on the Masada. Do you think I could forget that? Or what they did to my mother? To the people of Kefar Katan? Oh, no! I forget nothing! And you . . . all these months, waiting, wondering . . . and not a word, not a sign. Where have you been? What have you been doing? I want to know. I have a right to know!"

He grinned. "Well, I've been busy with your friend Bar Daroma."

"Making preparations?"

He nodded.

"Tell me, Simeon," she asked eagerly. "Tell me everything!"

And so he told her about the underground tunnels, and the caves with their caches of arms and supplies, and the secret military exercises that went on in the mountains surrounding Jerusalem. And as he spoke he saw the light return to her eyes, and the golden fire there was the same as danced in his own. And he was glad that it was he and not Akiva or someone else who brought forth this joy, and realized that the things she'd said in anger were the very things he wanted her to say. And he wondered why it meant so much to him.

Finally, when the candle was a mere stub in its holder, he said, "It's late. You must be tired. And cold. You're shivering."

"I'm all right. Go on. Tell me more. Tell me again." But she was in fact hugging herself, trembling from excitement as well as fatigue.

He put his cloak around her. "Go on, go to bed. I didn't realize it was so late. It isn't right for you to be here alone with me."

She rubbed her cheek against the rough wool covering her shoulders, smelling the familiar scent of sun and grass and sweat. His scent. "Why? I slept in your arms once."

He looked away. "That was different."

"Why? Why was it different?"

He studied her to see if she was playing with him. The cat eyes stared back, unblinking. He looked away again. "Go on, get out."

She smiled now, impishly. "You're in my room, Simeon."

He reddened, then rose to his feet. "In that case, I bid you good night."

"No! Oh, don't go! Please . . . I don't want you to go. . . ."

"I must."

"Then kiss me goodbye. You'll be gone in the morning. I know you will. When I awaken you'll be gone and you'll never come back!"

"I will. I promise I'll be back."

"Then kiss me. To seal your promise."

He let out his breath. "I'm beginning to think that old rabbi was right," he murmured. "You are a witch."

"I'm the same girl you once saved," she said earnestly. "My hair's a little longer, and I've got on a proper dress. But I'm the same."

"If you're the same, then I swear I never saw you before." He put his hands on either side of her face. "And I wish to God I hadn't seen you now."

She closed her eyes, feeling his thumb move across her cheek. His hands slid down to her throat and then back, lifting her hair. . . .

"Jara . . ."

She dared not open her eyes. She could hear his breathing as he drew her to him, feel his breath sweep across her lips. Then suddenly she was alone, standing in a vacuum of cold, empty air. She opened her eyes. He was at the door.

"Simeon!"

But he was already gone.

"YOU KNOW," Tobita said, "he's a nice-looking man. I confess I thought he'd be a monster, a great ugly hulk with a big Roman nose, or—well, I don't know what I thought. I've never seen an emperor before. And I tell you, he looks just like you and me. No airs. Pleasant as can be. Fancy that."

Jara did not reply.

"What's the matter with you, girl? You've been in a sulk since they arrived."

"It makes me sick, that's all. To see everyone running

around, bowing all the time, talking oh-so-respectfully, and oh-so-grateful for the presence of almighty Caesar. The man who destroyed our Temple, let me remind you. The Ravager of Jerusalem."

"Oh, be quiet! Hadrian wasn't even born then—or was just a babe. It's hard to tell how old he is," Tobita mused. "His hair is gray, but his face is youthful, and he's a splendid figure of a man."

"He likes boys."

"Boys!" The girl might as well have said "chickens." Tobita made a face. "Fech!" She looked at Jara. "I don't believe it! He's too manly."

"Simeon told me. The one sitting beside him—"

"Such a beautiful lad. I thought he was Hadrian's son."

"His name is Antinous."

"I don't care what his name is. If this platter is not served instantly, the food will grow cold. Come, take it in to them."

"Not I. May my hands fall off before I serve the Roman pig."

"Oh, you are stubborn!"

"Don't do it, Tobita!" the girl pleaded. "Don't fetch and carry for them!"

"Let's get one thing straight," Tobita said firmly. "I serve Akiva ben Joseph and whomever my master brings into this house, if that be his pleasure. I cherish my freedom no less than you, girl. But if the emperor of Rome comes in peace, a stranger in our land and in this house, then he will be accorded the same courtesy as any other guest. For each thing there is a time and a place. Now is the time to talk. And if talking means no bloodshed, no war, then I am glad to carry in to that dining hall fifty bowls of soup and a hundred platters of grilled fish. Now, will you help me?"

"No."

Tobita sighed. "How can one so young have such a hard heart? Oh, I know what you've been through. But you must change, Jara. You cannot live your life wrapped around a single idea. These last months I thought—"

"You thought I'd forgotten what the real world is like." Because this is . . . unreal, she thought, remembering Simeon. B'nei Berak. Akiva exchanging tales with the emperor of Rome. Rabbis Teradyon and Tarfon nodding politely to Tinneus Rufus, whom they cursed and called Tyrannus Rufus when he was not around. Beruria chatting with the governor's wife as though it did not matter how many slaves the woman owned. . . .

"I don't know what you're talking about. And I don't know what I'm doing standing here listening to you." But Tobita paused again at the curtain separating the kitchen from the entrance to the dining hall. "Are you sure about Hadrian? He really prefers boys?"

Jara nodded.

Tobita shook her head wonderingly, as though presented with a mystery she would never comprehend. "*Goyim*," she said finally, as if that explained all.

"IF YOUR GOD is so great," Hadrian wanted to know, "why then should he be envious of the gods other men worship? According to you they are nonexistent."

"In reply, allow me to tell you of a dream I had the other night," Akiva said. "There were two dogs, one named Rufus and the other Rufina—"

"What?" Startled, Tinneus Rufus protested with a not altogether amused laugh. "Can you not call the dogs by any other names than mine and my wife's?"

"I meant no insult," the rabbi assured him. "Yet see how disturbed you become when I call two nonexistent animals which I happened to see in a dream by the names you and your wife bear. How, then, shall the Holy One, blessed be He, not be offended when a piece of inert wood is called by His name?"

"Then let your God destroy his rivals," Hadrian said with the smile of a man who had accepted self-deification upon his completion of the Temple of Zeus Olympios, and who was accustomed to receive symbols of adulation from all parts of the empire acknowledging his "divinity."

"To destroy all that man worships, excellency, the Almighty would have to annihilate not only figures of wood and clay, but the sun, moon, and stars, which are also worshipped."

"Well, he could obliterate the former and spare the latter."

"To do so would only strengthen the false beliefs of those who worship those objects. For they would argue, 'There, you see? The stars cannot be destroyed.' "

"Your point is well taken, Akiva," the emperor acknowledged. "And yet it never ceases to amaze me that you—and your fellows who follow the teachings of Jesus of Nazareth —revere heaven and the angels which you say inhabit it, but treat with disdain the mightiest elements of the sky, which are the sun, the moon, and the stars. Can one conceive that the whole is divine and that parts of it are not? Is it logical to revere mysterious beings that suddenly appear before dazzled eyes—through the mist of sorcery, perhaps—deceptive visions, and not to think highly of what is both evident and splendid? I speak of the powers of nature. Those forces which supervise the rain, the clouds, the thunder and lightning, with all the fruits of the earth, those are the true heavenly angels." Pleased with his own speech, Hadrian made a slight gesture that cut off further debate. "All this talk has given me an appetite. I hope we will be treated to artichokes in the Jews' style. It is a most popular dish in Rome."

The Judeans present looked at one another in bewilderment. "Artichokes, you say?" Rabbi Tarfon asked. "Cooked by Jews?"

"If you will allow me," a pleasant voice broke in.

All turned toward the speaker.

"Ah, Andreas! Perhaps I have not expressed myself correctly. Perhaps the dish is called something else here," the emperor acknowledged.

"It does not exist, excellency," the young man replied with a slight smile. "The preparation of the vegetable in question—stuffed with garlic and herbs, then fried in oil, and served with a bit of lemon—is the invention of the Jews of Rome. You will not find anything like it in Judea."

"Indeed. What a disappointment."

"Perhaps Tobita—" Akiva began.

"No, no, we shall do without. I make it a point to eat only what is native to the area," Hadrian declared. "I simply thought—"

"You thought there was no difference between Jews of Rome and Judea," Andreas said. "A most natural error, excellency. The fact is, each community of Israelites has its own personality, habits, and bill of fare. The Jews of Alexandria are said to be more Egyptian than the descendants of Pharaoh, while those of Parthia have a distinct Babylonian character. The Judeans, all agree, are rather a class unto themselves. As for those of us who live in Rome—"

"One can hardly tell you apart from any citizen on the

Aventine,'' Hadrian admitted with a laugh. "By all the gods, Andreas—yours and mine!—you look more like a senator's son than all the progeny I've seen born to the purple.''

The young man accepted the compliment with another slight smile. He was, in fact, richly attired, the wine-colored tunic with its braiding of gold setting off his dark good looks. He was about twenty-eight, with curly black hair cut short in the Roman style and, again in the fashion of Rome, no beard. His eyes were also dark, the slight peak to his eyebrows, together with that fleeting, slightly crooked smile, conspiring to give a somewhat devilish look to what would otherwise have been a classically handsome face. He appeared to be of average height, smooth-muscled, and classically proportioned, so that while he could not have served as the model for a Roman sculptor intent on carving out a gladiator, he would have done nicely (as Hadrian, ever the admirer of beauty, had once pointed out) for some Greek artist wishing to depict a charioteer.

"It would seem that the Jews in Rome have become Romans, while the Romans in Judea . . .'' Tinneus Rufus allowed the sentence to remain uncompleted. He reached for his wine cup, grimacing slightly at the sweet drink. "Every day there come reports of this man or that running off to seek some miracle-worker who heals in the name of Jesus, or seeking out a rabbi for instruction in the laws of Moses. Even in high places . . .'' Again he left the thought unfinished.

Responding to the worried glances that passed among his colleagues, Akiva leaned forward and said, "You and I have had many pleasant discussions, yet our talks have in no way diminished your dedication to the empire or the certainty of your beliefs. Nor have I ever attempted to persuade you or anyone else to abandon his heritage. Unlike the Christians, whom you seem intent upon joining to us, we do not seek proselytes.'' He smiled apologetically. "It is hard enough for those born to it to be a Jew. Can we in good conscience ask others to share our lot?''

There was laughter at this.

"Well, you are clever, Akiva. I will give you that,'' Rufus said, raising his cup to the rabbi. "And some of what you say cannot be faulted by anyone. You have one saying in particular—what is it now? Something about a virtuous woman . . .''

" 'A virtuous woman in the house is like an altar in the Temple. She redeems all the sins of the family.' "

"Yes, that's it. What do you think, my dear?" Rufus asked, turning to his wife, who was staring straight ahead. "Let me ask you something," he continued, turning to Beruria, who was seated nearby. "According to the law of your people, after a woman has lain with a man, how long before she is judged 'clean'?"

The centurion Marcellus Quintus, who was also present, spoke up now. "From whence do we arrive at this subject?" he asked with a frown. He turned to Hadrian. "The question is indelicate, my lord, and totally out of place."

Hadrian, busy at this moment murmuring something to Antinous, who was in turn occupied in suppressing one of his frequent yawns, merely nodded, his attention passing quickly to the dish set before him, which he proceeded to attack with vigor.

"I merely wish to enlarge my sphere of knowledge, centurion. After all," Rufus said, "we are in the company of learned men and"—he nodded at Beruria and, with exaggerated civility, at his wife—"exceptional women."

"Perhaps," Beruria replied smoothly, "the best answer to your question is the one given by the philosopher Theano, who was the wife or, some say, the daughter of Pythagoras. When asked how many days after intercourse with a man a woman was, as you put it, 'clean,' Theano is said to have replied, 'If the man be the woman's husband, she is immediately clean. If he be a stranger, never.' "

WHILE THIS CONVERSATION was taking place, Andreas had become increasingly aware of a pair of eyes peering through the opening of the curtain hung across the entrance to the room. His first thought was that one or more of the servants sought a glimpse of the party. But as it became apparent that the eyes were the property of only one person and that the look in them was one of growing consternation, his interest was aroused.

Meanwhile, Jara, having recognized Marcellus Quintus, was debating what to do.

"What is it now?" Tobita asked. "You're as pale as a peeled potato."

"That centurion . . . he was in Tiberias the night I killed Valerens. He spoke to me."

Tobita's eyes grew wide.

"I'd better not go out there," Jara continued. "Don't let anyone back here."

The woman nodded.

As soon as she'd gone, Jara checked the rear entrance. Soldiers were all over the place, ensuring the safety of their emperor. If she ventured outside now they would most likely stop her, if only to tease or perhaps to set forth some lewd proposal. Even a casual word could be enough to draw the centurion's attention, to rekindle his memory.

"Hello."

She whirled about to find herself staring at the young man she had already marked as one of Hadrian's royal entourage. His eyes were the brightest, darkest eyes she'd ever seen. It was the cleft in his chin, however, that fascinated her. She'd never seen one before and wondered if it was a mark of some virtue or flaw in his character. He was certainly handsome, a fact she could not help noting without some resentment, as if beauty, considered a mark of God's favor, ought not to be attributed to one's enemies.

For his part, Andreas was equally transfixed. Before him stood a creature whose face and figure clearly transcended her homely attire. There was something more to the girl, something he could not yet define but which made her seem totally out of place in this spiritual and academic domain. He found himself struck with the desire to know all he could about her. He would have to tread with caution; she watched him as warily as the feline creature she resembled.

"I'd like some more wine," he said pleasantly. "The servants are all busy and everyone else is engrossed in talk." He held out his cup. "Will you fill this for me?"

"She doesn't understand Greek, Andreas." It was Beruria, alerted by Tobita. "I shall be glad to see to your needs."

"Thank you." He glanced again at Jara, who had not moved. "Perhaps if I spoke in Aramaic—"

"To a common servant girl? Whatever for?"

"My dear Beruria, this lovely creature is hardly common, and with the exception of yourself quite the most interesting thing in B'nei Berak. As for being a servant, may I ask why she has made no appearance in the dining hall?" He grinned. "Or is Akiva saving her for dessert?"

"She is so overwhelmed by the emperor's presence that Tobita fears she might drop or spill something, thereby causing an embarrassment."

Andreas looked at the girl again. She hardly appeared over-whelmed by anything. Yet . . . something moved behind that steady, almost glassy stare. What was it?

"She's very shy," Beruria was saying. "She hardly speaks to anyone."

He smiled now. "Well, we must remedy that."

"Have pity!" Beruria laughed. "You've already left a string of pining maidens from one end of the world to the other." She took his arm. "I'm going to insist you work your charm on no one but me while you are with us. After all, I don't often have the chance to converse with a handsome, witty man who will actually look me in the eyes when he speaks to me."

"Well, that's what you get for living in Judea. I told you to come to Rome."

"That was rather a long time ago, as I recall. We both were children. And if I'm not mistaken, you also asked me to marry you then."

"And you refused, thereby demonstrating at an early age the wisdom for which you have since become so famous."

They laughed together now. But as he allowed Beruria to lead him away, Andreas cast a last look at Jara, who remained immobile, returning his glance with her own inscrutable stare.

Jara did not relax her guarded posture until she was sure she was alone again. Still, she felt tense, skittish, unnerved not only by the presence of the centurion in the next room but also by the way Andreas had stared at her. Did he know? No, how could he? What had been in his eyes, then? It had fairly made her skin burn.

She made up her mind to avoid him, but when she finally stepped out of the house into the cover of night, he was waiting for her. This time he addressed her in Aramaic.

"Do you know your eyes shine in the dark like a cat's?"

She drew back, startled. He made no sound when he moved. Regaining her composure, she answered indifferently, "So I've been told."

"How are you called, Cat-Eyes?"

She glanced about nervously. They were too close to the house. The centurion might catch sight of her. "Walk a ways with me and I'll tell you."

An eyebrow went up. And Beruria had said she was shy! More intrigued than ever, Andreas followed the girl. When they were all but hidden in a grove of trees, he put out his hand to stop her. "I admit I'm not one for formalities, but before we begin I would like to know your name."

Jara stared at him. "Begin? Begin what?"

Before he could reply, a voice called out, "Stop! Who goes there?"

Andreas sighed. Trust the legion to be where it was least needed or wanted. "Put away your sword, centurion," he said as the approaching figure of Marcellus Quintus became visible. "As you can see, there's only—" He looked around. The girl had disappeared. "Me," he concluded wryly.

"Sorry. Can't be too careful. The emperor thinks he can just stroll about without a thought for his own safety. He doesn't know Judea."

"As you do, of course."

"As I do."

"But surely in the house of Akiva—"

"They're everywhere."

"I beg your pardon," Andreas said politely. "Who is everywhere?"

"Rebels. Assassins." He paused. "Sicarii."

"Sicarii?" Andreas studied the man. He appeared agitated, disturbed. "You must be joking. The Zealot Daggermen are long dead—or as old as Akiva, in which case I doubt Rome has anything to fear from them."

"Rome has more to fear than you may imagine," the man muttered. "This place is a curse. We come here thinking . . . And it all gets muddled somehow. We change. We become exactly what they think we are."

"Excuse me, centurion, are you sure you are well? Perhaps something at dinner—"

"I'm fine. But I admit the evening has been something of a strain. For a moment I even thought . . ." He sighed, rubbed his forehead. "I could have sworn I saw her." He studied Andreas. "Did you catch sight of a young girl with big, pale eyes—I don't know quite how to describe her—except to say that if you saw her you would not forget her."

"Sounds interesting."

"Dangerous, you mean. The female I have in mind killed the commander of the garrison in Tiberias. The man had the habit of taking young women on their wedding day—perfectly legal, of course, though I can't say much to my liking. Anyway, this one did him in."

"Well, I suppose we can't fault the young lady for avenging her honor."

"There was more to it than that. This was the work of rebels. I'm sure of it. It was carefully planned, even to obtaining a writ of safe conduct for the little murderess." He uttered a short, dry laugh. "I myself gave her the horse with which she escaped."

"What do you suppose happened to her?"

"Damned if I know. We searched her village—I don't know why—only a fool would have returned there." He paused. "The place was leveled. Very few survived."

"By your order."

"It was a capital offense. Yes, damn it! By my order!" He let out his breath. "By the gods, if I ever meet up with that bitch again, I'll strangle her with my own hands! Not for killing that bastard Valerens. Not even for making a fool of me. But for . . ." He stopped. "It was," he said again, "a capital offense."

Andreas did not reply.

The centurion sighed, shook his head. "I don't know what's happening to me. I've always thought of myself as a man who accepted all men, all peoples, for what they are, not for what is attributed to their race. I remember once, in Rome, seeing a play—Juvenal, I think—in which the Jew appeared as the most ridiculous, contemptible figure. 'The Dirty Jew.' It offended me. I could not help but wonder why a people that has never sought dominion over any other should be so reviled."

"I know the production of which you speak, although I did not see it. There was that very day, as I recall, a great show of events at the Circus Maximus. Men fighting beasts . . . then man against man, beast against beast. . . . For amusement's sake a team of dwarfs battled women. The arena had been sprinkled with gold dust. When the games were over, spectators jumped the stands and fought to retrieve a bit of the dirt, sifting through the dried blood and animal excrement for traces of that which glittered."

Quintus turned away in disgust. "That is not Rome. Not the real Rome."

"Any more, I suppose, than the man who destroyed a village for the sake of a single crime is the real Marcellus Quintus." There was that faint, crooked smile. "What is, is what is, centurion."

"I think I have spoken too openly with you," the soldier said now. "I should have guessed where your loyalties would lie."

"Not with a bunch of dirty peasants intent on suicide, I assure you. The glorious past of the Chosen People has never appeared all that glorious to me, and I'm not particularly interested in the restoration of what was at best second-rate. 'Jerusalem of Gold' . . . At its finest, could it compare with the Imperial City? As for the Temple, frankly I can do without the slaughtering of great numbers of birds and bulls upon a primitive altar. And I suspect God can as well. We're all a little older."

Quintus smiled wryly. "You have a unique view."

"I don't think so. Just before, the emperor was asking Akiva about the Eighteen Benedictions, the set of prayers which has replaced the daily sacrifice that took place in the Temple. Among other things, the *Shemoneh Esreh* calls for the reinstitution of the Temple service. But do you really think these rabbis want that to occur? Where would that leave them? Second-class, compared with the priests."

"I never thought of it that way."

"Believe me, centurion, the rabbinic powers will never sanction any action that holds within it the slightest promise of a return to the old days and the priestly hierarchy. And without that sanction the Jews will never unite in any significant numbers to be a real threat. So all you are left with are small gangs of bandits and hoodlums who no doubt call themselves patriots to mask their crimes. And you can easily take care of them, can't you?"

"Bandits, eh? Well, that's for certain. Three supply caravans have been waylaid within the last month. They're getting bolder," he mused. "Better organized. We found a cache of weapons hidden in one of the caves around Ein Gedi." He gave Andreas a quick look. "I don't suppose you know anything about that," he said, half-joking. "Your family, as I recall, has always had its channels of information."

"Enough to see us through four emperors," Andreas admitted. "But as for Judea . . ." He shook his head. "I am a stranger here, as alien to this place as it is to me." He indicated his attire. "And hardly the figure to inspire confidences from rebels."

"But you are a Jew."

"Well, let's just say the physical evidence of that fact remains hidden to the public."

Quintus smiled. "You're clever, Andreas. A bit too clever for my taste. That's why I can't help wondering . . ."

"What, centurion?"

"No." He seemed to correct himself. "If I have doubts, surely they would as well."

"They?" Andreas asked politely.

"The new Sicarii. I think they'd slit your throat as soon as look at you." He smiled again. "Good night, citizen."

"Centurion." Andreas watched the man depart. When he was sure there was no one else about, he said casually, "You can come out now."

There was a slight rustle of bush.

He turned around. "Quintus was right," he said, thinking how like a wild animal she looked with that curly mane and her eyes shining eerily in the darkness like the green-gold lights of the fireflies. "You are hard to forget."

She did not answer. She was listening for any signs that would mark the centurion's return.

"Well, aren't you going to thank me?"

"For what?"

"Saving your life."

Another gleam in the night as she held up the small dagger. "My life? You mean yours."

He let out a small whistle. "Charming. What other surprises have you got for me?"

"This isn't Rome. Some of us have learned it is as easy to kill as be killed."

"Easier, would be my guess. Are you really part of a rebel organization? They must be wonderful heroes, sending a girl to do their work."

"What do you know?" she asked contemptuously. "They're just 'dirty peasants' to you."

"Ah! So you do understand more than Aramaic. Another surprise."

"Perhaps. In any event, whatever I do or might have done is for myself."

"Such as killing a Roman officer. That was to save your honor, I suppose."

She did not answer.

"The pure, virtuous maiden defending her virginity . . ."

He leaned back against a tree and folded his arms across his chest. She thought she saw him smile. "No . . . somehow that image doesn't quite fit. I admit I was wrong about you just now. I think I understand why you were so anxious to be out of sight. Alas, the thought that motivated you was not the same as made me follow. Perhaps another time."

She started to move away, convinced now that he was not only an enemy but crazy as well. His voice stopped her.

"You're not like the other women around here, I think. Nor like the ones in Rome, would be my guess. In Judea, every girl dreams of marrying a scholar so she can spend the rest of her life toiling for him while he sits in the synagogue praying for the redemption of Israel. That is, when he isn't busy discussing with equally learned men such vital subjects as whether or not a proselyte has a share of the world to come. Now, in Rome, it's quite the opposite. There, all that is wanted is to marry a rich man, the richer the better. But you . . ."

"I'm not the least bit interested in what you think of me."

"Of course you are. There isn't a human being alive who doesn't enjoy hearing about himself."

"I'm sure that's true of you—"

"And you as well. Especially as you are at that age when you really aren't all that certain just who and what you are." There was that funny, crooked smile again. "Are you?"

She blinked.

"Well, I for one can't see you with some pale, burning-eyed boy. No, a rabbi's wife you'll never be—or pity the man who tries to think only of God with you around. Well, then, what is it little girls like you want? A rich, powerful man? No, I doubt you're clever enough to realize what money means. Or power. No, your dreams are full of heroes, I think. King David. Solomon. No, not Solomon. Too much brain, not enough muscle. The Maccabee. Yes, of course, the Maccabee. And most of all, best of all, the Hero-to-Come. The Messiah. For what is the Messiah to Jews, after all? Not some Divine Son of God, as the rest of the world thinks we believe, but the son of David. A son of Israel. A completely human figure who will take up arms against the world power and crush it, freeing Judea from its yoke of servitude and establishing the Kingdom of Israel which he shall govern with mercy and justice. He must be a man of dauntless courage, of course. All-powerful. Strong. Shoulders broad as a house. Like that fellow in

Caesarea, claiming to be a tenant farmer. Where is he, by the way? The kind of man," he continued, "who could overturn a horse or uproot a young cedar at full gallop. Like—what do they call him? Simeon ben Kosiba."

"What do you know of ben Kosiba?" she asked warily.

"He's the local Hercules, isn't he? More, to hear people talk."

"What people?"

"Just . . . people."

She shrugged. "I don't know what you're talking about."

He grinned now; his teeth were very white in the dark. "Now, why do I have the feeling that's not altogether true?"

"I'm sure I don't know. Perhaps you are accustomed to duplicity and, seeing it in yourself, are convinced the world abounds with it. In any case, as you seem to think you know everything about everyone—and especially about me—I expect you will come up with your own answer." And with that and another quick look around, she took her leave.

"Good night," he called after her. He was still smiling. "We'll meet again. You can be sure of it."

"Perhaps." The voice that floated back held the hint of a laugh. "When the Messiah comes."

THERE WAS a quality to the Judean night that Marcellus Quintus found both intriguing and disturbing. Darkness came too suddenly, after the merest hint of twilight, which was all the time it took for the sun to fall into the sea, wrenched from heaven as by some quick, violent hand. And as it fell, a trail of blood seemed to stain the sky. And then it was dark. Night. Light shining through all the little holes left where the sun had been torn away.

The night seemed to wrap itself around him. As Quintus moved across the quiet landscape, he felt as if he were pushing against soft walls, the wind always changing, with sometimes the scent of spice and leaf, sometimes the faint perfume of the sea.

It was like being in a woman, but with nothing to grab hold of, nothing to hold on to.

And so one seemed to fall, aroused but unfulfilled, wanting, needing to touch, to feel; and even that not enough.

What are these emotions? the centurion wondered. What

was he thinking, feeling? Was it because Livia was inside the house, talking, no doubt to Akiva, whom she loved as she would never love the man whose bed she shared or the man to whose bed she sometimes stole? Was it the memory of a girl who'd turned compassion to rage, letting loose all the naked violence within him? Or was it simply this place, this . . . Judea? He'd read the letters of the Romans who had been here before him: Vespasian, Titus, Lucilius Bassus, after the war, and Flavius Silva after Bassus. Commanders and military governors down through the reigns of Domitian, Nerva, and Trajan. Reports from centurions, letters from discharged soldiers living in the new colonies. In all of them he'd sensed something that he could not yet define, that intrigued him, made him want to come here not only because he believed in Hadrian's dream of a unified world, but because he'd had a whiff of some tantalizing mystery.

What had he found?

A country, already poor, being drained of every available resource.

Whose patriarchs preached peace but whose populace was restless, needing but the slightest spark to ignite them.

Whose faith carried with it the explicit call for freedom as well as human dignity.

Whose people in this context made bad slaves, troublesome servants, unwilling vassals quelled only by force.

Quintus sighed. So far his deductions hardly differed from those of the men who had gone before him. And still there was this sense of something beyond or beneath the obvious. Men came to Judea, and they changed somehow. He'd read it in their letters, felt it in himself.

We become what you think we are, he'd told Andreas.

Was it only faith in oneself that this small, insignificant slice of land was capable of shaking? Or was mighty Zeus himself in danger of being felled? Oh, there were statues and idols and charms enough, but how many men and women had come here worshipping Apollo and Venus, only to come away murmuring prayers to an invisible Lord, or claiming that a god had walked the earth in the person of one Jesus of Nazareth? There had been so many proselytes to the Hebrew faith that the emperor Domitian had prohibited conversion, rightly fearing the seeds of rebellion inherent in the religion's stand for equality. He had banished his own wife for her secret practice

of the faith and executed a relative, Flavius Clemens, for the
same crime. The Christians, persecuted by Nero, were less
feared. Hearkening to the message of Paul, an apostle of their
master, they seemed content to submit to Caesar, secure in
their reward after death.

Every Roman soldier ever stationed in Judea came to loathe
the place and—this was what Quintus sensed in all those letters—to fear it, or something in it. Images flashed before his
eyes: Cestius Gallus, at the start of the Great War, poised with
his troops before the Temple in Jerusalem, turning away for
reasons that would never be known. Flavius Silva, standing
silently atop the conquered Masada, confusion matched by a
sense of defeat that would follow him the rest of his days.
Titus, destroyer of Jerusalem, crying out on his deathbed that
he was being punished for only one crime he had committed—
which he failed to name. And all of them, all who had touched
Judea, taken sword and siege machine to her, ripped away the
veil to her Holy Place, carried away her sacred objects,
trampled her fertile fields—all of them, Pompey, Vespasian,
Titus, Bassus, Quietus, the list was endless—all, no matter
how history praised them otherwise and called them good or
even great, all had met with sudden, sometimes unexplained,
sometimes violent deaths.

And suddenly Quintus knew fear, not for himself but for
Hadrian, whom he loved. And the answer to the riddle that
had puzzled him for so long seemed as clear and evident as the
stars overhead.

We don't belong here, he thought. It was as simple as that.
Best to get out, to leave Judea and the Jews to themselves. Assured of their independence, they could become allies, thereby
providing the Parthian connection Rome sought. But Hadrian, who was so wise, must have sensed this already. Jerusalem was the beginning. Once that was returned, the Jews
would see they had nothing to fear from the Good Emperor.
As time went along, they would be allowed to form their own
government and be integrated within the empire as a member
nation rather than a vassal state. Hadrian would not make the
same mistake all the others had. He would not tax Rome further with the burden of maintaining Judea's occupation. The
Tenth Legion had been here well over a hundred years, so long
that its name, designated by the abbreviation LEG X FRET, the
last syllable standing for Fretensis, which was the Straits of

Messina, the legion's original and supposedly permanent garrison, might well be changed to one reflecting its presence in Judea. The temper of the troops had also changed, to one which Marcellus Quintus did not admire.

We've got to get out, he thought. *There's more to be gained than lost.*

But Hadrian would see that. No doubt, he already had.

THE EMPEROR was reading when Quintus entered the room. Antinous sat nearby, polishing a bow which had been presented to him upon the occasion of this visit. As always, Quintus was struck by the natural dignity of Rome's ruler, the way he graced his surroundings whatever and wherever they happened to be. Not for nothing had Hadrian earned the title "the Traveling Emperor." In nearly fifteen years of rule he had already passed two-thirds without fixed abode. During his journeys he had occupied palatial homes of Asiatic merchants, spartan Greek houses, handsome villas in Roman Gaul, even huts and farms. Quintus had stood beside him, ankle-deep in mud, cheerfully eating a plate of beans alongside his soldiers. He had watched over him, asleep by the fire after a day's hunt, stomach filled with roasted venison or boar. He had watched Hadrian preside at long, imperial repasts, spurning exotic delicacies for plain fare and impatient, Quintus knew, to be out of the place, out of Rome, and on the road again.

There had been others before Hadrian who had traveled the earth. But here the traveler was also the master, free not only to see but to change or even to create anew. Perhaps that was what most excited Hadrian. There was scarcely a town within the Empire that he would not visit or a detachment of troops he would not inspect. Wherever he went, he made it a point to intervene personally in the affairs of the place; he rebuilt cities and erected new ones, made roads, harbors, bridges, all the while seeking out men of learning, talking to them, continuing a lifelong study of art and the phenomena of nature.

Fortunately, because he was wont to favor roads off the beaten track, welcoming local accommodations as he found them, he was a man of stamina, in excellent health. Well built, of good complexion, he looked younger than his fifty-six years despite his gray hair, and appeared fit and strong. When he took to the sea it was in his own luxuriously outfitted ship equipped with gymnasium and library, but he had already become a legend for traveling on foot through the provinces, never minding cold or rough weather.

His quest for knowledge struck many as insatiable. It had taken him to Athens, Olympia, Pergamus, even to the heights of Mount Etna, and ultimately far into Egypt. Quintus knew the emperor was deeply interested in esoteric wisdom and the mystery religions such as the Mithraic cult, as well as dreams, omens, and astrology, and was therefore not surprised to observe that the papyrus now being studied so intently was an ancient Babylonian tract outlining various magical formulae. Still, the centurion said with a smile, "I would have thought you would be reading the works of the Hebrews, excellency, seeing as you like each thing in its place."

The emperor shook his head. "That gibberish! Jew or Christian, I can't make heads or tails of the nonsense they spout, and am at a loss to see how either sect can be so self-deluded as to believe they possess the highest wisdom."

The image of Livia flashed before Quintus' eyes, but he said nothing.

"It is the purest superstition, without a particle of sound judgment," Hadrian went on. "Especially the claims of the Jesus-believers. How many imposters in the world have claimed to be the son of God, descended from heaven!" He shrugged. "The Christians have no proof. The death of their savior was witnessed by many, his resurrection by only one. It might have been better had the reverse been true."

"The Jews also believe in the advent of a messiah," Quintus pointed out.

"Yes, but a completely human one. Akiva was very careful to make the distinction, albeit with some embarrassment. Obviously, the coming of such a man carries with it the implications of Rome's downfall. Our rabbi didn't wish to offend me, so he went on quickly to remind me of the Sibylline Oracles, which have prophesied that 'a man with the name of a sea' will restore Jerusalem, thereby precluding the need for a warring Son of David. I thanked him for the compliment. It is as close as I shall come, no doubt, to achieving deification here."

Antinous laughed.

"Dear Quintus, how do you stand it? How have I repaid your friendship and long years of service by sending you to this place filled with mad dreamers who speak of miracles and sons of heaven, where rebellion is an ever-agonizing itch, where there is so little beauty and even less sense?''

Quintus laughed now. "It's not so bad. One gets used to it. And I confess a certain fascination. . . ." He tried to explain. "In the wilderness, there is such strange beauty, and even Jerusalem, which you shall see tomorrow. . . . The city itself is in ruins, but the setting, excellency, and the view, the way the light falls upon the hills each afternoon . . .''

"Yes,'' Hadrian agreed, catching Quintus' excitement. "Pliny called it the most famous city of the East. And so it shall be again. I'm beginning to see it. Streets laid out at right angles in the best classical style. Shops, houses, and on the hill where their temple stood, a great monument to Jupiter.''

"To . . . Jupiter? But I thought . . . excellency . . .''

"That I would let the Jews have Jerusalem?''

"You said . . . they believe . . .''

"I said I would allow them to rebuild the city. And they shall. But by my design, Quintus, not theirs.''

The centurion swallowed. "There is the matter of Trajan's promise.''

"When my uncle undertook his expedition against the Parthians, he was aware of the need for full support and the devotion of the provinces. In addition there was—and is—a considerable settlement of Jews living in Mesopotamia. To that end, therefore, my uncle, the emperor Trajan, let it be known that Rome would permit the restoration of the sacrificial service in Jerusalem and the reconstruction of the Jewish Temple. He would have been mad to allow this actually to occur, and so would I.''

"Why?'' Antinous asked now. "You have never cared what gods people worship. You build pantheons consecrated to all the gods.''

"I have also built temples without images of any gods at all,'' Hadrian reminded the boy, "nor dedicated to any one particular deity, but where everyone could worship the god of his choice. In the end it is all the same,'' he said with a shrug, "whether one calls on Zeus, or Adonai, or Amnon as with the Egyptians, or Papai as with the Scythians. . . .''

"Then . . . why?'' Quintus asked, echoing Antinous' question. "All these years since the burning of their sanctuary, the Jews have prayed for nothing as they have for its reestablishment. You would win their devotion, their loyalty—''

"One doesn't win anything with these people. History has proven that."

Antinous smiled knowingly. "You don't like them, do you?"

"Like the Jews? What man of intelligence does? I had a discussion with Akiva," he went on, turning back to Quintus. "Thinking to catch him up in his obsession with circumcision, which, as you know, I look upon as an odious desecration of man's beauty, I asked which he considered more beautiful, the works of God or man. 'Man,' he replied to my surprise, saying nature only supplies us with the raw material as God commands, which we must then prepare according to the rules of art and good taste. 'Yes,' I said, 'but why did not God create man as he wished him to be?' 'Because,' Akiva answers, 'it is man's duty to perfect himself.' " Hadrian threw his arms up in the air. "What is one to think? Where is the logic? Do you know what he said about Homer? He said he thought Seneca was correct in saying the poet did much harm by attributing human nature to the gods instead of attributing divine natures to men!"

Antinous laughed.

"You're right," Hadrian said. "I don't like the Jews. Oh, I suppose I admire their tenacity, their faithfulness to their laws, but I don't like them, and it is clear to me that they must change." He got up and began to walk about the room. "As you know, centurion, it has always been the policy of Rome to grant our subject peoples those concessions that cost nothing and involve no danger. Therefore, you may well ask"—he stopped and patted Antinous' shoulder—"why not allow the Jews to have their Temple and Jerusalem? I will tell you why.

"I have looked carefully at their prayers, their festivals and holy days. All call for the rebirth of their nation or celebrate the existence of such in times past. The same word echoes throughout: freedom. Personal and collective. For themselves and all men. They do not seem to comprehend that the greatest freedom occurs only within the framework of order as set forth by an all-encompassing and compassionate government. Our government is the best example of this. Never before has the world seen such a power as Rome. Old enemies live at peace with one another under the mighty wings of our eagle. Roads, trade, language have bound the remotest provinces together. Places which once lay desolate are now covered with farms. Cultivated land replaces the forest, and flocks of tame animals oust the wild beast. Hills are planted, towns spring up. Everywhere there are signs of human habitation. Civilized government. Life. This, we have done. Our administration gives security. Order. Law. I will not allow this good work to be destroyed by one stubborn, selfish people.''

"What makes you think they can destroy it?'' Quintus asked.

"My uncle, Trajan, had good knowledge of the Jews which he passed along to me. Don't forget, his own father commanded the Tenth during Vespasian's war. Later, of course, Trajan experienced firsthand the ferocity of Jewish resistance in the Cyprus and Cyrene uprisings. I was involved there myself. Never mind that these rebellions were finally quelled. The cost to us was staggering, not only in moneys and men. Once again the Jews succeeded in damaging the reputation of our legions. And the restlessness which I sense spreading along our eastern frontier despite our benevolence, this, I blame on them.''

"Do you believe they wish to destroy Rome?''

"It is not their primary objective. But it is what they will accomplish if we allow them to have their way.''

Quintus was silent. He too felt a danger, but it was not the same as Hadrian feared. Yet what the emperor said made sense, more sense than his own vague and undefinable anxiety.

"Three times each day, my friend,'' the emperor was saying, "three times each day, every Jew throughout the world rises to his feet, if he is not already standing, faces east, and calls upon his God for the renewal of Israel, the rebuilding of Jerusalem, and the 'ingathering' of their 'exiles.' Oh, these rabbis are clever! They are clever, I tell you! For what we have is more than prayer. What we have, plain and simple, is a factor, brilliantly conceived, for unification. And it is the same with their laws, which, I assure you, render them no holier. Egyptian priests originated the rite of circumcision long before the Jews, as well as the abstention from eating pork. For that matter, the Pythagoreans dispense with animal food altogether. Nor is there any evidence of the Jews enjoying any special grace as a result of their obedience to these commandments. One can see what has become of them. What then do we have? A system of practical laws which, again, unite these people.''

"But to what good?" Quintus struggled to make clear all that was racing through his mind now. "We are agreed that Judea continues to be a troublesome area, if not overtly so, then, as you point out, the source of future rebellion. War, slavery, the confiscation of their land have not diminished the will of these people, nor, I suspect, their capacity for further struggle and suffering. We spoke of this before I ever set foot here, and since that time I have tried to give you my honest and, I believe, accurate appraisal of the situation. From a military point of view I can state unequivocally that the Judeans are no match for us. They irritate, they annoy, but they are capable only of hit-and-run attacks which are carried out by small bands of thieves and fanatics. Recent attacks show some common bond, some form of organization within these ruffian ranks, but history has proved the Jews are incapable of banding together in one great, unified offensive. The unity you speak of may exist, but not in a practical, military sense. Men like Akiva do not sanction the new Sicarii any more than they exhorted the Judeans to join with the Jews of Cyprus. As a result, the Jewish communities outside Judea would have no interest in lending the Judeans aid should war break out."

"What of Parthia?"

"The Jews in Parthia are content. They exist in strong number and enjoy favorable conditions. If they were to rise against Rome, it would be as Parthians, not Jews. I would further point out that even if the Judeans managed to move an army against us, it would be poorly trained and ill-equipped. They haven't had an organized fighting force since the time of the Maccabee. During the last war, they wasted most of their strength warring among themselves. Moreover, they have no system of conscription, rank, or strategy. They have no sense of obedience to officers or anyone even remotely equal to a good man in the field."

"Enter the Messiah," Hadrian said dryly, provoking another laugh from Antinous.

"Even if this warrior king should appear," Quintus said with a smile, "he wouldn't have much to work with."

"Rufus has said as much. He is not here now because he appeared a bit overcome by the wine. I sent him to bed. I trust relations between yourself and the governor are as they should be."

Quintus nodded.

"Good. Rufus knows his business, and he has behaved exactly as I wish him to. He may give the appearance of being a fool, but believe me, centurion, nothing misses his eye."

"I have no qualms regarding his service to the Empire. In any case, it is not for me to say."

"You may say anything you like. You are not simply another *primus pilus*. You are an old and dear friend. That is why I draw you into my confidence now. I know it seems that my refusal to return Jerusalem is an act of simple-minded repression, a reversal to the ways of those who ruled before me. Not so. But former harsh measures and my own attempts at benevolence have resulted in the same condition: status quo. No major outbreaks in Judea for more than sixty years. On the other hand, nothing to our benefit, and the constant danger of which we have spoken. We must find a new approach. We must do what no one has done before."

Quintus felt his whole being expand with warmth, relief, affection, admiration. Hadrian had seen it after all.

"One world. One people. That is what I want, what I have worked for. I know you share this dream, because you see the good in it not only for Rome, but for all men. But one group stands apart. It always has. It always will, unless we apply our will to it. We must draw Judea into the Empire. We must remove the factors which alienate the Jew from his fellow man, causing him to cling to his own kind. He may have his nameless, faceless God. But the laws and rites which bind him to an Israel that can never be, these must be removed. It is a kindness, believe me.

"No one knows better than I what it is like to be different, to be ridiculed, even despised. When I was quaestor, Trajan's reporter in the senate, I was cruelly mocked for my provincial dialect, having been born, as you know, in Spain. But I resolutely set about changing my manner of speech and learned to speak Latin correctly, although," he added, "Greek remains my favorite language."

"The language of poets," Antinous interjected.

"And lovers," Hadrian said with a fond smile. He turned back to Quintus. "The reestablishment of the Jews' Jerusalem would only propagate their vain dream of an independent Judea. On the other hand, resurrecting the old capital under a new name—'Aelia Capitolina'—as a Roman bastion under the very walls where so much good Roman blood was spilled, with a temple for Jupiter on the exact hill where once towered the Jews' monument to their God—this will symbolize our final victory.''

"Final?" Quintus asked.

"The edict against circumcision is to be promptly and thoroughly enforced. Future generations of Judean males must be spared the physical humiliation they now endure. They will enter the gymnasiums and baths with no sense of shame, no feeling of being different. This will lead to harmony on all sides.

"They are denied Jerusalem. Furthermore, I have instructed Rufus as to the disbanding of the conclave of rabbis in Jabneh. We don't want the place to become a second Jerusalem. They may reassemble, but in another area—and the setting must be changed every few years. The prerogatives of the Sanhedrin are to be limited, of course. We can go into this later. But it is especially forbidden for the rabbis to exercise regulation of their calendar. Rufus has pointed out to me that this function makes the conclave a legislature for all Jewry and that the attendant ceremonies are, again, symbols of the people's unity. Furthermore, neglect of their calendar will throw their system of festivals into confusion, and eventually these will be forgotten. Rather clever of Rufus.''

"Exceedingly.''

"You are too quiet, Quintus. What is it?''

"They will fight, excellency. They will never accept these measures.''

"You have already pointed out we have nothing to fear in that event. I suspect some will resist. Those too stupid to understand that all I am doing is endeavoring to take away their ridiculous restrictions and superstitions, to give the Jews civilized customs instead, thus improving an odious people.''

Quintus rubbed his forehead. It was late, and he suddenly felt very tired. Antinous, in fact, was yawning openly. Hadrian smiled at them both. "Go to bed," he told Quintus. "Get some sleep. I want to leave for Jerusalem first thing in the morning. I am anxious to see it. As soon as the orders for reconstruction are given, we shall set out for Egypt. I want you to come with us, Marcellus Quintus. You could do with a bit of change, and I have missed your company. Rufus can take care of things here.''

"They will fight," the centurion said again. He wanted to

say more, but suddenly nothing made sense. The emperor was
right; he needed to sleep, to rest. In fact, he needed to get
away. From Judea. From Livia, as well. Hadrian had seen
that. Hadrian saw so many things. Was it possible that a man
who saw so much, who understood so much, could be blind to
what seemed so evident?

The centurion rose to leave. "With your permission . . ."

Hadrian accompanied him to the door.

Outside, the air, which had turned cool, stung him to an
awareness of duty. There were no guards present. He turned
to the emperor with a puzzled stare. Hadrian smiled. "Nothing will happen," he said. "There are only students and old
men in this place."

"There must be Praetorians at this entrance," Quintus said
firmly. For a moment there had been a faint perfume such as
the scent of jasmine, and he had felt the presence of a figure
slipping away into the night. A woman. Perhaps one of the
servants seeking a glimpse of the emperor. Perhaps Livia,
seeking him out. But the thought that came most clearly now
was the memory of a girl with wild eyes and hair, and once
again Quintus felt a sense of dread and foreboding.

"You worry too much, old friend," Hadrian said.

"You are emperor of Rome," Quintus replied. "It is my
duty to serve you and protect you." Why did the words sound
hollow? "Where is your secretary, Phlegon?"

"Asleep in the adjoining room."

"Have Antinous wake him and send him to fetch the
guards. I will stay outside your door until he returns."

And so he remained for some time, outside, in the cold
night air, studying the stars.

Something he had read or heard long before he came to
Judea suddenly came to mind. It concerned the emperor
Caligula, who at one point decided to have a statue of himself
set up in the Temple in Jerusalem. When Petronius, governor
of Syria, arrived in Ptolemais, whence the statue was to be
sent to Judea, he found himself preceded by tens of thousands
of Jews who had quietly made their way to the town and
assembled there. They stood drawn up in good order, six detachments: old men, young men, boys, old women, young
women, and girls. They carried no weapons. They made it
clear they would offer no resistance. But if Caligula's statue
was to be carried up to their Holy City, it would have to be
over their bodies.

Undoubtedly, Quintus decided, Petronius' orders would have been to cut them down, had his dispatch on the crisis ever come into Caligula's hands. Fortunately for the Jews, the emperor was murdered by his bodyguard before it arrived.

But what would Hadrian's orders be in such an event? Quintus wondered. And would it come to that? And if it did, could he, Marcellus Quintus, once more cut down the defenseless?

The stars offered no answer. And if the God of the Jews was really somewhere up there in that bright, black sky, He too was silent. All that Quintus heard was the voice of Hadrian inside his head, repeating over and over, *Nothing will happen.* . . . *Nothing will happen.* . . .

THE NEXT MORNING Hadrian's entourage set out for Jerusalem, accompanied by Akiva and several of the other rabbis who had been present at dinner the previous evening, leaving Mesha with the honor of overseeing the school during Akiva's absence. He found to his surprise that Beruria had also remained in B'nei Berak. "I thought you'd be in Jerusalem with the others," he said, meeting her outside the great house.

She shook her head. "My father's anticipation is so great he could not bring himself to go. He has been in the synagogue since dawn."

"Our cause can have no better ally than the prayers of men like Rabbi Teradyon."

"Our cause," she repeated with a slight smile. "Sometimes you sound more like a Zealot than a man who aspires to the rabbinic order. If I did not see myself how wonderfully you approach the duties of a teacher, I would wonder where your heart really is, Mesha. In the classroom and synagogue . . . or in the hills with men like Simeon ben Kosiba."

"My heart is here, Beruria," he replied in a quiet voice. But his eyes seemed to emphasize his words with a look that made her cheeks turn pink. "I wasn't aware you'd observed me in the classroom," he went on.

"Several times. My father says you are gifted, that you are more ready for *semikhah* than most young men will ever be. The fact that Akiva leaves you in charge after such a short time shows how highly you are regarded. And you know what he and the others say about young teachers."

"Sour grapes and new wine."

"Exactly," she said with a laugh. "Well, I was curious to know why they were so impressed. I sat in the back, where you could not see me."

"And what is your opinion?"

"Oh, you are good, Mesha!" she responded eagerly. "I do not wonder you have won Akiva's admiration, or that your students love you. You have a way of making truly difficult subjects not just accessible but interesting. I myself like the way you clarify an issue from different standpoints. My father says you can substantiate as well as logically refute any opinion of the conclave. I do that too!" she exclaimed excitedly. "I mean, I am fond of taking first the pro, then the contra position," she added more demurely. But her enthusiasm could not be quelled. "And the tales you tell! What lovely stories! All about the fox and his many trials."

"You may not think they are so wonderful when I tell you I learned them from books belonging to Elisha ben Abuyah," he admitted sheepishly.

"The fables of Aesop . . . ah, yes! Now I see it! But you have changed them, Mesha. The Greek moralizes in worldly fashion, but you make use of the stories to illustrate Scripture. Oh, no! These fables, these *meshalim* are truly your own!"

He smiled appreciatively at the pun on his name, all the while thinking how splendid it was that she had grasped his method.

"Is it true you know three hundred tales pertaining to the fox?"

"Is it true you learned three hundred laws in one day?"

Her happy expression faded. She appeared startled. Then, lowering her eyes, she shook her head. "It was only a hundred."

Mesha could not help laughing. "No need to look so ashamed! That's still ten times the amount the rest of us can retain."

"Oh, it isn't that!" She sighed. "My brother and I made a wager. I only did it because he pushed me to it. And he knew all along . . . he knew. . . . Soon after, he disappeared. We heard he'd joined a band of rebels—or bandits, depending on who spoke of it. He was killed during one of their forays. And all because . . . Oh, it's so stupid! Even now I cannot think of it as anything but stupid, senseless, wasteful. . . ."

"You mustn't blame yourself."

"You don't understand. It's a trick, Mesha. It's just a trick of memory I happen to possess. I tried so many times to explain it to Avi, that my ability to remember things so easily doesn't make me wiser or better. But it was always so hard for him, you see. He would study and study, and the words would still elude him, slip out of his mind as easily as they came to mine. I was always first with the correct answer, the right precedent. I guess Avi just couldn't bear it any longer."

"But this is fascinating! Beruria, you must explain further."

"I told you, I don't know how it works. It's just a trick of nature. A talent, I suppose. I have but to look at a word, to glance at it, and it is locked forever in my mind. Even more than words," she mused. "If something catches my attention —days, weeks, years later I have but to think of the occasion and I can see it all as clearly as if it had only just occurred."

"So that's how you were able to learn a hundred laws in one day."

"Yes. But don't you see? Merely to recite Torah isn't enough. But to understand it and interpret it correctly . . . That's why I admire you so, Mesha. I mouth the words, but you speak them from your heart and soul, with every part of your being."

He did not acknowledge this praise, although in fact her confession moved him greatly. Instead he asked, "Can you really just glance at written words and know them completely?"

"Yes," she mourned.

"I don't believe it."

Sadness gave way to anger. "You accuse me of lying?"

"No, no," he said quickly, suppressing a smile. "It's just that what you claim is rather extraordinary, you will admit."

"Very well, I'll show you. Write something on your slate there. Anything, but be sure it is original. Make it as long as you wish and in any language you choose. I'll turn my back if you like."

He had already begun to fill the slate. "All right," he said finally.

"Hold it before me a moment, then remove it from my sight."

Again, he did as she commanded.

Looking him straight in the eyes, the young woman

promptly recited: "My dearest Beruria, I hope you will forgive this sham, but it is the only way I can find the courage to tell you that I love you and have loved you from our first meeting—" Suddenly aware of what she was saying, Beruria stopped, alarmed. "I—I cannot continue," she stammered.

"Why?"

"You—You know why. I cannot—I cannot say—"

"Then let me say it. 'You are beautiful to me in every way.' I dream about you, Beruria, hoping I'll awaken to see your long, dark hair spread out on the pillow beside me."

"That isn't on the slate," she whispered.

"I love to watch you read. I love the way you wrinkle your brow, and frown, and put your lips together in a way that begs to be kissed."

"Don't . . . please . . ."

"And I love the way the blood rushes to your face when I say these things to you."

"It's awful," she said helplessly. "I despise blushing."

"It's beautiful. You're beautiful. I love you. I want you to be my wife."

"No . . . no . . ."

"Beruria . . ."

And at last she was in his arms, and he was kissing her the way he'd dreamed of holding and kissing her. She seemed to melt against him; he was afraid if he let go she'd fall. Then suddenly a fire leaped out of her and her arms went around him, her passion equal to his. Just as suddenly she pulled away, her eyes big and dark in the pale, oval face.

"Don't run away." He caught her hand. "Beruria, don't go."

She shook her head.

"You're trembling. Don't go."

"I must."

"You haven't given me an answer."

She shook her head again. "No . . . no . . ."

"You don't mean that. You can't. You feel something for me. I know you do. Just now—"

"No!" She began to wring her hands nervously. "I—I'm not what you want—"

"You are exactly what I want."

"No, I—I'm too old."

"Old? You're a baby!"

"I'm not. Mesha, I'm twenty-six."

He shrugged. "So am I."

"You're twenty-four. I asked." She turned red again.

"What does it matter? You know it doesn't matter. Besides, that isn't it. What are you really afraid of?"

"Nothing. I'm not afraid. I'm not."

"You are. Of me?"

No answer.

"Or . . . yourself?" he asked slowly, remembering the way she'd come alive in his arms.

"No. No!"

He caught her to him again. "Tell me you feel nothing. Tell me, and I'll let you go."

"Stop . . . please . . ."

"I have heard that you will not marry until you meet a man who can teach you something you do not already know."

"Who told you that?" she asked angrily. She began to wring her hands again. "Why do they say those things about me?"

"By your own admission," he went on, "despite all your learning, you lack the understanding of Torah which you claim I have."

Her eyes widened. "I . . . I did say that. But . . . but it does not apply." She was caught now, struggling to escape the net he'd laid. "Your argument is vague. You have no irrefutable proof—"

"Very well, we will go on to something more. Something greater."

"What can be greater than the Law?" she asked, astonished.

"Love, Beruria. For it is love which leads to understanding. That is what I can teach you which you have not learned. What it is to love. And to be loved."

She started to say something, then stopped, confused. "Please," she said finally. "Let me go. I need to think."

This time he complied. But as he watched her hurry away, head down, distraught, it was all he could do to keep from going after her and telling her that what she needed most now was not to think, but simply to feel.

LEAVING MESHA, Beruria hastened to one of the schoolrooms

where Jara was waiting for her lesson in Greek. Despite a concerted effort to compose herself, Rabbi Teradyon's daughter
was having a hard time dwelling on the subject, and Jara, who
rarely missed the unusual, did not fail to take note of the
young woman's flushed and flustered appearance. As the
lesson progressed, it was clear to Jara that Beruria's thoughts
were elsewhere, but she misjudged their focus.

"Who is he?" she asked finally. Then, in response to
Beruria's blank stare: "The Roman who came into the
kitchen."

"Roman? Oh! You must mean Andreas."

"Who is he?"

"Well, for one thing he isn't a Roman. Well, I suppose he
is. But he is also one of us. That is, he follows the faith of
Israel."

"A proselyte?" Jara asked, wondering at Beruria's atypical
confusion in answering.

"No, of course not. Andreas comes from a distinguished
old family which has its roots in Jerusalem. The family left
Judea after the war and settled in Rome."

"Traitors," Jara said, her suspicions confirmed.

"Not at all," Beruria snapped. "Jara, many of our people
did not follow the ways of the Zealots and the Sicarii, but that
doesn't mean they were traitors. Rabbi ben Zakkai, for example, was a man of peace. If it were not for him and the scholars
who fled to Jabneh, our people would be in more disarray
than we are without the Temple."

"Ben Zakkai did not go to Rome," Jara reminded her.

"No, but if Rome had been the only place where the study
of Torah might have continued, then I am sure that is exactly
where he would have gone."

"And been a traitor."

"No! Can't you understand that there is more to being a
Jew than living in Judea? And do you think God looks down
upon us only from a spot in heaven directly above the Mount
Moriah? God is everywhere. The whole world is not large
enough to contain Him. Wherever we may be—Judea, Parthia, Rome, or the far-off Indies—so long as we are faithful to
the Lord's commandments and live as Torah tells us we must
live, then we are part of the Kingdom of Israel." Beruria
stopped. The suddenly cold and glazed expression in the girl's
eyes told her she was not getting through to her. *Mesha would*

know how to handle this, Beruria found herself thinking. *He would know how to make her understand.* And the thought of that young man unnerved her once again. "Where were we?" she asked, her face red. "We are far afield of our studies."

"You seem to know him well."

"Who? Whatever are you talking about?"

"The one from Rome. Andreas."

"We played together as children. He spent a summer with us—his father was here on business. They own a great many ships and much land. And before you go on about traitors again, let me tell you that his family has done as much for Judea as anyone. They have ransomed hundreds of slaves. Many a poor scholar would go hungry were it not for Andreas and his family. I'm surprised he hasn't married," she mused. "Every girl in Rome must be after him. He certainly is good-looking." She smiled. "And with the same mischievous look in his eyes I remember . . ."

"His chin is naked."

Beruria laughed. "Yes, it does seem strange, doesn't it? But you see, in Rome, the Jews all look like Romans. And they take two names, one which they use in public, and the other, a Hebrew name which they use at home and in the synagogue. It's safer that way. The Parthians do the same."

"I think that's cowardly."

"It's prudent, is what it is. One can't be fighting forever, Jara. Nothing would get done."

They both laughed now.

"How is it you've never married?" Jara asked, still smiling.

"Wh-Why do you ask that?" Startled by the question, Beruria pulled back, a lock of hair falling into her eyes. Nervously she pushed it back.

"You are beautiful and learned. I should think many men would want you for their wife."

"For their slave, you mean."

It was Jara's turn to be startled. Then she laughed. "I've never heard any woman say that!"

"That's because most women are too stupid to realize what getting married is all about." Beruria sighed. "I used to watch my mother, may she rest in peace, the way she worked and worried. . . . She did everything for my father. To this day he doesn't know what it is to do anything but read, think, study, teach Torah. If there were no one around to feed him, he'd starve. She did everything. And if once he called her from the kitchen to sip from his wine cup, it was as if he had accorded her the greatest honor you can imagine. Called from the kitchen! Like a servant! That's all she was. A servant. Teradyon's wife. Avi's mother. Never 'Beruria's mother,' '' she added with some bitterness. "Just as I am always 'Teradyon's daughter.' Never me, myself. Teradyon's daughter.'' She sighed again. "That's the way it is. We go from being someone's daughter to someone's wife, to someone's mother—provided, of course, that final someone is a son. Never ourselves. Never what we are apart from men—or from the particular men who dominate our lives. By these we are measured. Their worth, their very presence or absence determines our own worth in the eyes of the world. Well, I won't have it! If I can't be just Beruria, let them call me Teradyon's daughter the rest of my life. But that's all. One-third of a bad bargain is two-thirds better than the whole lot!''

Jara sat there, amazed. Finally she said, "But if you truly loved a man—and knew that he was worthy . . . I mean, somehow, it would be all right, I think. I mean, if you knew it was for someone—someone noble and wonderful . . .''

"You mean like Akiva and Rachel?'' Beruria let out a contemptuous snort. "Ah, yes, there's a romantic tale. There's the ideal love and marriage. The ideal woman, to hear men talk. Shall I tell you about them? She gave up everything for him. Everything. Her father was a wealthy man. And Akiva was nothing, a shepherd on the estate. But Rachel saw something in him, some hint of future greatness, and braved her family's wrath to marry him. She worked in the fields like a common peasant. She, who had been served by many. She bore children, and once, when there was nothing to feed them, she cut off her hair and sold it to buy food. And where was Akiva while all this was going on? Sitting at the feet of the sages in Jabneh, learning Torah. My mother said she never heard Rachel complain. She would never allow a word to be said against Akiva. In fact, it was she who made him go to school, and when he wanted to quit, to give up and return to the simple life of the *am ha-aretz*, Rachel would not allow it. Only then, my mother said, did she threaten to leave him. During their marriage he was away more than he was home, studying with first this one and then that one. His students grew to know Akiva better than his own children did. And as

he grew wiser and more learned, and more famous each day
for his wisdom and his learning, Rachel grew older and frailer.
She was always alone. That's how I think of her. Alone. Married, but to whom? A man who was never there.

"One day, years later, Akiva returned home. He had been
everywhere—Parthia, Antioch, even Rome, to intercede with
Caesar, who was about to enact many severe edicts against our
people. He returned a hero. Stories were told by the dozens as
to how he had alternately charmed and outwitted the great of
Rome. He also returned a wealthy man. Some say that his success brought about a reconciliation with Kalba Sabua,
Rachel's father. But I know for a fact that he received a large
bequest from Andreas' family and continues to draw funds
from them.

"In any event, he returned in triumph. Whatever town he
passed through, crowds thronged to see him and scholars ran
from the schools to join his retinue. At last he came to B'nei
Berak, where once more a multitude awaited him. Rachel was
there too. She tried to press through the crowd, but they
turned her away. Finally she managed to get close enough to
catch a glimpse of the man she loved and for whom she had
sacrificed so much. Still she could not reach him, held back by
Akiva's 'honor guard' of scholars and rabbis. They were
deeply affronted by the appearance of this worn, shabby creature who kept crying out that she must talk to their *rabban*,
their master. In the noise and confusion she slipped or was
pushed, and fell to the ground and lay there, all but trampled.
This, after all she had suffered on Akiva's account.''

"What happened then?"

Beruria looked at the girl. She would have preferred to end
the story there, but she was too honest to withhold what she
knew. "Somehow, Akiva saw her," she admitted grudgingly.
"Or perhaps he became aware that an accident had occurred.
My father says he pushed everyone away and raised her in his
arms. And when the others protested that it was unseemly for
so great a man to concern himself with this poor old woman,
he silenced them all with a look, my father says, that spoke
more than words could ever say. And he said . . . Akiva said,
'All that I am today I owe to her. She is worth more than all of
us together.' ''

Jara smiled, content. Suddenly her expression changed.
"Beruria . . . you're crying!"

"Because I'm a sentimental fool after all," the young woman said somewhat angrily. "And what does it prove? Akiva loved her. Very well. But all those years, those long years without him, alone, living in the most terrible poverty and with no one to turn to, no one beside her . . ." Beruria wiped her eyes. "Well, it is a good tale," she said, angry again. "Yes, I suppose he likes it. I wonder how he'd work his sly fox into that story!"

"Who? What fox do you mean?"

"Oh, never mind! Where were we? Oh, what does it matter? Why do you want to learn Greek? You know the rabbis frown on it. Now that we've rid you of your Galilean accent, your Aramaic is fine for everyday traffic. And you are learning Hebrew as well, which will make you an educated person in everyone's eyes."

"You don't understand. I don't care about reading Torah. I mean, I do," she said quickly, seeing Beruria's shocked expression, "but I must learn Greek and the language of Rome. That is what those in power speak." She did not want to admit she had spied on the emperor the night before, but to no avail, as she understood too little of what she'd heard to make any sense of it.

But Beruria had already guessed Jara's motives. "You want to help Simeon ben Kosiba, don't you? You think you can spy for him. Don't you realize how dangerous that could be?"

"We must free Judea."

Beruria stared at her a moment. Then she sighed. "What difference does it make who rules? Our condition, yours and mine, will remain the same."

Jara stared at this, shocked by the comment. She considered it a moment, then said with a small frown, "No."

Beruria laughed. "No? That's all you can say? That isn't much of an argument. If you want to debate the issue— although I am at a loss to understand why, as I speak for your benefit as well as mine—you must do better than that."

The girl reddened, but her chin was up. "I am not so learned as you," she said slowly. "And I am not so clever. And I have not given much thought, I admit, to what you call 'our condition.' When you are hungry most of the time, you think of other things. But this I know. The women who went before me were not slaves to men. Even when my grandmother was captured and sold, even then she was a queen. And my mother . . ." She swallowed. "Inside . . . inside her . . . she was free. As for myself, I have fetched and carried and served others, but no one has ever owned me and no one ever will. Like you, I lower my eyes for no one. And I will not walk behind any man. But," she added softly, "I would not like to walk always alone."

It was Beruria's turn to stare. She felt somewhat chastened by the girl's simple, direct statement and could not help admiring Jara's inner grace and determination to work for the good of all. There was nothing on her face, however, as she turned back to their lesson, to acknowledge the pertinence of Jara's last remark, although later she would recall the girl's words. And as she tossed and turned in her bed that night, Beruria thought of what she'd told Jara and what Mesha had said, wrestling like Jacob until daybreak with fears and questions that seemed to have no answer in any of the books she had read.

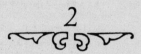

2

IT WAS LATE in the afternoon when Akiva reached the sea. He had walked for hours, nearly half the day.

He crossed the beach, making his way to a jetty of rocks where he stood for a long time, a tall, thin figure whose beard moved with the wind while all else was still. Finally, he turned away from the seemingly endless blue expanse at which he had been staring and walked along the shore for some distance, coming at last to sit on the sand near a line of scattered shells.

She had loved the sea.

What was it, he always wondered, that drew women to the sea, not like men who sailed the ocean, discontent on land, but with a oneness, a private understanding he himself had never been able to penetrate?

He was a man of earth with the soul of a shepherd, looking upward to the sky for God and to the world on which men walked for happiness. When he was young he had thought he needed nothing more than what he had. He had never felt poor, not even when there was little to eat and nothing he could call his own save the hills by day and the stars by night. So long as he'd had the stars, he could not be poor. And when Rachel had lain in his arms, he'd been the richest of men.

He remembered the first time he saw her, with her bright eyes and veil of hair black as night, her small breasts pushing against her robe . . . so impatient to be grown up and noticed. He let her play with a lamb. It was hers, after all. The flock, the field, the hut he slept in all belonged to her father, Kalba Sabua of Jerusalem.

The hut. Built of sunburned, unplastered bricks, window-less, a roof of clay and straw held up by branches and boughs

*that kept the sun out in summer, all but the worst rain in
winter. Straw mats covered the dirt floor. A year after they
were married there was enough saved to buy an earthenware
lamp; the next year, a bed, another luxury.*

In the beginning nothing mattered but the moments spent in
each other's arms. Even the war failed to touch them, and
when the estate was taken by the Romans, Akiva continued to
toil on it, having merely exchanged one employer for another.
With the birth of their first child, however, Rachel's outlook
altered. She wanted Akiva to go to school. It was their first
quarrel.

Akiva was content to have things remain as they were.
Moreover, like all *am ha-aretz*, he had a healthy dislike of
scholars and the rabbis of Jabneh, who were forever coming
up with new restrictions, regulations, and tithes, all of which
continued to benefit the survivors of the priestly class while
working against the poor and landless.

"I would as soon kick a scholar as be one," he told the dismayed Rachel. "If I had one in my hands now, I'd maul him
like a donkey."

"Which is all you'll ever be," she'd retorted. "An ass."

By the time she was pregnant with their second child, she'd
managed to wear him down. "Everyone comes to you. Whenever there's a problem or trouble, it is Akiva they seek. You
know how to talk to people. Better still, you know how to talk
for them. If you were at Jabneh you could speak for the op-
pressed, not only to ben Zakkai and Gamaliel, but perhaps
even to Rome."

"Those rabbis wouldn't listen to me."

"They would—if you were one of them."

And so he'd begun, going into the schoolroom to sit beside
his three-year-old son.

The curriculum of study in Judea had originated centuries
earlier in the public schools established by the priests of Israel
for the training of their own children. Therefore, when Akiva
had mastered the alphabet and learned to read he was not in-
troduced to the interesting narratives of Genesis, but to the
difficult technical laws of sacrifice in the Book of Leviticus.
Unaccustomed to the discipline of book learning, free to study
only after the day's labor, there he was struggling to remember
which offering was sacrificed at the door of the sanctuary; if
the offering of the high priest was a bullock or a ram; which
offerings were peace offerings, sin offerings, and guilt offer-

ings; which marriages were prohibited as incestuous; and whether the presence of yellow hair on a leper was a sign of disease or of healing.

And Rachel was pregnant again.

"I can't go on with it," he told her. "It makes no sense. The Temple doesn't even exist. Besides, it is clear to me now that we cannot continue as we are. The children must have a better life," he argued. "And now that I can read and write, I'll find better work. Jabneh is not for me."

But when he returned from seeking employment as a scribe, he found the house empty. Rachel had taken the children and gone to a cousin in the vicinity of Lod. He found her there one afternoon not unlike this one. She was drawing water from one of the wells that dotted the countryside. He sat beside her on the stones which formed the mouth of the well. For a long time neither spoke. Absently Akiva's fingers traced the deep grooves which marked the stones, even as now he played thoughtlessly with sand and bits of shell. Finally, for lack of what to say , or perhaps noticing for the first time how deeply etched the rocks were, he'd asked, "Who carved this stone?"

Rachel drew the bucket up. "The rope."

"How can that be?" he wondered. "Can soft rope cut hard stone?"

"It can," Rachel replied, "when it rubs steadily and constantly."

He'd sat there, silent, staring at the stones, thinking how long it had taken, how many generations and how many buckets lowered and raised to cut such long, deep crevices.

"Why do you wonder, Akiva?" Her voice came to him now, soft as the surf, soft as the wind that had touched her veil so long ago. "You, who believe all is possible in a world filled with God's love. Is it not written, 'The waters wear the stones'? So must you soften the hearts of those who oppress us. As you brought love and joy to a maiden who knew only loneliness in a house full of servants, as you tend your flock both gently and firmly, so now you must go forth and be what I know you can be. Go forth, my love. Go forth."

And so he had returned to his teacher and she to their home and he had learned, one by one, like soft rope drawing against stone, all the chapters of Torah. He mastered Leviticus, Exodus, Numbers, Deuteronomy. He mastered Genesis, and the Prophets, and the Hagiographa. And finally, at the age of forty, Akiva ben Joseph applied for admission to the rabbinical academy in Jabneh. Then followed the years in the company of men like Nahum of Gimso, famous for his learning, his poverty, and above all, his cheerful resignation in the face of disaster; Johanan ben Zakkai; Eliezer ben Hyrcanus; Tarfon, a man of priestly descent whose earthy, direct, and often brusque nature soon rendered him Akiva's confidant despite their many quarrels. There were others: Joshua ben Hananiah, who had spoken at Rimmon; Simeon ben Zoma; Simon ben Azzai, who became Akiva's son-in-law; Eleazar ben Azariah, the polished aristocrat who traced his ancestry back to Ezra the Scribe; and Gamaliel, descendant of the beloved Hillel, who became head of the conclave upon the death of ben Zakkai, and under whose leadership Akiva sailed to Rome.

Returning to Judea, the former shepherd found himself an acknowledged leader. For the next fifteen years, a period of unusual prosperity and peace, Akiva was able to devote himself to the formulation of his juristic principles, the clarification of his theological ideas, and the establishment of his school in B'nei Berak. And he could be with his Rachel. Never again would she work in the fields or sleep in a windowless hut. Never again would she cut her beautiful hair to sell for food. From Rome he brought her a comb of gold etched with a drawing of Jerusalem which she wore like a crown. *Those were the best years*, Akiva thought, staring at the sea. *Rachel, the children grown and wed, the students* . . . There was even the hope that Trajan would allow the restoration of Jerusalem. But then came the uprisings in the Diaspora. Trajan's promise went unfulfilled, and Lusius Quietus arrived. This, too, passed. Hadrian became emperor. He recalled Quietus, and once more the Jews were allowed to believe their city would be returned to them.

Where was the lie?

He never said it would be ours. He merely said it would be rebuilt.

Where was the lie?

Akiva shivered slightly as the wind rose from the sea. His bones felt stiff. He suddenly realized he would have difficulty getting up. For the first time he was feeling the burden of his years. It was more than age, however, more than the crushing realization of Hadrian's intent, more even than the loss of so many loved ones. Joshua ben Hananiah had died soon after the meeting at Rimmon. Akiva's own son had been dead little more than a year, felled by illness. Ben Azzai was gone too. And Rachel . . . No matter how many years passed, would he ever cease to feel that loss?

But it was more than that. His faith in his ability to serve his people and, most important, to serve the Lord, was shaken as it had never been. Even in those early days when he had thought himself ignorant and unable to learn, he had never lost the belief that somehow God would establish his path. But now . . .

His memory was clearly weakening. That bothered him. Arguments that had come with rapidity and ease in his prime were formulated more slowly now, sometimes with painful deliberation. More than once, knowing his students expected clear, definite expositions, he had found himself offering compromise. *Compromise.* That's what his whole life seemed to be about these last years. *Compromise . . . where there could be no compromise.*

"They say one of the marks of age is when a man starts talking to himself."

Akiva turned in the direction of the voice. Watching from a distance was a man of equally advanced years. His hair was white and curly; it looked as if a cloud had come to rest on his brow. He was clean-shaven. And his eyes were a bright, piercing blue.

Akiva smiled slightly. "I wasn't aware I had spoken aloud."

"Another mark of age. You're getting old, Akiva."

"Just what I was thinking. But then, you always were able to pluck men's thoughts from out of their heads."

"Men's thoughts, as you say. Not women's. I've never been able to fathom the female mind. I suspect therein lies the true mystery." Elisha ben Abuyah paused. "Well, did she talk to you?"

"Who?"

"Rachel. Did she call to you from the sea? You know that's why you've come here. In your way you're as great a blasphemer as I."

"Memory spoke. Rachel is dead."

"And God? Did God speak to you?"

Akiva was silent.

"No, I suppose not. He appears busy conversing with Hadrian."

"That is what Aher would say," the rabbi replied with some bitterness.

The apostate grinned. "That is indeed what he says. But perhaps you would like to know what your students say. They say you are afraid. They say your brain has become muddled, that you are no longer capable of giving guidance in the Law. They say you have renounced certain views which have been repeated in your name for decades. They say you do not keep your promise which you made at Rimmon."

Akiva sighed. "Mesha has told you this?"

"These are not his own thoughts. But he is worried about you."

Akiva nodded. "It is all true in any event. Do you know what I told one of the boys? 'You have dived into deep waters seeking pearls, but all you have come up with is a broken pot.' The look on his face . . . exactly as I know I must have looked when Gamaliel said those very words to me." He shook his head sorrowfully.

Ben Abuyah laughed. "Never mind, it will do him no harm."

"They speak of Rimmon, do they?" Akiva asked thoughtfully. "I suppose that's where they've gone, those who have left. To ben Kosiba or Bar Daroma or one of the others hiding in the hills."

"Fools."

"You thought they were fools to study the Law."

"Fools to study and fools to fight. For what? Hadrian has the right idea."

Akiva turned away. "Don't torment me. My heart is broken."

"To hell with your heart. Except there is no hell, Akiva. No hell, no heaven. No punishment. No reward. Not according to Epicurus, at any rate. Shall I tell you what the Greek says?"

Akiva did not reply.

"The world is only a kind of mechanism," Aher went on, "which is important for us to know insofar as is necessary to make use of it for our own satisfaction. Good and evil should be recognized merely within this context and dealt with only as they affect our lives."

"Mechanism," Akiva repeated. "Am I to believe we are God's toy?"

"You must leave God out of it. According to the teachings

of Democritus and Leucippus, there is no Creator. All bodies come into being by means of atoms and empty space. Because of the different motions of the atoms, which draw near, hook together, collide, and rebound from each other, worlds without number are generated in different parts of the limitless space which we in our primal Mosaic ignorance persist in calling 'heaven.' There is no heaven. Only space. The space between worlds.''

Akiva was staring at the sea. ''You need not expound your Epicurean philosophy to me. I know it well. Nothing comes from nothing, and nothing comes to an end in nothing. So what else is new?''

Aher laughed softly. ''Better. Much better. You are almost angry.''

Akiva smiled wanly.

''What are you going to do?''

''I don't know.''

''You made a promise at Rimmon. From what I hear, Simeon ben Kosiba is riding this way to collect on it.''

''Simeon. He knew. Even then, he knew. He saw it so clearly.''

''Is that what bothers you?''

Akiva shook his head. ''This isn't the first time I've been the fool. And if I live a little longer, it won't be the last.''

''Is it Rufus you fear? He'll put you away for good if he finds you are in collusion with rebels. He is not overly fond of you despite his apparent amicability.''

''You know it isn't that.''

''Then?''

''War . . . again.'' He sighed. ''What will be left this time? Rome has grown no weaker, and we are no stronger than when we challenged Caesar in the past. We are even fewer in number than before. What will be left?'' he asked again.

''Nothing,'' Aher answered matter-of-factly.

''But if we do not fight, also, nothing will be left.''

''Don't talk like a crazy Jew, Akiva. So a generation or two will not be circumcised. So Jerusalem gets a new name. So the calendar is abandoned, and the people go to the Roman courts instead of Jabneh. So your scholars will learn geometry instead of Deuteronomy. Maybe it's better that way. Maybe it's what God wants.''

''No!'' Akiva thundered. ''No!''

''Then where is a sign of His will? Show me, Akiva. I want

to believe. But I see nothing. Nothing. Give me a reason to think we must enter another long, horrific struggle to preserve a set of ancient rules and preposterous beliefs which have done nothing to advance the well-being, let alone the safety, of our people. Tell me what rewards the dead and the maimed have received for their defense of God and Israel. Are we free? Are we prosperous? Are we set above all others?"

"It will come," Akiva whispered. "The Day will come."

"What? The Day of the Messiah? Where are the signs? Do swords appear in heaven? Is the sun extinguished in the midst of its course? Does wood drip blood, do stones speak? Has the prophet Elijah appeared?"

Akiva stared at him like one awakening from a dream. "The Messiah . . ."

"Yes, where is he, this Son of David? Where is the Anointed One, the Redeemer of Jerusalem?"

Akiva was no longer listening. "Yes, you are right," he murmured with growing excitement. "Surely the time is now. Surely now . . ."

It was the other's turn to stare. "You can't mean what I think you mean."

"I must think it through. Perhaps another envoy to Hadrian . . . I did not impress him. Someone younger, perhaps, more cultured, refined . . ." He sighed. "What am I saying? There is no hope from that quarter. The emperor has made up his mind. Andreas writes there is no possibility of dissuading him." He looked straight into the other's sharp blue eyes and nodded. "It may be we must fight. I cannot quarrel now with those who wish it."

"War . . . for a speck of flesh."

"For the covenant."

"For a city that is already no more than a heap of stones and sand."

"For Jerusalem."

"For a way of life that sets us apart from all the nations on this earth."

"For Israel!"

"Akiva—"

"I must go." His voice had become brisk, young. "There is much to do. I must meet with all the leaders of the rebel groups. If there is one that seems . . . If I have a sense . . ." He did not finish the sentence. He smiled. "Goodbye."

"Wait—"

Akiva turned back.

"Have you forgotten Gamaliel's prophecy? 'The days of the Messiah will be among the most difficult in history. The redemption of Israel will come about through widespread war and suffering such as no generation would seek of its own accord.' "

Akiva nodded. " 'I see the House of Assembly turned into a brothel,' " he quoted softly, " 'the men of Galilee wandering from city to city, yet receiving no kindness. The wisdom of the scribes will decay, the pious will be despised, and he who withdraws from evil will be thought a madman.' "

The two men looked at each other for a long moment. Then Akiva raised his hand in a gesture of farewell and turned back toward B'nei Berak.

Elisha ben Abuyah watched him go off. He could not help thinking of something else Gamaliel had said: "Akiva ben Joseph will ponder a matter most carefully and critically before he acts. But once the choice is made, he fights with his heart rather than his head."

THE GIRL RAN to meet him. Akiva could not help smiling at the image Jara presented, at her youth and beauty and especially her high spirits. She was in a state of some excitement, a mood, he realized, which matched his own.

"Simeon ben Kosiba is here."

Akiva nodded, smiling again at the girl's bright eyes.

She smiled too. "You're feeling better, aren't you?"

"Yes. How did you know?"

"By the way you walk. When you left this morning, you were a very old man. Now you are young again."

The rabbi laughed. "Young? I've never been young. I was born old. Didn't you know?"

Jara laughed too, and Akiva took her hand and walked with her to the great house where Simeon ben Kosiba awaited him.

SIMEON REMAINED in B'nei Berak for some days, secluded with Akiva. What transpired during these meetings remained a secret, but for Jara it was enough that Simeon was near. There was little doubt in her mind that preparations were being made for the kind of confrontation with Rome of which she had long dreamed, and when Aaron ben Levi, known as Bar

Daroma, suddenly appeared in B'nei Berak, followed by the brothers of Kefar Haruba, her suspicions were confirmed. She had discovered to her surprise that many of the young scholars at the academy shared her hopes, especially one Simon bar Yohai, who, along with Mesha, oversaw classroom activity while Akiva was conferring with Judea's known rebels. Bar Yohai's hatred of Rome, caused by the death of his father at legion hands, was intense. During Hadrian's visit he had been unabashedly vocal regarding his feelings for the Empire, and as soon as the emperor's decision on Jerusalem was known, he had urged Akiva to sound the call for war. But no pronouncement was made. Workers were arriving in Jerusalem by the scores now; Rufus' men were raiding towns and villages to see that the edict prohibiting circumcision was not disobeyed, and the rabbinic court of justice at Jabneh had been disbanded. Still, Akiva issued no pronouncement.

"At least he is himself again," Mesha remarked.

"Who? Akiva?" Bar Yohai was pacing restlessly outside the room where the rabbi was talking with ben Kosiba again. "Yes, but he has done nothing. Nothing! How long must we wait?"

Jara heard them. "It's going to be all right," she said. "I have faith in him."

"Who?" Mesha asked this time, knowing her feelings. "Simeon or Akiva?"

"Both," she said firmly.

Two days passed; three. Men came and left B'nei Berak. Akiva remained sequestered, and despite Mesha's most imaginative efforts in the classroom, his students fidgeted with excitement, curiosity, and apprehension. Spirited debates took place in every corner of the academy, a condition which, to hear the reports that came to B'nei Berak at this time, was being repeated throughout the country. Yet no one sounded the ram's horn; no one stepped forth to blow the *shofar* in the ancient call to battle. With a certain smugness Tinneus Rufus was able to report to Hadrian, now somewhere in Egypt, that Caesar's orders were being carried out with a minimum of opposition, albeit with the usual whining and sullenness to be expected from the Jews.

It was, as men would say, the calm before the storm.

* * *

A WEDDING was taking place in Tur Malka. It was the custom there to set a cock and a hen before the bridal procession as a symbol of the biblical commandment to "be fruitful and multiply." A Roman patrol happened to be in the area and through accident or mischief killed the birds, which so enraged the villagers they attacked the soldiers and sent them running. That evening, however, while the Jews were dancing and making merry, the legionaries returned in greater strength, and what had begun as a celebration of life ended in calamity and mourning.

It was not a simple massacre. The Jews of Tur Malka fought back, inflicting considerable damage. But in the process, Bar Daroma was killed.

FAR INTO THE NIGHT the oil lamps burned, illuminating the windows of Akiva's academy like beacons. Outside, Obodas sat cross-legged on the ground, playing on his flute, while Jara sat nearby, listening dreamily to the haunting music and thinking of Simeon, who was inside the house conferring with Akiva. She saw even less of him now, but at dinner she was sure to be the one who served him; and who could say if it was accident or not when her hand brushed his as she set the wine cup before him, or a tawny lock escaped her veil to touch his cheek as she leaned forward to fill the cup? Despite his solemn expression and attention to Akiva's discourse, wasn't there a momentary flicker of Simeon's eyes when Jara was around, as though he was ever aware where she was? Hardly a word passed between them during this time, yet Jara had never felt so happy.

A week passed, and then suddenly all the newcomers to B'nei Berak rode away, leaving the academy strangely quiet and somewhat melancholy. Akiva seemed to be in the throes of despair and uncertainty again.

The rabbi was convinced now of the necessity of armed resistance despite the tragedy of Tur Malka—or perhaps because of it. And he was confident now of the integrity of the men to whom he had spoken these last weeks. Moreover, Simeon ben Kosiba, explaining how he thought a war against Rome ought to be waged, made victory seem quite feasible. He had further outlined the kind of government he foresaw following that victory. Akiva was impressed. He had known Simeon for many years and had always found him to be an exceptionally clear-thinking individual, but he had not dreamed there was so much to the man. He saw too that following the death of Bar Daroma, the other rebel leaders looked to Simeon for leadership. Certainly there was a power emanating from the auburn-haired giant that went beyond physical strength. But then, Akiva recalled, Simeon's uncle, Rabbi Eleazar of Modi'in, had always believed his nephew was special. How disappointed he had been when Simeon chose not to enter the course of studies leading to ordination but had gone off instead to Ein Gedi to work with his wife's family. His wife . . . yes, there was that tragedy. No need to dwell on it now. The important thing was it had not broken Simeon or warped his judgment. He was a competent leader of men. An intelligent one. And most important, as much as he hated the Romans, he cared more for the people of Judea, so that he would not be reckless with life.

Why do I vacillate? Akiva wondered. *What choice is there? We must fight now or be forever cursed, if not by Rome and all the nations of the world, then by the Almighty and surely by ourselves. But oh! can we bear it again! All that has been built to be felled once more, the ground torn asunder . . . human beings, so many human beings to suffer and die . . .*

A sign.

Give me a sign, Lord.

I must have a sign.

It was at this moment Akiva caught sight of Jara. She was leaning against the fig tree, embracing it with one hand while the other appeared to move up and down as though she were writing something on the trunk. Curious, the rabbi moved closer. "What are you writing, child?"

She did not answer.

"*Shin,*" he said, recognizing the shape of the Hebrew letter. "*Shin* and . . . *dalet.*"

"Oh," Jara said with a laugh. "Is that what it is? I didn't realize." She laughed again, shyly. "There's a mark on Simeon's right arm just above the wrist. I guess it does look like a *shin* and *dalet.*" Then, realizing what she'd said and how she had revealed herself, she blushed and ran off.

Akiva remained where he was, as rooted to the ground as the tree at which he stared. He seemed to see the letters the girl had drawn emblazoned on the trunk as if they had been carved there or scorched with fire—as if they were written in the clouds, on the grass, dancing in the air before his eyes as they were marked on the strong right arm of Simeon ben Kosiba.

Shin. Dalet.

Letters of the holy alphabet.

Shin. Dalet.

Shaddai. One of the divine names of the Almighty.

And he had wanted a sign.

THREE WAFERS of unleavened bread rested on the platter. Akiva removed the middle *matzah* and broke it in two, wrapping the larger half in a cloth which he then set aside. He removed the roasted shankbone which lay to the right of the *matzot*, commemorating the paschal sacrifice which would have been offered upon the Temple altar, and the roasted egg, symbolic of the spring, which lay to the left. Rabbis Teradyon and Tarfon then lifted up the platter, and all present in the great dining hall of B'nei Berak recited together:

This is the bread of poverty which our forefathers ate in the land of Egypt. Let all who are hungry enter and eat. Let all who are needy come to our Passover feast. This year we are here; next year may we be in Jerusalem. This year we are slaves; next year may we be free men.

A hush fell over the assembly. Then Akiva, a smile on his lips, eyes merry, gestured for Tobita's young grandson to come forward. Shyly the boy complied. Encouraged by Akiva's warm manner as well as the walnuts which the rabbi surreptitiously pressed into his hand, the four-year-old began to ask those questions without which no seder could proceed, beginning with the query: "Why is this night different from all other nights?"

There was a murmur of approval when the child ·finished reciting the *Mah Nishtannah* and retreated to his father's proud, encompassing arm. Akiva began to narrate the account of the Exodus. But no one had watched these proceedings with more satisfaction than Tobita, who stood in the doorway to the kitchen, arms folded across her ample bosom. Weeks of cleaning had left the academy and its surroundings sparkling. And if the men who sat at the seder table felt kinship with their brothers across the world, so too did the women of B'nei Berak feel as one with their female counterparts. For it would not be false to say that every house in every Jewish community had been turned inside out and upside down in preparation for the Passover. Cooking utensils had been scalded, scoured, and scrubbed, if not altogether replaced. Cupboards had been cleaned out, linen washed, and everything that could be dusted had been dusted. Stacks of *matzot* had been baked and stored during the thirty days preceding the holiday, all according to detailed specifications and with great care. The *matzot mitzvah*, however, which Akiva and his guests partook of this night, had been baked that very afternoon, which in the days of the Temple had been the time for sacrificing the paschal lamb. While the seemingly indefatigable Tobita had worked the dough, kneading it continuously lest leavening set in, Jara had been at her side, pitcher in hand, guarding the batter from any sudden heat, pouring cold water into it at Tobita's command. Next to Tobita another servant assisted, rolling the water out of the dough and thinning it into cakes, which were then passed along to Beruria, who quickly decorated them with a comblike implement, outlining in perforated holes the likenesses of doves, fishes, and flowers. The figured cakes had caused some controversy at the table, Rabbi Tarfon wondering if they were permitted. A full discussion on the subject would have taken place had not Akiva settled the matter somewhat hastily by recalling decorated *matzot* at the house of Rabbi Gamaliel. His impatience and general demeanor made Tarfon wonder if there was not more to this seder than might be expected, particularly in view of the variety of guests present. Not only had many of Judea's prominent rabbis gathered at B'nei Berak, brought by unusually urgent invitation, but Akiva had also invited an assortment of men who in the most charitable of terms were no more than *am ha-aretz* and, in plain fact, outlaws.

But if Tarfon, the man Akiva affectionately called ha-Zaken, "the Elder," was upset by the company he was in (and if so, he did not show it), then Jara was ecstatic. All during the telling of the *Haggadah*, or Passover narrative, her eyes never left the person of Simeon ben Kosiba, who sat respectfully silent beside his uncle, Rabbi Eleazar of Modi'in.

The seder had progressed to the reciting of the *Hallel*, consisting of Psalms 113 and 114, after which the meal was to be served. But as Jara felt Tobita tug her arm, the signal to help bring out the food, she sensed a murmur pass among the assembly. She turned her attention back to Akiva and realized with surprise that he was adding his own words to the traditional rite.

"Therefore, O Lord," the rabbi was saying, "bring us in peace to the other set feasts which come to meet us, while we rejoice in the building up of Thy city and are joyful in Thy worship. And may we eat there"— he paused significantly— "*in Jerusalem*, of the sacrifices and Passover offerings. We praise Thee for our redemption and for the ransoming of our soul. Blessed art Thou, O Lord, Who hast redeemed Israel!"

The murmur grew.

"What trick is this?" Tarfon was frowning. "Have you gone mad? Jerusalem is not returned to us. How can we make sacrifice in the Temple or eat there of the Passover offerings? How can we rejoice in the building up of David's city by these monsters of Rome—may I ruin my son if they mean any good by it—knowing how and to what purpose it will be used?"

Akiva's eyes twinkled. He appeared so joyous as to give credit to Tarfon's assertion that he had indeed lost his powers of reason. But all he said was, "Let us dine now and speak afterward. All will be made known to you as it is to me."

With expectations now of some great revelation, the participants in the seder at B'nei Berak turned to the feast set before them, continuing to talk and to wonder and attempting to surmise Akiva's meaning throughout the meal.

When the last plate had been cleared away, leaving the linen cloths covering the long tables still speckled with *matzah* crumbs and the scarlet stains of spilled wine, and the great *Hallel* had been recited, indicating that the seder had now been performed according to Law and statute, Akiva rose again to address the assembly.

"We are gathered tonight," he began, "for the Feast of Passover, which commemorates a very special event. That event is the Exodus from Egypt, a great deliverance which transformed a horde of slaves not only into free men but into a people. A nation. For truly it may be said that the welding of people into a people must take place in its deliverance.

"We are instructed that every person in every generation must regard himself as having been personally freed from bondage. And for this we give thanks. We sing a song that since the days of the Temple has come to be known as the *Dayyeinu*. It begins with the words 'How many are the favors that God has conferred upon us,' and goes on, as you well know, to enumerate the stages of our redemption from Pharaoh. After each stage we sing *dayyeinu*—'it is enough'—meaning that if the Almighty had done nothing more for us than this one thing, we should be content.'' He paused. "No." He shook his head. "No! And again, no! *Lo dayyeinu*. Not enough! We cannot be content. For while it is true that in every generation men have risen to destroy us and in every generation God saved us, it is also true that we must be worthy of God's help. Even as we sit here, men toil to build a Jerusalem that shall be foreign to us, a desecration of our holy site. The laws which bind us together are threatened. The very sign of our covenant with the Almighty has been forbidden to us by pagans who imagine they are our masters.

"Rome thinks very little of us. They think we are no match for them. Well, why not? We are poor, and they have every resource at their command. Our strength is debilitated by years of war, slavery, and oppression. We have no army. And —let us make no mistake about it—if we challenge Caesar once again, we will be faced yet again with the double burden of attack and defense, of striking at the enemy while preserving our homes and families. This is a terrifying task. Who would not be afraid faced with such a challenge? I tell you plainly, I am. And yet it must be done. It is time, my children, to be a people again. It is time to be a nation.''

As the rabbi sat down, the murmur in the dining hall began anew. Akiva's words were tantamount to a call for war. Rabbi Tarfon appeared shocked, Rabbi Yossi startled. Rabbi Teradyon seemed to nod; his face was the picture of perfect peace. Beruria looked quickly at Mesha, who was studying Akiva with a thoughtful expression; next to him Simon bar Yohai was beaming.

As Beruria had looked instinctively to Mesha, so Jara's gaze flew to Simeon ben Kosiba. A slow smile was spreading across his face. He seemed to sense Jara's stare and turned toward her. Still smiling, he made a "thumb's up" gesture. And if Jara had loved him before, then she loved him more now and vowed to herself that she would always love him.

"Akiva . . ." Tarfon was pale. "Master . . . my heart bleeds like yours at the events of these last weeks. But war! You know what it will mean. We both know. We must find another way. There must be another way."

Jara slipped out the door and into the night. The debate would go on forever. She was in no mood to hear scholars whining. It was enough to know that Akiva had kept his word. Nothing would stop Simeon now.

Simeon.

She stood there in the darkness, her heart beating like a war drum, every nerve, every muscle of her body straining to be near him, to be touched by him.

And he had seen her. He had looked for her and seen her and smiled and made that funny little signal just for her.

Just for her.

A sudden burst of sound broke from the dining hall. Tobita emerged holding her grandson in her arms. Her face was flushed. "It is too much," she murmured. "Too much . . ."

"What is it? What's happened now?"

"So much noise for the little ones. Those men, they forget that children are present, the way they carry on. . . ." She took a deep breath. "It's the Messiah, he says." Her voice was low, hushed. "The King Messiah."

Without waiting to hear more, Jara ran back into the house just in time to see Simeon standing before Akiva, the rabbi's long hands placed on each of ben Kosiba's broad shoulders.

"And it is said: *There shall step forth a star out of Jacob, and a scepter shall rise out of Israel.* . . .

"Go thou forth, Simeon of the line of David, no longer to be called ben Kosiba, but *Bar Kokhba*, 'Son of a Star.' " Akiva took a cruse of oil and dipped his fingers into it, applying the liquid to Simeon's brow and head like a wreath. "Thou art consecrated to God and Israel. May the Almighty grant wondrous victories to thee and deal graciously with thee, *ha-mashi'ah*, our Anointed King. Go thou forth in strength and wisdom, remembering always: *Justice . . . justice shalt thou follow!*"

Jara stood transfixed. The entire hall was still. And in that moment of hushed silence she saw Simeon turn slightly and catch sight of her. Their eyes locked for one fraction of a second; yet in that moment she felt her whole being fly out and merge with his, and knew that whatever might happen she was a part of him and he of her. Throughout her life no moment of physical union would ever surpass that sense of oneness with another human being.

And then, like the sea crashing onto a silent beach, a great cheer swept over the room. Simon bar Yohai had risen to his feet and now he began to sing: *"Da-vid, melekh Yisrael! Hai! Hai! Vi-ki-yom!"* Others took up the song, and there was clapping and singing and even weeping with joy.

Rabbi Teradyon, nodding, smiling, was humming, tapping his finger on the table in rhythm. Disturbed, yet obviously moved, Tarfon sat with tears in his eyes. Rabbi Yossi appeared to be in shock. Eleazar ha-Kohen of Modi'in seemed oblivious to the noise; his head was bowed in prayer. Johanan ben Torta looked stern and shook his head in disbelief.

Akiva embraced Simeon, who returned the gesture somewhat stiffly, apparently surprised and ill at ease with the honor and title accorded him. Simeon turned around to view his audience of fervent supporters. Unconsciously he wiped a drop of oil from his forehead. Then, realizing what he had done, he stared at his hand, rubbing his fingers together. He looked up again, and as it became apparent that he wished to say something, the revelers began to hush one another and grow still.

Simeon nodded curtly. He swallowed, looked around. He nodded again. "I will do my best," he said. And with that terse statement, his face reddening, the man who would henceforth be known to all as Bar Kokhba strode from the room.

Rabbi Yossi turned to Akiva. "Eloquent he's not," he remarked.

Akiva smiled; he was content. "Not with words perhaps, but with deeds," he replied.

Tarfon sighed. "God help us."

JARA DID NOT WASTE a moment in following Simeon outside. He took no notice of her presence, however, and they walked for some time in silence, she scrambling to keep up with his long strides. The lighted windows of Akiva's academy retreated until they were mere spots of light no larger than the stars overhead, and the noise of debate and celebration mingled with the rush of surf in the distance ahead.

They were on a hill with a view of the sea. Simeon paused, staring at the black horizon, the moon shooting silver streaks across the water. He turned as though suddenly aware he was not alone, then looked away again. Jara said nothing, but she wondered at the tight set of his jaw and distracted expression.

It didn't make sense; he ought to have been joyous—jubilant
—or at least as excited as everyone else. She watched him wipe
the remaining oil from his forehead and then stare at his hand
as he'd done before. His fingers curled into a fist. "Damn!"
he exclaimed.

Her mouth fell open.

"Damn," he said again.

"Why aren't you happy?" she wondered.

He stared at her. "I didn't want this."

"But you did! We all did! Now that Akiva is with us, all
Israel will rise against Rome!"

"Not that. This—this king business. I don't want it. I don't
like it."

She smiled now. "But it's true, Simeon. I knew it from the
first moment we met. You will save our people. You are he for
whom we have waited." *For whom I have waited.*

"The Messiah." He let out a bitter laugh. "No, I'm not he.
I am not God's man."

She laughed now. "You are the people's man. You are Bar
Kokhba!"

He looked at her in surprise; then he laughed too.

"What does it matter how Akiva calls you so long as the
people believe there's a chance to be free? That's all that matters, isn't it? To be free!"

"It means so much to you," he said in wonder. "I've never
known a female like you. Most women are afraid of war."

"I'm not."

"Because you don't know what war is."

"I know enough. Anyway, anything's better than what we
have now, living like this, always at the mercy of others, begging and crawling and"—she recalled Hadrian's visit to B'nei
Berak—"serving those pigs!"

"Don't talk like a child."

She stepped back, shocked. "Why are you acting like this?"
she asked finally. "Are you frightened?"

"And if I told you I was, would you hate me?"

"No," she answered. "I would never hate you, Simeon."

"Maybe you should."

"Never." She shook her head. "Never."

He looked away. The sound of the sea filled the night as
they stood in silence. Finally Simeon said, "I was married
once. I had a home, a family. My wife's name was Ruth."

She had not expected this. Everything else—her excitement and happiness at the evening's events and now being alone with him—was suddenly dissipated, leaving her to shiver slightly in the wind from the sea. Her voice sounded hollow when she spoke. "Was she beautiful?"

"To me she was."

Jara sat down on a rock and hugged her knees. The night had become cold indeed.

"She was like a little brown bird," Simeon went on, "always singing, and with a smile sweet as sunshine. She came to the King's Mountains from Ein Gedi, to stay with her uncle, who was kin of my mother. Her parents sent her away because they feared the soldiers—there's a garrison in Ein Gedi, like the one in Tiberias. Ruth's father was afraid harm would come to her because she was too gentle and too giving and trusted everyone. I called her 'little cousin,' and I grew to love her just like everyone else who knew her. And we were betrothed."

Jara nodded dumbly.

"We returned to Ein Gedi, which she loved, and I worked the land with her father and brothers. I can still smell the balsam that grows there. Soon there was a child. A son. My son. But not long after the boy was born, I received word that my mother was dying. I returned to Kosiba and stayed with her until she passed away, and then another thirty days of mourning. When I returned home I found I had no home. No wife." His voice was flat. "No son."

"What happened?"

"For as long as I can remember there have been rumors that gold was smuggled from the Temple during the war with Rome, and hidden in Ein Gedi. At one point the Sicarii on the Masada attacked the oasis, and most people seemed to think it was for this. One night, some members of the *cohors milaria thracium* got drunk enough to decide they would find the Temple treasure. They started the quest with their usual unimaginative method—by abusing whomever they ran across in an attempt to extract information. Someone led them to my house. I am of the line of David, you see. The anointed line. If anyone knew where gold was buried, surely the king's descendant would. But all they found was Ruth." He paused. "Her father tried to protect her. They killed him too. Her brothers fought back; my neighbors ran to aid them. Masbelah,

Jonathan bar Be'ayan . . . good men. I shall always be indebted to them. It is on my account they they have become outlaws. Well, as you know, striking a Roman soldier is punishable by death. The whole garrison turned out. They weren't quite as thorough as they'd been in your little village. They didn't level the area or kill everyone, because Ein Gedi is of value to them and they need people to work it. A Jew may be worthless as far as the world is concerned, but balsam is not. Gold, spices, whatever the market calls for is always worth more than blood. I learned that in Ein Gedi." He let out his breath slowly. "And I learned something else. I learned that I have no love for the Creator of atrocities. Oh, I know that evil is done by men. But men were created by God. And if, as we are taught, all is foreseen . . . if He knows . . ." He did not finish the sentence, but his eyes had taken on the look of a man facing an adversary. "Night came. A night like this . . . with stars in the sky, the sea somewhere . . . perversely beautiful. Nothing stopped. The world went on. That's something else you learn. The world keeps going. My world was shattered; it lay all around me in bits and pieces of bloodied flesh. But the sun and the moon would continue to give forth light, and birds would sing and grass would grow, and soon enough"—he let out a dry laugh—"by noon the next day or sometime thereafter I'd thirst for water, hunger for bread, and want—someday—to know a woman again. But not that night. Not that night in Ein Gedi."

She sat very still, listening to all that he said.

"It was over by the time I got there. The killing, even some of the burying. But not the mourning. 'Three days for weeping, seven days for lamenting, and thirty days to refrain from cutting the hair.' I had been through it for my mother, and now I was to begin again. For eleven months I would recite the *Kaddish* at daily, Sabbath, and festival services, as we are bidden to do after the death of a parent. Only now the words would encompass wife, son, brothers, friends. That night, though, that night when I rode into Ein Gedi, when I saw them all . . . people standing like stricken animals, moving about on numb feet, mumbling their prayers. . . . When I saw that afflicted crowd who in the midst of their grief and anger could yet proclaim to God their faith in Him, who called out through their tears, 'Blessed be the name of the Eternal!'—I rebelled, and I have rebelled ever since.

"In the years that have passed I have witnessed many such scenes. The men who killed my wife and son in Ein Gedi I sought out and killed in turn. And there have been others. And no doubt there will be more. And the ledger is never balanced. Not because of Ruth and the baby, but because of the rest along the way. Strangers and friends who fight and fall. I have known many. And in the days ahead I will know more. But from that night in Ein Gedi, from that time to this day, I say *Kaddish* for no one. I make no prayer for the dead."

Jara did not move or utter a sound. When Simeon turned to her, he could read nothing in her face. There was only the eerie quality of her pale, catlike eyes reflecting whatever light there was in the darkness, as if some fire from heaven had fallen across the face of a pagan idol.

"I do not pray," he said. "I do not love God, and I will not pray to Him. But something should be said in view of what Akiva has declared and the hard days before us. So listen now, listen to what Bar Kokhba asks of God. For this one time and this one time only will I call upon Him." And turning away from the green-gold eyes with their fixed stare, which more and more he found comforting as well as exciting, he lifted up his head and raised that fist whose arm bore the mark of *Adonai*, and cried out, "Hear me now, God of Abraham! Hear me! I have no illusions about You! I know how You work—and I think You don't give a damn one way or the other! So don't help me. *Just don't help them!*"

And as he had told her, despite this blasphemy the world went on. The stars and the moon did not disappear from above, and the sky was not split by lightning. There was no thunder to roar disapproval, only the sound of crickets and the hushabye whisper of the sea.

Jara rose now and went to him, still silent, but her heart was beating so fast and loud that Simeon might have heard it had his own not pounded with equal force. He took her in his arms, seeming to groan a bit as their bodies came together. "I need you," he whispered hoarsely. "I need you."

She closed her eyes, floating in the heat of his touch, feeling the strong hands move up her back to her shoulders, down across her breasts to her waist. But just as his face came close to hers, she opened her eyes and pulled back slightly. He stopped. "I'm not Ruth," she said succinctly.

"Damn you!" He twisted his hand in her hair and brought her lips to his. "I know who you are," he muttered angrily.

And then, finally, his mouth was on hers.

ALL THROUGH THE NIGHT the rabbis at B'nei Berak debated the consequences of Akiva's pronouncement and what lay ahead. Primary to the discussion was Akiva's assertion that the messianic era had been wrongly confused with the Future World, or *olam ha-ba*. Henceforth the two were to be carefully distinguished. Simeon ben Kosiba would lead the way to political freedom, but the world cataclysm prophesied in so many apocalyptic writings would be brought about by God Himself. This explanation did little to appease Johanan ben Torta, who at one point remarked acidly, "Akiva, grass will grow from your cheeks and the Messiah will still not have come!" And so it went, until Mesha, taking note of the dawn slipping through the windows, said gently, "Masters, it is time for morning prayer."

As the rabbis dispersed, Mesha went into the kitchen. His emotions were at a high pitch. Akiva had not only anointed ben Kosiba, he had also ordained Mesha and Simeon bar Yohai as rabbis. He had likewise renamed Mesha, declaring that henceforth the young man should be known as Rabbi Meir, "the illuminator," because he had "enlightened even the eyes of the sages" with his masterful interpretations of the Law.

Mesha was excited, but he was also hungry. In search of a bit of leftover chicken or a stray *matzah*, he found instead Beruria, asleep at the kitchen table, her head pillowed on her arms. Her veil had fallen back, and the new sun cast a sheen on her hair, which was caught in one thick dark braid shiny as Sabbath bread. He watched her a moment, then went over to her and gently touched her shoulder.

She woke, lifted her head, opened her eyes, and smiled sleepily at him.

"It's morning," he said softly. "Have you been here all night?"

She nodded.

He shook his head in mock disapproval, but smiled.

"Isn't it wonderful?" she said sleepily.

"You mean about Bar Kokhba?"

"No . . . you. Mesha. Rabbi Meir." She sighed happily. "I'm so proud of you."

Tears came to his eyes. "Are you?"

"Yes . . . yes . . ."

He sat down beside her. "Then, will you be my wife?"

She nodded. "Yes." She yawned. "Yes," she said again, smiling.

He put his arm around her now. She leaned her head against his shoulder, yawned again, and closed her eyes. And so they sat as the sun filled the room.

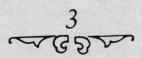

3

"THE KING MESSIAH is come! A star has risen out of Jacob, and his name shall be Bar Kokhba!"

With these words the sword of Judea was once again unleashed. Feelings and longings that had been dammed up for generations now burst forth unchecked. In towns and villages from Dan to Beersheva, Jews rose as one against their enemies, cutting down not only the legionaries among them but also the equally despised *matziqim*, estate owners who had seized Jewish property after the war and either expelled the original owners or forced them to work as laborers. Military veterans and settlers, as well as Roman aristocrats who had received land grants from the emperor, these "colonists" were the first to suffer the wrath of Bar Kokhba's followers.

The revolt extended speedily, the troops of Tinneus Rufus proving no match for the Judeans. Jericho was secured, likewise Ein Gedi, Tekoa, and all the hill country stretching north of Lydda, southward to the Dead Sea. The port of Jaffa was closed. Town after town declared itself "free." As news of the Judeans' astonishing successes reached across the sea, volunteers from Jewish communities abroad set out to join their brothers, the memory of the violent aftermath of the uprising against Trajan still fresh in their minds. The rebellion had their full sympathy, even if there was not universal agreement as to the naming of one Simeon ben Kosiba as Israel's anointed Messiah, or, for that matter, as to the political versus the eschatological nature of that office. But the feeling against Hadrian was strong enough to quell those doubts. Before his departure from Judea, the emperor had visited Tiberias, where he had erected a Hadrianeium in his own honor. This manifestation of emperor worship on the soil of Israel was considered a grave affront by the Jews of the Diaspora. Nor was the visit to Egypt without incident. Antinous, the imperial favorite, had drowned in the Nile, whereupon the grieving Hadrian ordered the establishment of a memorial city in Egypt and a divine cult in Antinous' memory to be spread throughout the East. If any doubt had ever been entertained by any Jew as to the final consequence of a policy which appeared devoted to the propagation, strengthening, and glorification of idol worship, culminating in the self-deification of Hadrian and his homosexual lover, it was dissipated by the even more pertinent knowledge that Jerusalem was to be converted into a pagan center and circumcision prohibited.

THE CURTAINS of gauze hung about the room stirred gently, long white lengths of cloth so thin and transparent as to be wafted by the slightest breath, gentle ghosts giving silent testimony to that world of shadows wherein Gods could be summoned forth in a bowl of water on a marble table.

The Egyptian conjurer made three passes over the silver bowl. His voice spiraled like the smoke of the incense nearby. "I call upon you, Zeus-Helios-Mithras, Serapis, unconquerable, Meliouchos, Melekertes, Meligenetor. . . . Appear and pay heed to him who was manifest before fire and snow . . . Bainchoo'och, for you are the one who made light and snow appear, terrible-eyed Thunderer and Lightning-giver. . . ."

Quintus yawned. He put his hand over his mouth, thereby managing to stifle the sneeze that was about to follow. Incense always made him want to sneeze. Self-conscious, he looked around. Hadrian was sitting still as stone, his face pale, his eyes haunted, burned out. Before him was the table with its oracle-producing bowl. To one side sat a boy of seven or eight, black as night, his eyes glazed in trance, the whites glistening like pearls. Across from him, Ostanas, seer of the Delta, droned on. Quintus shifted restlessly in his seat, caught sight of Phlegon, Hadrian's secretary, beckoning, and gratefully took his leave. Hadrian, the boy, and the magician appeared to take no notice of his departure.

Publius Marcellus, legate of Syria, who, like Quintus, had been invited to join the royal entourage in Egypt, was waiting.

He had his helmet under one arm and a rolled parchment in his hand. He handed the document to Quintus. "Take a look at this."

Quintus unrolled the letter. " '. . . town after town has declared openly for Bar Kokhba. The garrison at Ein Gedi has been expelled. Jaffa has closed her harbor to our ships. A patrol sent forth last week has not been heard from. A cohort of the Sixth, on its way to aid the garrison at Ein Gedi, was intercepted and cut to pieces. Two cohorts of the Tenth on a routine patrol suffered heavy losses while going through what were thought to be peaceful villages. The entire nation is armed and fighting against us. Reinforcements are required.' "

"I don't know what's gotten into Rufus!" Publius Marcellus exclaimed. "You'd think he'd be able to handle things better than this. 'The entire nation armed'! With what? I know for a fact nothing's gone out of my territory, and after the war with Trajan the Jews here in Egypt are too weak to take care of themselves, let alone get involved in another revolt. Unless . . . Parthia . . ."

Quintus shook his head. "They've been preparing for this a long time."

"And Rufus couldn't see it coming? Where were his spies? I was under the impression he had an arsenal of informers."

Quintus recalled the hill country, that long stretch of low-lying mountains with its hundreds of inaccessible villages and thousands of hidden caves. Tur Malka, it was called. King's Mountain. How many caches of arms had been stored in those caves? How many rebels trained in those villages?

"Personally, I think Rufus is exaggerating," Marcellus was saying. "I think he feels left out of things and wants a bit of attention. 'The entire nation'! What nation? Well, I'm off in any event. Judea is undermanned, that's all."

"The garrison at Jerusalem was doubled before I left."

"So it was. I'd forgotten. Well, detachments of the Twenty-second Legion Deiotariana will put an end to this nonsense." He stopped. "From the look on your face, I gather you think not."

"We've lost Ein Gedi. They can bring supplies from across the Dead Sea. And Jaffa . . ."

"Well, it won't do them any good now. I'm on my way. Look, Quintus, I know what's waiting there. I may not like the Jews, but I don't underestimate them. When they take it into their fool heads to fight, there's no stopping them half-way—especially when they think they've got their messiah. They've done plenty of damage to our legions in the past, and for all I've said, I know them—and Rufus—well enough to know that the military governor of Judea would not be asking for help if he didn't need it. But there's no way this thing can continue once my forces arrive. In sheer numbers alone the Judeans will be sorely outmatched." He nodded at the white curtain behind Quintus. "I must speak to the emperor now."

Quintus drew aside the cloth. The little black boy was mumbling incoherently now. Marcellus' mouth fell open. "Don't tell me that's Antinous' replacement!"

"No, merely a means by which to reach Antinous. If he can be reached."

Marcellus stared a moment longer. "Ah, yes," he said thoughtfully. "The emperor was saying only yesterday that when inquiry was made at Trallis into the probable issue of the Mithraditic war, a young boy was used to obtain an oracle from the god Serapis. The boy gazed at an image of Mercury which was reflected in a bowl of water and straightaway foretold the future in a hundred and sixty lines of verse."

The two men exchanged glances.

"It is documented by the philosopher Varro," Publius Marcellus added. He drew the curtain closed. "I do not doubt you wish to return to Judea, Quintus. But you must stay here, with Hadrian. Antinous' death has cut him deeply."

"Yes, I know."

"He will get over it. Men do not die for love. Boys like Antinous, perhaps. But not men. And the emperor is a man. A very great man."

"Yes."

"He counts you his true friend. Remain close to him. Not only for his sake, but for the good of Rome."

Quintus took a deep breath. "I might serve Rome better in Judea. I have some knowledge of the Jews and this Bar Kokhba."

"Bar Kokhba. The Jews' messiah . . ." The Roman shook his head. "Will they never get over their superstitious folly? It will take more than one man, I tell you, even the so-called Son of David, ever to defeat Rome."

*   *   *

AT THAT VERY MOMENT the "Son of David" was riding in triumph to B'nei Berak. All along the way, people ran to greet the rebel army, laughing, cheering, the air filled with flowers and song. Simeon's expression was stern, solemn, but his eyes shone.

Joshua ben Galgola, "chief of camp" for the district of Herodium, leaned over. "You might at least smile," he said with a grin.

"They're crazy," Simeon muttered. "They act as if we've won the war. They think it's all over. It's just begun."

"You and I know that," ben Galgola replied good-naturedly. "But there's no harm in letting them have this moment." He shook his head in wonder as the realization struck. "Simeon, can you believe it? For the first time in over two hundred years we're our own masters! For God's sake, smile!"

Instead Simeon turned to Obodas, who was riding behind. "Someday this will be for you," he promised the Nabatean. "We will get your land back, my brother, and you will rule as your family has always ruled."

Obodas did not reply, but his eyes were full of emotion. He nodded, the pact between himself and the big Judean once more affirmed.

"Well, that should make you smile," Joshua ben Galgola exclaimed, pointing to a hill not far ahead where he had spotted the lithe figure of the young female known as Jara. He grinned, knowing Simeon's fondness for the girl, whose courage back in the days before the Brothers became a real army had won the hearts of all ben Kosiba's followers. "If a mere slip of a girl could defend herself against a Roman commander, how then should men be afraid?" they had asked those who hesitated to join their ranks. That was two years ago; and the girl—that scrawny creature by Simeon's side at the Valley of Rimmon—had become a woman and a beauty. Joshua ben Galgola for one did not wonder that Bar Kokhba took whatever opportunity there was to ride to B'nei Berak, even during these past months of heavy fighting. There was nothing unnatural in Judea's military commander conferring with the Jews' spiritual leader; most took it as a good sign. But, Joshua thought, staring now with appreciation at the radiant face of the girl on the hill, was it Akiva whom Simeon really went to see? He grinned again and laughed aloud, returning Jara's wave as he did. "I wager that's a sight would gladden the heart of any man,'' he told Simeon.

Unable to restrain herself any longer, Jara ran from the mount where she had positioned herself in order to have a clear view of the approaching troops.

"Simeon! Simeon!"

He could not help it. Smiling now, ben Kosiba swept the girl up onto his horse amid a roar of approval from his own men, followed by the cheers of those watching. The act was so spontaneous, the gesture so instinctive and Jara so lovely, the very epitome of all that was young and fresh and beautiful, that even the most staid of scholars in that crowd felt as if their own hearts' longings had been fulfilled. No matter that the female's veil had been lost and her hair flowed free, drenched with sunlight. It was the symbol of themselves: the very soul of Judea had been freed. Now the *Shekhinah*, the Bride of God, rode forth among them, her beauty safe forever in the strong arms of Bar Kokhba.

Someone threw a flower wreath that Jara caught and placed on Simeon's head to the accompaniment of another great cheer.

"Get that thing off me," he muttered.

"You are the King Messiah. You ought to have a crown."

"I am not a king," he said through clenched teeth that were bared in a fixed smile. "And if anyone should have his head covered it's you," he continued in her ear. "Running at me like that . . . Half the world saw your legs."

"Are they too ugly to be seen?"

"You know they're not," he growled. "And anyway, that isn't the point. You don't want people to think you are wanton, do you?"

"I don't care what people think. And neither, I thought, did you."

"What I feel about such things doesn't matter anymore," he replied in a low, angry voice. "There's Akiva. Come on, off with you. Obodas will come for you later," he whispered hurriedly.

She slid off the horse, taken aback by his last remark. She wasn't sure she understood what he meant by it. Her instincts, however, told her it signaled a change. The question was, in what?

Thoughtfully, Jara studied Simeon as he dismounted some yards away and walked with new formality and great respect toward the waiting rabbi.

*   *   *

As THOUGH to allay whatever sudden fears she might have, the sound of Obodas' flute came softly through the window, like a bird that had flown from a faraway land, far and yet near, carrying the desert moon in its beak. Quickly Jara took up her veil, covered her hair, and followed the song out the door. Swiftly she ran to her lover.

He was on the hill by the sea. The moon had not been stolen after all; there it was, opal-edged, embraced by shimmering clouds above the silver water.

Salty kisses by the sea . . . a faint smell of flowers embroidering the night like petals on velvet in a later time . . . far away the music of the desert . . .

She was in his arms again, lost but not unsure in the moment. The whole world dwindled to nothing but the touch of his lips, the feel of his hands, the weight and the warmth of him.

A moment . . . moments . . . that was all they had, all they'd ever had. It wasn't enough, it would never be enough. One night to last weeks, maybe months. Waiting . . . always waiting, wanting to be with him, to be near him, to touch him, to absorb him into herself, not just for the pleasure of it but for his strength, for the strength he gave her, knowing that what she took she returned, that he needed her as much as she needed him.

Hungry. They were hungry people, the blood in them never flowing so strong, so fierce and green as now in the hot course of love.

"Jara, wait . . . we must talk."

"Later," she murmured, lost in the kiss they'd shared. "Later . . ."

"No, now." Gently but firmly Simeon put his hands on her shoulders and held her away from him. "We can't continue like this," he managed to say at last.

She stood there, still flushed from the heat of their embrace. "I don't know what you mean," she said breathlessly.

He swallowed, torn between the desire to take her in his arms again and the need to speak. "This thing between us," he muttered. "It cannot continue."

She stiffened, the cool edge of the sea wind cutting close to her heart, returning the feelings she'd had earlier in the day. "Why not?"

"It's wrong—"

"It isn't! I love you, Simeon."

He shook his head. "What if I get you with child?"

"I don't care!" She wanted to laugh. If that was what was bothering him . . . "Don't you see? I would be proud."

"Jara . . ." He shook his head again, sighed. "No. I cannot let it come to that. It would be wrong of me. . . . It's no good like this," he concluded.

"It is," she insisted, smiling. "You know it is. It's good, Simeon," she said in a low, throaty murmur, her arms finding their way around his neck once more, her mouth nearing his. "It's good. . . ."

He pulled away. "Stop it! Listen to me. . . ." His hands gripped her shoulders again. He was staring at her as though caught in some private struggle.

"Don't send me away," she whispered, frightened now. "You're all that I have, the only one. . . ." The fear was rising. "Don't send me away," she said again. "I don't care what anyone thinks of me. I don't care! I'll be your woman. I'll be your whore! I'll come to you whenever you want, wherever—"

"Will you listen?" he thundered. He drew in his breath. "By the Almighty, girl, give a man a chance! You will not be anyone's whore," he continued angrily, glaring at her. "Now just shut up and listen! We cannot go on as we are," he went on firmly in a lower voice. "It will only lead to—No, stop! You will not run away! You will listen to me!" Strong hands held the trembling girl in place. Another deep breath. "I think of you . . . I think of you too much. All the way here I thought of you and how much I wanted you . . . and of the consequences should you . . . that is . . . you've been through so much already. And I don't like deceit. I like things open, plain. So I have decided. You will become my wife."

"Your . . . wife!"

He nodded. He seemed relieved. "I tell you plainly I don't know what kind of marriage ours will be. Even before . . . I was never much of a husband. And now, with all that is ahead of us . . . It's going to be hard, Jara, harder than you can imagine."

"But we've won! The legions are gone—or locked away in their garrisons, afraid to come out."

"All we've won is time. The legions will come out of their fortresses once troops arrive from Syria and Egypt and the other outposts. And make no mistake, those troops will arrive unless we can close off all our borders, including the ones to the sea." He sighed ruefully. "For a long time I didn't want to think of marriage. And then I couldn't allow myself to think of it. I don't know what I'm thinking of now. Except maybe how much I want you. God help me, but I want you!"

She returned his kiss with ardor, buoyed by happiness as much as by passion.

"We've got to secure Caesarea," he said finally. "And the Egyptian border as well. I set out in the morning. When I return we will be betrothed." He gripped her arms. "We'll be married in Jerusalem."

"Jerusalem!"

He grinned. "If I'm not killed first."

"You won't be. I know you won't."

"Even so, you may find yourself a widow soon after you become a bride. Jerusalem doesn't end it unless Hadrian by some miracle agrees to a treaty respecting our sovereignty as well as our religion."

"What if he doesn't?"

"Then we keep on fighting. We have no choice, especially now. That's why you must understand what lies ahead. All my days will be spent waging war—in pursuit, if I'm lucky, and not pursued."

"I'll go with you," she said eagerly.

"The battlefield is no place for a woman."

"If it's as you say, then all Judea will soon be a battlefield. I want to be with you. I'll follow you wherever you go."

He shook his head, but he was smiling. "What have I gotten myself into?" He drew her close again, touched her hair. "You are too willful, too bold—and too beautiful—ever to give a man any peace. But I will have you!" This time his mouth came down hard and hungry. As they slipped to the ground, he murmured, "When I return we will be betrothed."

SIMEON'S ANALYSIS of the military situation proved correct. Although he was never able to secure Caesarea for more than a short period, he did manage to hold off the reinforcements sent to aid the beleaguered Romans. In late summer of the one hundred and thirty-second year of the Common Era, the centurion Marcellus Quintus brought startling news to the emperor Hadrian, who was still reposing in Egypt. He was met at the door to the imperial chamber by Phlegon. The old man shook his head, putting a finger to his lips.

"I must see the emperor."

"Not now. Not now, centurion."

"Now!"

"He is unwell—"

Quintus pushed past and strode determinedly to the emperor's couch. "I must speak with you, excellency."

Hadrian opened his eyes. "Why, of course," he said calmly.

"I did not mean to disturb your rest."

"I have no rest, Quintus." He looked away. "My limbs are numb, yet sleep does not come. Only thoughts . . . and dreams awake."

"You must shake off this melancholy, sire. For the good of Rome. What's done is done. The boy is dead."

"No . . . no, that's just it. Antinous is not dead. He is here, with me. Every moment I see him, beautiful beyond compare. Was ever anyone so beautiful?" He sighed. "I used to think that a sense of beauty would serve me in place of virtue. Evidently the gods have seen fit to punish me for this view . . . most cruelly. And now Antinous is one of them. A god. I have made him a god. Like the Christians with their Jesus, whom they claim rose up after death. So, too, Antinous will live. A god . . . ." He took the death mask of the boy into his hands. "See what a god he is. . . ."

Quintus' jaw tightened. "We must speak of other things, excellency."

"Other things." Hadrian sighed wearily. "You mean Judea, of course."

"Yes."

"Judea. Always it is Judea. Was ever a curse upon the world as these Jews be! They killed Antinous. I know it. He wasn't the same when we left Judea. He'd changed somehow. He looked upon himself with loathing, at once fearing he had lost my love while seeming to tremble when I touched him. That brave, beautiful boy . . . ."

"Excellency, Publius Marcellus has arrived. Rufus is with him. You must call together all your senior officers—"

"Marcellus is back, is he? Good. I can't wait to hear how the Jews have been destroyed."

"The Jews have not been destroyed. Marcellus' detachments were routed by bands ten times their number. Additional legions are requested—"

"Routed? Impossible!"

"It is a fact. I suggest the Twelfth Fulminata and the Sixth Ferrata be dispatched immediately."

"Routed . . ." Hadrian put down Antinous' death mask. "It would seem," he said with a sigh, "that the Jews' rebellion has gotten out of hand."

"We can no longer speak of rebellion, sire," Quintus said. "This is war."

THE KING'S MOUNTAIN, Jara had learned, was not one place but many. There were hundreds of villages in the hilly region surrounding Jerusalem, which was called in Hebrew *Har ha-Melekh* and in Aramaic *Tur Malka*, and which stretched from Gibeah of Saul in the north to Solomon's Pools in the south, and from Kiriath-Jearim in the west to the ascent of Adummim in the east. Every hill seemed to have its own pyramid of dwellings and terraced fields that often appeared to hang from the very clouds or to be perched impossibly atop the precipices: human nests of stone and straw. Although the area immediately surrounding Jerusalem had been stripped bare by Titus, olive groves and scattered cypresses planted after the war pushed toward the sun, reaffirming the belief of the old Jew who, when asked why at the age of eighty he had planted a carob tree, replied, "The world was not desolate when I came into it. As my father planted for me, so must I plant for my children."

The air had become noticeably cooler as Akiva's party made its way up into the hills leading to the village of Kobi, where for the moment Bar Kokhba was headquartered. Simeon had no real place of administration. He changed locations frequently, suddenly, so that no one could be sure where he might be at any given time except that he was usually to be found somewhere in the mountains about Jerusalem.

Several months had passed since Simeon had asked Jara to become his wife, during which time he had continued to consolidate his victories and, to the great joy of his countrymen, had driven the legions from Jerusalem. Contrary to expectations, Bar Kokhba did not position himself thereafter in the

Holy City, considered the Eternal Capital of the Jewish nation. Many considered this curious, and it so concerned the rabbis that Akiva now felt it necessary for the man he had proclaimed Messiah to explain himself. Moreover, scant progress was being made toward the rebuilding of Jerusalem and its Temple, which for many had been the primary reason for going to war. These concerns were etched on Akiva's face as they entered Kobi. Jara rode behind the rabbi, impatient, her state of breathless anticipation a mixture perhaps of anxiousness to see Simeon again and the altitude of the place. She had persuaded Akiva to allow her to come on this journey on the pretext of being permitted to make her first pilgrimage to Jerusalem; and indeed the City of David held great meaning for her: Simeon had said they would be wed there. But meanwhile, they were not yet betrothed.

The village had been turned into an armed camp. Clusters of men were grouped here and there. One crowd seemed to follow with great interest some activity taking place in its center, as evidenced by the variety of cheers, groans, and exclamations that issued from it. Curious to know what was causing all the excitement, Jara paused and managed to catch sight of two men wrestling in the center of the human ring. She recognized Samson immediately. His opponent was a slender but well-built young man with dark, curly hair, deeply tanned skin, and a great grinning flash of white teeth above a short, black beard. He was extremely agile and surprisingly strong. To Jara's astonishment he managed to lift the big smith completely off his feet and flip him backward to the ground. Samson lay there a moment, dazed, then shook his head as if to clear it. A smile spread over his features. "Well done," he conceded. "Well done."

The young man grinned. "I should have warned you. It's a family talent."

"I still don't know how you did it."

The other laughed and put out a hand to help the big man up. "You did it, Samson. I simply turned your own strength against you. Like this!" As the smith took his hand, the fellow jerked back and Samson flew forward, to the laughter of all who were watching.

Jara could not help smiling too; the effect was so comical. She wondered who it was could beat Samson so thoroughly. There was something familiar about him.

"Where is Bar Kokhba?" Akiva was asking.

"Come," Obodas replied. "I shall take you to him." He put up his hand to keep Jara from following. "No, little cat," he said softly. "Not now."

She frowned slightly, then, sensing several pairs of eyes directed her way, turned aside. Impatient as she was to see Simeon, she would behave before these men with the decorum befitting the soon-to-be wife of their leader. No more running to greet Simeon with her skirts held up in her hands. No more fly-away veils and leaps into his outstretched arms. At least not in public. He had made it clear he did not like such behavior, and she had decided that he was right. At sixteen she was too old to act in such a manner. Still, when she did see him at last, there was no telling how she would behave. She longed to see him. Oh, why hadn't he come back for her as he'd promised? The last few weeks had been peaceful ones. . . .

With a sigh Jara led the donkey she had been riding over to a clump of sycamore and tethered it to one of the trees. Doing so, she again became aware of being stared at and, turning, saw a boy of her own age or thereabouts watching her with great interest. She gave him a friendly nod, then checked the donkey's rope; when she looked up again the boy was gone.

Tirza, Shem's wife, waved from a short distance. "Come to the house," she called. "There's food and wine."

Smiling now, Jara ran to greet the woman, instantly forgetting the stately manner she had determined to adopt for herself.

"I must find the children," Tirza said. "They are always wandering off, and there are too many swords lying around for anyone's good. Everywhere you look swords and lances, and now these Parthian bows. . . ." She clucked her tongue disapprovingly. "Well, here, there is some bread and cheese on the table. Help yourself. I'll be right back."

Jara watched her hurry out of the house, then looked about, content. It was a modest dwelling, at once homey and homely. To the orphaned girl, however, it seemed as if there could be no finer place in all the world. She quickly drifted into a happy daydream in which she imagined Simeon sitting at the table—there ought to be flowers in the pitcher—herself preparing his meal, a baby gurgling in the next room. . . .

Her heart took a small leap. At this very moment Simeon might be saying the words to Akiva that would make that dream come true. At this very moment her betrothal and marriage to Bar Kokhba might well be in the process of being planned. Soon it would be announced. Of course, Akiva would want to talk about Jerusalem first. But then—"That looks good. Do you mind if I have some?"

She looked up, startled. It was the young wrestler who had thrown Samson. Only now she knew who he was.

"You've got a beard," she said.

Andreas grinned. "For the moment."

She blinked, unsure.

"Cut me a bit of that loaf, will you? My hands are dirty. I don't want to spoil it all."

"Go and wash."

"Too hungry. Besides, you might be gone by the time I got back. You have a way of disappearing the moment one looks away."

She handed him a piece of bread. "Here."

"A little cheese perhaps," he prompted.

"The cheese is not mine to give. Nor the bread."

"Yes, it's Tirza's. I know. She won't mind. Anything for the Cause. Oh, come on, don't be shy! Pretend you're my wife or something."

"In a pig's eye!" Nevertheless she spread some cheese on the bread, and after a moment's hesitation took a salted olive from the dish and deftly cut the flesh from the pit, arranging the morsels atop the cheese in a pretty pattern.

Andreas watched admiringly. "You handle a knife well." He grinned again. "But as I recall, you've had some fine practice with a blade."

She stuck the *sica* through the sandwich and offered it to him on the point of the knife.

He laughed cautiously but took it from her. "Mmmm," he murmured, biting down, his dark eyes never leaving her face. "Good."

"The olive will make you thirsty."

"Right." He helped himself to the wine, grimaced. "Where's the water? Ah, here it is."

"You've got the pitcher dirty."

"So I have." He looked down at his hands. "The soil of *Eretz Yisrael*. Sacred, isn't it?"

"To some of us."

Another grin.

"What are you doing here?"

"What do you mean, what am I doing here? I'm a Jew, aren't I?"

"Are you?"

He nodded solemnly. "I give you my word." But his dark eyes were merry. "Want to see?"

She reddened. "You wouldn't talk like that if I were one of your fine Roman ladies."

"Don't be so sure. There's nothing a fine Roman lady loves so much as being treated like a—" He stopped.

"Go on," she said, eyes narrowing dangerously. "Finish what you started to say."

"Not while you've got that knife in your hands. I may be all sorts of things, but I'm not stupid. Anyway, I was out of line, I admit it. I apologize. Now, can we be friends?"

"Definitely not."

He sighed. "You're awfully hard on me. Why?"

"I don't like you," she said flatly. "And I don't trust you." She bit into an olive. "I heard what you said to the centurion in B'nei Berak. Simeon ought to be told."

His eyes met hers without so much as a blink. "Bar Kokhba knows all there is to know about me. I don't play false with men I respect. In any event I haven't much changed my mind. This war of liberation has about as much chance as a virgin with ten gladiators."

"There isn't a Roman in all Judea dares show himself," she retorted angrily. "Jerusalem is ours—"

"Yes, but for how long? Why do you think Simeon hasn't set up camp in the Holy City? Why do you think he is so reluctant to spare any men for the rebuilding of the Temple? Because he's smart enough to know what's coming. Rome hasn't even begun to use her muscle. No, I take that back," he amended. "Rufus' reinforcements were substantial, and they were outfought." He nodded. "I daresay the whole world has been surprised. I know I was," he added with a laugh. "But that doesn't mean Hadrian has given up," he went on. "And now we're talking about an endless supply of arms, equipment, and the best-trained troops in the world against—"

" 'A pack of dirty peasants bent on suicide.' Misguided fools. Dreamers and dunces. Why don't you say it? It's what you're thinking. Well, let me tell you something. Until Simeon came along we were nothing. Nothing," she repeated. "I grew up seeing men groveling in the dust every day, running at the turn of a leaf, afraid to speak out even when their women were abused. That's changed now. We aren't a pack of anything. We are a people. With purpose and pride and reason to fight. But you . . . Why are you here? You care nothing for Israel. Your life in Rome must be a fine one." Her eyes narrowed again. "Why have you come back to Judea?"

"I have my reasons," he said calmly.

"What are they?" she demanded.

"I really don't feel like telling you." He tipped her chin back with his finger. "Even if you are the most beautiful girl I've ever seen. Ah," he said with that crooked smile. " 'Haughty indeed are the daughters of Israel!' " He planted a light kiss on her nose. "Thanks for the food." And he was gone.

DAY WOULD SOON be night; still, Akiva remained with Simeon, and Jara had seen nothing of either. "Doesn't Simeon know I'm here?" she asked Samson.

"Why, yes, I suppose," the smith replied. "But you must realize that Bar Kokhba has little time to spare. He has much to consider—especially now, with Parthia showing interest in our cause."

"It would be wonderful if Parthia were to join us. She is as strong as Rome."

"And as likely to swallow us up if we're not careful. Simeon must consider that. But it is good that the Jews of Parthia lend their support. They are rich. And there are many of them." He gestured toward the boy Jara had seen earlier, who was now grooming a black stallion nearby. "That's the son of the *Resh ha-Galut*, exilarch of all the Parthian Jews, descended, they say, from King David himself. He has sent the boy as a sign of his commitment."

"What a beautiful horse. . . ."

"Their steeds are the Parthians' pride. You wouldn't believe how well the lad rides or the tricks he can do," the smith said admiringly. "So young, and a prince at that. . . ." Samson shook his head in wonder. "Andreas is the only one can keep up with him. Rides like the devil himself, that no-good son of Satan," he added with a fond grin.

Jara sniffed. "I wish you'd beaten him. He could use a good fall."

Samson laughed good-naturedly.

She did not want to talk about Andreas. She wanted to see Simeon.

"I wonder where Obodas is. It will soon be dark." She sighed. "Well, he warned me. He said it would be like this." She laughed. "And not yet married!"

"You know Bar Kokhba is to wed?" Samson asked, surprised.

She laughed again. "Of course."

"But I thought—" He stopped. "Never mind. I should have realized nothing is unknown in the household of Akiva."

Before Jara could digest this strange remark, she caught sight of Obodas and waved vigorously. The Nabatean appeared not to see her, but the gesture startled the black stallion, who reared up on his hind legs, whinnying nervously. The young Parthian quickly caught the animal's reins and, speaking softly, managed to calm him. When the horse was quiet again, the boy nodded reassuringly to Jara, who had watched in consternation.

"I'm sorry," she said, dismayed.

The Parthian nodded again, this time with a shy smile. But his eyes were bright with the interest he had earlier shown.

The next morning as if by signal, all the Brothers rode out of the village: Legionaries had been spotted to the south. It was night when the men returned, their number less than when they had set out, not because of the enemy but because their commander had reportedly changed his plans and decided to spend the next few days in the area of Ein Gedi. Disappointed as she was at having failed to meet with Simeon and unable to discover whether he had made mention to Akiva of their betrothal, as the rabbi, having apparently forgotten all about her presence in Kobi, had set out for Jerusalem without her, Jara attempted to make some use of her sojourn in the mountains by helping the sick and wounded. There were always children to be tended, little ones whose cuts and scrapes could be soothed and healed with the salves she drew from the earth. Tirza, pregnant again, was grateful for the herb drink that calmed her rebellious stomach. And men who had fought with Bar Kokhba were glad to have old wounds rechecked, as grateful for Jara's light touch as for her tender look, which seemed to surface only when she was with children or immersed in acts of healing.

It was while making the rounds of her "patients" that Jara

came upon Andreas, who was lying out in the open near a fire, propped up on one elbow. Startled, she stopped and saw that his tunic was torn at the shoulder and stained with dried blood. She knelt beside him. "What happened to you?"

"Nothing, really. A passing stroke from a legionary who was quicker on his feet than I anticipated." He flinched slightly as she touched the wound. "I'm all right, I tell you. Just tired. It was a long ride back."

"That was yesterday. Why did you wait so long? Never mind. The cut isn't deep, but it should have been cleaned." She put her hand on his forehead. "You're feverish."

He smiled. "A natural consequence of your presence."

She gave him a withering look. "Stay where you are. I'll be right back."

"I assure you I have no intention of going anyplace," he said, and closed his eyes. When he opened them again, he saw that she had already washed his shoulder and wrapped it in clean cloth. She was preparing a drink of sorts. "I must have fallen asleep," he murmured.

"Good. Sleep heals."

He sat up. She had covered him with a light blanket. "I feel like an idiot." He eyed the cup in her hands cautiously. "What's that?"

"It will work against the fever. Drink," she commanded.

Andreas hesitated.

Jara smiled slightly. "Are you afraid I'll poison you?" she asked.

He raised an eyebrow at this but downed the brew obediently. "Not bad," he said when he'd finished. "What is it?"

"Herbs, water . . . A kind of tea."

He gestured toward his bandaged shoulder. "How is it you know about these things?"

"My father was a physician. I used to watch him. You'd better lie down now. Here, let me fold this cloak into a pillow."

Smiling his lopsided smile, he settled back on the ground. "Mmm," he murmured as she put her hand on his forehead again. "Delicious."

She withdrew her hand hurriedly. "I daresay you'll live," she remarked icily.

"Of course I'll live." He laughed softly. The pain in his shoulder was beginning to fade. "If you call this living."

She tried not to smile. "You find Judea hard?"

"Hard place, hard people. You most of all. Don't go. . . ." He caught her arm. "Come here," he murmured. "Come back to me. Closer. That's it. There's something I've been wanting to do. . . ." Reaching up now, he pushed the veil back from her head and filled his hand with the soft weight of her hair.

"Don't," she said softly. But she did not move. "What will those around us think?"

"They will think I want to make love to you."

"Make . . . love?"

"To lie with you. I want to lie with you. . . ."

She pushed his hand away now and, rising angrily, said, "Be glad the Roman stung you. If he hadn't, I would. And with better aim."

He grinned as she strode away. But the potion she'd given him had taken effect, and in another moment he was asleep.

TWO MORE DAYS PASSED, and suddenly Akiva was back, in good spirits but preoccupied. He seemed surprised to see Jara, as if he had forgotten it was he who had brought her to Kobi. Jara was less concerned with this slight than the matter of her betrothal to Simeon. It was one thing for Rabban Akiva to forget her presence, but quite another for the man she loved! "Where is Simeon?" she wanted to know. "When is he coming back? What did he say about me?"

The rabbi was astonished at her forwardness. "My dear child, do you imagine men have nothing to do than chat with young girls while a war is taking place? I know how much Simeon means to you," he said more kindly. "After all, he saved your life. But now he must think of thousands of lives."

She gave an impatient toss of her head. "Yes, I know. But didn't he say anything to you about—" A thought struck her. "Does he know I'm here?"

"Yes, of course. He inquired as to your well-being."

"That's all? That's all he said? And you say he knows I'm here?"

"My dear child . . ." Akiva paused. He was not blind to the girl's feelings for Bar Kokhba, nor unaware of the affection she generated in the man she was so anxious to see. As he'd said, Simeon had literally rescued Jara at a most perilous and frightening time in her young life; it was only natural that a bond exist between them. But that bond, he suddenly worried, might be stronger than he'd imagined. At least on Jara's part. "It would be best for you to put Simeon far from your thoughts," he said at last.

"I can't do that." She smiled. "And I'm sure Simeon wouldn't want me to." The smile faded. Akiva was staring strangely at her. She didn't like that look; she didn't know what it meant. "It's because legionaries were reported in the South," she said suddenly. "He had to ride out before he could. But you'll see, when he returns from Ein Gedi—"

"Bar Kokhba is no longer in Ein Gedi," Simon bar Yohai, passing, said. "He was here during the night but rode out again before dawn."

Jara blinked.

"Come," Akiva said. "We must be on our way. I will take you to Jerusalem," he said, remembering the purpose of her presence away from B'nei Berak and thinking this would cheer her.

Jara nodded dumbly. A funny, cold feeling was beginning to grip her.

As Jara went to fetch the donkey, Andreas reappeared, recovered from his wound and the brief illness that had attended it. He seemed his usual jaunty self. He was leading a pretty white mare. "Here," he said. "A gift from an admirer."

"I don't want anything from you."

"Who said it was from me?" he wanted to know.

She turned back, studied him, then looked at the horse. "Who, then?"

"I told you, an admirer." One side of his mouth turned up. "Someone whose heart you've stolen away."

Jara answered this bit of mockery with a disgusted look. Then, slowly, she began to smile. An admirer. Someone whose heart she'd stolen. Who could that be but Simeon? The horse was from Simeon; it had to be. It was his way of making amends, of showing that he cared. He simply hadn't had a chance to mention their betrothal, what with the fighting still going on and Akiva obsessed with Jerusalem. What did it matter so long as he loved her?

Everything was all right now. And if the business of war prevented Simeon from seeing her, why, then, she would just have to find a way—again—of seeking him out. Still smiling, she took the reins from Andreas.

"Let me help you up," he offered. "Do you think you'll be able to ride? This isn't a little donkey, you know."

"I know." She pushed his hands away from her waist.

"Be careful, now. This is a very sensitive breed, a very fine animal."

"Too fine for the likes of me?"

"I didn't say that. But if you must know, I can't see the good of giving a horse to a girl, especially in Judea. And with men on foot facing Roman cavalry." He shook his head. "It's a strange power you've got, Jara, to bewitch men so."

"You know my name."

"And I'll wager you know mine." He grinned. "Where might that lead, do you think?"

"Nowhere. You can be sure of it."

He laughed. "Well, be careful anyway. If you've never ridden—"

"I've ridden a horse before," she told him pointedly. "A centurion's horse. All the way from Tiberias to the Valley of Rimmon." She looked down at him from atop the mare. "You can let go of the reins."

"I'd like to rein you in," he murmured.

"What?"

"Nothing."

"By the way, where did Simeon go?" she asked casually.

"Kosiba. I'm to meet him there later."

"Ah, yes! I thought that was what Akiva said. To the north, isn't it?"

"No, just south of here." There was that funny crooked smile again. "Why?"

She shrugged. "No matter." She turned the horse around and started after the others.

"You might say thank you!" Andreas called after her, indicating the mare.

Jara laughed. "I intend to!"

"YOU SEEM in much better spirits," Simon bar Yohai remarked later to Jara as they walked along the road.

"I am," she said happily. "I mean, I suddenly realized that I've been acting like a selfish child, thinking only of myself. Bar Kokhba belongs to everyone now. It's just that I thought—" She broke off with a laugh. "Well, but look!" She pointed to the mare which she had tied to Akiva's cart. "See what Simeon has given to me!"

"The mare is from Bar Kokhba?" His eyebrows shot up. "I wondered where you got it. That's a strange gift for a girl. Besides, it's one of the Parthian horses, isn't it? Well, it must have been one of the dowry presents. Still, it's odd that Bar Kokhba would give you a horse."

"Dowry presents? What dowry presents?"

"From the exilarch," Bar Yohai said. "Simeon is to marry one of the daughters of the *Resh ha-Galut*."

Jara halted abruptly. She stared at the young man. "No . . . that isn't possible."

"What do you mean, isn't possible? I tell you it's true. The exilarch has sent—"

But she had already run to Akiva. "Rabban! Rabban! Is it so? Simeon is to marry a Parthian?"

"Why, yes," he answered, taken by surprise. "Yes, it is so."

"No!" Her face turned pale. "No, it can't be!"

"Jara—My child—"

"He loves me! You know he loves me! He said we would be betrothed! I don't believe you! I don't believe you!"

"But it is true," Akiva said. He looked around. "You must calm yourself. This is unseemly—"

"No! No!" She sucked in her breath, eyes wild, accusing. "This is your doing. You forced him to it! You're making Simeon do it just to get the Parthians to fight! You're making him do this!"

"Child . . . no one is forcing Simeon to anything. The proposition was put to him by his uncle, and he agreed—"

"I don't believe you! I don't believe you!" She ran back to the horse and, before anyone could say anything or stop her, rode off in a dusty gallop.

SHE APPEARED in the mountain village of Kosiba just as Simeon was going to his own horse. The sight of her on the white mare, her hair undone and tangled by the wind, her

green-gold eyes bright with fear as much as fury, was enough
to make those who saw her clutch at whatever amulets they
wore or murmur a prayer to *Adonai*. Simeon, however,
showed no emotion. He did not ask why she had come or what
she needed to know. The look in her eyes told all. He nodded
slightly, lifted her from the horse, and set her on the ground,
holding her another moment to be sure she had her balance.
Still without a word between them, he led her away from the
others and, after a moment's hesitation, brought her into a
small, empty house.

She sank down on a stool, exhausted.

"How did you know where to find me?"

She made a slight gesture, waving the question aside; it
seemed so inconsequential in light of what had happened.

"What is it you want me to say to you?" he asked quietly
after a pause.

"I want . . ." She caught her breath, began again. "I want
to know if it is true that you are going to marry the exilarch's
daughter," she said carefully, trying to keep the trembling
from her voice. "And if it is true, I want to know why you did
not tell me so yourself."

"It has only just been arranged. A matter of weeks since—"
He broke off. "I give you my word, Jara. I had no thought of
it or any indication of the possibility when we were last
together."

"Then it is true. . . ."

"Yes."

She turned away, unwilling for him to see her cry. But he
was beside her in that moment, gathering her up in his arms,
kissing the hot tears that coursed down her cheeks. "Jara,
Jara . . . nothing has changed," he whispered. "The way I feel
about you . . . nothing has changed. I know that now."

"But you're marrying someone else. . . ."

"Yes. I must. You've got to understand."

"I don't," she said simply. "I don't."

He sighed. "Don't you see? It isn't me that's getting married. It isn't Simeon. It's . . . *Bar Kokhba*. The head of the independent nation of Judea. Israel," he corrected himself
absently. "Akiva is right. We must call ourselves Israel again,
as in the days of David."

"What are you talking about?" she asked numbly.

"I'm talking about politics, Jara. And war. And freedom.

Love has nothing to do with any of it." He gripped her arms, forcing her to look at him. "Our feelings, yours and mine, don't matter anymore. What matters is that the exilarch will send money and men, and hopefully persuade the king of Parthia that our fight is an opportunity to wrest power from Rome. As a sign of his good will and to seal the bond between the Judean house of David and his own house, which is also descended from David, the *Resh ha-Galut* offers one of his daughters in marriage. That's all there is to it."

"All!"

"I should have told you. . . ."

"That's why you wouldn't see me at Kobi." She was beginning to understand now. "Why you avoided me . . ." Anger was beginning to replace shock. "Do you know how that makes me feel?"

"I'm sorry."

"All this time I thought . . . You never intended to marry me."

"That's not true."

"Liar! *Bar Kokhba*." She fairly spat the name. "Son of a Star! *Bar Koziba!* That's the name for you! Son of Lies!"

"I don't know why you're carrying on like this," he said angrily. "I told you, nothing has changed. I still want you."

"Want," she repeated bitterly. "I suppose that's like war and politics. Love has nothing to do with it."

"You said you didn't care," he reminded her. " 'I'll be your woman,' you said. 'I'll be your whore—' "

Her slap silenced him.

They stood there, glaring at each other. Finally he said, "I'm sorry."

"Sorry," she whispered. "Yes . . . you will be sorry. You love me, Simeon. You may say you want me, but it isn't only that. You love me," she said again, "as you never loved your precious Ruth, and as you will never love your Parthian bride. You don't have to say the words. You've never had to say them. Because I can feel what I am to you, and I know what you are to me. Because I am you."

"Jara . . ." As though to prove the truth of what she said, her pain was mirrored now in his eyes. But Jara could not respond to this show of emotion. She was beyond forgiving. Rage and shame and the love she still felt for Simeon had twisted inside her into a rope that would strangle her if she didn't first use it to thrash at him. A cold fire leaped into her eyes as she said, "This was your mother's house, wasn't it? Well, I swear to you now in the house of your mother—I swear to you now, Simeon ben Kosiba, not by the God whom you fear but by all that is holy to me—someday you'll beg for my love!"

He turned white.

"I swear it. Someday you'll beg!"

She ran from the house now, nearly bumping into Andreas, who stepped back just in time. She stopped, glared at him. He returned the look politely, his dark eyes noncommittal. If he'd heard any of what had transpired between herself and Simeon, he gave no indication of it, nor ever would.

BOOK III

1

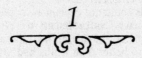

IN THE one hundred and thirty-third year of the Common Era—year two of the war that would be known to history as Bar Kokhba's Rebellion—and in the seventeenth year of the emperor Hadrian's reign, the province of Judea was no more. The tiny country had declared itself the "free and independent land of Israel." Coins declaring the "Freedom of Jerusalem" and "the Redemption of Israel" were struck, an administration set up. The head of the fledgling government, whose name appeared on the new shekels, was known to be one Simeon ben Kosiba, who had taken for himself or been given the title of *Nasi*, a term, meaning prince or president, that was generally used to designate the head of the Sanhedrin. Another name appearing on the new nation's coins was that of one "Eleazar the Priest," indicating the Jews' determination to return to a society ruled by both secular and religious authority, each office acting as a check upon the other, as in the days of David. And, as in that long-ago time when the tribes of Israel had been nearly invincible, the world once more learned the strength and valor of the Jewish warrior.

The defeat of Tinneus Rufus' troops, astonishing as it was, could be rationalized at first by Hadrian's generals. After all, they argued, the elements of concealment and surprise were in themselves superb weapons. When these were combined with the talents of someone who, as the centurion Marcellus Quintus said, knew the area, "every hill and cave, as well as he knows his own face," and who also appeared to have some knowledge of the workings of the legions, the opponent became formidable. It was also agreed that the auxiliary gar-

risons, all of which the rebels had succeeded in isolating, forcing out, and then cutting up, were notoriously inadequate. At
a tactical disadvantage without them, further hampered by the
difficult terrain, was it any wonder that Rufus' legions could
not respond to the crisis effectively?

But the generals could not explain away the fact that, when
"superior" legionary reinforcements were rushed from the
neighboring provinces, the tide, in fact, did not turn. Publius
Marcellus fared no better than Rufus had. The Third Legion
Gallica from Syria, the Second Legion Traiana from Egypt,
and other succeeding legions were demolished. The Tenth
Legion, which was forced finally to evacuate Jerusalem, survived to fight another day. But in the wooded entry to Judea's
highlands the road to Jerusalem called Sh'ar ha-Hai, an extraordinary event took place. The Twenty-second Legion
Deiotariana was totally annihilated and thereafter ceased to
exist, its very name permanently and visibly erased from the
inscription affixed to Caesarea's aqueduct. An entire Roman
legion had been wiped out by the forces of Bar Kokhba.

"THEY TRICKED ME," Hadrian said. "They lied. All that talk
of peace—guarantees of loyalty—and all the time they were
planning this. For how long? Since Trajan? Since Masada?"

"They've been preparing for years," Tinneus Rufus agreed.
"It's clear to me now. Ever since Vespasian, the Jews have
been bound to make weapons for us. The records show that
for any number of years their smiths have been turning out
such rotten stuff we've had to reject it. It's my guess they took
back all that we turned down only to put it right for their own
use. That cave you found stashed with weapons, those
underground passages—you said it was the work of bandits,"
he accused Quintus. "Bandits!"

The centurion did not reply. He was used to commanders
berating others for their own mistakes. He gave Hadrian a
knowing look, but for once the emperor did not respond in
kind.

"Are they getting outside help?" Hadrian wanted to know.
"They must be getting outside help. To destroy an entire
legion . . ."

Publius Marcellus shook his head.

"What about the Nabateans?"

"Content to be part of our Empire. Grateful to be free of the petty intrigues and murderous conspiracies of their old kings."

"Parthia. Surely Parthia has a hand in this."

Again the governor of Syria shook his head. "As I have assured you many times, excellency, there is no evidence of large-scale Parthian involvement. To be sure, there is evidence of Parthian warfare. I've seen it myself. Extraordinary feats of marksmanship accomplished while on the back of a galloping horse . . . the famous 'Parthian shot'—yes, I saw it myself. In the midst of a retreating gallop, this fellow turns completely around in his saddle to send off an arrow, hitting the man beside me square in the chest. Absolutely amazing. But such are isolated incidents—the work, I would say, of Parthian Jews sympathetic to the revolt."

"Jews!"

"They are skilled fighters, excellency. The Parthian kings have long been afraid of their Jewish soldiers as well as relied upon their strength and ferocity."

"The question is, will all of Parthia enter the conflict?"

"Doubtless they are watching. And waiting."

Silence at this. Parthia was a force to be reckoned with. It was the only competitor for world supremacy equal to Rome; it was always a potential and often a very real enemy.

"It's only the Jews," Tinneus Rufus said finally. "Nobody will join the Judeans but Jews, and apart from recruiting some of their own from Parthia, who else have they got? The Jews of Rome are not likely to give us any trouble. They're too smart for that. As for the Egyptian community, what remains of it has been rendered impotent as a result of their war against your uncle Trajan. There are, in fact, no more Jews anywhere in Cyprus or Cyrene."

"No, they're all living in Jaffa," Hadrian retorted. "Illegal refugees, malcontents . . . Quietus was right. I ought to have done away with them at once instead of allowing them to find refuge in Judea. I daresay they're the ones behind this."

"No," Quintus mused, hardly aware he was speaking aloud. "Certainly Bar Kokhba has reaped a fair amount of experienced manpower due to the earlier revolt, but the Jews have in fact become masters of the kind of warfare they call 'Sicarii,' ever since the fall of Jerusalem. Even after Masada, pockets of resistance had to be continually and systematically

ferreted out and destroyed." He suddenly remembered the
words that had been told to him when he first came to Judea.
"They just don't give up. . . ."

"Yes, it's obvious these loathsome people have been longing for a new war," Hadrian snapped. "Which is why all of
you here were given the positions you have. To control them.
To stop this from happening."

Silence filled the room. Suddenly—again, almost to himself
—Marcellus Quintus asked, "What is it the Jews want? Why
is it we never ask ourselves that question? They're not like the
Gauls or the Germans or the Thracians. They don't want to
conquer the world, or to rule Rome, but only to rule themselves. And to worship their God in their own way." He
looked around. The room was still quiet; no one was looking
at him.

"What the Jews want is of no importance whatsoever,"
Publius Marcellus declared succinctly. He turned to Hadrian.
"Frankly, I've always been of the opinion that Judea simply
does not pay its way. Because of the troublesome nature of the
inhabitants, we've always been forced to station more men
there than a province that size should require. And when you
double the garrisons, you double the taxes back home. The
money the Jews bring in hardly makes up the difference. And
they contribute no troops," he pointed out. "They refuse to
integrate themselves into our world. They are at odds with the
Samaritans in their midst, the Christians, and our own colonists."

"I quite agree," the emperor said. "For all that, Judea remains vital to our interests. The land is of strategic importance
to our frontiers. We cannot afford to lose it."

"We don't have to lose it," Quintus said. "We can take it
again with force. But there is another way. A better way, I
think."

Hadrian nodded for the centurion to continue.

"We haven't allowed the Jews their own king since Herod,
because the line proved too weak or too untrustworthy. But
this Bar Kokhba . . . You've got a man now who's strong, able
to unite his people—"

"But not all the people of Judea," Tinneus Rufus broke in.
"I have a letter from the leaders of the Christian communities
disallowing any sympathy or cooperation with the revolt.
They denounce the rebels most strongly and express fear that

they may suffer for refusing to join Bar Kokhba's army. And there is also the matter of our own settlers in the province, who have suffered grievously in this disturbance. Shall we desert them? You must realize, centurion, that Judea today is not the Judea of Herod.''

"It's a matter of precedent anyway," Publius Marcellus said now. "Come to terms with one ragged little province and where does that leave you with all the rest? Frankly, I'd be glad to see the Jews eliminated completely. I have no personal animosity, but politically and economically we would do better without them.''

Hadrian closed his eyes. "You miss the point," he said. "All of you. This rebellion, this war of Bar Cochebas, or whatever the fellow calls himself, represents more than a challenge to Rome. It is a challenge to all that we represent. It is the Jews' culture, their way of life, their *thinking* against all that man has achieved, guided by the Greeks and now brought to fruition through our strength and abilities." His eyes had opened as he spoke; they sought out the death mask of Antinous, which was ever near. The emperor extended his hand, touched the likeness of the drowned boy lovingly. "All that is great and beautiful the Jews would destroy," Hadrian said softly. "Well . . . I will destroy them.''

MARCELLUS QUINTUS was correct in suspecting that the man who led the Judeans in their stunning victories had good knowledge of the Roman army. For years Simeon had watched the peacetime exercises of Judea's military occupiers. Three times each month the garrisons spilled their infantry out on ten mile route marches. Simeon made it his business to tag along unseen. He'd noted how the rate of marching was purposely varied by the officers so as to give the troops practice in rapid advancement and retreat. He saw that a good deal of time was given over to open-order fighting, to reinforcing the front line, and to adopting formations that would repel ambushes. Dressed in his farmers' clothes, he'd watched the arms drills of the soldiers at Ein Gedi; he'd even helped set up the stakes and sods used as targets, silent when the soldiers spoke to him or called to him laughingly as "that stupid bull," all the while watching the practice, seeing how thrusts aimed at vital points were particularly encouraged. And later, when he

barked at his own training recruits—"At the left knee—point!
At the throat—jab!''—he was echoing the instructions of
some of Rome's most grizzled veterans.

Simeon had learned to recognize the phalanx formation:
eight deep, spear-throwers in the front, lancers in the rear. He
saw that the front ranks did not throw their spears but rather
used them to stab the horses of attacking cavalry, while the
lancers behind them hurled their weapons over the heads of
their comrades. And he knew that the *pilum*, or throwing
spear, and the *gladius*, or Spanish sword, were used only by
the legionaries, distinguishing them from the generally less
formidable auxiliaries, who used the *hasta*, or thrusting spear,
and the *spatha*, or long sword.

Experience revealed the method of the legions' advance. In
"safe country," the army marched in one long column with a
vanguard of scouts, light-armed troops and archers drawn
from the auxiliary cohorts; cavalry on the flank; allied troops,
baggage animals, and so on in the rear. The legionaries, the
hard core of Rome's formidable fighting machine, were always in the center of the column, where, protected by auxiliary infantry and cavalry, they had time to deploy. In difficult
terrain, however, and once the possibility of attacks by
Simeon's rebels became stronger, the order of march, Simeon
observed, was easily converted into an order of battle: generally a hollow square formation with troops divided into four
parallel columns. It was Mesha, in fact, who explained how
this formation could be transformed into the three lines of
defense known as the triple *acies*.

The young man appeared in camp one day quite unex-
pectedly. Simeon welcomed him heartily, saying he was in
need of a good secretary, as he had neither the time nor the patience to attend to the letters necessitated by the administrative
business of his new office. "There are problems I hadn't even
thought about," he confessed, running his hand through his
hair in a gesture that combined exhaustion with exasperation.
"Parcels of land to be given under contract . . . local officials
to be appointed, disputes to be settled, taxes to be set and collected, coins to be minted. . . . I've organized the country into
four major districts with a military as well as civil administration for each. Here, take a look at this map. Galilee. Samaria.
Judea. Ein Gedi. We're getting most of our supplies from the

South. But it's all paperwork and more paperwork. You don't know how glad I am to see you."

But Mesha had no intention of working as a scribe. "I can help you," he declared, ignoring the map. "I can help you in a way you've never dreamed."

Simeon sighed. "I need your pen, not your piety, Mesha. Or should I say, Rabbi Meir?" He smiled thinly. "I have all the prayers in the world, thanks to my uncle, the priest Eleazar. He is in constant touch with the Almighty, or so I am told."

"Simeon, listen to me—"

"If you've come about Jerusalem," was the brusque reply, "you are welcome to go there yourself, lay stone for the Temple, whatever. As you like. I will not be drawn into that business, as I hope I have made clear to everyone. I haven't the men, the time, or the inclination. Nor do I have any intention of setting up headquarters in Jerusalem. I won't be a sitting pigeon for anyone. Not even God. The key to our defense is mobility—something your rabbis don't seem to understand."

"I understand very well. I also know the war is not over. Rome will be back. With more men, more machines, and more determination to break us."

"You see that. Good."

"And I can help. I know the workings of the legions. I know the workings of the legionary's mind. I know how he thinks, how he is trained to think."

Simeon received this with an amused smile. "Your knowledge has fast become legend, Mesha, but no rabbi can tell me—"

The young man did not let him finish. "The *orbis*," he said. "It's a kind of half-square or circle formation used in retreat under fire. The baggage train is always left outside, abandoned if necessary. A good way to catch supplies."

The smile vanished.

"The *testudo*," Mesha continued. "Closely linked together, those in the front rank lock their shields together above their heads. It could be used in a retreat, but it is generally used in an advance, say, in the siege of a town or camp."

A thoughtful nod. "Go on."

"The officers. *Legati* are nearly always political appointments with little military experience. The tribunes are young but not always stupid. There are two kinds, anyway. The one is only in for a year before proceeding to the political *cursus honorum* of senators, but the other, *tribuni angusticlavi* —they've got a narrow stripe on their tunics—they aspire to the equestrian *cursus* and must hold two additional posts: commanding an auxiliary cohort or infantry unit and then a cavalry unit. They're eager, determined to make good, and often reckless. But it's the centurions you must beware of. They're the heart and soul of it. The key to the Roman military is the centurions as well as the disciplined obedience of the common soldiers. And they are very disciplined. Do you know what the penalty is for a cohort or legion which deserts or mutinies or is simply guilty of insubordination? *Decimatio.* Every tenth man steps forward to be beaten or stoned to death by his own comrades."

Simeon ran a finger over his mouth. "Well, it seems you do know something about the Roman army. Tell me, where does a rabbi learn this? Surely not in Akiva's school. Nor even with the one called Aher."

"My father . . ." A deep breath, and then at last it was out. "My father was a legionary. The Fifth. Macedonica. Both my parents were proselytes."

"I see." A soft whistle, then a friendly grin. "I wondered where you got that fine Roman nose."

A dark flush spread over the young man's face. "Few people know what I've told you. It isn't something I talk about."

Simeon shrugged. "Why not? Be proud. Always be proud of what you are."

The set of Mesha's features, together with the look in his eyes, revealed to Simeon a certain private struggle. But ben Kosiba had neither the time nor the inclination, as he'd said earlier regarding other matters, to help the rabbi work it out. So he merely said briefly, "Take it as God's will. You're right. I can use you."

BERURIA HAD COME to him, distraught, pale, nervously picking at her fingers. "I can't," she said finally. "I can't marry you. You must release me from our betrothal."

"What is it?" His hands went out to her arms to steady her.

"Don't touch me, please. When you touch me I can't think, I become confused. . . ."

He let his hands drop.

"That's it, you see. I can't change. I don't want to change. And I will, I know, if I become your wife. I'll be like my mother. Like Rachel. Like all women." She shook her head. "I can't. I won't."

"Beruria . . ."

"Let me go," she begged. "Release me from my vow. I've never asked anything from a man, but I ask you now . . . I must be free. I must be free."

He had not replied. He had simply walked away. The next morning when it became known that he would not be teaching his customary classes, that, according to the announcement made by Akiva, Rabbi Meir had been granted a leave of absence from the academy of B'nei Berak, she came again to him. "I did not mean for you to go," she said, concerned. "There is no reason for you to leave. You are greatly needed here."

"I thought my presence disturbed you."

"What I feel is less important than your duty to God."

"What you feel is all that is important," he shot back in a burst of anger he could no longer contain. "What people feel is all that really matters, Beruria. It's the only truth. The rest is garbage. The mind plays tricks, games—but what you feel inside, that's what counts, that's what's true." He threw his writing materials into the bundle of possessions he was packing and tied it all up. "Goodbye."

"Where are you going?" she asked, alarmed now. "Will you teach?"

"I'm through with teaching. I'm sick of words. I'm weary of ideas. Right now I need to touch, to move, to fight!"

"This isn't you," she said softly.

"Isn't it? Isn't this what you're afraid of? I'm a man, Beruria. Isn't that what frightens you?"

"No," she said shaking her head. "Not this violence in you. It was never that."

"It should have been that. You're right, there is violence in me. Generations of violence that all the prayers in the world can never wash clean."

"You frighten me now. I don't understand."

"You don't have to. Not anymore. I'll exorcise my demons alone, as I should have from the very beginning. With Simeon."

She grew pale at this. "You're going off to Simeon. . . ."

"Yes. Yes! It's where I belong."

"You're just saying that to make me . . . You know how I feel about my brother. And now you want this on my head as well," she accused. "Oh, Mesha! If anything happened to you . . . Mesha, please, not that!"

"What I do no longer concerns you, Beruria."

"You'll be killed! Mesha, please, don't do this. You know it's only to spite me."

"No. It isn't to spite you." His voice was calm now. "How could I dare believe someone like you could love someone like me?"

She opened her mouth, but no words came out. It was only after he'd gone that she could whisper to the empty room, "I do . . . I love you, Mesha. . . . I love you."

AND SO HE SAT in the dark now, somewhere in the hills outside Jerusalem, with no synagogue or school save God's own night, and thought about her and all the events that had led him to this moment.

EVEN AS Hadrian and his staff debated the proper course of action to take against the Jewish insurgents, determining finally to recall Julius Severus, Rome's ablest general, from Britain, similar arguments were taking place in Judea, as leaders of the Christian communities met in what was for them an unusual spirit of cooperation.

In the first half of the second century, the followers of Jesus were already divided into factions. There were the original believers: Judeans who still thought of themselves as Jews and were faithful to the laws of Torah while accepting the mission of Jesus as teacher, prophet, or even as a messianic figure. The rabbis called them *minim*, meaning "heretics," and sought to exclude them from synagogue service by inserting phrases in the daily prayers that adherents to the new faith could not utter in good conscience. Those Greeks, Romans, and others who had embraced the teaching of Paul, the "Apostle of the

Pagans,'' were called by the rabbis ''sectarians,'' which seemed to include Gnostics as well as Christians. The men of Jabneh were inclined to be less critical of Gentiles who believed in the Christ, seeing this turn to monotheism as at least a step upward from antique notions; but they had nothing but contempt for Jewish apostates, a condition which was echoed by the Gentile Christians.

''They use the Gospel according to Matthew only, and they persist in repudiating Paul,'' Quadranus of Sepphoris was heard to complain regarding several Ebionites who were sitting together in what appeared to be an isolated group. ''How can we trust them when they even refuse to give up circumcision?''

Aristedes of Neapolis nodded agreement. ''They deny the Lord was born of a virgin and the Holy Spirit—''

''Peace, peace,'' a man named Galen urged softly. ''We are not met today to berate the differences among us, but to decide how we must act regarding that which threatens us all, which is this war.''

''I am involved in no war with Rome,'' Quadranus declared. ''I have already informed the emperor, on behalf of our brethren in Sepphoris, that we have nothing in common with these rebel Jews, either politically or philosophically.''

''Tinneus Rufus has been likewise informed,'' Aristedes said. ''We have always cooperated with the governor, and there is no reason to deviate now.''

''There is every reason.'' A young man detached himself from the Ebionite group and stepped forward. ''Can we allow Jerusalem to be defiled, shrines to Venus and Zeus erected on the very places where Jesus walked, where he died? Can we allow the Law of Torah, the Law which he followed, to be cast into the dust?''

''We are not justified by observance of Torah,'' Quadranus said disdainfully, ''but through faith in Jesus Christ.''

'' 'Think not that I have come to abolish the Law, but to fulfill it,' '' the young man countered, quoting Matthew.

''Peace, peace,'' Galen said again.

''There can be no peace,'' Quadranus snapped, ''until these false brethren recognize the Lord's own truth. All the precepts of the Torah—observance of the Sabbath, circumcision, dietary laws, and so forth—were given by God to the Jews because of their sins, to soften their callous hearts. Genuinely righteous men have no need of any of that. After all," he said with a shrug, "the generations from Adam to Abraham were not circumcised. In any event, Christ has redeemed us and thus delivered us from the yoke of the Torah. So you see," he said to the young Ebionite, "there is no reason for a true Christian to war with Rome."

"But it was the Romans who crucified our Master," another of the Judeo-Christians protested. "It is Rome that persecutes us now! Let the Tiber overflow—let drought, earthquake, famine, or plague appear, and at once the cry is raised: 'Throw the Christians to the lions!' "

"The Jews crucified Jesus," Aristedes said deliberately. "And they are the ones at fault in the persecution of our Roman brethren. Can you doubt it? You know very well how they curse us in their synagogues."

"The *birkat ha-minim* is a benediction against all heretics," a voice said now. "It is directed impartially against 'slanderers,' 'informers,' and the 'kingdom of arrogance.' I should hate to think, Aristedes, that you or anyone here could be taking that personally."

The young Ebionite who had first stood up smiled at the newcomer. "Jacob . . ."

"The fact remains," Quadranus continued, "that it is more to our benefit to align ourselves with Rome than to maintain any kind of bond with a people for which no nation on earth does not feel scorn and contempt."

"I do not think the Jews are the recipients of 'scorn and contempt,' as you put it," the one called Jacob said thoughtfully. "Not at this moment, anyway. Not with an entire Roman legion eradicated by Bar Kokhba."

"Bar Kokhba! How do you even dare say that name? The 'Messiah'! Blasphemy!"

"He's right in that, Jacob," Galen said now. "No matter how some of us may feel about Rome and Hadrian, we cannot, as Christians, give our allegiance to a man who claims he is the Messiah. The promised Son was Jesus. For us there can be no other. There is only one Son of God, born of the virgin Mary—"

"You don't know what you're talking about," the young Ebionite burst in. "You don't even read Hebrew! You read the Greek texts, and they're all wrong! The word in Isaiah is *almah*—'young woman,' not 'virgin'!"

"Daniel, sshh." A pat on the shoulder, and the agitated Judeo-Christian was still. Jacob turned back to the others. "What has been decided?"

"We will not fight alongside the troops of Simeon ben Kosiba," Galen replied.

"He has declared that all who are not with him are against him," Jacob reminded the Christian.

"Yes, and I expect we shall be harassed for our position."

"If he has the time for it," Jacob said with a slight smile. "Somehow I believe the new administration has more to do than persecute us."

"Nevertheless," Quadranus said dramatically, "we must prepare ourselves for the martyrdom which no doubt we will suffer as a result of our pacifist stance."

Jacob stared at the man a moment. Then, as though replying to something he saw in Quadranus' eyes, he said quietly, "But you have not taken the road of peace. You plan to aid the Romans, as you have in the past, by whatever means you can. You are thinking ahead . . . to Jerusalem . . . to a new bishop of the city . . . one whom Hadrian would tolerate . . . a Christian who was never a Jew. . . ."

Quadranus, who had returned Jacob's stare like one hypnotized, flushed deeply.

Jacob turned to the others. "Who else would fight on the side of Caesar?"

"No one," Galen said. He looked around. "No one," he said again. "We are agreed to behave as our fathers did during the earlier war with Rome. We will stay outside the conflict."

"That may not be possible," Jacob said, with another look at Quadranus.

"Then you do think ben Kosiba will not tolerate our position."

"I think he will not tolerate spies and informers and saboteurs. If he has reason to believe we are supplying Hadrian with a fifth column, then, yes, I think he will be unmerciful toward us."

"It is not so, Jacob. The community as a whole will not commit itself to such action. We wish only to live in peace. You have spoken before with the rabbis. You must talk to them now. Tell them we will take no sides."

"Yes," Aristedes said suddenly. "You must find Simeon ben Kosiba and tell him as well. He will believe you. You will show him how you can heal wounds by the touch of your hands, and he will believe what you say.''

"He will believe what I say," Jacob told the man, "if I believe what I say."

Aristedes returned the level gaze. "Do you doubt Galen?" he asked deliberately.

"No," Jacob said after a pause. "I do not doubt Galen."

The meeting now dispersed. Quadranus and Aristedes watched the Ebionites depart, led by Jacob of Kefar Sakanya, the "miracle-worker" who spoke with rabbis. "We must not have further contact with those people," Quadranus said in a low tone. "So long as they cling to their old ways, the curse that lies upon the Jews lies upon us all. Do not draw near to those who maintain that their Torah is the same as yours," he admonished the others. "Christ has come. The tablets of Moses are broken."

"I DO NOT TRUST Quadranus," Daniel said as he and Jacob walked along the road. "He is forever plotting against one and all. He says it is for love of Christ, but it is only for himself."

Jacob nodded. "Perhaps, someday, through love of Christ he will see the error of his ways," he replied calmly.

"I doubt it. He seeks power, not peace. Oh, how I hate those who distort our Lord's mission for their own purpose! I could easily hate Quadranus as much as Rome!"

"You must keep such feelings from your heart. They eat at the body as well as the soul. They will sap your strength, and you must remain strong, Daniel. You have a wife and child now. Suzannah is still uncertain about many things. Your strength is her strength. And all strength rests upon the love that is within us."

The young man sighed. "I know you are right. But when I think how she must have suffered . . .''

"Our Lord suffered too, yet never stopped loving all mankind. Think of his words, as Matthew, whom you are so fond of quoting, tells us," Jacob said now with a smile. " 'Ye have heard that it hath been said, thou shalt love thy neighbor and hate thine enemy. But I say unto you, *Love your enemies.*' "

"Jacob, you're as bad as the others," Daniel reprimanded with a shake of his head. "The words 'and hate thine enemy' never appear in Torah—not in Hebrew and not even in the Greek texts."

"Then I am as bad as Matthew," Jacob replied with a laugh. "Well, I confess I've never found God in words. In dreams, yes, visions . . ."

"Is it true that you have actually seen Jesus? That your power to heal and to see men's thoughts comes from the Christ?"

"All power comes from God," Jacob said, and fell silent.

"Well," Daniel said, "you had better make use of all your powers when you see ben Kosiba. They say he can be very cruel."

"Do you really think Akiva ben Joseph would give his blessing to a cruel man?"

"Akiva was alone in proclaiming him Israel's Messiah. The people may have flocked to Bar Kokhba's banner, but the other rabbis have not."

Jacob smiled. "Akiva is worth all the others together. No," he said, growing thoughtful. "I have nothing to fear from Simeon ben Kosiba." He stared ahead, as though seeing something far in the distance. "It is not Bar Kokhba I need fear," he repeated, almost to himself.

2

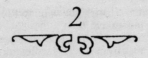

To JARA'S SURPRISE the world did not end when Simeon married the Parthian princess. It was true she lost her appetite for some weeks, seeming to exist in a state somewhere between sleep and waking, with not much energy for anything and with a rather constant ache not around her heart but around her stomach, as though she'd swallowed something broken and jagged. Meanwhile, the days were glorious: warm and bright, full of butterflies and birds whose airy flight and delicate song seemed to her unkind and callous. And while the rest of the country appeared for the most part intoxicated with their new-won freedom, celebrating the wedding of the *Nasi*, boasting of the prowess shown to Rome and indeed the world, Jara was quiet, her joy in Israel's triumph diminished by her own sense of loss.

She told herself the pain would go away. Nothing lasts forever, the Old One used to say. She found herself thinking more and more of the ancient woman who had raised her, remembering Arnon and Batya, and Sharona, and Kefar Katan, reliving all the old hurts, as though by reopening those wounds she might forget her new ones.

And then one day, quite simply, she was all right. Maybe it was the smell of the Sabbath bread baking in the clay oven, or the smile Akiva gave her. Or maybe it was the sudden presence of Andreas in B'nei Berak, his mischievous eyes and teasing smile a not unwelcome tonic. She still didn't like or trust him—and she was sure she never would—but she had to admit he was interesting. And perhaps he would cheer up Beruria, whose lips seemed to have grown thinner, her back straighter, and her manner sterner since the departure of Rabbi Meir.

"You're looking as beautiful as ever," Andreas commented. His dark eyes traveled the length of Jara's body, then returned to her face. "No scars showing," he said with his crooked smile.

She turned red. "I wish you wouldn't look at me that way. You make me feel naked."

He grinned now. "Would that you were, would that you were. . . ."

"One of these days I'm going to slap you."

"Good."

Her eyebrows went up.

"For the slap to give you pleasure," he explained, "what comes before must give me pleasure."

"You are really vile."

"So you keep telling me. And here I thought all my heroics for God and Simeon would win your admiration."

"What heroics? So far as I can tell, all you've done is grow a beard."

Akiva's appearance did not permit a reply, but as Andreas left with the rabbi, he turned back a moment and winked at Jara. She sniffed contemptuously, but the fact was she felt revitalized by their encounter and did not mind when they met again.

"I've got something for you," Andreas told her later, after dinner.

"Another present from the Parthian?" The mare had not been from Simeon after all; it was a gift from the exilarch's son, brother of the girl ben Kosiba had married. He had sent other tokens: a vial of perfume; a comb for her hair encrusted with irregular pearls; a length of silken fabric shot with threads of gold.

He smiled. "Not this time, though I'm sure if Rami knew I was seeing you, he would have burdened me with some heavy proof of love."

She lowered her eyes. "I don't know what he expects of me."

"Rami wants you for his bride."

"But I'm not a princess."

"Doesn't matter. And anyway, he's already got a royal wife or two. Don't look so shocked. There's nothing in Torah against a man having more than one wife. The rabbis here frown on the custom, but our Oriental cousins see nothing wrong in it."

"But . . . but he's just a child!"

"Well, Rami is old enough to kill his share of legionaries and father a few baby exilarchs. You ought to consider it," he advised her. "The *Resh ha-Galut* is rich as Croesus. Besides, you'd be right in the bosom of Simeon's family." He stopped. The sudden pain in her eyes made him regret his last remark.

"You said you had something for me." Her voice was cold.

"Yes." He gave her a small sack whose jingling contents gave evidence of the coins inside, and a letter. "Can you read?"

"Of course I can read," she snapped. But her eyes stayed so long on the parchment that he had begun to wonder if she could indeed decipher the message, when finally she looked up, obviously disturbed. She stared at Andreas a moment, then handed him the letter.

" 'I, Jara, daughter of Benjamin,' " he read, " 'have received from my guardian Simeon, son of Kosiba, the sum of twenty denarii from the first of Tammuz until the thirtieth of Elul, year two of the Freedom of Israel, which are three whole months. Babeli, son of Menahem, has written this.' " He looked up. "You are to sign this, I suppose, for me to return to Simeon. What's wrong? Isn't it enough? It's a very generous sum, seems to me."

She turned on him in a fury. "How dare he appoint himself my guardian? He's nothing to me, nothing! He thinks because he is *Nasi* he can do this? He is nothing, I tell you! Nothing! While his fathers were tending goats, mine were pouring oil upon the Temple altar! How dare he send money to me! Let Simeon ben Kosiba return the land and estates of Judea to its rightful owners, and we shall see who has money to send to others!"

He stared at her with growing interest.

"My guardian, is he? We shall see about that! Why is he doing this?" she asked Andreas tearfully, her anger beginning to merge with other emotions. "Why is he doing this to me?"

"I would suppose to facilitate your marriage to Rami. He is protecting you, Jara, in more ways than one."

"I don't need his protection. I don't want it! And I'm not marrying that boy! Why are people forever marrying me off? Why can't they leave me alone as they do Beruria? Nobody makes decisions for her."

"You are a very different sort from Beruria," Andreas replied. "And Beruria is the exception, not the rule. There are many clever, learned women, but there is only one Beruria."

Jara sighed. "In one way at least I am becoming like her," she said grimly.

"How so?"

"I think I am beginning to hate all men."

He laughed. "Now that would be a pity."

"Would it? Why?"

"Because if ever any female was made to be held and kissed, it is you, Jara." He seemed to shrug slightly, and again there was that crooked half-smile. "Some women are just not meant to be virgins."

"Oh," she said through clenched teeth. "I do hate you!"

"Sorry. I thought you were one of those rare people who appreciate honesty."

"Honesty! I doubt you know the meaning of the word. Any more than the one you serve," she added bitterly. "Whoever that may be."

"Rome, or Bar Kokhba," he said thoughtfully. "You still are not certain which side I am for."

"Whatever I may feel for Simeon ben Kosiba," she replied evenly, "I have less love for spies and traitors, and Romanized Jews who may be either or both those things."

"I see." He stood up. "You know, for one whose back is up at the merest hint of some imagined insult, you're damn quick to toss out injury to others. It's a bad habit. One I am beginning to find less and less amusing." He nodded in the direction of Simeon's letter, which was lying beside the untouched pouch. "If you don't want Simeon's money or protection, I suggest you tell him so yourself. He's in Jaffa." He paused at the door. "I hate unfinished business."

HE WAS GONE the next morning. Despite her hostility, Jara was sorry to see him leave. There was something exciting about Andreas; a feeling of danger hovered about him that was not like the danger one felt with the soldiers, but rather . . . well, what was it? Jara was not sure. She knew she didn't like him (how could she?), and yet she almost hoped the figure coming over the hill was the young man returned.

It wasn't. The man who came up to her was approaching

fifty, not thirty, his long, fine hair a pale shade of brown inter-mixed with white. His eyes were light, but whether blue or green or gray she could not tell. He leaned on his traveler's staff, catching his breath a bit, and smiled.

Jara nodded politely. "*Shalom*."

"*Shalom*. Peace unto you from God and our Lord Jesus Christ."

Her eyes widened, but she said nothing.

"This is the house of Akiva ben Joseph, is it not?"

Again she nodded, remaining silent.

"Is the rabbi at home? I must speak with him."

Still she did not reply.

"Are you afraid to talk to me?" Jacob of Kefar Sakanya asked. "Are you forbidden to converse with Christians?"

"No," she said slowly, staring into his eyes. "I am just wondering what I should say to you. I am trying to decide if you mean harm to anyone here."

"And what have you decided?"

"Akiva is not at the academy," she said after another pause. "He is at Lod, I think. In truth, I do not know. He may be at Lod, or elsewhere. But he is not here."

Jacob nodded. "May I have something to drink?"

"Yes. Of course."

Tobita was less generous. "I know who you are," she said to the stranger. "If you try to work any of your magic in my kitchen, you will find yourself on the wrong end of my pots. I know all the ways to ward off the evil eye, so none of your nonsense. This house is blessed. Beware."

"What are you going on about?" Jara whispered to the woman.

"He utters charms over wounds," Tobita said in a loud voice. He is a healer, or so the *minim* say. A sorcerer, more likely, and come to do no good."

Jara stared at the Christian with open curiosity. He seemed gently amused by Tobita's outburst. "Is it true?" Jara asked. "Can you heal the sick with magic?"

"Only God works magic."

"But can you really work cures?"

"I am sometimes an instrument by which men are healed."

She brought a pitcher of cold milk to him. "My father was a physician." She sat down beside him. "Tell me how you do it."

"Don't talk to him," Tobita warned. "He will fill your head with rubbish. Don't look into his eyes, or he will make you do whatever he wants."

This admonition only made Jara even more curious, and she did in fact stare deeply at the man. Having been called a witch so often in her life, she was eager now to see what the devil was really like.

Jacob was amused.

Fearful now of the girl's interest in the "Christian magician," Tobita left the room to seek a rabbi. Jara hardly noticed her departure.

"What do you see?" Jacob asked.

Jara continued to stare into his eyes. "I know you from somewhere," she said slowly.

Jacob nodded. "Perhaps."

"Can you really heal the sick?"

"Why do you ask? Is there someone you wish me to aid?"

"Oh, no! Besides, you would never be allowed. The laying on of hands is forbidden."

He appeared to grow sad at this.

"Why do you want to see Akiva?"

"I must get a message to Simeon ben Kosiba."

"Why don't you take it to Simeon, then?"

"He is hard to find. First he is in one place, then another. And I do not know if I would be welcome."

"Bar Kokhba talks to all men."

"Since the war there is little love for those of my belief."

"Because you work for our enemies. The Romans are always boasting of their Christian informers."

"There are Samaritan spies, and Greek spies, and spies who are Jews as well. The acts of a few men should not condemn a whole community."

"Your community, as you put it, does not seem to care much for freedom."

Before he could reply, Tobita burst into the room with Simon bar Yohai at her side. "What do you want here?" the rabbi asked brusquely.

"He wants to see the *Nasi*," Jara explained. She turned back to Jacob. "I'll take you to him."

"No," bar Yohai said.

But she had already made up her mind to go to Jaffa, as much for her own sake as for the Christian's.

* * *

THEY FOLLOWED the sun to the sea. Despite the urgency of his mission—and Jara felt it must be urgent for the man to go where he would be at the very best unwelcome—Jacob of Kefar Sakanya was in no hurry. He seemed to enjoy the flat semitropical plain, its species of plants and trees, its warm sun, and the scent of ocean that grew stronger as they approached Jaffa.

It was one of the oldest cities in the world. Built on a hill jutting out slightly from the coastline and overlooking the open sea, the port town had been the site where Jonah, unwilling to fulfill his mission to Nineveh, had boarded the ship for Tarshish. It was among the Canaanite cities conquered in 1469 B.C.E. by Thutmosis III, who, like Ali Baba, took the town by cunning, smuggling his soldiers into its fort in baskets. The rock upon which Andromeda was bound was at Jaffa, and it was here that Peter heard the voice calling him to convert pagans to Christianity.

In the earlier war with Rome, the city had been destroyed, but it was rebuilt during the reign of Vespasian. The guard from the Tenth Legion was gone now. The city had always been a busy, noisy place with certain distinct neighborhoods. The refugees from Alexandria and Cyrenaica, who had been among the first to join Bar Kokhba's troops, clearly predominated, their accented tongue loudly evident in the market. The Christian quarter was quiet, many of its inhabitants having fled with the legionaries.

Jacob led the way to the fortress where presumably the *Nasi* would be headquartered. He was less a stranger to the city than Jara. She walked beside him, studying him curiously now and then. He had been studying her as well, she knew. She did not find his gaze disconcerting; and while she continued to wonder about his healing powers, she refrained from questioning him about them during their journey, most of which had been spent thinking about Simeon.

Why hadn't he been open with her, told her directly what must be before she'd had to learn the truth from others? The deed itself, his marriage to another, could be no greater betrayal than the way he had avoided her at Kobi. What had he been afraid of? she wondered even now as she had so many times. What had Simeon thought she would do? He had been the one to speak of marriage. She'd never asked for it. It hadn't mattered. Could words spoken before a God neither of them loved bring them any closer together than they had been?

I used to wake sometimes at night knowing you were thinking of me. . . . I could feel the rough wool of your cloak under my cheek and smell out over the hot land and it would come to me, the smell of blood and sweat and the sound of arrows flying through the air. . . . The earth beneath my feet trembled with the weight of stones flung and spoke to me of the battle you were fighting. . . .

I was with you. And you knew it. At least I thought you knew it. Just as I have always known when you were thinking about me. . . .

"The people in B'nei Berak are angry with you for coming with me," Jacob said.

"What? Oh . . ." Jara shrugged.

"Not so much because it is unseemly for a young woman to go off alone with a stranger," he went on, "as because I am what I am."

"It is both, I should think," she answered realistically.

"The displeasure of the community does not bother you?"

"It is nothing new, although I haven't been faced with it for a very long time."

"You are not afraid to be with me?"

"No."

"You are not afraid of a Christian?"

Surprise. "No."

"You are not afraid of men?"

Scorn this time. "No."

"Can it be because you have faith in me, faith in the providence of God, or faith in that little knife you wear at your waist?"

She looked up in surprise. "How did you—"

"I would not harm you," he assured her.

"I know that."

"How do you know?"

"Just a feeling I have. The same feeling that tells me you are not an enemy—except to the synagogue, and that doesn't much bother me. That's why I decided to bring you to Simeon."

He frowned. "I am not Torah's enemy."

She laughed. "Aren't you?"

"I am a Jew."

"No, you're not."

"I am. So was Jesus."

She shrugged again, as if to say she didn't much care one way or the other.

"I am sorry if by helping me you bring trouble upon yourself," Jacob said now, "but I do thank you for it."

She stared at him, again wondering why he seemed so familiar to her.

Getting to see the *Nasi* proved to be no simple matter. At first the armed guards were reluctant to admit Bar Kokhba was in Jaffa, but when Jara produced the letter proving Simeon was her guardian, they ushered her and Jacob into the fortress. The pair sat down to wait. There was a line of petitioners in the hallway, arguing among themselves over whose turn it was and the relative merits of their cases. Jara was oblivious to them. For the moment, too, she had forgotten even Simeon. The building brought back memories of the palace in Tiberias and what she had encountered there. Her fists began to close.

Jacob saw the girl's body stiffen. Her pupils had become dilated, a line of sweat breaking out on her upper lip. He touched her hand. She was trembling.

As the Christian healer's hand covered her own, Jara started, like an animal surprised. Then she felt warmth return to her fingers; they opened. Her shoulders relaxed.

"What were you thinking?" Jacob asked softly.

"I was remembering . . . another palace. A hallway like this one. Soldiers . . ." She closed her eyes, opened them, a deep breath escaping her lips. "Strange," she murmured, staring at one of the guards. "I know he is a Jew. And yet I find myself afraid. As if . . . as if he were not my own kind."

"All the armies of the world have but one face," Jacob said. "But the soldiers of peace shall be blessed."

She stared at him. His hand had been so warm, like fire without flame, drawing the fear from her, sucking out the ugly memories, burning them away. She felt drained, like one from whom a fever has fled. She looked at Jacob's hands.

Obodas was standing before her. "Come," he said.

She rose to her feet slowly, looking back at the Christian, who sat quietly. Jacob nodded for her to leave, the bob of his head seeming to signify that he would be all right without her.

Jara nodded too and followed the Nabatean down the hall.

*   *   *

AT FIRST SIGHT of him all else was forgotten. Was it truly nearly a year since she'd last laid eyes on him? Was it possible she had managed to survive, to live each day in all that time without once seeing him, touching him?

He moved toward her with that purposeful stride she remembered so well, the powerful arms and shoulders her bulwark against the hostile world; then suddenly he stopped.

She had wanted him to think she felt nothing in his presence, but she only succeeded in appearing defiant. For Simeon, however, that show of pride was more touching than any tears or trembling lips. He ached to take her in his arms.

They stood there, stiff, still, the air between them like a wall; while at their feet the shadows of man and woman merged, as if their souls had fled their wooden bodies to touch as flesh could not.

He had the letter in his hand. She held out the pouch of shekels and very deliberately dropped it on the floor. His face darkened. "You're being foolish."

"I don't want your money."

"I will not have you be a charity case. As your guardian—"

"You are not my guardian!"

"As your guardian," he continued after a pause, "I intend to see you are well provided for."

"You are not my guardian," she said again, taking a step toward him, her chin raised belligerently.

"Aren't I?" he answered huskily. "Who've you got, then, Jara? Who have you got but me?"

"Akiva. Tobita. Beruria. Samson—"

"None of them knows you as I do. No one knows how you think, how you feel, the way I do. I should never have let you go. All these months—it's as if some part of me was missing. I didn't realize what it was until now, seeing you again." He turned away, unwilling for her to see the emotion he could not keep from his eyes. "You're not going back to Akiva," he said brusquely. "You're staying with me."

Her heart soared, but she forced herself to inquire coolly, "As what?"

He busied himself with the papers on his desk. "As my ward, of course. As a member of my family."

"Your family?" She let out a laugh. "What do you want me to do, Simeon? Play handmaid to your wife during the day and take care of you at night? You're mad."

His face became dark with anger again. "Don't talk like that. That is no way for you to talk."

"I talk plainly, Simeon ben Kosiba. As you once did. I don't lie. Not to myself or anyone else."

"I'm not lying to you. I want to take care of you. I intend to see that you are taken care of whether you agree or not."

"You have no right—"

"I have the right and the power. I am *Nasi* of all Israel. I can give you land, money—or I can have you thrown in jail. Do you understand?" He spoke deliberately. "I am the law, Jara. I am the government."

"And I suppose now you also believe you are the Messiah," she said disgustedly.

"I've done as much as any man can against the most powerful empire in the world," he reminded her.

She sighed. "Yes, you have." Slowly she raised her eyes to his. "Whatever else . . . I thank you for that."

He started to put out his hand to her, then stopped himself. "I don't want your thanks. I just want you to be happy."

She turned away now, for the tears would come after all. "I am happy," she whispered. "We are free. We are Israel. That's all that matters, isn't it?"

He did not reply. When at last she could turn and look at him again, he was gone.

Obodas came into the room. Jara stared at the Nabatean blankly, tears starting up in her eyes again. "I love him," she said helplessly. "I love him."

HE LEFT JAFFA that very day. Jara rode with Obodas in a chariot taken from the Romans. Despite her show of defiance, she did not protest at being taken along. The fact was she did not want to be parted from Simeon again, and as much as she dreaded seeing him with his wife, it was somehow better than not seeing him at all. This feeling she kept hidden, and when Simeon rode back from the front of the line to see how she fared, she turned away and sulked like a captive.

They camped for the night. Jara sat close to Obodas, listening as he played his flute, thinking of all the other times she had heard those melodies and how the music was so seductive and yet so sad. Simeon appeared to have vanished, to have disappeared into the very night. She did not recognize the two men sitting on the other side of the fire, but they did not seem to find her presence odd. She wondered if everything Simeon did now, every order and command, was accepted without question. Did these two really believe Bar Kokhba was sent to them by God?

They entered Jericho the next day. During the earlier war with Rome, Vespasian had wintered there, setting up a camp whose garrison massacred nearby Gerasa, sojourning from this base to the Dead Sea, where he had prisoners with their hands tied behind them thrown into the water to see if they would float.

The warmth of Jericho's air and its abundant waters had long attracted settlers. It was one of civilization's oldest settlements, older even than Jaffa. In the time of Herod wealthy Jerusalemites built villas on the oasis, where they might escape from the wind and occasional snow of David's city. Some of these estates had survived the war with Rome. It was to one such place that Jara was now delivered.

The furnishings were princely and exotic: trappings of Babylonian embroidery, intricately carved wood, and hammered metal. Incense holders of gold and silver filigree were everywhere, their perfume mingling with the smell of balsam outside, heavy in the sultry air.

"She must have brought half of Parthia with her," a voice said.

Jara spun around. Obodas had disappeared. Andreas stood there.

"Well, what do you think?"

"It's very grand," Jara said, looking around. She smiled. "Pretty."

"Yes, a woman would like it. A bit ornate for my taste, but it does have a certain character."

"Does Simeon live here?"

"Well, his wife does. Hey! Wait! Come back!"

But she was already out the door.

Andreas caught her by the arm. "Where do you think you're going?"

"Far away from here." She blinked; the sun was strong.

"You can't just go wandering around."

"I'm not going to wander. I'm going back to Akiva."

"I'm surprised you came here in the first place."

"I didn't have much choice."

"Ah, I see. Your 'guardian's' command."

"The *Nasi*'s command." She looked around, trying to get her bearings. "But this is too much," she muttered. "I will not stay in the same house with—with—"

"Her name is Sarai. She's small, dark, pretty in a childish way. Doesn't say much, but then she's a female, and females aren't supposed to talk. She's only twelve, Jara."

She blinked again.

"You're hesitating."

"No. I'm getting out of here. Will you take me to B'nei Berak?"

There was that crooked half-smile. "Do you really want me to?"

Before she could reply, several women had come up to her; they whisked her back into the house. "Wh-What are they doing?" she called out to Andreas as they bustled her off.

He laughed. "Wait and see. You may even like it."

SHE WAS BATHED, perfumed, and wrapped in an improvised toga of white linen. The silken robes she had been offered lay in a heap on the pallet. She had pushed the maidservants out the door and twice ignored the summons for her appearance. Now Simeon stood in the room. He seemed oblivious to her naked shoulders, unmoved by her shining hair and glowing skin. "Why aren't you dressed?" he wanted to know.

"I want my own clothes."

He turned to the servant huddled behind him. "Where are her clothes?"

The woman stammered that they had been washed but were not yet dry.

"Wear those," he said pointing to the colorful puddle on her bed. "They're good enough, I imagine."

"No."

"You're acting like a child," he said flatly. "Get dressed and get out there. Rami is waiting."

The mention of the young Parthian put her in a rage. Andreas was right. Simeon was planning to marry her off. "Why don't you just pull me out like this?" She purposely let the wrap slip lower until one breast was nearly exposed. "As King Ahasuerus did to Vashti—since it seems you have become a Persian tyrant."

His jaw tightened. "What do you mean by that?"

"Is that what we fought for? Palaces, dresses of silk, royal weddings? Jerusalem is still in ruins. The people cry out for the Temple to be restored. And there is no peace agreement with Rome. And you sit here like some Oriental monarch disposing of me as if—as if—'' She could not go on.

He stared at her, then, without saying anything, turned and left the room.

''OBODAS, WHAT HAPPENED to the Christian?''

They were on the road again. After Simeon left, there were no further summonses for her presence, and she spent the night alone, dining in her room without once seeing Simeon's wife. In the morning, however, she caught a glimpse of a small creature, heavily veiled, whose shy glance reminded her of Rami. The young Parthian rode ahead now, obviously as much at ease on the back of his horse as others were on foot. Every now and then he altered the animal's gait, or did stunts that evoked the admiration of the men in the company and were ovbiously meant to win Jara's attention. She smiled wanly at the boy. Simeon had vanished again; Andreas was also absent. She had no idea where she was being taken. Suddenly she remembered the ''healer'' who had gone with her to Jaffa.

''What did he want? He never did say.''

The Nabatean looked surprised, as if only now recalling the Christian.

''His name was Jacob, I think,'' Jara persisted.

''I don't know. I will try to find out.''

THE CITY OF BETAR stood on the heights of a mountain approximately seven miles southwest of Jerusalem. It was a walled city with a great fortress and bounded by the Sorek Valley on the east, north, and west. A better place of defense would be hard to find, and it was not difficult to see why Bar Kokhba preferred it to nearby Jerusalem.

It was well populated, with many schools and synagogues. The northern half of the spur on which the city was located was a kind of garden suburb whose residents, in the days when the Temple stood, had derived their livelihood from the sale of their produce in Jerusalem's famed markets. The fertile fields, watered by the spring that flowed from a rock southeast of the spur and was Betar's main source of water, were as green as they had ever been and a source of delight to all who saw them.

The place fairly glowed with prosperity and contentment. The marketplace was rich with foodstuffs. Baskets overflowed with grapes, purple and green, each one big as a man's thumb. Scarlet and yellow flowers peeked out from courtyard gates. In the doorway of one house, a little girl sat on her mother's lap, the woman humming as she braided the child's hair. From another window came the measured sound of students reciting the alphabet, and from yet another opening the voices of men in prayer.

Men and women going about their daily business, children playing and studying, stalls brimming with fruits and vegetables more fragrant and beautiful than any perfumer or jeweler's ware . . .

What a wonderful place to be, Jara thought. The air was clear, the streets were clean, and the people . . . the people looked happy, she thought. And proud. Not vainly so, but as if they knew they had hold of something precious.

This is the face of freedom, she thought. *This is what it looks like*. And she knew that what they had fought for was real and worth whatever it cost. And she thought of Simeon and wished she had not said to him the things she'd said.

But her benevolent mood vanished when she learned that Jacob of Kefar Sakanya was being kept in chains.

"I brought him to Jaffa," she told Obodas, horrified. "I said Simeon would hear him, that he would not harm him."

"He works for Rome," the Nabatean replied.

"I don't believe it. They just say that because he is a Christian."

Obodas shook his head. "It was a Christian who pointed him out. One of your people who turned to the Christ to make his wife happy but has since divorced her and returned to the synagogue."

She couldn't help laughing. "And Simeon believes him?"

"It would appear so."

"Has Simeon met the Christian? Has he talked to him at all?"

"No. But this man is well known. Many fear him. They say he can bewitch animals and snakes."

"Pooh to that!" But his words made her remember something. She knew now why Jacob had seemed familiar to her. "He's not evil," she said, "and I think Simeon should at least hear whatever he has to say. Jacob knew he might be imprisoned for trying to see Bar Kokhba," she said suddenly. "It was brave of him to try, and I am at least partly responsible for his predicament now. I've got to help him, Obodas. And you must help me."

IT WAS A MEASURE of his regard for her that Simeon had the Christian brought to Betar.

He did not look mistreated, and she was thankful for that.

"I'm sorry," Jara said. "Truly, I am."

"It was not your doing that imprisoned me," Jacob said. "And it was your word that set me free. You need offer no apology. I owe you my thanks."

She smiled. "I know now where I have seen you. It was by the waters of the Jordan. I was escaping the soldiers. A lion came out of the brush. I stopped, waited. . . . I dared not move. Then I saw you. You said something, too softly for me to hear. The beast looked at you, and then disappeared back among the trees. Still, I waited. I closed my eyes, I think. When I opened them you were gone. I thought perhaps it was a dream . . . You . . . the lion. But I could see the animal's tracks on the ground. His scent lingered in the air. There was no trace of any man. Yet I know it was you."

"I saw a boy stumbling through the brush," Jacob wondered.

She grinned now. "That was me."

"How can that be?" He was genuinely confused.

And so she told him how she had been taken to the commander's palace and there killed the man and fled from the place. When she finished he said, "You must pray to be forgiven."

She was astonished. "For what?"

"You have taken a life."

She could only stare at him.

"In Christ all our sins are absolved," he went on. He spoke softly, with no hint of rancor, only a kind of sweet and grave certainty. "You must come to Christ, Jara, and you will be forgiven."

She continued to stare at him; but whereas before that deep and gentle gaze had drawn her to him, now she faced him with the inscrutable expression others found so disconcerting. The wall had gone up.

Jacob was not put off. "You may have the eyes of a cat," he said, "but your heart is human. I know you suffer from the guilt of murder. I saw your torment in Jaffa."

"Florus Valerens deserved to die," she said flatly.

" 'Justice is mine, sayeth the Lord.' "

"Don't make me laugh."

She turned away, then suddenly whirled back to face him again. She was breathing quickly now, her teeth bared slightly. "Sometimes I see his face . . . the look in his eyes when the knife went into him, the blood spurting from the wound . . . the smell of that room. . . . But I'm not sorry Valerens is dead. I'm not sorry I killed him. I'm only sorry I didn't do it sooner, before he touched me."

"Because the act of fornication was odious to you?"

"No," she said deliberately. "Because I like it."

Again his gaze sought to draw her out, to draw her near, but she resisted. He who had always been able to discern truth from falsehood could not tell now if the girl had spoken to shock him or confessed her innermost feelings. The green-gold eyes were like stones, and Jacob saw in them a kindred power. Her resistance was as strong as his faith. Only time would tell which one of them would prevail.

"I HAVE HAD WORD from Akiva," Simeon ben Kosiba said. "He is concerned about your whereabouts and well-being. All of B'nei Berak buzzes with rumor."

"What am I supposed to have done now?" Jara wanted to know.

"Did you run off with the Christian?"

"I was bringing him to you," she explained with some exasperation. "Or tried to at any rate. Your men locked him up in Jaffa."

"I locked him up in Jaffa. I."

"Then you're as stupid as those around you."

"Watch it, Jara," he warned.

"What are you going to do, kill me? Lock me up too? Wouldn't that interfere with your plans for a strong Parthian alliance?"

"Don't think so highly of yourself. With that sharp tongue, any arrangement that includes you would probably set the exilarch on my back along with everyone else."

"Everyone else?"

"The rabbis are disenchanted with me," he said wryly. "They don't seem to care that for the first time in a hundred generations we are our own masters, that the land of Israel is once more owned by the people of Israel. All they seem to care about is seeing Jerusalem rebuilt. And a new Temple." He sighed. "How I wish the Temple was rebuilt, just so Tarfon and ben Torta and the rest would go and fight with the priests —which you can be sure they'll do—and leave me alone!"

They exchanged sympathetic glances. For a moment it was like old times, the two of them against the world. Another moment and he would reach for her, draw her roughly into his arms, bury his face in the tawny curls on her shoulder. The way she'd looked a Jericho, wrapped in nothing but a length of gauzy linen, her skin still wet from bathing and the smell of flowers coming from her . . . If only that damn servant hadn't been there. . . .

Simeon looked away. "What is between you and the Christian?" he asked brusquely.

"Nothing," Jara replied, startled by the question. She recalled Jacob's words to her, his talk of "guilt" and "murder" and "Christ." "Nothing," she said again, tightly.

"You went with him."

"I told you—"

"Only a *zonah*—a whore—would go off with a stranger. But this man is no stranger to us. He is a Christian. Worse, he is one of those who follow Jesus but still claim to be Jews. They call themselves Ebionites, or Nazarenes, or Elchasites— and while they quarrel among themselves and with the sectarians, they are one when it comes to you and me."

"He is not an informer—"

"I didn't say that. These people will do anything and everything they can to make you one of them. They will turn your head backward and forward and upside-down until you don't know who you are. Jacob of Kefar Sakanya has more power than most to do this. He can bend people to his will. I don't want that to happen to you."

"What makes you think it can?"

"Because you're angry. With me. With a lot of things. With Akiva too, maybe."

"What makes you think I like Jacob of Kefar Sakanya any better?"

"Do you?"

There was no answer, and there was no way he could read her eyes.

"You're right," he said, returning to the brusque, impersonal voice of Bar Kokhba. "The man is not an informer. He came to tell me the *minim* have agreed not to work against us. On the other hand, they cannot in good conscience accept conscription into our army. That is not considered working against us, I suppose," he added wryly. "So I think I'll keep our friend Jacob with me a while to see if his word is good. Meanwhile, I have informed Akiva that you are here, that I have assumed your guardianship and will soon arrange a befitting betrothal. Jericho was a mistake," he conceded. "But I thought it would give you and Rami a chance to become acquainted. And . . . my wife . . . is very lonely," he added lamely. He looked away. "She is with child. . . ."

The words hung heavy in the air.

He cleared his throat. "You will remain in Betar. And you will keep away from the Christian. For your own protection—"

"Don't tell me what to do." She had risen and was facing him squarely. "You have no right. Do you understand? You have no right to tell me anything."

"Jara . . ."

"I will stay in Betar because Betar pleases me. And if I want to talk to the Christian, then I will talk to the Christian. And yes, I will talk to the Parthian boy too. Why not? At least I can make the *Nasi* happy on that account."

But for some reason that did not make him happy.

"Oh yes," she said softly, studying his expression with some satisfaction. "Do you remember what I told you once? Well, you will beg, Simeon. . . . Oh, yes! You will beg. . . ."

THE STALLION was restless, kicking pebbles with its right hind leg, its sleek head now held high, now lowered. Suddenly it rose up, pawing the air, sending the curious onlookers scurrying. Shouts of alarm and warnings added to the animal's confusion. The tether rope strained, but just when it seemed the animal would break loose and set off on a wild gallop through the marketplace, Andreas appeared, pushing his way through the crowd. He made his way up to the horse, now dodging the kicking legs, now whistling softly. Suddenly he leaped up and caught hold of the bridle. This firmly in hand, he maneuvered the stallion around so that the sun was in its eyes. Stunned by the light, the animal ceased all motion. Andreas then proceeded to stroke its neck, all the while speaking softly until finally the stallion was docile again. Still holding firmly to the bridle, Andreas called for someone to untie the rope. This done, he mounted the horse and rode away from the awed spectators. Coming upon Jara, who had watched the entire incident with great interest, he pulled the horse up, leaned casually over its neck, and said without benefit of greeting, "So you have decided to remain with Simeon after all."

She flushed. Why did he always make her hate him whenever she almost decided he wasn't so bad as she'd thought? How she'd like to wipe that horrible, knowing smile from his face! "You shouldn't bring that animal to a public place," she said sternly. "People could have been hurt."

He looked around unperturbed. "Well, it would have been their own fault for taunting the poor beast," he said calmly. "You'd think they'd never seen a horse before."

"Horses are for the rich," she said icily. "And for Romans."

"*Pingg!*" he exclaimed, indicating the flight of an arrow that had found its mark. The lopsided smile broadened.

Disgusted, she started to walk away. Horse and rider followed.

"Horses are for Parthians too," he teased, riding alongside her now. "Have you thought about becoming Rami's princess? Or are you determined to get Simeon back?"

She was silent a moment. "His wife is with child."

"Ah! I didn't know. Well, that should make him very happy. It would make any man happy, I suppose. The exilarch will be pleased," he added. "Don't worry, Jara." There was that crooked half-smile again. "Little Sarai's pregnancy won't lessen your attractiveness to Simeon. It will probably enhance it."

"He doesn't even see me," she murmured, thinking of Jericho and Simeon's impervious manner. She had stood before him practically naked and he'd not even so much as blinked. In Betar all he'd done was rail at her. There had been a moment when she thought . . . but his hands had never left his side. "He looks at me but doesn't see me."

"Oh, Simeon sees you, all right! A man would have to be blind not to. Even the Christian, I'll wager, finds you disturbing to his prayers."

She looked up in surprise.

"Poor Jacob. I can see him now, shivering with the horror of his own lust, beseeching Jesus to deliver him from the sins of Lilith."

"You're really vile. He's not like that at all. Even if he does carry on a bit," she added, thinking of the Christian's entreaties. "Anyway, how do you know about him?" she asked curiously.

"There's very little I don't know, Jara."

"Oh, you're so smug! You think you've got everyone fooled—well, not me!"

With something like an oath, he dismounted and caught her by the arm. "Just what does that mean? You think because I can see ahead to the ultimate tragedy of this venture—this pathetic war of Bar Kokhba—that I am capable of betraying my own people?"

"Pathetic?" She seized on the word. "How dare you say that! You're the one who's pathetic, with your fine Roman manners and ways, wrestling with Samson as if you were in the arena, riding horses like some fancy centurion! You don't belong here. You never will."

"That may be true," he admitted quietly. "The fact is, we're both aliens, Jara. Wanderers. Searching for the home we never had and may never find." His smile seemed to mock himself as well as her. "We don't fit in anyplace."

"That's not true. I'm happy now. In Betar. I belong here," she said firmly. "I know I do."

"Because . . . Simeon is here?"

"No," she said truthfully. "It has nothing to do with Simeon. Not in the way you think it does."

He mounted the stallion again, looked around. "A city on a mountaintop. Still, it's a very ordinary town, Jara. Closer to the clouds perhaps, but no nearer to heaven. The same restrictions prevail as in all the dusty villages below." For once the dark eyes did not taunt or tease or mock. "You don't belong here. I see you and wonder how you'd look without that veil on your head . . . dressed in something soft and colorful instead of the plain, heavy garments you wear. I think how your eyes would shine presented with the rich variety of a city like Rome or Alexandria or the capitals of Parthia and Greece.

How your tongue would take to different foods . . . how your mouth, stained with wine, would taste.''

She stared up at him, fascinated. For a moment there was the memory of the boats in Tiberias, sailing away while she stood on the shore. . . .

"You don't belong here," he said again. "You talk of freedom, but you don't know what it is. There are all kinds of slaves, Jara. Slaves to Caesar. Slaves to God. Slaves to custom and society. You're a rebel against all three, not just Rome, as you think."

"What . . . what makes you say so?" she asked faintly.

"I've seen the look in your eyes when men call on the Lord, and there's no need to debate your feelings concerning the Empire. As for the society," he continued, "you obviously don't give a damn for what people think. You refuse the protection of marriage, go off with a Christian. . . ." He shook his head. "Hardly prudent behavior. The world can be a cruel place for a woman."

"Oh, leave me alone," she said irritably. "You're always discussing me. Why are you always discussing me?"

"Because you interest me. Or perhaps, 'intrigue' is the better word."

"Well, you don't interest me," she said turning away once more.

Andreas laughed softly. "You'll never get me to believe that. And one of these days, when you've finished with Simeon and Jacob, when you've finished searching for a father, I'm going to hold you in my arms and—"

She whirled around. But this time the sun was full in her face, so that like the stallion earlier she was blinded and momentarily stunned. And in that moment she felt herself swept up into a kiss unlike any she had ever known. She felt as if her mouth were being raped. And yet, what was the heat that rose in her, enveloping her . . . ?

She wrenched away. "Let me go," she gasped.

Still he held her, his arms surprisingly strong. Her feet dangled above the ground. "You're not really going to tell me you don't like it, are you?" he murmured, bringing his face close again.

She kicked the air, as the stallion had, pulling back and at the same time pushing down on the arms encircling her waist. Seeing finally that her struggles were to no avail, she went limp in his embrace and, looking straight into his eyes, those dark, devil eyes, said coldly, "Do as you like. It's not the first time I've had to tolerate someone I despise."

Immediately he released her, his handsome features drawn tight. He stared at her a moment, and then, without another word, he rode away.

Well, Jara thought, picking herself up off the ground where she had fallen when Andreas had let go, at least she had finally managed to wipe the smile off his face.

THE DAYS that followed were a kind of respite. For the moment no battle raged on the soil of Israel, although members of Simeon's army—the "Brothers," as they called themselves —kept a watchful eye on the ports and borders. People were once again thronging to Jerusalem, resettling there, often in houses abandoned by the legion, which in turn had taken these dwellings from the victims of Titus' assault sixty years earlier. Temple Hill became the site of feverish activity; boundary stones marking the dimensions of the new Temple began to appear, with various sections curtained off for worship.

Survivors of the priestly class began to show themselves; Jehoiarib came down from Meron; Jedaiah from Sepphoris; and so on down to the last of the twenty-four classes. Simeon's uncle, Eleazar of Modi'in, took charge of coordinating religious activity, and as he was both a rabbi and a descendant of priests, no one appeared to find fault with this bit of nepotism. Indeed, it was considered a good sign, for Eleazar the Priest, as he was now called, was not only highly regarded by the sages of Jabneh but generally revered for his saintly demeanor. Men like Rabbi Tarfon and Johanan ben Torta even hoped that some of his uncle's piousness might adhere to the *Nasi*, who, Akiva's proclamation notwithstanding, seemed less like the Messiah they had imagined than a very earthy and brusque military commander not much different from Rome's generals. Simeon did not bother himself with winning their favor. If the adulation of the *am ha-aretz* meant little to him, except as support for his troops, the opinions of the rabbis meant even less. So long as the country did not divide and turn upon itself as it had in the civil turmoil of John of Gischala and Simon bar Gioras during the earlier war with Rome, he did not concern himself with political or meta-physical debate. There was too much to do, for one thing. The Parthians had yet to be won over, and the day when Hadrian's forces would

return was drawing ever closer. Some way had to be found to
fight effectively against the massed troops he would soon have
to face. But despite the best efforts of himself, trusted comrades in arms like Masbelah and Obodas, and the keen minds
of Mesha and Andreas, none of them could come up with any
better methods of meeting the legions—given their own capa-
bilities—than they had already used. Simeon did not doubt for
a minute that, without additional help, the strategy that had so
far proved successful would eventually fail. None of the men
at these war sessions doubted it. The fact was, as Simeon said
wryly to Mesha, everyone in Israel was expecting outside help,
namely God. As for himself, Simeon confided, he would settle
for the Parthians.

There were those of the opinion that a new Temple speedily
rebuilt would ensure the Lord's favor; certainly the administration ought to be moved to the Holy City with all speed. But
Simeon preferred Betar, and Jara, who had gone with Akiva
to Jerusalem and there found nothing in the jumble of dust,
the crumbling walls, and the tents of the new settlers to kindle
imagination or longing, was inclined to agree. In Betar, she
felt she had come home. It was a feeling, as she'd told Andreas, that had nothing to do with Simeon and certainly was
not motivated by the tactical considerations of ben Kosiba.
She only knew she felt happy here, and whether this was
because she took pleasure in the peace and prosperity of the
place or delight in the sight of the surrounding hills turning to
gold each afternoon, or, despite her words, some satisfaction
that Simeon was here and his wife in Jericho, who could say?

She roamed the city, content. There was diversity here. For
all its isolated position Betar was far less provincial than B'nei
Berak; its proximity to Jerusalem had in earlier times given the
wealthy suburb a degree of sophistication that still remained.
In fact, since the destruction of the Holy City, Betar had in
many ways become what Jerusalem once was. And as the
place became known as the *Nasi*'s seat, more and more diverse
types made entry through the city's gates, seeking audience
with Bar Kokhba.

Jacob of Kefar Sakanya was sequestered in a small house
not far from the villa used as ben Kosiba's headquarters. He
was under guard, but Jara encountered no difficulty in seeing
him. The Christian received her gladly. "I prayed you would
come," he said.

"Did you? Why?"

"You are in my thoughts."

The cat's eyes became half-lidded; they seemed to glitter faintly as she studied the man. Had Andreas been right?

Once again Jacob was able to reach inside her mind. "You disturb the thoughts of many," he said. "Men lust for you. You wonder now if this is so with me."

"Yes."

Instead of answering he asked, "Do you take pleasure in arousing men?"

"I don't know," she said, surprised by the question. "I've never thought about it." But even as she answered him, she saw Simeon in her mind's eye and turned away, her face reddening.

"Why did you come?" he asked after a pause. "I thought you were angry with me."

"I feel responsible for you. I know you are being kept against your will."

"Not against my will."

"Well, under guard, anyway," she replied, confused. "I thought perhaps you'd want to get word to your family."

"There is only my sister, Elisheba. She is used to my disappearances and does not worry. She knows I am in the hands of the Christ."

"Look, you'd better not talk that way around here," Jara warned in a low voice.

Jacob smiled. "I am already in jeopardy for my beliefs. It would do no good to pretend or say other than what I know is true."

"You don't understand," Jara said, exasperated. "They will think you are a spy."

"I am sure 'they' think so already. But what about you? Aren't you afraid what 'they' will think of you for being my friend?"

"I didn't say I was your friend," she pointed out. "I said I feel responsible for you."

"I see."

"Well, do you want my help or not?"

"I would like your company. I would like to talk."

Again the lids of the green-gold eyes narrowed. "About what? Jesus?"

"Not if you don't want me to."

"I would like to know how you heal the sick," she said after a pause.

"Come here and I will show you. Come closer, yes. . . ."

She moved toward him slowly.

Jacob took her hands in his. Again Jara felt the tingling warmth she had experienced in Jaffa. A tremor went through her. "It's in your fingers," she said slowly. "A kind of fire . . ." She looked up, still curious. "Has it always been so?"

"Yes." He let go of her hands and moved away as though to grant some respite from the magnetic field he generated. "When I was a child I didn't understand. I was afraid. Then I came to realize it was the Christ working through me, and that I could do good."

"Do good?"

"Heal the sick."

She nodded. "Do your hands always feel like that?" she asked after a pause. "Sort of warm and tingly?"

"Christ is always in my heart, but the power comes and goes."

"What makes it come?"

"Need."

Suddenly her eyes took on the inscrutable stare that, even more than their pale color or oblique slant, made them so catlike. "Need," she repeated. "Whose?" she asked with a slight curl of lip. "Yours or mine?"

Jacob blinked. He had faced adversaries before, learned rabbinical minds, stubborn hearts, mean and petty natures who worshipped evil out of ignorance, but he had never met anyone like the young girl who stood before him now. She was part child, part woman—part devil, he feared. How else to explain that chilling glance or the words that cut straight to the core? She was too young to be so strong. Unless another Power possessed her and spoke now through the slender female body. Could that small hand wield the dagger at her waist unless directed by some outside force?

He said a silent prayer.

Jara turned away. She appeared bored.

"Don't go," Jacob said almost desperately. "Stay with me. Pray with me."

"I don't pray," she said flatly. She turned back as a thought had struck her. "I am not a witch," she explained. "I just don't pray."

Jacob nodded dumbly. He looked so forlorn that Jara had to laugh. "I like you," she said, smiling. "I don't know why,

but I do. And I will be your friend, if you like." What he had
said about his childhood had touched her. "So long as you
don't go on about God and the Christ," she warned.
"Because I have no taste for miracles and stories of angels and
such."

"You felt the power."

"The Old One once told me of a woman from her village
across the Great Sea who healed people by the laying on of
hands. She worshipped the Good Goddess. There have been
others . . . Greeks, Egyptians. My father spoke of them. So I
don't doubt your power." She shrugged. "I just don't know
where it comes from. Nor do I care, so long as you don't use it
against anyone here."

"There are other things I can do," he said, wanting her to
understand and at the same time ashamed of his need to prove
himself to her.

She nodded. "You draw people's thoughts from them.
Akiva can too. But he doesn't make a fuss about it and get all
sober and solemn. You hardly know what he's doing until
later, when you realize you've emptied your heart to him, told
him things you never thought you'd ever say aloud and never
meant to say at all."

He stared at her, stricken. Vanity, he thought. His humility
had been but a form of vanity; he saw that now. But how
could she know this?

"You oughtn't to take yourself so seriously," Jara went on.
"But I suppose with the power you have and all the *minim*
treating you like a god, it would be difficult not to." She
cocked her head. "Yes, I should think you would need a
friend."

He took a deep breath, let it escape slowly. Years seemed to
float away with the air; suddenly, he felt quite young. "A no-
nonsense friend," he said, smiling.

"Yes," Jara agreed. "A no-nonsense friend."

THEY MET OFTEN; they talked. Jacob ceased to believe that
Jara was an agent of evil, but her godlessness disturbed him.
He sensed a torment deep within the girl that went far beyond
her feelings for Simeon and, he was forced to admit, was not
caused by guilt over the death of Florus Valerens. "I had to
kill him," she explained simply. "For all of us." But then a
look came into her eyes that Jacob was unable to fathom, and

the inscrutable stare—the wall—returned.

He knew she was in love with ben Kosiba. "I'll always love him," she admitted. "No matter what he's done to me. No matter what he does."

"But you seek revenge," Jacob pointed out.

"I hate him for what he did. He didn't just betray me, he betrayed *us*, what we are together. He must pay for that."

"Soon enough, I fear. Hadrian is bound to return."

"No! Not that! You don't understand, Jacob. Whatever is between Simeon and me, nothing must happen to him that would endanger Israel. He is the only one who can lead us against Rome. You've seen what he's accomplished. And it isn't only in battle. Right now, here in Betar, he is drawing up documents that will give the land back to the people so they will never be slaves to anyone. He works so hard and long. Obodas says he barely has time for food or sleep." She sighed. "I wish I could help him. I feel so useless. How I wish I were a man!"

"But you said Simeon believes your marriage to the Parthian—"

"That will do nothing for our cause, I can assure you. Rami may be the son of the exilarch, but the exilarch is a Jew like the rest of us. He doesn't rule Parthia. I don't know why Simeon doesn't send an envoy directly to the Parthian king, one monarch to another. It seems to me this reliance on the exilarch lessens our sovereignty."

"Have you told this to the *Nasi?*" Jacob asked admiringly.

She shrugged. "Who's going to listen to a girl? In the old days, perhaps . . . but he is *Nasi* now. He is Bar Kokhba."

"Wisdom ought to be appreciated for its own sake."

"Not when it comes from a female. Unless you're Beruria," she added. "The Old One used to say there isn't a man on earth half so smart as any woman around." She grinned at his expression. "The Old One said that Jesus was just another tale told by men, and that if the Eternal One really wanted to help, He would have sent a Son *and* a Daughter." She laughed. "The Old One was kind of crazy," she said fondly.

"Is that what you believe?" Jacob asked, careful not to allow fear or shock to appear in his eyes. He must tread carefully with this girl or he would lose her.

"I don't believe in gods *or* demons, if that's what you want to know. Nothing above and nothing below. Just people, most of them terrible."

"Does it matter, then, who rules? Or which Temple rises in Jerusalem? How can you be so passionate about a war whose sole aim is to make the Law of Moses triumphant?"

"That isn't at all what it's about. Well, maybe so. But not for me. Of course it matters who rules. The Romans took our land. They treated us horribly. What right do they have—what right has anyone—to make slaves of others? I watched them ride into our village. . . ." She swallowed and was still a moment. "Do you know what I remember?" she said finally. "I remember after . . . after they took Sharona . . . for days the children were beaten. I'd walk by a house and hear a child crying. At first I thought it was fear, remembering the way the soldiers had come and taken Sharona and beaten Samson. But then I saw my own brother, Arnon. . . . He was always so gentle with Avi. And suddenly—the boy had done nothing really, spilled his cup of milk, something like that—suddenly, Arnon just reached out and slapped Avi. Hard. Even Batya, his wife, was shocked. And I looked at Arnon's face and I saw how tight and tense it was. He'd looked that way from the moment the soldiers came. All that anger and hate inside . . . and all he could do was let it out on a child. His own son. And I realized it was the children who suffered most. Not just because there was little to eat while the Romans had plenty, or because all they might look forward to was growing up to labor for others without thanks or reward, or be raped or killed . . . but because so long as their parents were treated like animals, they had no parents. They were orphans. Like me."

"Jara . . ." Jacob took her hands in his; once again she felt the comforting warmth of that magnetic touch. "Whatever befalls us, we are God's children. His love can sustain us when there is no other love. His love is all we really need."

"We need each other," she said firmly. "And I need Simeon."

"You don't." He tightened his grip. "You may think you do, but you don't. You're strong, Jara. God's strength is in you, I see that now. And I see that you serve God, though you may not think so yourself. But you must come to Him with love, the same love that He has for you. Or you will never be at peace."

"The only peace I want is the guarantee that the legions will never ever come back."

"You know they will."

"This last time, then, and never again. We're free, Jacob. We're free now and we must remain free. That's all that matters."

SHE TRIED to persuade him to win the *minim* over to Simeon's camp. "This is your land too," she argued. "Surely you have also suffered under Rome. Why won't you fight with us?"

Jacob explained that there were Christians, who agreed with her. "My young friend Daniel has said those very words," he told Jara. "His wife was probably a victim of the soldiers."

"Probably?"

"We found her wandering near Capernaum, dazed and bruised. She appears to have lost all memory of what befell her or indeed her own identity. David calls her Suzannah, because he found her 'by the water.' "

Jara sighed.

"She is happy now, though, praise the Lord. She has Daniel and the baby and the Christ."

SHE FINALLY ALLOWED him to speak to her of Jesus. And so it came about that Jacob told her the story of the carpenter's son who died on the cross. "In a way he was like you, Jara. All Jesus wanted was a better world."

She did not comment, but neither did her eyes become as guarded as they had in the past. Her look was open, thoughtful; and Jacob's heart was lifted.

"I WANT YOU to stay away from the Christian," Simeon said.

"No."

"Don't go against me, Jara." His voice was tight, the muscles of his jaw working. "My position is difficult enough without having to answer for you."

She shrugged. "Don't answer for me."

"By God, girl! Who and where do you think you are?" he exploded. "You're not a child anymore! You're a grown woman. Unwed. Without family, save for my guardianship, which itself," he added, "is causing no end of talk."

That interested her. "What sort of talk?"

He ignored the question. "I'm announcing your betrothal

to Rami. I'll answer for your dowry.''

She took a step toward him, fists clenched. "Don't arrange my life, Simeon. Not you.''

"All right.'' He took a deep breath. "All right. If you won't wed Rami, then go on back to B'nei Berak, and let Akiva make a marriage for you. One way or the other, it must be settled. I can't worry about you any longer. Once my son is born—''

He might as well have struck her. "I'll marry whomever I like,'' she managed to say. "And I don't need you or Akiva or anyone else to find me a husband.'' Her chin came up. "Jacob has asked me to be his wife.''

"I'm sure he has,'' Simeon remarked dryly. The idea of her marrying the Christian was so preposterous he failed to exhibit the shock and astonishment Jara would have liked to see. Her face reddened. "M-Maybe that's what I'll do,'' she stammered.

"Don't be an idiot. If you marry one of the *minim*, you cast yourself out forever. You become one of them.'' He stopped, stared at her. "Is that it? Have you become one of them?''

"Now you're the idiot.''

A sigh of relief escaped him. "All right,'' he said brusquely. "No more games. I want this settled today.''

"All right,'' she echoed.

"Which is it to be, then?''

"Jacob of Kefar Sakanya,'' she said deliberately. "As soon as you release him, we will go to the village where his sister, Elisheba, lives. There we will be betrothed and married.''

"In that case I won't release him,'' Simeon said after a pause. "Congratulations. You've just sentenced the man to eternal imprisonment.''

"You can't!''

"I will not allow you to do this. I'm not going to let you throw your life away out of spite. This isn't just getting married to someone, Jara. You know what he is, what he believes. You're one of them or you're one of us. You can't be both.'' He let out a harsh laugh. "You don't even love the man.''

"How do you know?''

"Because you belong to me and you always will.''

"I hate you. . . .''

"I know.'' He sighed. "Jara, I know. . . . But you're mine, all the same.'' He paused. "Forget the Christian.''

She shook her head.

"You little fool, will you give up raging against the world? I can make you a princess! What are you proving by this? By God, I'd respect you if it were out of genuine belief. I'd hate it, but I'd respect it. But you don't give a damn about the man or his faith."

"How do you know? Maybe I've come to Christ."

"Liar. The only thing you believe is what you can grab with your hands and cram into your mouth."

"I'm not an animal!"

"Yes, you are. Just like me. Just like all of us, Greek, Roman, Christian, Jew. The only thing that keeps any of us from tearing each other apart is believing in Law or God, one or the other. And you don't believe in either."

"I believed in you, Simeon," she said bitterly.

"I'm not a god!" He began to pace up and down. "I'm wasting time," he muttered. "I haven't time for this." He came to a halt. "All right. You want me to believe you're ready to give up your friends, to give up even the appearance of following the faith of your fathers, and run off to the *minim*. All right, then, show me you're one of them. *Show me.* That knife stuck in your belt, the knife of the Sicarii, the weapon your grandfather Eleazar ben Ya'ir used . . . throw it on the floor! Get rid of it, Jara! Forget about a nation called Israel. Turn your back on all they died for at Jerusalem and Masada. You're a Christian now. You don't need justice and freedom here on earth. You've only to wait for heaven. You don't even need to do anything to get there. Someone named Jesus did it for you. All you've got to do is believe that and pray to your Christ. You don't even have to follow Torah anymore. Just say, 'I believe in Christ,' and you're saved. I have to admit it sounds wonderful. But first, throw away the *sica*. Throw away the knife."

She stared at him, frozen, pale. And then, suddenly—so suddenly she would not be able to recall later how it happened —suddenly she was in his arms, and his mouth was tearing at hers, and all the months without him were as though they had never been.

"Jara . . . Jara . . ."

"You love me. . . ." Never mind that his hands were hard, unrelenting, his mouth so brutal she could feel the blood start from her lip; she wanted to laugh, to cry. "You love me. . . . You do. . . ."

"Yes." It was like a groan. "Yes. . . ."

"Then say it. Say it," she demanded fiercely.

"I love you. I love you."

She closed her eyes, threw back her head. His mouth was on her throat. They were together again, as they had once been, as they were meant to be. But it wasn't the same. It could never be the same. He had seen to that.

"Do you want me?" she whispered. "Do you want me . . . now, Simeon?"

"Yes . . . yes. . . ."

"Then beg." Her fingers dug into his arms. "You must beg for it."

It was the tone of her voice more than the words she spoke that arrested him. He pulled back to look at her, puzzled.

"I swore. . . ." she hissed. "If you want me, you must beg."

He straightened, stared at her, his jaw tight, his eyes burning. Finally in a hoarse voice he said, "Bitch. You bitch."

She smiled, but there was no joy in her heart. She felt leaden. "Well?"

"Get out of here, Jara. Go back to B'nei Berak or go with the *minim*, I don't care. Go on, go with your Christian! Go to hell with him! Go!"

3

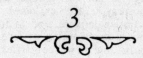

AT THE FOOT of Mount Tabor, in the Lower Galilee, below the mountain's steep slopes crowded with oak and the terebinth, the village lay, a dark carpet of fertile soil. There were almond trees here, and wild flowers, and the thorny jujube; the mandrake grew in spring, with its heady fragrance and legendary medicinal and aphrodisiac powers. None of it was unfamiliar to Jara: not the trees or the flowers or the hills. Not the mud when it rained and the small, stark houses, often little more than huts. Not the barefoot children or the smell of scorched bread or the all-consuming darkness of night. Not the look or the taste or the stench of poverty. It all reminded her of the little village where she'd been born.

Nor did living among the *Ebionim* prove to be a totally strange experience. The sect was after all made up of Judeo-Christians who still followed the ways set forth by Moses. Newborn males were circumcised, the dietary laws of *kashrut* were observed, the Sabbath was kept. But the day following the Sabbath, called in Greek *Kyriake*, meaning the "Lord's Day," in commemoration of their Savior's resurrection, was also a time for gathering. By midmorning the constituents would be assembled in the house of Jacob's sister, Elisheba. There would be the reading of "the memories of the apostles" and "writings of the prophets," such as the various epistles or perhaps the prophecies of Hermas. Then would follow a homily, prayers for the chief intentions of the Church, and the kiss of peace. The eucharistic prayer would be said, the people answering "Amen." Then the consecrated bread and wine would be distributed, alms were collected for those in need,

269

and sometimes a communal meal was served.

Jara was an observer at these gatherings more than an actual participant, for these were the days of her "instruction." "Those who are convinced and believe the truths revealed by Jesus and his apostles, and who promise to live in this way, shall be taught to pray," Jacob explained. "Then you shall fast, and while fasting implore God to forgive your sins. You will be baptized in the waters of repentance. You will receive the Eucharist. And we will be married."

Jara nodded. She was in no hurry.

She hadn't realized Jacob would expect her to undergo actual conversion to the faith of those she still called *minim*. But the very idea of "bringing her to Christ" seemed to fill him with a kind of ecstasy. His voice throbbed with emotion as he described her baptism in the Jordan and the accompanying rites. She would be anointed with oil as a sign of the gift of the Spirit. Jacob would touch her forehead with the mark of the cross, the *sphragis*, which was not yet the symbol of crucifixion but meant the Hebrew *tav*, symbol of the Name of God.

"Then shall your body be adorned all in white, and I will place a crown of leaves on your hair." He took her hands in his. "We will drink of the cup of milk and honey. . . ." He raised her palms to his lips, but before he dared touch his mouth to her flesh, he seemed to catch himself and put her away from him. It was the closest he had yet come to physical intimacy with his bride-to-be.

Jacob's attitude was an echo of the Ebionite regard for virginity and chastity, which was not far distant from the earlier notions of the Essenes, the austere Jewish sect that had congregated on the shore of the Dead Sea and ostensibly vanished after the fall of Masada. Even the name Ebion, "Community of the Poor," was not dissimilar to the way in which the inhabitants of Qumran had referred to themselves. And like the Essenes, the Ebionites pooled their belongings.

None of the Judeo-Christians, who were perhaps most like the first followers of the Nazarene, frowned on marriage. There was, however, the pervasive thought that total service to God was somehow lessened by human ties. The attitude of Jesus toward his own family was often cited, which was totally contrary to rabbinic views, but, again, in keeping with Essene philosophy. Perhaps it was this that had kept Jacob from taking a wife these many years, or perhaps it was some primal fear that his "power" would diminish or depart following union with a female. In any event, his life, which had been singularly chaste, had changed upon meeting Jara. More and more it began to seem to him that his own salvation as much as hers lay in her acceptance of God and the teachings of Jesus.

Wisely, Jacob refrained from preaching. His world of the Divine was one of dream and vision and the strange electric force of his hands to banish illness. Like Elisha ben Abuyah and Akiva and so many others, he had speculated upon the mysterious workings of creation and the question of good and evil within all the framework of mystic thought. The ideas of the Nicolaitans; of the Gnostic Cerinthus, who had been a contemporary of John; of Simon Magus and the Samaritan Messianists; of Simon's disciple Menander; and of Saturninus of Antioch, the present leader of Gnosticism—all the apocalyptic writings, oracles, and mystic speculation of an age fairly bursting with sect, cult, and mystery worship were not unknown to Jacob of Kefar Sakanya. And like Akiva, he had survived, strong in the certainty of his faith, which in these last years saw a Christ transcendent over the views of most Judeo-Christians. Still, he lived among them, not yet comfortable with the Greco-Roman absorption of his Lord.

Jara knew none of this, although she suspected Jacob was not a typical Ebionite or even a typical Christian. She spent most of her time now with his sister, Elisheba, who personified the chaste "righteous widow" (she had never been married), her entire life devoted to Church and community. Jara found her to be kind, soft-spoken, and dull beyond words. None of Jacob's charismatic powers appeared present in this plain, sweet lady who spent her days tending the sick (in the normal, mundane manner as opposed to her brother's spectacular method), preparing and serving communal meals, and in all other ways caring for others. She wasted no time pressing Jara into like service and found the girl amenable to all tasks but one: Jara would not wash the dead.

"She says she is of the priestly line," Elisheba told her brother with some dismay. "And . . ." she hesitated. "When I spoke to her of baptism, she looked away. I thought at first she did not hear me, so I repeated my words. Again she did not answer. Jacob, I do not think her heart is with us. She is willing enough in most things to serve, but her heart is not with the Lord. I think you ought to speak to her."

* * *

"I CAN'T," Jara said firmly. "I cannot wash the dead. I am descended from a house of priests."

"But your father was a physician," Jacob reminded her. "Surely he had occasion to touch a corpse. And you, you have killed a man."

"It's not the same. I can't explain it, but I can't do it, Jacob. Something inside me . . . I know it is forbidden to me. I just know it."

"The *Kohanim* are no more, Jara."

"What are you talking about? There are priests in Jerusalem right now. They've been giving Simeon ever so much trouble—" She stopped.

"They are false priests and false servants of God, as their predecessors were."

"Don't talk to me of God," she snapped. "Have you ever heard some of your people praying at the bedside of the sick or the dead? They pray to your Jesus just as if they thought *he* was a god. You told me he was a teacher."

"No, much more than that."

"There, you see? I don't know what you believe or what you expect me to believe. I don't think you are what you say you are," she continued suspiciously.

"I told you—"

"You told me you were a Jew. You're not."

"Then I am a Christian."

"Those books in your room aren't Christian scrolls. I know what they are. I heard Beruria and Mesha speak of them. They are of magic."

He shook his head. "They are only philosophical writings. Once I even spoke with Akiva regarding their theories. There is mention of dual forces, but—"

"Is that where you get your power?"

"My 'strength' comes from Christ."

"Why won't you use it on Sharona?"

"Her name is Suzannah."

"Her name is Sharona. I know who she is even if she doesn't."

"Have you spoken to her again?"

"Yes." She looked away. "She doesn't remember anything."

"Perhaps it is better so. What did you tell her?"

"Nothing, really. I just asked her some questions. She

doesn't know me at all. It's so strange. . . ."

"She's happy now, Jara."

"Yes," she mused. "She seems to be. The baby is lovely.
He has blue eyes. My father had blue eyes."

"What is it then you want, Jara?" Jacob asked after a
pause.

"I don't know! I just hate lying, that's all!"

"What is the lie?"

"I don't know." She sighed. "Talk to me, Jacob. I'm so
miserable. Daniel says Simeon is trying to secure the coastal
plain again. He says there have been sea battles with the
Romans off Jaffa and Caesarea. But no one else here will tell
me anything! They won't even speak of the war. All those
prayers and never a word for Israel! It drives me mad!"

"Simeon ben Kosiba's Israel is not our Israel, Jara."

"But it's mine! It's my Israel!" Her eyes widened as she saw
the look on his face. She ran to him, threw herself at his knees
in remorse. "Oh, Jacob, I'm sorry! I'm so sorry. I try . . . but
I just don't belong here. I thought it wouldn't matter—Jesus
or *Yahweh*—But I can't pray to either, and I can't lie to you. I
don't want to be a bad person. But if being good means I must
bow my head and pray to nothing I can believe in, then that is
how it must be. Maybe I am bad. I came with you to spite
Simeon. And I said I'd marry you because I was curious. I
wanted to know if the power in your hands is in all your body,
if it would enter into me, too. There, I've said it. Now you
know what I'm like."

In answer he took her hands in his and raised her to her feet.
She shivered as he touched her.

"You will be baptized in the Jordan," he told her. "Then
we shall be married. And you will know all you want to
know."

"Jacob," she began desperately.

"You must believe, Jara. You must believe in something."

She shook her head.

"Otherwise you are nothing. You are no one."

She raised her head at this. "I am the granddaughter of
Eleazar ben Ya'ir and Alexandra of the house of Harsom. I
am of priestly descent. I am of the line of David—"

"Dead people," Jacob said gently. "All dead. Who are
you? What are you?"

She drew back, stunned.

"Who are you?" he repeated. "Who are you, Jara?"

"Jara," she said now angrily. "My name is Jara. I am a woman. And I am a Jew. And I don't want your Christ. I don't need your Jesus dying on the cross. I don't want anyone dying for my sins or because of them! And I don't want any God that kills babies and innocent people! You and Akiva and everyone else can have all the gods you like and any heaven thereafter—because all I want is a little piece of this world with a fire and food and someone to love, someone who loves me, someone to hold in the night, someone to cry with and laugh with. Oh! Oh, how I want to laugh! Yes! And to sing and dance! And I want to touch and kiss! You've never kissed me, Jacob. You never touch me if you can help it. All you want to do is pray with me. I don't want to pray. I don't care about any hereafter. I want to live! Now!"

He covered his face with his hands.

Jara stared at him, dismayed. Finally she whispered, "I don't want to hurt you. You're good and kind. . . . But I can't lie. I am what I am."

He gripped her arms now. His eyes were filled with tears. "All that you seek is God. God is life. God is love. Soon you will understand that. Soon you will see the truth."

BUT AS THE DAYS passed, it became clearer to her that she could not dwell among the Ebionites, not only because she could not bring herself to mouth their beliefs, but because she could not divorce herself from the political struggle at hand.

The air was charged with events. Travelers reported sighting the legions on the southern border. The roads were once again filled with armed men, converging from the Galilee and from every part of the land to join Bar Kokhba outside Jerusalem. Their faces were grim, determined, they would not willingly lose what they had gained. Jara watched them pass, her heart flying after them. Restless, she turned back to the house, entered it slowly, and dutifully set about preparing the soup to be served to the faithful. It would be another dreary evening filled with readings from Matthew, most likely, prayer, and perhaps the recitation of some new miracle performed in the name of Jesus. There would be no sly play on words or witty exchange like the ones between Akiva and Tarfon, or Beruria and one of the other rabbis. No sudden outbreak of dancing among the scholars as the meaning behind a law became clear to them, Rabbi Yossi the Galilean joining them, his frail arms raised high, a smile of pure joy lighting his thin face. No lovely animal fables told by Mesha. No exotic tales from Obodas, or the music from his reed pipe filling the night while Simeon spoke in low, urgent tones to the eager young men at B'nei Berak, promising freedom and Jerusalem if they but had the courage to fight for them.

She even missed Tobita; the woman would shun her now. Simon bar Yohai would never speak to her again.

I need a home, she thought, staring with unblinking eyes at the vermilion horizon. She stood there in the doorway, arms folded across her chest, and watched the sun bleed to night. And she thought now of Betar, and the supper she would lay for Simeon if she could. It would be a cozy house, neither small nor grand but with a courtyard where the children could play. . . .

Where was he now? In Jericho, dining with his pregnant bride, his silent, obedient, Parthian princess?

Suddenly the image of Andreas flashed before her. She could see his wicked eyes, and he was laughing at her like a demon. . . .

And there was Jacob with his gentle gaze, his long fingers with their strange fire. Jacob with his magic books and his dreams and his talk of Christ. *I saw you before I ever knew you* he'd told her. *Not by the Jordan but in a dream long ago. You will be with me at the end of days.*

A figure cut across the night, running up to the doorway. It was the young woman called Suzannah.

Sharona.

"You needn't hurry so," Jara said, pleased to see her. "It is still early. The service hasn't begun."

"Oh," came the breathless reply, "I'd forgotten about the service. For a moment though, I thought . . . that is, seeing you . . . I felt sure I . . . I . . ." She broke off, confused. "Now I don't know what I thought."

"Perhaps I seem familiar to you," Jara said carefully.

"Yes. No. I'm not sure. . . ."

"Well, you look familiar to me." Jacob had come to the door; Jara could sense his presence behind her. "We may have seen each other before. On the road, perhaps, or in the market of Tiberias. I was born in the Galilee. In a place called—"

"I don't know." The young woman shook her head. "I can't remember."

Daniel, her husband, appeared. He was carrying the baby. Instantly all doubt and confusion vanished from Sharona-Suzannah's eyes. Smiling, she took the child in her arms and, with Daniel's hand placed protectively on her shoulder, entered the house.

Jara sighed.

"Come," Jacob said gently. "The others will be arriving soon. It will do you good to feel their love. Your heart needs lifting. Perhaps, tonight, you will pray with us."

"I don't pray. You know that."

"Say the words. Just say the words, and the Spirit will enter in you."

She turned away from the hills, which had become black and foreboding. The scene inside was not unpleasant. Elisheba and Sharona were lighting the candles and oil lamps; Daniel was playing with the baby. The evening was warm, but Jara felt cold.

I want to go home, she thought. *Only I don't know where that is. I only know where it is not.*

THEY WERE ALL ABED when the knock on the door came. Jacob rose and went to greet the visitors. "Welcome in the name of the Christ," he said.

"Peace," Quadranus, the sectarian adverse to dealings with Judeo-Christians, replied. "In the name of the Son of God," he added pointedly.

Jacob gestured for the man and his companions to enter.

"Forgive the late hour," Quadranus said, "but we have ridden here with all haste, as the news we bring is of great importance. Hadrian is returned."

Jacob nodded. He lit the oil lamp on the table and then another in a wall niche. The light cast an eerie glow on the grim faces of the men. "You seem as little astonished by the emperor's return as by my appearance," the sectarian remarked.

"Both were expected."

"I see. Then you are a realist after all, despite the aura with which your followers surround you."

"I have no followers. I am a simple man with a gift for healing, which the Lord in His mercy gave me in order to help others."

"You are not the only one who serves God."

"No," Jacob agreed. "We each serve as best we can."

"And now is the time to do great service for the Lord."

"How do you mean?"

"By helping to destroy the Jews. Rome has had enough of these troublemakers. They have condemned themselves to annihilation by this revolt."

"If it be the will of God."

"It *is* the will of God! And now we must join our will to His through God's instrument, Hadrian."

"It was decided—"

"Nothing was decided."

"I went to ben Kosiba," Jacob said, frowning now. "I gave him my word."

"Yes, I'm surprised you came away alive. And with the man's own niece, I hear. You do have your ways, don't you? . . . Perhaps the stories about you are true after all. You work magic. . . ."

"What is it you want from me?" Jacob asked now.

"The girl, for one thing. I need to bargain. Some of my people have been imprisoned by this false and perfidious 'Messiah,' who seems to take great delight in persecuting anyone who dares speak the name of Jesus."

"What is the charge against your men? Heresy or treason?"

"Does it matter? They are in jail because they are Christians."

"They are in jail, I think, because they are spies and Roman informers."

"Just as you were, eh, Jacob? Oh yes, I know all about that."

"I'm sure you do," was the quiet reply.

"Let it be a warning. Don't work against me. I serve the Lord. All that matters to me is to do Christ's will. And I know that his way, his truth, must be revealed to all the world for the good of all men. Simeon ben Kosiba is not the Messiah. He is the enemy of God, and all who fight under his banner fight against God." He paused. "I know that you and your kind look down on me because I am not born to the race of Abraham. Because my flesh is whole and I eat the meat of idolaters. But I love Jesus. And the Christ is with me. Your Jewish pride and arrogance have no place within the church of my Lord. Your ways are old, rotten ways. They have no place in the New Jerusalem when God comes again."

"What then will you do with Jesus when the Christ returns?" Jacob asked. "For my ways were his ways."

"His way is a New Way, Jacob. Come with us and live eternally. Fight me and you will not survive."

Jacob was about to reply when Jara, who had heard the talk, entered the room. Quadranus turned his attention to her. "Is this the female?" he asked.

"This is Jara. She is to be my wife."

Quadranus' eyebrows lifted at this. "So? After all these years . . . can it be you are not so pure as your people believe?"

"The union of marriage is holy."

"The union of God and man is holier." He looked again at Jara. "Strange eyes. Has she received the baptism?"

"Not yet."

"You must renounce your evil upbringing," Quadranus said to her now, "and pledge yourself to Christ Jesus."

Jara looked at Jacob.

"Let me hear you say it," Quadranus urged. "Then I will know you come to God with a pure heart and are not sent by Beelzebub or his agent Simeon ben Kosiba."

"Who are you?" Jara asked coldly.

The question took Quadranus by surprise.

"The hour is late," Jacob said quietly to the sectarians. "You have traveled a long way, brothers. Sleep now."

But Quadranus would not take his glance away from Jara. "I do not like her looks," he announced. "She has the haughty eye of the Jewess. She does not serve the Lamb." He turned his suspicious gaze on Jacob. "And now I wonder. . . . Do you?"

"It is late," Jacob said again. He nodded for Jara to leave the room. "Let us talk in the morning. The women will prepare your bed."

"No," Quadranus said. "I will not sleep here. Don't send her away," he said as Jacob again motioned for Jara to leave. "I want to look into her face." He took a cautious step toward the girl. "I want to see the yellow light of her eyes and know it is the spark of the Heavenly Spirit and not the glow of

hellfire. Is it so, healer? Is it, magician? No!" He drew away
from Jacob's hand. "Don't touch me. I know of your power.
You will not touch me." Wrapping his cloak tightly about
him, he left, followed by his wide-eyed companions.

Jara watched them go, amazed.

"Don't be afraid," Jacob said.

"I'm not," she assured him. "Who was that terrible man?
He reminds me of Rabbi Kawzbeel. . . ." She turned around
to Jacob. "They'll be back."

"Yes, in the morning. Quadranus will want to speak to all
the congregation."

"No." She shook her head. "Tonight."

Jacob did not reply.

"He hates you. I saw it in his eyes. He means to kill you."

"No. . . ."

"You know it is so. Surely you see it."

"The people want peace," he said as if he had not heard
her. "The way of Christ is the way of peace. Quadranus must
not be allowed to sway them."

She sighed. He would not run away. He would face the man
in the morning before all the assembly of Ebionites. If he lived
until morning. "Why don't you 'heal' the sectarian of his feelings toward you?" she asked, only half-teasing. "You're
always telling me that hatred is a disease."

"He will not let me touch him. That is how it is with some.
They will not allow themselves to be touched. They will not let
their hearts be opened."

She looked away. His point was not lost to her, but she had
nothing to say on the matter. She was more concerned with
making him understand the danger he faced. But nothing she
said could persuade Jacob to take any action to protect
himself against Quadranus.

SHE WOKE with a start, sensing their presence even before she
heard the muffled exchange of words, followed by what
sounded like a groan and then a dull thud. She sat up, tensed,
listening.

Silence. Nothing in the night.

Suddenly the three men burst into her room. But she had
already found the little dagger and was up on her knees
waiting for them. They halted, stopped by the gleam of the

blade and the eerie quality of her eyes. Then Quadranus hissed, "What are you waiting for? Kill her." They seemed to hesitate, and suddenly there was the sound of Elisheba's screams piercing the darkness. The two men ran, leaving Quadranus to face her alone.

Jara let out her breath slowly. She was breathing evenly now, waiting. The dagger felt good in her hand. She almost smiled.

Quadranus had no weapon. He would have to strangle her, quickly, before Elisheba's cries brought others. He took a step forward, his hands raised, then stopped.

It wasn't the knife. It wasn't even her eyes.

Her lips had parted, her teeth were slightly bared. Her breath came and went, softly menacing, like that of a beast before it sprang. Even her posture was animallike.

"Witch," Quadranus whispered. "Daughter of hell!"

Other cries were added to Elisheba's now. Quadranus bolted from the room, pushing aside those who had come to stop him. He ran out of the house and disappeared into the night.

JACOB HAD BEEN STABBED a number of times, but miraculously, he was still alive. One look at his crimson chest told Jara there was no hope of recovery; still, she set about trying to staunch his wounds, oblivious to Elisheba's sobs and the murmur and weeping of the others who had rushed to the scene. Daniel paced the floor, grim and ashen, his own tunic stained with blood.

Jacob's eyes were open and clear. He seemed to be in no pain—or beyond it—and with no alarm on his features at the approach of death. He watched Jara's efficient motions a moment, then made a slight gesture for her to desist. He turned his head slightly, saying to the others, "Leave us."

As always, they obeyed him, some believing perhaps that their healer would now work a miracle upon himself.

The eyes of the Christian and the girl met.

"You knew they would return," she said at last. "Without my warning, which you would not heed. Why did you allow this to happen? Why?"

"To prove . . . to you . . ."

"What? What, Jacob?"

He swallowed. "The power . . . You must receive it now . . . to heal me."

"There is nothing I can do," she said gently. She took his hands in hers; they were cold, with little life in them, much less the fire she'd once felt. "There is nothing anyone can do now."

"Yes . . . yes . . . I will tell you . . . what . . . to do." His voice was barely a whisper.

"All right," she sighed.

"Hold my hands."

She started at this.

"Have you done so? I cannot feel . . ."

"Yes. I have done so."

He closed his eyes, and she thought he had died, so cold were his hands, his face gray in the first dawning light of day. But at last he looked at her and said in a voice surprisingly strong, "Lay your hands on my wounds, Jara."

"Wh-why?"

"Take my strength . . . and say, 'In the name of Jesus'—"

She drew away. "No . . ."

"You must. It is the only way."

"No . . ."

"Don't be afraid. . . ."

"There is nothing I can do," she stammered. "Nothing anyone can do. . . ."

"Yes . . . if you believe. Only believe . . . and we are both saved. Now and forever. Accept the Christ . . . and you will gain the world to come."

"While despising myself in this one. . . ." She shook her head, tears in her eyes now. "No, Jacob. Not even for you."

"You can heal me . . . if you believe."

"I believe in my people," she cried now in despair. Her voice sank to a whisper. "I cannot betray them."

"There is no . . . betrayal."

"The laying on of hands is forbidden. I cannot invoke the name of your Jesus without making of him a god. There is but One God, and we may serve no other. . . ."

He opened his eyes. He seemed puzzled by her words, and then suddenly he smiled. She didn't even realize what she was reciting through her tears.

"Jara," he managed to say. "Stubborn, stiff-necked . . ." His face seemed to take on the glow of the morning light that

was slowly filling the room. "Is it any wonder God loves you
. . . chose you . . . ?" His whole body seemed to sigh. "His
people . . . His . . . eternal . . . people."

JACOB WAS LAID in the ground, his body wrapped in white
linen upon which Elisheba had stitched a cross.

Jara wandered away from the mourners, who were praying
softly now, in unison, as they stood around the healer's grave
at the foot of Mount Tabor. The wind of the hills pulled and
tugged at her veil, and finally she ceased to hold tight to it, letting it slip away and trail from one hand like a wing or a sail
fluttering behind as she walked. Soon the comb that held her
curls in a thick coil came loose, and she pulled it out so that
her hair tumbled down onto her shoulders as it had when she
was a child.

She walked and walked, letting the wind push her in any
direction it chose, climbing one hill and then another, not
really caring what lay ahead and not wanting to think of what
was behind.

She couldn't return to B'nei Berak; Betar was out of the
question. She couldn't stay with Elisheba, because it was certain Quadranus would come back. Even Daniel had said she
must leave. "The sectarian ran out of the house shouting that
you murdered Jacob," the young Ebionite told her.

"But you know that isn't true."

"Truth doesn't mean much in times like these or in the
hands of a man like Quadranus, especially when he must cover
his own crimes."

Where was she to go?

Tiberias was not far. If the woman Ziva still lived there,
perhaps she would give Jara shelter. There was bound to be
someone in the city who had need of a maidservant.

For the moment, though, she didn't want to think about the
future. She just wanted to walk and to feel the wind and to say
goodbye to Jacob in her own way.

She had gone nearly an hour's distance when she saw the
two men looking down from the hill to the road below. They
were only a few yards away, their backs to her, but it did not
take longer than a second to recognize their leather cuirasses,
their curved and oblong shields, the short, broad swords, and
the hobnailed boots called *caligae*.

Legionaries.

Quickly she took shelter behind a tree, digging her nails into the bark in an effort to calm the trembling that overtook her. She bit her lip.

They were back. How many? From where? There had been no sounds of war, no reports of any fighting in the North— only sea battles at Caesarea and Jaffa, whose outcome was unknown.

No thought of Tiberias now. Somehow she had to reach Simeon. But how?

Cautiously she peeked out from behind the tree. The soldiers were still there, talking casually now, anticipating no threat.

Jara lay her cheek against the bark of the terebinth, wondering what she should do. Determining finally that it was best to make her way back to the village and from there try to get word to one of the settlements sympathetic to Bar Kokhba, she started to turn when a hand covered her mouth and another caught her around the waist. Before she could flail at her attacker, she was flat on the ground, the man on top of her, his palm muffling her cries. Slowly he raised a finger to his lips, and then slowly removed his other hand from her mouth. She gasped, her eyes wide.

It was Andreas.

HE LAY BESIDE HER in the grass and bush, one leg thrown over her, his torso still covering hers as he raised his head to sight the soldiers.

She didn't move; she lay there, watching him.

Suddenly he looked at her and then, slowly, his eyes never leaving hers, brought his face down until their lips were touching. His mouth brushed hers, then lingered a moment. And then another moment. And then a longer one still. . . .

"What are you doing?" she whispered.

"Taking advantage," he whispered back, kissing her yet again.

She closed her eyes. "You—You'll get us both killed," she whispered weakly.

"Just say I'm raping you," he advised her. "Ravishing the natives is in the line of duty." Another kiss. And another. "Anyway, they're gone."

She pushed him away, saw now that he was dressed like a legionary. "You—You—" she began angrily.

"Sshh. You can tell me later. First let's get out of here before we're surrounded by Praetorians." He grabbed her hand, pulled her to her feet. "Where's your husband?"

"Jacob's dead."

"You really have the touch of Midas, don't you?" he murmured.

"What's that?"

"Never mind. Let's get to my horse."

She hesitated.

"Make up your mind fast. Do you want to come with me or not?"

"Yes. Yes!"

It was only after they'd ridden for some hours that she even thought to ask where they were going. Andreas grinned. "Where every good Jew should go at least once, Jara. Jerusalem!"

4

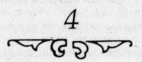

MARCELLUS QUINTUS made a last check of the palace corridor. The hour was late, the place quiet. He could almost hear the water of the Lake of Galilee slapping gently on the beach below. The Praetorian standing guard at the emperor's door leaned drowsily against the wall. He straightened at the centurion's approach. Quintus nodded. "All is well?"

"All is well, sir."

The door opened slightly, revealing Hadrian, who beckoned to Quintus. Another nod at the guard, and Quintus was inside the room.

"I see you can't sleep either," Hadrian said. "What is it, old friend? Surely not fear. Anticipation?"

"I don't know. Just restless, I suppose. In a curious way I'm glad to be back," he admitted.

"Judea is a curse," Hadrian replied grimly with a slight shudder. "Even this palace—it was Herod's, wasn't it? I swear to the gods I can feel the presence of that old madman in every shadow. Something about this place . . . What is it I've heard said about Tiberias? Something about the whole city being built on the bones of dead men."

"The rabbis claim it is the site of an ancient burial ground. They refuse to set foot here."

"Which was probably what Herod intended," Hadrian said with a laugh. "Do you think this Bar Kokhba fellow has the same idea?"

"Bar Kokhba won't attack, if that's what you mean. He doesn't appear to be predisposed toward the taking of fortified cities. In any case, he's never had to. He's gone in only

285

where the people have declared for him.''

"But he must know we're here."

"I would think so. But in all our encounters with the man, he's made it obvious that he only fights on his own terms and in his own way.'' Quintus walked to the window and peered out at the town spread below. "He avoids the cities," he mused. "No information has yet appeared to indicate his army is centered in any one place or garrison. Instead he's apparently divided his followers into hundreds of units posted on mountain ridges or placed in ambush positions. He knows how to exploit the hills and defiles in order to pin us down with the javelin and sling, which are the weapons best used by the Jews. The man's brilliant,'' he conceded. "A superb fighter. I wish he were one of us.''

"What do you think of Severus' plan?"

"I think the general's approach is correct, excellency. The terrain here does not favor massive infighting. And we've already seen to our misfortune that when we advance in large, compact formations, they take us quite easily, holding their positions at points which force our attack. They make use of two units, one before and one behind, so that we are unable to turn flank without danger of attack on the open flank or rear.'' He shook his head. "And as suddenly as they appear, they disappear, withdrawing to their mountains, where they hide themselves in cliffs and caverns, making use of underground passages that enable them to turn up again at some other position. Bar Kokhba himself has been reported at places miles apart within the space of an hour.''

"A magician!"

"A damn clever fighter."

"Not clever enough in the long run, Quintus. I have brought up reinforcements from every part of the empire. Twelve legions in all, composed of their full complement or detachments thereof. And I have the utmost confidence in Julius Severus. Moreover, his British auxiliaries are accustomed to fighting on difficult terrain. And his plan to cut the Jews off into small, separate groups that we shall then defeat one by one makes even more sense to me, now that I've heard you. Yes,'' he continued thoughtfully, "we'll isolate them—each one of those 'hundreds' of units—and then we'll starve them out until they are too exhausted to resist attack. One by one the 'legions' of Bar Kokhba will be defeated. And finally, the man himself.''

"It will take time, excellency," Quintus cautioned. "Severus has made that clear to you, I hope. Time and patience. And more than likely we will suffer heavy losses."

"So long as we win. Understand, Quintus. I don't care how much time it takes or how many men we lose. It will not be said that the Empire became less under Hadrian, that Rome's frontiers, which failed to expand under my uncle Trajan, shrank even more during my reign. I owe that much to my family," he said with a thin smile.

But Quintus, for once, did not respond to his emperor's attempt at humor. He was disturbed by the gleam in Hadrian's eye, the near-fanatic determination etched on the features of this once-benevolent being whom Quintus had believed to be the most intelligent and humane person alive. Moreover, any command beginning with the words "I don't care how many men we lose" was profoundly disturbing to hear. Still, Severus' plan of action was the only feasible one. Perhaps the victory Hadrian desired would come about sooner than Quintus foresaw. Success bred success, but a few devastating defeats for Bar Kokhba, who had hitherto enjoyed complete victory, might turn his followers against him, make them realize their "Messiah" was not only human but vulnerable. Hadrian seemed to read Quintus' thoughts. "I like Rufus' ideas," he confided. "The campaign to discredit Bar Kokhba makes excellent sense. Any man who believes he is fighting for his God will attack more ferociously and defend himself more strongly than a soldier working for pay. We've always seen that with the Jews. The battle for Jerusalem is not so far in the past that we may forget the zeal of its defenders or the determination of those on the Masada. And now that the Jews believe their Messiah is come, well . . . So, while one campaign is waged in the field, another must begin that will show this Bar Kokhba person to be nothing but a scoundrel—a criminal with no thought for the people's good. Rufus says the Christians will be good allies in this."

"Not necessarily," Quintus replied, uneasy at this new tactic.

"Then we must see that they are. Set the followers of Jesus to fighting with the Jews anyway you can. And while we're at it, let's not forget the rabbis. Akiva must be discredited, along with the man he has named to lead his sorry race."

"That will not be an easy thing to do," Quintus replied, even more astonished. "Akiva is greatly loved."

"He is old," Hadrian said impatiently. "Senile. What man of sense would trust his judgment? And from what Rufus has told me, it would not take very much to get those rabbis quarreling among themselves, especially when they realize what Akiva and his 'Son of a Star' have stirred up."

"With all respect, excellency, this is no task for me," Quintus said stiffly. "I am a soldier, at ease only in the field. . . ."

"Well, leave it to Rufus, then. I'm sure he knows what to do. And we must give him this chance to redeem himself. How is his wife?"

"What?"

"Rufina Livia. Is she settled comfortably?"

"Yes. Yes, I suppose so. . . ."

"Well, see that she is taken care of. A plain, melancholy little creature . . . but with the most pleasant speaking voice. I hope what I have heard said of her is not true."

"What?" Quintus asked again.

"That she practices the ways of the Jews in secret. That Akiva has bewitched her, or she him—although I find that hard to believe on either account. Still . . . there's something to be used. If it were let out that Akiva succumbed to the charms of the Roman governor's wife . . ." The emperor started to laugh. "No, no, it's too mad. That old man. Still . . . old men do make fools of themselves." He laughed again.

"There is the matter of the lady's honor," Quintus said now.

Hadrian sighed. "Well, we'll see." He yawned. "It really is late, isn't it?"

Quintus moved to the door. "Good night, excellency."

"Good night." He smiled. "And thank you."

"For what, excellency?"

"For reminding me—without saying a word—of all that is right with Rome. There are too many Rufuses and not enough Quintuses, I fear. But you see, my friend—try to understand—I need you both. The sooner this thing is righted, the sooner you and I can get about the business of building the kind of world mankind needs."

Quintus nodded. But for once those words invoking the old dream of "one world, one people" sounded hollow, even empty. Hadrian's golden age would be paved over the bodies of many stout soldiers along with the men, women, and children of Judea. As he made his way to the chamber where

Rufina Livia awaited him, Quintus kept seeing the face of the emperor as it had looked just at the moment when, leaving his room, he had turned to close the door behind him. Hadrian was staring at an object which Quintus knew to be Antinous' death mask. Such a range of emotions played over the emperor's face—love succeeded by sorrow, then hate, then a kind of fierce determination—that Quintus, for one brief, terrified moment, feared for Hadrian's sanity. Just as quickly he dismissed that notion, although he continued to feel chilled by it. What Hadrian had felt for Antinous may indeed have been an excess of love, he told himself, but that in no way diminished the need to end the war begun by the Jews with a finality that could not be questioned.

Livia had fallen asleep. He stared at the figure curled up in the bed, touched by the vulnerability of her pale face, so childlike in sleep. Rufus was still in Antioch, his return to Judea only a matter of days, perhaps hours. There was always so little time. And yet, he hated waking her.

She sensed his presence; she opened her eyes, and he came to her. For a brief span of time, until the morning, there would be no Hadrian, no war, no Rufus, no place called Israel, and no Rome. They would ride the bed like a ship alone on a dream-colored sea, like an island refuge far from the hungry beasts Duty and Country, safe even from the gods.

5

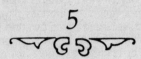

JARA FOLLOWED Andreas down the streets of the ruined city, through the hazardous piles of debris and rubble. Before she realized it, she'd lost her footing and fallen into a ditch. "Be careful," Andreas warned as he helped her out. "There are pits like this everywhere. The legionaries never gave up digging for treasure, even though most of it must have been carted off with Titus. Stories still persist that tons of gold are buried beneath Jerusalem."

"I wouldn't mind finding some," she said wistfully.

"Really?" He was surprised. "I thought money didn't mean anything to you."

"One thing I realized living among the *Ebionim*—I don't like being poor," she said grimly. "In fact, I hate it."

"Well, well." He laughed softly. "You are growing up, aren't you?"

"That doesn't mean I want to be like you," she retorted. "I'd never keep a slave."

"Neither would I. Lazy rascals. You get better work from a freeman. So you want to be rich," he mused.

"I didn't say that." But she blushed.

"Oh, don't go stupid on me again, Jara. Let me believe for a little while at least that there's some intelligence lurking behind that stare."

"I know I'm not clever like Beruria—"

"Oh, you're clever, all right. You've got all the instincts and cunning of a fine little animal. You're a true survivor. But you're not too smart."

"I'm not an animal." Simeon had called her that.

"Yes, you are. A beautiful, willful animal. You act without

290

thinking. Refusing to marry Rami was bad enough, but going off with the 'healer' was incredibly stupid.''

"Jacob was a good person," she said softly. "He was kind and good."

"No doubt. But he wasn't the man for you. And now you've cut yourself off from everyone. You've caused Akiva no end of grief," he added.

"Akiva?" It was her turn to be surprised. "Why should he grieve?"

"Because he cares about you."

"If he loves me, why did he arrange for Simeon to marry the Parthian?" she demanded angrily.

Andreas shook his head, somewhat disgusted and unwilling now to continue the conversation.

They resumed walking. After a while Jara said, "I'm not one of the *minim*."

"I know that."

"Not that there's anything very horrible about what they believe—although I hated all that preaching about masters being obeyed without question—'the good ones and the bad.' I'll never understand how anyone can accept injustice on earth for some promise of heaven."

" 'Servants, obey in all fear. . . .' How does it go? 'Be obedient to every human command, whether it be the king as the supreme power or the rulers that he has appointed.' And, oh yes—'Slaves, obey in everything those who are your earthly masters, with fear and trembling, in singleness of heart as to Christ. . . .' ''

Jara stared at him. "How do you know—"

"I told you once. There's very little I don't know." He grinned. "It isn't just Caesar the Christians have in mind. There's the matter of women. I can imagine how enchanted you were to hear 'Let a woman learn in silence with all submissiveness. I permit no woman to teach or to have authority over men; she is to keep silent.' Paul, I believe."

Jara nodded. "But most of it is about being kind to one another and doing good, much like the laws of Torah."

"That's true."

She sighed. "But I couldn't do it. If Jacob hadn't been killed, I would have had to make him see that. I couldn't let them baptize me. And in the end I couldn't say . . . what he wanted me to say."

"What was that?"

She sighed again. "He was dying. He said I could heal him if I asked in the name of Jesus."

Andreas turned around now, his interest aroused. "What did you do?"

"I just told you. I couldn't do it."

"Pity," he said after a pause.

"What do you mean?"

"You ought to have accommodated him," he said, walking on again. "If he'd lived it would have been a miracle. If not, Jacob would have died an enlightened man. Either way it would have been interesting."

"You're horrible," she whispered, close to tears. "Horrible . . ."

"I know," he admitted. "I have a perverse nature. It's just that I'm always so damn curious to see how things turn out. I don't like it about myself, but there you are." He turned around again, stopped, startled by the look in her eyes. "I'm sorry, Jara. I shouldn't have spoken to you like that. After all, you've just lost a husband."

"No," she corrected him quietly. "I have lost a friend."

WHEN, IN THE EARLIER WAR with Rome, Jerusalem was finally captured, and in the words of the historian Flavius Josephus, "there was no one left for the soldiers to kill or plunder, not a soul on which to vent their fury; for mercy would never have made them keep their hands off anyone if action was possible," Titus ordered the entire city as well as the Sanctuary razed to the ground. Only the towers of Phasael, Hippicus, and Miriamne, and the stretch of wall enclosing both Jerusalem and the Temple on the west, were left. Some said it was as protection for the garrison that remained; some said to show later generations what a proud and mighty city had been humbled. But a legend persisted that the destruction of the Western Wall had been entrusted to one of Titus' allies, an Arab king named Pangar, who for some unknown and private reason refused to carry out the task and was subsequently executed.

Apart from the three towers and the Western Wall, all the rest of the fortifications encircling Jerusalem had been leveled so completely that, again in Josephus' words, "no one visiting the spot would believe it had once been inhabited." For more than six decades the Holy City had remained a place of weeds, dust, and dirt, its ruins utilized for makeshift brothels to accommodate the Tenth Legion, and to shelter wild animals, squatters, beggars, madmen, and those few saints who still found glory in the sight of the Temple Mount and dedicated their lives to perpetual mourning and prayer. And if all that was left to these pious souls was a span of wall, then that was where they made their way daily, staining the stone with their tears so that it soon came to be called by jeering legionaries the Wailing Wall—pressing their bodies against the great limestone blocks as if they hoped the beating of their own hearts might bring back to life all that had once stood.

When it was certain that Titus had vanquished all Judea, many Christians who had fled to Pella during the war reestablished their community in Jerusalem, complete with a bishop. Fearing Bar Kokhba, they had abandoned the city once more. The dwellings they left were quickly appropriated by Jews who began to stream back following the evacuation of the Tenth Legion. The soldiers also left buildings, which had housed their common-law families (legionaries were forbidden to marry) and which were claimed by the original dispossessed in the natural evolution of conquered and reconquered cities.

Before Hadrian's departure for Egypt, the ceremony marking the rebuilding of Jerusalem as Aelia Capitolina had taken place and the actual process of that rebuilding begun. But now, on the spot where the emperor had planned his temple to Zeus, a rude Sanctuary stood, a rough affair of poles and curtains and limestone blocks marking the various courts and rooms to be erected. The actual sacrificial cult had not yet been reestablished; the new Temple served as a kind of synagogue or place of prayer. But for the first time in many years the voices of the Levites rang out at dawn and dusk and intermittently throughout the day, the beauty of the hymns they sang tinged with new poignancy, golden as the afternoon settling on the surrounding hills.

"There's Jerusalem's treasure," Andreas said, pointing to the sky and the hills, which seemed now to melt together, cloaked in light. "There's the real gold of the city."

Jara looked up at the sky and in so doing missed seeing the half-buried limestone block in her path, stumbled over it, and would have fallen again if Andreas had not caught her arm. "This place is a mess," she said, wrinkling her nose. "I still don't know why such a fuss is made about Jerusalem. Betar is much nicer." She looked around with distaste. "There's nothing here but crumbling walls and scraggly plants and a few pathetic houses."

"That's because you only see as far as your nose. Look again. Look hard. Listen to the song of the Levites, and see Jerusalem as it once was."

"I don't know how it once was," she replied crossly. "I never saw it. And all I see now is filth and—"

"Sshh. Look, Jara. Listen to the Levites, and look. Over there, see . . . there was Herod's palace, built of rare stone, with rooms without number, no two alike, and furnishings of gold and silver. On every side were pillared colonnades and green lawns with copses of trees traversed by long walks. There were pools and bronze statues through which the water flowed. Tame pigeons flew about. There were guest rooms with one hundred beds."

"All of which the Romans destroyed."

"No," he said, laughing, "not Rome. The palace was fired by the Sicarii." He took her hand. "Come. Look. Over there was the Gymnasium built before the Maccabee. And there, the Upper Market with all its treasures . . . white glass, jellied wine, the best pickled olives and smoked fish in all the world. Bracelets, necklaces, brooches, perfumes . . . silk from across the Great Sea, linen from Egypt, damask from Syria, embroidered pieces known as 'Babylonian' tapestry. Every kind of known spice could be purchased in one of the Seven Markets. And the air itself was sweet with incense, the scent carrying from the Temple as far as Jericho. And the Temple itself—"

"How do you know all this?" Jara asked, curious. "You were not even born here."

"Josephus, mostly. He was a historian—a Jew—who lived during the war with Rome and wrote about it. Along the way he described Jerusalem quite carefully."

"I know who Josephus was."

"Do you? I didn't think you would. Curious."

"There's nothing curious about knowing your enemies. Flavius Josephus was a traitor."

Andreas sighed. "I suppose so." He let go of her hand.

"Now where are you going?"

"We are in what was, I believe, the Upper City, where the

priests and the great houses of Israel had their villas. Phiabi, Kathros, Ananias . . ." He broke off, turning to the right and then to the left. "It should be around here somewhere," he muttered, "if anything's left of it. . . ."

"What? What are you looking for?"

"The house of the priest Matthias. According to my calculations . . ." Again he didn't finish, being too busy now poking through bushes grown wild. Suddenly he disappeared over a low-lying wall covered with Latin graffiti.

"Where are you?" Jara called. "What are you doing?"

No answer. In the distance came the faint howl of a dog or jackal. A sudden wind marking the onset of evening made her shiver. Frightened now, she scrambled over the wall and saw him standing before the rusty remains of a huge iron gate. He appeared to be studying a motif wrought in the metal.

"What is it? What are you looking at?"

"The figure of the new moon. . . ." He smiled his lopsided smile. "Well, well . . . 'And it shall be a sign for all who pass,' " he recited softly, " 'that here the weary are welcome, the widow and orphan shall have refuge, and all who love wisdom will find sustenance and spirited conversation.' This," Andreas said, turning to Jara, "was once the villa of the great house of Harsom."

But even before he'd finished speaking, she had begun to move toward the gate. Silently she touched it. Her fingers found the insignia; they clutched at the slice of moon caught within the metal circle. She closed her eyes and then slowly pressed her lips to it.

Andreas was so busy looking around that he did not notice her actions. "You know," he said, "the house of Harsom was so rich—" He stopped. She'd swung open the gate and was slowly entering the courtyard of the once great villa.

The place was small by any measure, for a plot of land in the City of David was the most desirable real estate in the country; even the houses of the high priests and members of the royal family were crowded together, the balcony of one sometimes overlapping the courtyard of another.

Softly, slowly, silently, Jara covered every inch of ground, touching the broken sundial, the roses and jasmine grown wild, the crumbling remains of the wall. Finally, with a small sigh, she sat down on an overturned limestone block carved like the capital of a pillar, and leaned back against the shell of the house of the priest Shammai of the family Harsom. Wild roses climbed the wall, making an arch above her head. The afternoon sun seemed to turn her eyes to glass, staining her fair skin with the golden purity of a dying day.

Andreas watched, transfixed by the grace with which she moved even as she appeared transfixed by the place and all it once held. She seemed to recede from the present, and all the words of Josephus, all the images that had burned so brightly in Andreas' brain for so many years, now took on new light and meaning. Suddenly there was more in the air than the song of the Levites carried to this ruined garden on the twilight wind. Andreas could hear the high priest instructing his servants to light the braziers against the dark and, in the distance, voices of the sages, still debating as they walked home from the Council of Hewn Rock, the Great Sanhedrin. Shutters were being drawn across the market's stalls. . . . A tutor spoke in Greek to the young daughter of a rich Jerusalemite. . . .

A thousand images were whirling around the courtyard like leaves blown by the wind. Noises, smells, snatches of conversation—a thousand ghosts whirling in a misty vapor of memory and dream, pulled out of time into the vortex of this garden, all swirling about the figure of a girl sitting amid wild roses.

Finally she raised her eyes to his. There was a tranquillity in her gaze that he had never seen before. She welcomed the ghosts.

"Tell me," he said simply.

She nodded.

"YOU SEEM TO KNOW of the house of Harsom," Jara said, "so I need not remind you of the wealth my family possessed or the renown in which they were held not only by our own people but by the rulers of Egypt, Greece, and Rome. The ships of Harsom sailed to every corner of the world. The first fortune, I am told, was in pearls. . . .

"But commerce was only a part of it. There were priests too, and philosophers. Philo of Alexandria was said to be kin." She looked around sadly. "And now there is only this. . . ."

"You said your family . . ." Andreas prompted.

"Yes. I am of the house of Harsom. Why does that seem so strange to you?" she asked suddenly. "Because when you first met me, I was working in the kitchen, a common servant?"

"There is nothing common about you, Jara," he replied softly. "From the moment I saw you, I knew you didn't belong in Akiva's kitchen. And I know the fortunes of war can turn princes into slaves as well as make kings of others. But it was my understanding that, in Judea, not one member of the house of Harsom survived the war with Rome. Moreover, your friend Samson told me you are a daughter of the Sicarii, which"—he added, smiling wryly and gesturing toward the small dagger at her waist—"I can well believe."

"What do you know of Masada?"

He was taken aback by the question. "As much as anyone, I suppose. Again, thanks to Josephus. The fortress was taken early in the war by the Sicarii, who made it their headquarters. After Jerusalem, the place became a refuge for others as well."

"For three years they held out against Rome. They were the last. And finally, rather than surrender, they killed themselves—nearly a thousand men, women, and children."

" 'But an old woman escaped,' " Andreas quoted from memory, " 'along with another who was related to Eleazar, and five little children. They had hidden themselves in the water cisterns. . . .' "

"Eleazar. Eleazar ben Ya'ir, leader of the Sicarii. He was my grandfather. His wife, my grandmother, was Alexandra of the house of Harsom."

Andreas did not reply. But his eyes, which had become riveted to her, urged her to continue.

"She was born in Caesarea and somehow survived the massacre of the Jews there when the Greeks of the city conspired with the Romans. She managed to escape to Jerusalem but was later captured and returned to Caesarea, where Vespasian gave her in marriage to another prisoner, Josef ben Matthias. Your Flavius Josephus. When my grandmother saw that he was a traitor, she left him and made her way to the Masada, accompanied by the Old One, who had been her nurse. It was on the Masada that she became the wife of Eleazar ben Ya'ir, who was himself of the priestly line. She bore him a son named Benjamin. In the last hour of the Roman assault, she gave the baby to the Old One and bade her hide with him in the cisterns, saying he must always be made aware of the blood from which he came. And then she took her place beside her husband and was killed by him and died with him."

"The baby, Benjamin—"

"Was my father. The other children were Avigael, daughter of Shem and Rebekah; Leah, daughter of Sheptai and Hadassah; Yeshua, son of Baruch and Hava; and Sara, daughter of Zebulon and Batsheva, who became my father's first wife. Also in the cistern was Miriam, cousin to Eleazar ben Ya'ir, and the boy David."

"That makes eight people, not seven, as Josephus wrote," Andreas wondered.

"When the Old One and the others showed themselves, the soldiers would have fallen on Miriam and killed the children if the boy, David, hadn't fought them. He was only fourteen, but he was a *bacchur*, a warrior, and he slew one of the Romans before the rest killed him. But Flavius Silva, the Roman general, heard the commotion, which was in the midst of a great silence, as all the rest of the people on the Masada were already dead. He came to see what had occurred. The Old One and Miriam told him, and he learned then how the Jews of Masada had stolen his victory from him."

Andreas shook his head in amazement. "Incredible! The way you say it, knowing all the names . . ."

"The Old One would never let me forget. She was always telling me things. She said she'd chosen me of all the children to remember. She used to say I had eyes like her mistress, Devorah, who was, I think, my great-grandmother and of the line of David. . . ."

"The Old One? The woman who survived Masada? Impossible! How could you have spoken to her? She must have been nearly a hundred years old when you were born!"

Jara laughed. "I used to think she would never die. I thought she would live forever, like a tree or stone. I used to think that if she did die, then she would turn into a stone like Lot's wife. Even now," she admitted, "I can't think of her in the ground. It's more as if she *were* the ground. It's difficult to explain. . . ."

But Andreas was hearing so many astonishing things that this scarcely seemed strange. "What happened after Masada?" he wanted to know.

"There was a physician in Silva's camp, a Jew named Solomon ben Ya'ish. He was allowed to take the children, and he and the Old One made their way to the Galilee, which held no memories for either of them. Miriam was sent to Rome. I don't know what became of her. My father, Benjamin, son of

Eleazar ben Ya'ir and Alexandra of the house of Harsom, became the son of Solomon ben Ya'ish. He also became a physician and had three wives, the last of whom was my mother." She looked around the ruined courtyard. "This was his legacy. And now it is mine."

"What are you going to do with it?" he asked after a pause.

"I don't know. But I won't give it up."

Andreas was silent. "If you are truly the granddaughter of Alexandra of the house of Harsom," he said finally, "then your inheritance is greater than this ruined villa. Your family held property all over the world."

"I don't care about the rest of the world. I only care for this."

Again he fell silent. He seemed to be looking at her strangely, but perhaps it was only the fading light that made it seem so. "Well," he said at last, "we'd best be on our way."

"I'm staying here."

"You can't," he said firmly. "There isn't even a roof—"

"Yes, there is. Look. Back there. See? Someone's made a kind of lean-to."

"Which means someone has already claimed your 'legacy.' Stay where you are. I'll take a look. . . ."

She followed him anyway. "A woman and a child . . ."

Andreas frowned. "They look ill."

Jara went over to the woman, who was lying on the ground with her knees pulled up to her chest. Every now and again, her legs jerked spasmodically. The child, a girl of two or three, lay nearby, her eyes open, wide with fear.

"What is it?" Andreas asked.

"I don't know. She's shaking and in a fever."

"Well, come on. We can locate a doctor by the Temple area, I'm certain."

"We can't just leave them. The child is frightened."

"Jara, I must find Simeon."

"Well, all right then, you go."

"I don't want to leave you here."

"I'll be all right." There was a water jar. She poured some water into a clay cup she found nearby and brought it to the woman's mouth.

"No, I'm not leaving you." He grabbed her hand, pulled her to her feet. "We'll find a physician, I promise you. But you're not staying here."

"The child—"

Even as she spoke the little girl began to retch, vomiting a kind of mucus. There was the smell of blood. Jara started to go to her, but Andreas pulled her back. "No," he said. "Stay away. It's plague, Jara."

She wrenched loose. Before he could stop her, she was kneeling by the child, holding the small head in her hands, murmuring endearments. "Find a doctor if you can," she told Andreas. "Better yet, bring more water and fire to light this oil lamp. It's so dark I can hardly see."

He hesitated only a moment. Then, taking off his cloak and spreading it over the child, who was shivering now and whimpering pitifully, he said, "I'll be back," and disappeared into the hastily fallen night.

IN THE MOONLIGHT, the courtyard with its broken pillars and wild roses seemed to take on an even more unreal quality; it seemed like a place awakened from a hundred-year sleep, and the girl who came out of the shadows in answer to Andreas' call like a ghost or specter with her pale eyes and white skin. She stood some yards away from him, nodding in greeting to the doctor he had brought. "Everything is fine," she said calmly. "The fever is passed. You had better go, Andreas. You have information for Simeon. You must find him."

"He's not in Jerusalem. I'm going to ride to Betar. Come with me."

"No, I want to stay here. Please go."

"Jara," he began impatiently, then shrugged. He had already lost too much time. "All right. Do as you like. I'll be back for you."

"As you wish."

Her voice was calm; why then did he feel there was something strange about her? It was the moonlight, no doubt, and this garden with its ghosts. "I'll be back," he said again, and smiled that crooked smile of his. "Don't disappear."

"Go. Please go."

He felt the anger rise in him. She had backed away from the hand extended in what he thought was no more than comradely farewell. Damn the bitch. Was there no getting to her? And after all the trouble he'd had finding the physician and then locating this shambles of a villa again. "Goodbye," he said curtly and, turning his back on her (for good, he thought), made his way out of the courtyard.

The doctor, who had gone to examine the woman and child, now emerged from behind the villa. He walked slowly to Jara's side and said, "They're both dead."

"I know."

"Do you understand the cause?" he asked cautiously, his tone indicating his suspicions.

"Yes," she said, still staring at the dark where Andreas had disappeared. "Cholera."

SHE WATCHED the flames climb the night like fingers spread against all the demons of darkness, like flowers bursting into fiery bloom only to wither within the hour like her newborn dreams. She herself had torched the place, knowing it must be done, and when she wept she could not be certain if it was for one small child killed by the cholera or for all the dead she would never know but whose presence she had felt for one magical moment in the garden she had now destroyed.

Morning found her huddled in a corner of the courtyard, wrapped in the cloak the doctor had given her, her eyes still red from tears and smoke, her nostrils smarting from the stench of charred flesh and scorched earth. Soon after dawn, the physician returned with food and water. He was grateful she understood that she must remain isolated until it could be learned whether she had contracted the disease. "There are too many people in the city," he told her. "They come from everywhere, wanting to rebuild the Temple. And there are not enough proper places for them to live and do their normal functions. When the Temple stood, Jerusalem had the best sewers in the country," he said solemnly. "Why, people were inspected at the very gates to the city to be sure they were free of disease before being allowed to enter. The streets were swept every day. And woe to the officials who did not keep the water sources and conduits clean and flowing. Well," he said with a sigh. "We shall see. Thanks to the Eternal we are not in the midst of the rainy season. We may yet be able to contain this plague. I will return in a few hours. If there is blood in your stool, you must tell me. I will try to find another garment for you to wear. It is best that you burn your robe."

He left then, and the day crawled on. She boiled some of the water he'd brought her, washed her hands with the cooled liquid, boiled some more, and drank that. She did not touch the round of bread. By afternoon she had not vomited or defecated in an uncontrolled manner. When the doctor returned, he found her sitting on the limestone capital, still as a statue. "Are you well?" he asked.

"Yes."

"How have you passed the time?"

"Thinking. Dreaming . . ."

He smiled. "Young women are always dreaming. What do you dream about? Bar Kokhba?"

She looked at him, startled out of her reverie. "No," she said. "No . . ."

He'd brought another robe. After he left, she put it on, setting fire to her own garment and thinking how many times in her life she'd put on borrowed clothes. On the fifteenth of Av, when the young maidens of Israel "went forth and danced in a circle in the vineyards," it was mandatory to wear a borrowed dress. The rabbis had decreed this in order that the daughters of wealthy men should not put their poorer cousins to shame. Beruria had made a lovely robe for the occasion with a sash of silk embroidered with pomegranate flowers; likewise, Jara had sewn a pretty garment that curiously fit Beruria as nicely as Beruria's gown did Jara. How happy they'd been then. Beruria had felt it was beneath her dignity to dance, but she'd seemed more than content talking with Mesha, her dark eyes bright and her cheeks red as the pomegranates on the silk sash. But Jara had danced and danced, and though she'd never once looked at him, she'd known Simeon had eyes only for her and that he knew she was dancing only for him.

They'd all been so happy. Tinneus Rufus had run from Simeon's army like a frightened dog. All over the country people were speaking of freedom and the redemption of Jerusalem. . . .

And now the Romans were back. Simeon was married to another. The Romans were back, Jerusalem was still a dung heap, and a child had died for no good reason or cause. She herself might be dying, the cholera festering even now in her body. Jacob was dead. Sharona, daughter of priests and kings, was someone else, stranger to her own heritage. There was nothing left of the house of Harsom.

She started to tremble. She felt giddy, faint. She could still smell burned flesh in the air, and the odor nauseated her. She staggered to the pot of water that she'd suspended over a small fire, balancing it on four rocks she'd found and laid out in a kind of primitive hearth. A dead insect floated on top of the water. She turned away, holding her stomach, bowels and gut rebelling simultaneously. But as she turned, she caught sight of the metal gate with its new-moon insignia. She drew in her breath, the sound echoing in the silence like an astonished sigh. Then she took another breath and, still staring at the gate, another, longer one. Still breathing deeply, she straightened, feeling her body relax, become hers again.

The gate. That was all that was left. All the ships and gold and words and hopes and laughter; the books and jewels and grand villas; the priestly garments; the irreplacable manuscripts; the scrolls of correspondence with kings and generals and philosophers, prophets, sages; the country estates; the mosaic-floored courtyards; the knowledge, the memories of a dynasty risen from sand to embrace the civilized world were gone. Slaughtered in Caesarea. Dead in Jerusalem, on Masada, in the Galilee. Murdered in Alexandria, Cyprus and Cyrene. . . .

All gone. Nothing left but a gate.

"I am left," she said suddenly, fiercely. She said it again. "I am left. I am here."

She started to walk around the courtyard, her blood warming, the chill leaving. "I am here," she told the stones and the charred grass and soot-darkened wall. "I am here," she told the gate. "I'm alive, and I'm not going to die."

No, she wasn't going to die. She had survived the Roman commander who'd kidnapped her, the animal haunts of the banks of the Jordan, Samaritan bandits, and a crazed sectarian who had wanted to strangle her. She'd even survived a broken heart.

She started to laugh. She felt fine. She had never felt better. And if some dark force thought she'd gone through everything only to die in the lost courtyard of her own family, stricken by disease cruelly placed, then that malevolent fate was wrong.

"Damn you!" she cried, shaking her fist as Simeon had the night he had shouted, "Don't help me, God. Just don't help them!"

"Damn you, world," Jara said. "I'm going to live! I'm going to live just to spite you!"

SHE WAS WAITING for the doctor. "I'm not sick," she told

him. "I haven't got the cholera, and I won't get it. I want to leave this place now."

He believed her.

THE DEAD WOMAN and child proved not to be isolated cases. The cholera had already spread, and only the strict sanitary observances central to Jewish belief kept the disease from being even more destructive than it was.

The conception of personal cleanliness as a prerequisite of holiness was an essential part of Torah. Many of the commandments whose stated intention was ritual purity were in fact intended to inhibit the spread of many of the diseases prevalent in neighboring countries.

In the Temple period, the laws pertaining to social hygiene had been enforced by the priests, who had no authority as physicians but rather held the position of health wardens of the community. After the destruction of the Second Temple, this concern passed to the rabbis, whose attitude toward the sanctity of life and the importance of health would be frequently expressed in the Talmud, reflecting the view of the beloved Hillel, who was said to have maintained that the act of bathing was equivalent to caring for a vessel containing the divine spirit. The rabbinic stress on the connection between cleanliness and holiness was emphasized by many injunctions, such as the commandment to wash one's face, hands, and feet daily in honor of one's Maker. It was a particularly important religious duty to wash one's hands before eating a meal, and the protection of foodstuffs was also required. Slaughtered animals were examined for various signs of disease; it was forbidden to drink any liquid left uncovered overnight; food had to be served on clean plates, and all edibles were to be kept from flies, which were considered carriers of illness. No carcass, grave, or tannery could be placed "within fifty ells" of a human dwelling; streets and marketplaces were to be kept clean; the digging of wells in the neighborhood of cemeteries or refuse dumps was forbidden; and no scholar would live in a city lacking a doctor or bathhouse.

From the time of the Bible, the Jews were aware that contagious diseases were spread by direct contact with infected persons as well as by clothing, household utensils, and other objects. To prevent epidemics, they therefore compiled a series of sanitary regulations that included such precautionary isolation as Jara had endured. Anyone coming into contact with a corpse or carrion or suffering purulent discharges from any part of his body was required to undergo a thorough cleansing of himself and his belongings before being allowed back into the community. As in the time of Joshua, even the garments, weapons, and utensils of Bar Kokhba's soldiers were cleansed and disinfected upon their return from battle to prevent the spread of any disease that might have been picked up from the enemy.

The cholera was seen as a sign. The Romans were back, and now a plague had fallen on the Holy City. Was it God's way of saying they followed a false messiah? Where was Bar Kokhba now? Why wasn't he in Jerusalem? He didn't like the City of David. He had done nothing to help rebuild the Temple, nothing to restore the city itself. And now this had happened. Too many people, living like animals in the ruins of a destroyed place, thinking themselves blessed for being here. Bar Kokhba. *Bar Koziba.* Liar. Deceiver.

And what of Akiva, who had proclaimed Simeon the "Son of a Star"? The plague was upon him too, and all at B'nei Berak. Scholars dropped daily, all "Akiva's soldiers." This filthy disease . . . It was past believing that it could strike at Rabban Akiva, who would not even share a wine cup with another without first wiping the rim. It was a sign. It had to be a sign.

Jara heard the mumblings as she went among the ill and dying. The physician allowed her to accompany him, convinced that she was somehow immune from disease. For three weeks she stayed at his side, assisting in the quarantines that took place, the burning or scalding of infected garments and utensils, and the scrubbing and smoking out of houses suspected of infection. Sometimes, rarely, the cholera could be beaten, washed out of the bodies it ravaged by great quantities of broth and boiled water. When death came, it came quickly. If the patient was strong and fought the disease, holding desperately on to life, then after a time herb potions could be given to soothe the stomach, and eggs for strength. But there was no telling who would live and who would die, Jara reflected. It all seemed random to her: chance, luck, a matter of heartless fate. Sometimes she would stare at a corpse, wondering what sins the dead man had committed to die so, only to hear a nearby mourner reciting a litany of praise for the deceased's good deeds. And then she remembered the child she'd torched in the garden of the house of Harsom, wondering what sins that small body could possibly have been punished for, and concluded as she had done long ago that the world was a place of orphans who had only each other to care for and protect and mourn them.

ON THE FIRST DAY of the fourth week of the epidemic, just as it appeared to abate, the physician began to vomit, and died the next day. The following morning Jara felt dizzy. She managed to rise from the bed that she had been given in the doctor's house, only to break out in a cold sweat. Gritting her teeth, she started for the door but had gone only a few steps before she fainted. As the darkness enveloped her, she heard her own voice whirling around her, growing more and more distant, saying, "No . . . no . . . no . . ."

6

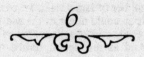

THE LEGIONS had begun their advance. Splitting into small task units the vastly reinforced Roman army, which, in addition to the six legions already in the country, now included five more from the eastern Danube and one from Cappadocia, with some sixty to seventy thousand auxiliary troops, Severus set about reducing the rebel strongpoints and villages, forcing Simeon's fighters back step by step. In the first year of the war, the forces of Bar Kokhba had taken control of over fifty fortified sites and nearly a thousand towns and settlements scattered throughout Judea, Galilee, and Samaria. Now, one by one, these enclaves of freedom began to fall back into Roman hands. Ceaselessly, Severus sent his "commandos" into the hills to ferret out the insurgents from their hideouts. Soldiers swept through town and village, searching every house and street for Bar Kokhba's men, to be executed without trial or killed when they resisted capture. No prisoners were taken. Interrogation was minimal. Rome was making a clean sweep.

There were no open, pitched battles; Severus was determined to avoid them at this time. Cities like Tiberius had no real defending army for the Romans to confront, Simeon having long ago decided against deployment of that kind. The plague, moreover, made ben Kosiba cautious. Fearing to contaminate or be contaminated by the other regions of the country, he remained in the vicinity of Jerusalem during the initial stages of the Roman advance, unable to aid those under attack. Twenty-four thousand Jews died during this period through sickness or enemy assault. The faith—in the righteousness both of their cause and of their leader—of those who survived was sorely tested and in many cases lost. Akiva, too, was now perceived by many to have fallen victim to the delusions of old age.

And so the Galilee fell. But its reconquest was not without cost. For every soldier of Israel slain, Severus lost at least one of his own. Hadrian could now ride the width of the northern country unhampered by rebel activity, but he'd paid dearly for that privilege. And as the legions turned south, still under Severus' "seek and destroy" orders, their mission would become even more difficult. The war was far from over; and the fighting would become fiercer, trickier, and yet more costly for all concerned.

THE DARKNESS was disappearing, the dreams at last dispersing. The voices and faces that had come and gone, so dimly perceived, receded into a silence so sudden, so all-consuming, that the shock of that utter quiet woke her at last.

The room was bright with sunlight. Someone was sweeping; she could see the particles of dust swept up into the air, dancing in the beams that fell through the open window. She heard the sound of the woman's broom and then, from somewhere out the window, a chanting of prayer in a childish, singsong voice. The air smelled so clean it stung her nostrils.

Jara closed her eyes again. She felt tired. Was it possible to feel so tired and still be alive? Her legs felt leaden under the linen coverlet, light as the fabric was.

She opened her eyes again, this time to find Tobita staring at her.

"Well," the woman said, "so you're not dead after all."

Jara did not reply; she was too busy studying Tobita's eyes for some sign of the woman's feelings for her. It was hard to tell.

Tobita's hand went to the girl's forehead and then to her neck in the age-old way of women seeking signs of illness. Satisfied as to the coolness of Jara's skin, Tobita next whisked away the linen "fever cloth" and replaced it with a warmer blanket.

"Where are my clothes?" Jara asked weakly.

"They were burned. We shall find you something to wear, never fear."

"It was the cholera, then?"

"No. What it was no one can say. Sheer exhaustion, I should think, after the running about you've done, my girl."

"Don't hate me, Tobita," Jara blurted, bursting into tears. "Please don't hate me."

"Hate you?" It was Tobita's turn to become misty-eyed. "Hate you, how could I hate you?" she said, gathering the girl up in her arms. "Poor, wild, misbegotten creature . . . with no mother to love you or tell you what's right. And that big brute—I don't care if he is the *Nasi*—treating you the way he has. Oh, my poor girl! My poor child!" And she rocked Jara in her arms and wept with her until they both felt cozy and warm.

"Then you're not angry with me," Jara said at last, happily.

"Yes, indeed, I was very angry," Tobita answered sternly. "But when I heard what you had done in Jerusalem," she said, her eyes softening again, "and when they brought you here and I saw you—so sick you were, so pale, and still, and your flesh on fire . . ." She shook her head. "Surely God has punished you enough, I am satisfied as to that. And now we must make you strong again. You must eat something. Look at you! Nothing but skin and bones! Not even a quarter of a chicken are you!"

"How did I get here?" Jara asked when Tobita had returned with broth and bread.

"How? They brought you, of course."

They? She was too tired to pursue the matter and too hungry to speak. Tobita's soup was pure nectar. But after a few spoonfuls she fell back, too weak to continue eating.

"Here, let me help you." The woman propped her up and began to feed her again. "You must eat. You must grow strong. This is no time for any of us to be weak. Too many have died."

"What's happened? You must tell me what's happened, Tobita. Where is Akiva? They said he'd been struck by the plague."

"Not my master, not him, blessed be the Eternal. Though how any of us have survived is a miracle indeed. So many struck down. Old, young . . ."

"Then it did spread beyond Jerusalem . . .?"

"It was everywhere. It's always like that when they come,

those barbarians with their swords and hobnailed boots. It's civilization they're bringing to the world. Yes, indeed, all sorts of laws and bridges and fine roads—and every kind of disease you can imagine."

"You think the Romans brought the cholera? Not God?"

"All I know is, war and pestilence are never strangers. Here, eat some of this bread. You must have something solid in your belly."

"Where is Akiva?" she asked again.

"Off to Betar. The Sanhedrin has reassembled there. He left right after the wedding. Ah, I see by your face you don't know what I'm talking about. Well, how could you? Rest, and I will tell you everything. Only let me fetch an egg for you, and then we'll talk."

"IT WAS ONLY a day or two after the cholera had ceased, and that was the eighteenth day of Iyyar. I remember the date exactly because Rabban declared the time a holiday, a thanksgiving to mark the passing of the plague. Well, as I told you, sometime thereafter, who should show up but young Rabbi Meir? Only from the looks of him you would never guess he was a rabbi at all. Brown as a berry, with his hands looped easy as you please in that wide leather belt around his hips. Those long fingers had felt the hilt of a sword, not a writing pen, in the months he'd been away. Well, more than one scholar has joined up with Bar Kokhba, and with Akiva's blessings at that. Still, it was a shock. And none more surprised—or should I say disturbed—than Rabbi Teradyon's daughter, Beruria. How she stared at him! And he at her. What a look there was in his eyes! As if he would have eaten her up on the spot. And she! Well, Beruria's a cool one. I always said butter wouldn't melt in her mouth. But you could see, ah, what you could see in those dark eyes of hers! She was frightened. It was the first time, I think, any of us had ever seen her so unsure. But all the same, she could not look away from him. And I tell you—because a woman knows—I tell you she was drawn to him despite his appearance, or maybe even because of it. In any event she turned red as blood.

"Next thing you know they're getting married. And how that came about is a story."

"But they were betrothed," Jara broke in. "It is only

natural they would wed. And about time, I should think. The betrothal year was long over.''

"Exactly what the young rabbi told Beruria. I could hear them, you see, busy as I was with my cleaning chores. But there must have been some pact between them that there would never be a wedding. 'You agreed,' I heard her say.

" 'I agreed to nothing,' young Mesha replies. 'The year is up and you are going to become my wife.'

"Well, more words pass between them, and next thing you know Beruria is flying from the room, pale as a peeled potato. But the wedding did indeed take place.''

"How did she look?" Jara asked eagerly.

"Like a piece of stone, with her mouth set in that thin line and her eyes staring straight ahead. She'd done nothing at all to make herself beautiful. Her dress was plain as can be. Mesha didn't smile much either. The two of them looked so stern you would have thought they were on their way to the Sanhedrin as opposing parties of some terrible dispute, instead of bride and groom.'' Tobita threw back her head and laughed heartily at the picture of Beruria and Mesha getting married.

"It doesn't sound very amusing," Jara wondered.

"Because you don't know the whole of it, my girl." Tobita leaned forward confidentially. "He forced her to it. She had no choice. 'Marry me,' he said, 'or your father will pay the price of a broken betrothal.' ''

"But Rabbi Teradyon hasn't a bean!"

"Exactly what Beruria said. 'There's the house,' Mesha said. And he told her he'd take that in payment for the broken contract.''

"I can't believe he would do such a thing.''

"Neither could Beruria. But the young rabbi made it very clear that he would.'' Tobita chuckled. "Oh, he knew what he was doing, all right! I always say God doesn't make scholars from ignoramuses. Although from the looks of that wedding one could wonder. Poor Rabbi Yossi. He was so confused. He kept shaking his head through the whole thing, doubtless remembering his own wife, who had never given him a day's happiness. 'Teradyon,' I heard him say to the bride's father, 'you had better go and sit in mourning for this marriage, because those two are going to kill each other!' ''

"And did they?" Jara asked, like a child listening to a bed-time tale.

Tobita laughed knowingly. "Well, something went on that night, that's for certain. All eyes were on the house, but nary a peep was heard all through the evening and into the next morning. The sun rose, and no sign from the bridal chamber. Morning prayers came and went without benefit of Rabbi Meir's appearance. And then, past noon it was, who should come ambling to the well but Beruria with a sparkle to her eye and her lips pink as a spring flower. 'Good morning, dear Tobita,' she fair purrs. (And this said with the sun high in the sky, mind you!) 'Isn't it a most bee-yoo-ti-ful day!' " Tobita started to laugh again. "And it's been like that ever since. And do you know what else I've noticed? Since her marriage to Mesha, Beruria never blushes!"

This time Jara laughed with her, and the two of them went at it until there were tears in their eyes again. But suddenly, in the midst of the gaiety, Tobita said sternly, "Here now, what are you laughing at? You oughtn't to understand a word of this! Never mind," she said, softening again and drawing Jara to her ample bosom once more. "You must forget him," she murmured, stroking the girl's hair. "It's no good thinking about it and doing foolish things. You only hurt yourself. Now God has brought you back to us, and you must get well and strong again and go about the business of making your life. The world is full of men. What do you want with him anyway? He has no time for anyone. You think he loves that little mouse he married? He loves Israel. He's married to Israel."

"He loves me," Jara whispered. "No matter what I do. Just as I love him no matter what he's done to me. Maybe it isn't love. Maybe it's something else. All I know is, Simeon is part of me. And I'm part of him, no matter how hard he may try to forget I exist."

"Well," Tobita said, sighing, "the Lord knows that man has enough to think about. So many dead. . . . Never mind. Simeon will turn things around soon enough. These new soldiers of Rome have worked their mischief, but they have yet to meet up with Bar Kokhba! All will be well," she said firmly. "You'll see. You'll yet wed a nice young man, and Caesar himself will bow to the *Nasi*. God won't desert us. We are His people, aren't we? You'll see," she said again, cheerfully. "All will be well."

A day or so later, when Jara was up and about, she learned

from one of the other servants that Tobita's grandson—the little boy who had brought the woman such pleasure and pride that Passover night when Simeon became "Bar Kokhba"—had died of the cholera.

SLOWLY THE ROMAN WAR MACHINE was working its way south. There would be no lightning sweep across the land of Israel, but Severus was being true to his word. He had assured Hadrian he would "annihilate, exterminate, and eradicate" Bar Kokhba's troops, and that, in a very precise, methodical, and grueling manner, was what he had proceeded to do, inching his way toward Jerusalem, which, despite its unfortified condition, was regarded as the heart and soul of the Jewish state.

The number of dead on both sides grew. But if Rome's losses were greater numerically, the Jews (as Severus had calculated) were proportionately harder hit. No one was more aware of this than Simeon. Hadrian and his generals might count slain troops as mere fractions of a sum, but for the man called Bar Kokhba, as indeed for all Jews, each life lost to the legion sword was a slash upon the very soul of Israel. It was perhaps hardest for Simeon, who'd known so many of the dead. He was never heard to utter a single prayer for the fallen, unlike David, who had wept for Saul and Jonathan. But, while delivered in his customary, brusque manner, his orders to retrieve dead comrades for burial regardless of danger, in accordance with the Law of Torah, left those who knew him well in little doubt that his resolve was not shaken but that his heart indeed was sore.

Jara saw it in his eyes. Months had passed since they parted in anger, how many months she could not say. So much had transpired in that time—her sojourn among the Ebionites, Jacob's murder, the horror-filled days (or were they weeks?) when the plague had raged through Jerusalem, her own illness—that it seemed to her whole years had gone by. Certainly she felt years older. Simeon did not look older except for his eyes. . . .

If she could but kiss those eyes. If things could be as they were at the beginning, before he became the man called Bar Kokhba. . . .

He was dictating a letter to his old friends Jonathan bar

Be'ayan and Masbelah, whom he had appointed joint commanders of Ein Gedi, unaware of Jara's silent entry into the room that served as headquarters in his camp outside Jerusalem. As always, Simeon had no real place of administration, preferring to move freely and unannounced among the districts under his control. Localities in these districts were administered in turn by community leaders working with Bar Kokhba's military commanders.

Immersed in matters of administration, he had not heard her enter the room or taken notice of her presence. As he continued to speak, however, he seemed to become aware of Jara, turned slightly, saw her, and after a moment's pause continued speaking.

"You had better send another letter, Samuel. I want the wheat of one Tahnun bar Yishmael confiscated and sent personally to me under guard. This thing has gone on long enough. They are sitting there in Ein Gedi, eating and drinking what belongs to all Israel," he said with some bitterness, "without a thought for their brothers. And tell them if they don't know how to handle those idiots in Tekoa—I do! As for Yeshua bar Tadmoraya, I want him put under guard and brought here. I want to see his eyes when I question him."

"Shall I bring this letter to you when it is written?" Samuel bar Ami, one of the *Nasi's* many secretaries, asked.

"No, sign it yourself." Simeon looked at Jara. He was impatient now to be done with dictation. "Wait. Something else." He handed the adjutant a rolled papyrus. "That is for bar Be'ayan. He is to do whatever Elisha commands. No questions. All right, you can go." They were alone now.

"Trouble?" she asked.

"Always." He scanned her figure briefly. "You look fine."

"Thank you. I am well."

He nodded. "I didn't think any plague could kill you."

"No? Why not?"

"Hadn't you heard? Only the good die young." But there was a fond look in his eyes.

Jara smiled.

"Besides, it will take more than the cholera to finish off the likes of you and me," he added gruffly. "Won't it?"

"I suppose so."

"What are you up to now?" he asked.

"I am with Akiva."

"Yes, I know."

Her eyes searched his questioningly. He turned away. "Still working with Tobita? Or has Akiva finally persuaded you to marry one of his students? What happened to your Christian?"

"Jacob is dead. One of the sectarians murdered him. Because he would not counsel war against you," she added pointedly.

Simeon turned back but did not say anything.

"They only want peace," she said softly. "They believe life on earth is of no consequence and that war accomplishes nothing."

"I know what the *minim* believe."

"Those who agree with our cause will not join us because the people call you *ha-mashi'ah*. They say that to follow you is to deny their own messiah. But they do not love Rome."

"Some of them do," he contradicted sternly, "and have been working against us from the start."

"Only a handful. You can't persecute all the Christians because of those few."

"Who said I was?"

"I have heard stories—"

"Stories! Jara, if you believe all the tales told about Bar Kokhba—" He shook his head in disgust. "Do you know what the rabbis say? They say that in order to join my army, a man must cut off his little finger. According to them I've got twenty thousand warriors, each missing a finger!" He shook his head again. "Makes sense, doesn't it? Fighting men with crippled hands!" He ran his own hand through his hair, a gesture of incredulity coupled with anger and disgust. He sighed. Suddenly he turned back and, after staring at her a moment, called "Samuel! Samuel!"

The secretary returned hastily.

"Another letter. No, I'll write this one myself. Just give me the materials." Papyrus and pen were hurriedly produced, and Bar Kokhba quickly scrawled a brief note, which he then handed to bar Ami. "No, wait. Read it to her."

Samuel bar Ami stared at Jara, puzzled, but obeyed Simeon's order. " 'Simeon, son of Kosiba, to Joshua, son of Galgola, and to the men of Kefar Habbaruk,' " he read. " 'Greetings. I take heaven as witness against me that if anyone of the Galileans who are among you should be ill-

treated, I will put fetters on your feet as I did to ben Aphlul.'
Signed, Simeon, son of Kosiba. . . ."

Simeon nodded. "All right. That's all. Have it dispatched
immediately."

"Well," he said to Jara, when they were alone again, "are
you satisfied?"

"There are other places where the *minim* live—"

"Jara, I don't give a damn about the *minim*. I never have.
So long as they don't get in my way. In any case, most of their
villages are back in Roman hands. No doubt your friends
are moaning to Hadrian now that I victimized them most
cruelly."

"They're not like that."

"We'll see." Silence. "Well, is that it? Have you got what
you came for?"

"No, I—I mean, that isn't why I'm here. I came with
Akiva."

"Ah, yes. The rabbi is on his way to Betar, where the Council meets."

"Simeon, couldn't you persuade him to remain in Betar?"

"Why should I do that?"

"Because he'd be safe there."

"What makes you think he isn't safe in B'nei Berak? Or are
you another one who's begun to see legionaries coming over
every hill?"

"You know I'm not. But how can you stop them? Even
winter hasn't slowed their advance."

"A bit. It slowed them a bit."

"Slowed, but not stopped," Obodas said, coming into the
room.

"Thank you," Simeon said dryly, acknowledging the Nabatean's presence.

"Once they cross the Plain of Esdraelon, they'll start chop-
ping us up here as they did to the Galilee," Jara said.

"It won't be so easy in the South."

"Oh, Simeon, who's to defend B'nei Berak?" Jara exclaimed. "Akiva's 'soldiers'?"

"Yes, damn it! Let the scholars defend themselves! Let
them fight for Israel!"

"They're willing! And many have done so. But what chance
would they have?"

"We've fought the legions before," Simeon replied grimly.

"This is different," Obodas said. "For every one we slay, a dozen more appear. And when they are dead, there are still others, more and yet more."

"All right!" Simeon exploded. "All right," he repeated in a calmer voice. "It's true. God knows it's true. They don't seem to care how many they lose if they can get at us. And nothing stops them. Rain, mud, mountain . . . still they come. Fifty soldiers' bodies strewn across a field and twenty of our men dead. Only twenty to their fifty. But oh! that twenty!"

"If they invade the King's Mountain, whole villages will be wiped out," Jara said. "You know what happened at Tur Malka."

He did not reply.

"You must hold the Romans back."

"Damn you, girl," he said through clenched teeth. "You never cease being a thorn in my side. Do you think I don't know that? But you've just heard Obodas and me. What chance do you think we've got meeting the legions face on? I've gone over it again and again in my head—even before they came back. *We've fought the only way we can fight and win.* The only way we know how to fight. From the hills and mountains, springing at them from the entrance of some narrow defile, surprising their rear. . . . We've fought like the Sicarii fought, with the sling and the lance and the dagger. We have no siege machines. Our archers can't compare to their Idumaean auxiliary. Because of the laws of *kashrut*, we've never been meat hunters. With all the training in the use of the bow—which I've insisted on—we have a mere handful of dead-shots against the number Hadrian enjoys. And there is the matter of formation. No, no . . . it's impossible. It would be over in moments. There'd be nothing left of us. Maybe Hadrian doesn't give a damn how many soldiers he loses, but I do! I won't sentence my men to suicide."

"You sentence us all if you just sit and wait for them to come to you," Jara retorted.

"You don't understand," he muttered, dismissing her with a wave of his hand.

"I do understand! I'm not stupid! If meeting the Romans in open fight will prove so disastrous, then why haven't they pushed for it? I've spoken to Mesha. He says the Roman general appears to be avoiding any kind of pitched battle. Why? According to you, he would have an easy time of it."

Simeon stared at her. He looked at Obodas.

"Long ago," the Nabatean said, "when we first met, you said to me, 'I do not want the slow death.' You were alone in the desert. A snake had bitten you. 'Kill me,' you said. 'Kill me now if I am to die. It is better to go quickly than to die a slow and terrible death.' "

"Nobody's dying," Simeon said after a pause. "Listen to me, both of you. This war is far from over."

HE KNEW she was right. She'd burrowed right into his brain, ferreting out that one puzzling fact he wrestled with night after sleepless night. Why hadn't Severus opted for open battle?

But perhaps he had.

Perhaps the moves up to now were meant only to flush out the bulk of Jewish fighters, to force all the Brothers out of their mountain and desert hideouts for that one grand, mismatched confrontation.

In which case, rushing now to stop the Roman advance into the South, meeting the legions in the Plain of Esdraelon known as Armageddon, before which the Roman troops were so conveniently paused, was playing into Severus' hands.

Still, the girl was right. If Severus invaded the southern districts—not just Tur Malka, but Tekoa, and particularly Ein Gedi, which was not only a military but an economic bastion of the state—wholesale destruction would take place. The Romans were so wonderfully free from prejudice, Simeon mused wryly. They bestowed citizenship and conducted massacres with equal impartiality.

Both sides would be desperate. In the end it would not be soldiers who suffered most but the women and children, the old and the weak caught in the middle.

There was no choice. He had to draw Severus away from the inhabited areas. Which was probably what the Roman had counted on all along.

Ben Kosiba drew in his breath. It was at best a gamble. A terrifying gamble. But Jara and Obodas were right: It was better than waiting. And if he failed, at least he would have taken Severus away from the towns and villages. But if he won, if he could strike a decisive blow, then perhaps terms could be arranged. Surely there must be senators in Rome who were appalled at the troops lost in their old province of Judea, numbers so disparate from the size and importance of such a small area. Surely some men in the senate were rational enough to recognize the independence of Israel in return for a pledge of friendship or guarantee against Parthia. After the lack of assistance Parthia was giving the struggling state, Simeon had little compunction on that score.

It had been a waiting game after all. He'd known all along the kind of war he must wage could not continue indefinitely with success. But there were all those hints from Parthia, those subtly worded messages that might or might not be promises but surely were encouragement. He'd begun by hoping Parthia would enter the conflict, and then he thought that, seeing the Jews' resolve, other subject nations would rise against Rome. But none had. Israel was alone.

As it had always been.

As it would always be.

A FEW DAYS LATER, Simeon showed up in B'nei Berak. He came unannounced to the kitchen where Jara was working. Her hair was tied up in a kerchief; the escaping tendrils framing her face made him think of the youngster he'd encountered on the road long ago. It all flashed before him: the girl in the shepherd's tunic . . . the small, pale face stoically absorbing the curses of a half-demented rabbi . . . the way she'd clung to him sobbing herself finally to sleep. . . .

And the sight of her beneath the great fig tree, miraculously transformed from a dirty child into a beautiful, nubile creature.

All the memories came flooding back, breaking through everything to glisten finally in his eyes. *I'm tired*, he thought defensively, needing to justify the sudden rush of unchecked emotion. And still the images persisted: the sound of the sea and the feel of her against him . . . passion unleased at the first embrace, only to become woman's rage . . . the same angry tiger-eyes turned on him at Jericho as he'd seen first in the Valley of Rimmon.

Rimmon . . .

The pictures stopped. *I must be mad*, he thought, hesitating even as he moved toward her.

She looked up, saw him.

There was no turning back. . . .

"I have a man who is in Caesarea now," he told her, "who goes by the name Elisha. I need to convey a message to him."

She waited, alert, poised, a momentary spark lighting the great cat-eyes, only to be swept away by a blink that rendered them inscrutable once more.

Simeon smiled slightly. Once again their relationship had shifted, but the steel thread uniting them, that bond forged of so much more than just the time they'd had as lovers, was taut again and so tight now the movement of the air could make music on it. She knew without his saying exactly what he wanted of her, what he was offering as well as asking.

"HE'S CRAZY!" Tobita exclaimed when she heard that Jara was setting out for Caesarea. "You can't go! You mustn't! That terrible city! There isn't a God-fearing Jew alive there. Nothing but Greeks and Syrians—and now the Romans are back, they as well! What can he be thinking of? Sending a girl to do his business! Who's going to tell me Simeon ben Kosiba hasn't a multitude of men to do his bidding? Why must he send you? Can it be true what they say, that Bar Kokhba cares not a whit whom he uses or how, so long as he achieves what he wants? Has it come to that? No!" She shook her head, mouth set. "Oh no! I will not allow it! It is too dangerous. Do you hear? It is much too dangerous!" And she poked the air with the knife that had just carved a chicken into eight neat parts, to emphasize these last words.

"There's nothing you can do to stop me," Jara said calmly, "so you may as well put that down. Besides, it isn't as dangerous as it sounds. Obodas will accompany me."

"If he is going, why must you?"

"Because a 'Christian' serving girl should be able to find her way into the governor's palace without much trouble."

"The governor's palace!" Tobita closed her eyes and muttered a short prayer. "Does Akiva know about this?" she asked, opening her eyes again, only to narrow them in suspicion.

"Yes."

"Well?" the good woman demanded.

Jara shrugged slightly. "It's necessary. Don't be cross with me," she said, throwing her arms around the woman. "This isn't the same as when I last went away."

"It isn't you I'm angry with," Tobita replied. "It's Simeon ben Kosiba. What can he be thinking of?"

"Don't you see?" Jara hugged her again. "It's all he can give me."

"Give you! Give you what? The chance to be killed?"

"No. The chance finally to do something! Oh, Tobita, I've wanted so to be part of all that's happening, not just to serve soup, and throw flowers at Bar Kokhba's soldiers!"

"I don't understand." The woman was clearly confused. "What do you want? To fight? To take a sword in your hand?"

"I would if I had to. No . . . it's just that I want so much more than what I have or what I am. I know I should not complain—and I'm not, truly. You are kind to me, and Akiva is good to take me in. I've learned to read and to write. I have shelter and food, and a warm blanket on my bed, and all this with no family or husband."

"What do you mean, no family? We are your family," Tobita protested.

"Yes, yes . . . I only mean there's something in me—I don't know what it is—that wants . . . I don't know how to say it. I'm not sure I know what it is. But Simeon does. He understands. He knows who I am."

Tobita shook her head. "Bar Kokhba may know who you are, but I pray he knows what he's doing. And you," she added.

Jara assured the woman that all would be well, but later, on the road with Obodas, she began to wonder about her mission. She had no idea who Elisha was. "You will recognize him when you see him," was all Simeon would say.

"It is better not to know too much," Obodas told her as they camped for the night by the fire he'd made. "In case you are discovered. There are many cruel ways by which men obtain information," he added matter-of-factly.

"I would tell them nothing."

"You would," he said in the same matter-of-fact tone. "You would."

Jara did not reply. Tobita had been right; there was danger. It didn't matter, though. If she could help Simeon . . .

"What does 'Now must the crane look into the lion's mouth' mean?" she asked after a pause.

"It is better not to know too much," he said again.

She fell silent once more, going over in her mind all that had to be relayed to Elisha. "The crane in the lion's mouth." . . . Where had she heard that before?

"Tell me about yourself, Obodas," she said, snuggling against the rolled blanket. "Tell me how you came to know Simeon."

The Nabatean had taken out the reed pipe he always carried with him. Before answering her, he proceeded to play upon it, and as he did the mist of the night became a desert haze. Without a word spoken, the richness and the beauty of a civilization that had blossomed briefly in the waste of the Negev like some rare, exquisite flower began to be evoked. It was perhaps fitting that this transmission of sense and image came about through Obodas' music, for the Nabatu, as they called themselves in their own inscriptions, left no historical documents to mankind.

They were a storybook people with almost magical accomplishments, hewing towers and temples out of solid rock, transforming desert wasteland into terraced gardens, fabricating delicate pottery of exquisite design. Moving in from the spawning grounds of Arabia in the second century B.C.E., the Nabataei, as the Hellenized world would call them, had seized Edom and Moab, the Negev and Sinai, as well as other lands, prospering quickly as tradesmen, farmers, engineers, architects, and artists of genius—only to be thrust back by the Romans into limbo.

The Judeans and the Nabateans knew each other well and ofttimes intermarried. Herod Antipas, son of Herod the Great (whose mother was a Nabatean), married the daughter of the powerful Nabatean king Aretas IV. He divorced her in order to wed his niece and sister-in-law, Herodias, which not only cost John the Baptist his head but caused Aretas to dispatch a punitive expedition that soundly thrashed the army of his former son-in-law. He was not the first Nabatean king to defeat Judean forces. By the time of the birth of Jesus, the desert kingdom had become a formidable power in the affairs of the area, partly because it was situated on the trade route between Arabia and Syria. Heavily laden caravans carrying not only spices and incense but also goods from Africa, India, and even China converged on the Nabatean capital, Petra, the "rose-red city, half as old as Time."

It was not really that old, but it was beautiful, fantastically beautiful, the buildings carved out of solid rock, aglow with the pinks and purples and yellows and blues of the naturally striated stone, and further adorned with the same grace and delicacy as could be found on any painted piece of eggshell-thin Nabatean pottery. In Obodas' music, Jara could hear the water trickling onto gardens blanketing a hot, stony valley, the life-giving water that no one would ever know better than the Nabatu how to wrest from the arid environment.

All this was in Obodas' music as well as something else, seductive, female. When he put away his flute and said, "That was a song of the goddess Atargatis," Jara was not surprised. Then, at her urging, he told her of the being whom his people worshipped in the form of a mermaid, her face covered with leaves so as to be unseen. He told her also of Dushara, who, like the Hebrew God of Sinai, could not be looked upon or represented in human terms; he was worshipped in the shape of an unhewn four-cornered stone.

"In many ways your people and mine are much alike," Obodas said. "But you have something here"—he touched his heart—"that we do not. We are an easy people. We love our gods, but if the Romans tell us Zeus is good, we worship Zeus, and for many, Dushara is forgotten or puts on the mask of Zeus. When the Romans came and my people saw they would not be destroyed nor driven away, that life would go on as it always had, they did not care. To bow to Petra or to bow to Rome"—he shrugged—"it is all the same to them so long as they are left to themselves. That is how they are."

"And you?" Jara asked.

"I am a king," Obodas said. "That is different."

"You . . . are king of the Nabateans?" She sat up, eyes wide.

"I am the first-born of Rabel II. But my brother rules. Such as he is allowed to do," he added. "The Kingdom of the Nabatu is but a part of the Roman Province of Arabia since it was declared so by the emperor Trajan. We could have resisted," he said, anticipating her question. "Petra lies in a great, bare basin surrounded by mountains. The only approach is through a single, narrow cleft. Even if the Romans had sealed off this pass, we would not have starved to death. Only if they could take the water from us. And no one can do that. But the people did not wish to resist. They saw no good in doing so." He spread his hands as if to say that was all there was to it.

"And you?" Jara asked.

"I see that change will come. For while it is true that Caesar interferes little in the affairs of the Negev, it is also true that Rome does what is good for Rome, not for the Nabatu. The capital of Caesar's Province will become Bozrah in Syria. Already trade departs from Petra. Soon, too, the people will leave. We will be no more what we are. The Nabatu will be swept away.

"My brother does not see this. Nor does he object to dancing like a doll on the end of Caesar's strings. He conspired with the Romans to kill me. And so I was taken from the palace and brought far away from the city, my hands and feet bound, and left to die in the desert. But as you can see, I did not die.

"There were three of them," he recalled. "One was young, hardly a man. One cursed all the time. And one was silent. He died silently, the others with a curse and a whimper. And then Simeon ben Kosiba cut the ropes from my hands and feet, and gave me water to drink, and spoke to me.

"His wife and child were dead. He had nothing. Like me. We were brothers. He had gone into the desert like the prophets of your people. What he sought there is not for me to say. But he saved my life."

"You said something once about a snake," Jara interjected.

"It coiled itself around him while we slept. The movement of his waking stirred it to attack. It bit him—here, on his arm. Ben Kosiba gave me his knife and bade me kill him. But I cut into the wound and sucked the poison from it, and he lived. Then the fever came upon him, and he shivered and sweated for two nights. By the third sunrise he was well."

"You saved his life," Jara said.

"As he did mine."

"That funny mark on Simeon's arm," she said suddenly. "I thought it was a birthmark—"

"The scar of the snake and the knife." Obodas nodded. "The wound healed strangely. Like scribe's work."

Jara was about to agree, but felt too drowsy now to say anything. Obodas began to play upon his flute again, and she drifted off to sleep wondering at the odd fashion in which a snakebite had left its mark and what a curious thing it was for a desert people to worship a fish goddess.

MORNING DAWNED with a chill. The fire had gone out, and the first thing Jara saw as she opened her eyes was the hobnailed boot of a legionary alongside her head. Quickly she was up, but before she could stand, an arm caught her around the waist and set her on her feet.

"That's better," the soldier drawled. "Now we can get a look at you."

Ignoring him, she searched instead for Obodas, saw him spread-eagled on the ground, a knife held at his throat.

The legionary followed her gaze. "Not to worry, miss. He won't hurt you."

Bewildered, she turned back to the Roman.

"Can't you see she doesn't understand what you're saying?" one of the men holding Obodas said now. "You've got to talk in their language." He got up and took a step toward her. "*Shalom. Shalom.*"

Jara swallowed. "*Shalom,*" she said breathlessly, adding quickly, "peace in the name of the Christ."

The soldier's eyes widened. He was young, not much more than twenty, with fair hair and a fresh sunburn.

"What does she say?" the legionary with Jara wanted to know.

"She's a Christian. Let me have a word with her. I'm sure she'll tell us all we want to know."

"Whatever you say, corporal." There was an amused sound to the sergeant's voice. He let go of Jara's arm now and motioned for her to go over to the fair-haired Roman. But after a few moments he barked impatiently, "Well?"

The young corporal hastened back. "Like I said, she's a Christian. Looking for work in Caesarea. Her husband's dead. The Nabatean offered to show her the way. She says he's harmless."

"In my arse he is. Well, let the bugger up."

"Shall we let him go?"

"No, we'd better take him in with us. The girl too." He'd had the chance to look Jara over and said now with an ap-

preciative gleam in his eye, "Needs to earn her keep, does she?
Well, we can see to that. All right . . . come on. Let's move
it!"

Jara and Obodas were allowed to gather up their belongings
while the soldiers stamped out all remains of the fire. As Jara
bent to pick up her cloak, the young corporal kneeled down
alongside her. "Don't be afraid," he whispered. "I won't let
any harm come to you." She looked questioningly at him, but
he said no more. As he rolled up her cloak, however, he appeared to scratch something in the dirt. Then, hastily, he stood
up and walked away. Jara leaned forward and saw the outline
of a fish. As she retrieved her cloak, she allowed a corner of
the fabric to fall across and sweep away the sign the Christian
had given her.

THE CAMP WAS a perfectly square stockade inside which, with
mathematical precision, tents were erected in the neat,
prescribed order of Roman camps everywhere. From this arrangement, this carefully structured habitat which was, in effect, a temporary town, and whose dimensions—whether in
Gaul, Britain, Africa, or Syria—deviated not a whit from one
another or from the soldiers' quarters on the banks of the
Tiber, cities such as London would rise.

There were two main paths in the camp, crossing at right
angles. The *via praetoria* ran east to west. The *via principalis*,
which was the troop commander's road, ran north to south.
Here, in this command post with its court and *dias*, its altars
for the legion's sacrifices, its *auguratorium* from which the
priests of the camp could determine omens by watching the
flight of birds, or the stars—here inside his comfortably furnished tent, Sextus Julius Severus sat with his officers and ad-
visers.

It was an amazing group. Staring into the faces of that
assembly, Jara felt as if she had been ushered into some hellish
tribunal, confronted by all her enemies as in some nightmare
vision. Evening had fallen by the time they'd reached the
Roman position, and the glow of the oil lamps only served to
make more pronounced each sinister shadow and dark stare of
the men before her. She saw only three: the centurion whose
face was as firmly implanted in her memory as the night in
Tiberias when she'd killed Florus Valerens; the sectarian

who'd murdered Jacob, and—his dark, devil eyes boring into hers—the traitor, oh, damnable traitor! Andreas.

The path to the *praetorium* had been lit by torches. Truly, she had descended to Hades.

"What have we here?" The hard sound of Latin cut through her shock.

The sergeant made his report. When he was done, Severus said, "I see no reason to detain the girl or the man." He had barely glanced at Jara, but was studying Obodas. "The people of Petra are peaceful members of the Empire. What is your profession?" he asked the Nabatean.

"Dinnerware, excellency. Plates and bowls of fine work."

"There was nothing on him when we found them," the sergeant said, his face red. "Not a jug or jar."

Severus looked at Quintus.

"There was talk once, before the war, of a Nabatean who rode with Simeon ben Kosiba," the centurion mused. He turned to Obodas. "Where are your wares?"

"I must settle an account in Caesarea," Obodas explained. "There are moneys owed me. My letters mean nothing. My wife said it would be so. Now I must go myself to collect from the Greek who robbed me. You know how it is."

Andreas laughed. "I thought you people were better businessmen than that! Working on account . . ." He shook his head. "Better let him go and collect what's due him, general." He grinned. "Or his wife will have his head!"

Severus smiled and made a motion to dismiss Obodas, who said now, "With your permission, excellency, I will pass the night here and set out in the morning for Caesarea."

The Roman nodded, and Obodas was led out of the tent.

"Now for the girl," Severus began rather wearily, wishing the sergeant had done what he obviously wanted to do out on the road instead of bringing the female to camp and making a case of it.

"I know this female," Quadranus broke in excitedly. "I know who she is."

Severus turned to him in surprise.

"She is a witch. A murderer." The sectarian paused dramatically. "She is the daughter of Bar Kokhba!"

There was stunned silence. Jara looked at Quintus, but he said nothing. Suddenly the sound of Andreas' laughter broke the tension. He poured himself a cup of wine and drank it.

"You find this information amusing?" Severus asked, not certain himself whether the Christian was declaring a fact or indulging in some kind of fanciful religious rhetoric.

"Considering that Bar Kokhba's wife is no more than thirteen years of age, and this creature is, I should guess, closer to twenty, why, yes. With all due respect"—he raised the cup to Quadranus— "yes, it is rather amusing."

"Men may wed more than once," Severus said.

"That is true," Andreas acknowledged. He found himself being stared at by Marcellus Quintus now and said quickly, "It occurs to me I did hear once that ben Kosiba had been married in his youth. But all his family are said to have been killed by legionaries. That is what started him on this dreary business," he added. "Or so I've heard."

"You've lived among the rebels for over three years," Severus remarked. "It seems to me you ought to know a bit more than you do."

"Let me remind you I was kidnapped. A prisoner, although free to move about. But still, a hostage. Even though my family has paid my ransom thrice over, Bar Kokhba refused to release me, hoping to extract even more from them."

"Rather unsporting."

"It's the Sicarii method of funding. The historian Josephus, so well beloved by the emperor Vespasian, made note of it in his works. Alas, I have seen the proof of it. I am afraid, however, that we are not the inexhaustible treasury these peasants imagine my family to be. Had I not managed to escape when I did, it is certain Bar Kokhba would have soon decided to slit the throat of the bird who'd ceased producing golden eggs."

"Your captivity has not dulled your wit," Quintus remarked somewhat dryly.

"Indeed it is a pleasure to speak a civilized tongue once more. And to be away from the company of animals like that bitch there"—he indicated Jara—"who naturally does not understand a word we're saying. By all the gods, how I long for Rome!"

"She may be an animal," Severus said, coming closer to Jara now, "but she is indeed an attractive one. Look at those eyes. . . . There was a female in Britain, daughter of a Druid chief—there's a pack of savages for you. . . ." He did not continue.

"She is a witch!" Quadranus came forward again. "I tell you she is kin to Simeon ben Kosiba!"

"It may be so," Quintus agreed slowly, his face expressionless. "I think I've seen her before . . . in a village suspected of harboring rebels. I seem to remember her face." He took a step nearer. "Yes . . ."

"Now that I think on it," Andreas said suddenly, "it seems to me there was some talk of a girl in Bar Kokhba's camp. She does look familiar. You know, you're right," he said to Quintus, smiling crookedly, his eyes on Jara. "Now that I see her in this light . . . one could hardly forget that face."

THE YOUNG CORPORAL arranged to guard her. He was a rarity in the enlisted ranks: a true Roman, born in the Imperial City. The days of Rome's "citizen army" were a thing of the past; most of the soldiers that made up Hadrian's troops were peasants recruited from some frontier district that they were required to defend against the barbarians beyond the Empire's demarcation line—from whom in fact they differed very little. They signed up for twenty years, at the end of which they would be awarded land in the place or province where they had spent most of their lives and become farmers again. If a legionary's booty was good, he could settle down in style. But first, there were those twenty years of soldiering, which the fair-haired boy with Jara had just begun. "Don't worry," he told her once more. "Unless it's the general himself, no one will get into the tent. You're safe so long as I'm about." But sometime close to midnight she was awakened by a man's hand on her shoulder.

"Sshh," Andreas said before she could make a sound. "Don't speak. Come with me."

"What do you want?"

"Sshh. Not so loud. I'm getting us out of here."

"Us?"

"Sshh. Come."

She hesitated. The corporal's body lay in a corner of the tent where Andreas had dragged him. "Is he dead?"

"No. Why? Would you feel better if I killed him?"

"No," she said hastily and, with another glance at the unconscious soldier, followed Andreas out the tent.

They stole through the camp, silent as thieves, making their way to a clump of trees a short distance away where a pair of horses were tethered.

"Where's Obodas?"

"He's all right. Don't worry about him."

They untied the animals, led them still a further distance from the camp. Then they mounted and rode like furies into the welcoming night.

FROM THE TOWER WALL guarding the city of Betar, Simeon ben Kosiba counted the stars and studied the moon. "Where is she now?" he asked finally.

"She is with Andreas." Obodas took a step toward him. "He has persuaded the Roman general to allow them to escape in hopes of finding you."

Simeon nodded, his eyes still on the moon.

"The legions are further south than we thought," the Nabatean said. "Only Hadrian remains in Tiberias."

"You're sure she's safe."

"She is with Andreas," Obodas said again, as if that answered the question. "He is quick and clever."

"Clever," Simeon echoed with some bitterness. "How I hate being 'clever.' She may die for our cunning."

"Not so," Obodas replied, and he recounted with admiration the way Jara had answered the soldiers. "Rome cannot destroy her," he said finally, "any more than the snake could kill you. It is not in the stars," he concluded, pointing upward.

Simeon looked away. "What else?"

"I took care of the sectarian. They will not find the body."

Ben Kosiba nodded. He was still thinking of Jara. The plan had been for Obodas, not Andreas, to escape with her. The thought of the girl alone for some days with that young man did not exactly thrill him. "You're sure she's safe," he growled.

The Nabatean smiled slightly. "Safe from the Romans," he said.

JARA SAT with her elbows on her knees and her chin in the palm of one hand, staring at the sea.

"The horses are all right," Andreas said, coming up to her.

"They just need to rest. And so do we," he added.

She looked around. "We're too visible here."

"We won't be missed until morning. Besides, this area is quite safe."

"Is it? The Romans guard the sea."

"Well . . ." He cleared his throat. "I don't see any ships, do you? And I doubt anyone aboard one would be much interested in a man and a woman alone on the shore." He grinned. "Not the way you imagine."

She turned away, disgusted. "Is that all you ever think about?"

"When I'm with you, it seems. By the way, I forgive you."

She turned back, mouth open.

"In Jerusalem," he explained. "I misunderstood. I thought you were just being wretched again. I didn't realize you were trying to save me from the cholera." He leaned forward slightly, the half-smile playing about his lips. "You were trying to save me, weren't you?"

"You had information for Simeon."

"Oh. I see."

"But maybe I was wrong. Perhaps . . . I don't know. I'm confused," she said under her breath.

"About what? Seeing me with Severus? Surely you understand—"

"I understand nothing! Not . . . this. Not all of it. I heard what you told the Roman general. Just as I heard what you said once to another Roman—the centurion—when you came to B'nei Berak with Hadrian."

"Jara, I got you out of the Roman camp—"

"It's a trap. It's a trick of some kind. I can feel it. And I never go against my feelings. It's the one thing I know I can trust."

"You can trust me," he said quietly.

"Can I?" She stood up, looked around again. "This place is too open. The escape, the horses waiting . . . it was so easy." She looked back at Andreas. "They're following us, aren't they?"

He did not answer.

"What did you say to make them let us go?" she demanded.

"I said you would lead them to Simeon."

"I won't!"

"Of course you won't. Jara, I don't need you for that. I

could lead Severus straightway to Bar Kokhba's camp if I cared to."

"Then . . . what?"

"You're right. It is a trick. You and I are to make Severus think Simeon's encampment is where it is not."

"I don't believe you."

"Yes, you do. You were sent out by Simeon—"

"Not for that."

"Yes, for that. That was the second—actually, the primary part of your task. The first part was to deliver a message to Elisha. I am Elisha. Obodas told me what I needed to know." He paused. "Frankly, I didn't expect to see you. It was a shock, I can tell you that. But it worked out well. Especially after that crazy sectarian started carrying on. I had no trouble at all persuading Severus how 'valuable' you could be. I'm not quite sure, though, why Quintus went along with it," he mused. "I thought he would give us some trouble. But he seemed almost anxious to be rid of you."

She was no longer listening. She had sat down on the boulder she'd perched on earlier and was staring at the sea again. "Why didn't he tell me . . . ?"

"In these things it's better not to know too much. Damned if I understand why Simeon decided to use you," he wondered softly. "He must be feeling desperate."

"Use!" She pounced on the word. "Yes, that's just what he's done. Again!" She stood up angrily. "Everybody lies," she whispered, blinking back tears. "Why does everybody lie?"

"I'm not lying to you, Jara. I never have." He caught hold of her arm. "This is a perilous business. I don't pretend it isn't. How we've managed to get this far without harm coming to either of us is something of a miracle. And we're not out of danger." He paused. "If you choose to, you can go on back to Akiva. I can probably manage to persuade Severus that I know where Bar Kokhba is waiting for him and finish this alone."

Jara did not answer; she appeared to hesitate.

"You know," Andreas said, "for so long as I've known you, you've acted out of anger and spite. That's why I said you weren't too smart, not because you haven't the learning of Beruria. The first time I ever saw you behave out of something other than those childish, selfish instincts of yours was in

Jerusalem—and I didn't realize until later what you were doing and why. You probably saved my life. From what I hear, you saved many others or at least helped them as much as you were able.

"You can leave now, Jara. I won't blame you if you do, not because Simeon may or may not have lied to you, but because, as I said, this is hard, dangerous work."

She turned back. "What is it all about?"

"Simeon needs time. That's all I can tell you. A few more days. We can give that to him."

She turned away again, the look in her eyes cold evidence of what she'd like to give Simeon ben Kosiba.

"Funny," Andreas murmured, smiling crookedly. "I never imagined a time would come when I'd be trying to persuade you to do something for Israel. But that's what is really at stake, Jara. Not you and Simeon. You talk about being the granddaughter of Eleazar ben Ya'ir and Alexandra of the house of Harsom. You might want to think about the path they'd choose now. Think what your grandmother would do."

Slowly Jara turned back to him. Then, slowly, she nodded.

"Good," Andreas said. "Very good!" In the moonlight his dark eyes seemed aglow and his straight, even teeth shone white as he grinned at her. "Between the two of us we're going to lead the Roman army on one damn fine merry chase!"

7

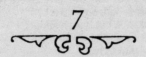

"WHERE IS AKIVA? Where is he?"

The students in Rabbi Meir's classroom turned around as one. Mesha, who had been conferring privately with one boy, their heads bent together over a portion of Torah, looked up, startled.

"Where is Akiva ben Joseph?" the intruder demanded to know. "I must speak with him."

Mesha hurried to his side. "He is not here, rabban."

It was Aher's turn to be startled. He took a step back as though recoiling from the title his former pupil accorded him. "Where is he, then?" he asked gruffly. "In Antioch, trying to raise more volunteers for his Son of a Star? In Parthia? They're still sitting *sheva* in Alexandria for all the dead lost in the last war, so he can't have gone there," ben Abuyah added bitterly. "Well, what are you looking at?" He turned on the young scholars who were staring at him as though they'd seen the devil. "Look at yourselves, sitting there like sheep, learning useless prayers to mumble to the wind. Words flung into the wind, that's all they are. Why don't you learn a decent trade? Yes, you, with those long fingers! Become a weaver—there's a useful profession. And you, a mason—yes, that means something! And the rest of you! Get up from your seats and go out into the world!"

Gently but firmly Mesha led the distraught man outside and closed the door. "What is it?" he asked softly. "What has happened?"

"I'm sorry," ben Abuyah said, his voice dropping to a

334

whisper. "Forgive me." He stared at the door to the school.
"I didn't mean to frighten them. I only want to save
them. . . ."

"From what, rabban?"

Aher did not answer.

"Come to the house," Mesha said. "Sit and rest. You have
had a long and hard ride. Come and sit with me, and we will
talk as we used to do."

BERURIA SET OUT the cups warily, unsure how to regard the
visitor. Ben Abuyah was notorious for his apostasy, his frequent association with harlots, and his preoccupation with all
the species of metaphysics and esoteric knowledge that the
sages of Israel were unanimous in declaring dangerous to
one's well-being.

"Your father was an intelligent man," ben Abuyah was saying now to Mesha. "A thinking soldier. That is a rare combination. He wanted to know about the faith of the Jews—the
strange obsession which led men to chant hymns of blessing to
their Eternal Lord while the flames of a sacked city leaped
around them, to slit the throats of their own children on a
desert mountaintop before serving Rome, to rise up again and
yet again in angry defiance of what the rest of the world had
learned to accept. I, in turn, wanted to learn more about the
worship of his gods. At the time, the cult of Mithras intrigued
me. But I digress. . . .

"A curious thing happened. The more that your father and
I spoke, the closer he came to the God of Moses, while I was
drawing further and further away. I think in the end he believed that by instructing you, I might find again what he perceived me to have lost."

"Perhaps someday you will," Mesha said.

The white head shook in denial. "My way is set. Learning in
youth is like writing in ink on clean paper. In old age it is like
writing on blotted paper." But there was such an air of regret
in his voice that Beruria found courage to ask, "Why did you
forsake the path of a *tanna*?"

"Why did I stop teaching?" He turned to the young
woman. "Yes, you would like to know that. Beruria. Lovely
Beruria, whose knowledge of the Law is known far and wide,

and whose sagacity—yes, sagacity—makes even the Sanhedrin tremble with admiration. They say you lay *tefillin* like a man," he said suddenly.

Beruria's chin came up. "Michal, daughter of King Saul and wife of King David, did so as well."

"My wife is excellent at quoting precedent," Mesha said with a grin.

But Aher was not listening. He was staring at Beruria with the same look in his eyes as he had had in the classroom earlier. "Why do you want it?" he wondered. "With all that knowledge up here"—he tapped his head—"and in here"—he indicated his stomach—"you who have the ultimate wisdom, the real mystery inside you, eternal and everlasting . . . why degrade yourself to be as those who are weaker than yourself? Why do you bind yourself with the leather boxes and straps of *Yahweh*, why do you harness your soul? Why do you cry that you are not counted in *minyan?* Why do you ache that you cannot be a rabbi, when in truth you ought to be a priestess of Astarte, men worshipping at your feet!"

Beruria had drawn back, her face gone white at this heresy.

"And bringing infants in arms," Mesha continued calmly, "to be killed in front of the goddess or perhaps before Baal-Hamon or Moloch and burned in a brazier whenever danger or draught or pestilence threatened."

"You think Israel does not sacrifice its children?" Ben Abuyah turned on him. "Not in the *tophets* of Carthage perhaps, but everywhere else." He stopped, put his hand before his eyes. "Forgive me," he said as he had earlier. "My days are weary, my nights so filled with dreams. . . ." He sat down heavily. "I do not sleep well of late. Too many dreams. And always, I see Akiva. . . ." He looked up. "Where did you say he had gone? To Jerusalem. . . ." He let out a laugh. "I wonder how it sits with him, the priests rearing their heads again. I wonder what he truly feels . . . Akiva, who so loves his shepherds and farmers and tradesmen, having put back in power the class he always despised!" He smiled at Beruria, who was regarding him now with open fascination. "You want to know why I left the path of my fathers. Well, first let me tell you my father was a Jerusalemite, a wealthy man imbued with the culture of the Greeks and fond of all the arts. Fond of women too. Beautiful women. Now, my mother was beautiful. And learned. Like all the women of her class she was schooled in several languages as well as music. She was a pious woman withal. She observed the laws of Torah, performed many *mitzvot*, but she also sat at dinner with my father and wore the dress considered fashionable in the civilized world. They say the virtue of a house rests upon the shoulders of the wife. In which case one may say my mother bore a heavy burden well. My father loved her, but he did not often look away from a pretty face or leave the pursuit of pleasure to others. And so it may be said I have not left the path of my father but, indeed, especially when I was younger, followed it with zeal.''

"Surely lying with women did not cause you to become an apostate,'' Beruria said, looking him straight in the eye.

"No,'' ben Abuyah replied, his blue eyes bright. "But women have always been a source of trouble for me, as for most men. In any case,'' he continued, "you are correct. I did not fall from grace through the efforts or the effects of any Eve.''

"To fall from grace one must first be in it,'' Beruria observed tartly. "Perhaps you would have done better to heed the ways of Eve rather than Adam. From what you say, your mother would appear to have been a better example than your father.''

"And now you sound like my daughter. She has almost given up on saving me, I think. But nothing I do can save her. She is determined to make her little son—my grandchild—a rabbi. Whenever he sucks at her breast she recites Torah to him, saying this is the true milk of life. Poor little Jacob. . . .''

"Poor indeed,'' Beruria shot back. "I think he receives riches far greater than you had in your youth.''

"What brings you to B'nei Berak?'' Mesha interrupted. "You still have not told me the reason for your coming here.'' He did not say it, but both he and Beruria surmised the matter to be of some urgency for Aher to put himself in the very setting where it was most likely he would be shunned.

"A whim,'' the retrograde replied flippantly. "I have a reputation for eccentricity which I must maintain.'' Suddenly he leaned forward and said in a voice low with intensity, "Run, Mesha. Run as fast and as far away as you can. There's no profit to it. Only suffering and more suffering. Suffering without end. For what? For nothing.''

"Rabban . . .''

"You think God is on your side, that Akiva's Anointed is the Lord's Anointed, but it isn't so. Haven't you seen enough? The plague, all those people dying . . . the legions returned, stronger than before, laying waste to all we have. . . . And in my dreams I see even more. The tongues of the sages dragged in the dust by dogs. . . . Your father—" He turned to Beruria. "The scroll he worships will be his shroud! And Akiva . . ." He buried his head in his hands. "Akiva . . ."

Beruria and Mesha were silent, she still with horror.

Ben Abuyah raised his head. "Akiva's a fool," he said flatly. "His Son of a Star is a fool. Your father was a fool, Mesha. And you are a fool. Run. Run, I tell you."

"Rabban," Mesha began, "we are not fools in that we do not fear the legions—"

"The legions!" The words came out in anguish. "The legions of Rome today, the legions of Hell tomorrow!" Ben Abuyah's white head shook, his blue eyes glittered. "There's no profit to it. Neither here nor in the world to come. Why do you want it, Mesha? *Rabbi Meir.* Listen to me! Bar Kokhba, Akiva, the sword or the Book—it's all lies. Go. Be a farmer. A tailor. A baker of bread. Build houses, mend wagons, do something useful! Something with meaning! You serve only the wind now. And the wind will throw all your prayers back in your face. You will cry to God, but only the hills will hear you and the rivers will turn red with blood. For nothing."

"Do not speak so," Mesha said gently.

"You must listen to me! And run. Run, while you can!"

"Where?" Mesha asked simply. "Where can we go? For a Jew, there is no place. Parthia, perhaps, for a little while. Some far-off land across the sea. . . . But in the end it would be the same. In the end we must face what we are, and perhaps choose between that and something else. But we can't run from ourselves and what we believe. I don't know what God intends for us," he continued. He nodded slightly. "I have my fears about the outcome of this war, not because of ben Kosiba's abilities or our virtue as a people, but because I know what we are facing. And still I hope and pray. But whatever happens, this much I know: Simeon ben Kosiba stood up to Caesar when no one else would. While others wept, he made a fist and shouted, 'No!' He wasn't afraid to fight. He wasn't afraid," he repeated. "He made men of us again."

"If that is what being a man is," Beruria could not help commenting.

"It's part of it," Mesha said, turning to her with a level gaze. "Yes. Fighting for what you believe is part of being a man." He turned back to Elisha ben Abuyah. "And it's part of being a Jew."

MESHA WALKED beside his old teacher as ben Abuyah rode out of B'nei Berak. "I wish you would stay the night," he said. He looked up at the sky and smiled. "Even the sun hurries to the Sabbath meal."

"*Shabbat.* I'd forgotten. All the days are as one to me now." Ben Abuyah looked up at the sky also. Even as he spoke, darkness was falling upon them in that quick descent to night typical of that part of the world.

"What are you reading now?" Mesha asked conversationally. "Something new brought back from Antioch?"

"As a matter of fact I've gotten hold of a very interesting document: the 'Sacred History of Euhemerus,' in which the author recounts the deeds of Uranus, Cronus, and Zeus as he found them recorded on a column of gold on some island in the Indian Ocean." Beruria would be lighting the Sabbath candles by now; why wasn't Mesha hurrying home to her? "Euhemerus claims that all three gods were mortal men who had died like men, and only after death attained the rank of gods because they had benefited humanity." They were nearing the marker beyond which to set foot on the Sabbath was a transgression, such distance being accounted as "travel," which was forbidden on the day of rest. Ben Abuyah looked quickly at Mesha, who appeared to take no notice of the sign but was listening studiously to his former teacher. "One might find a parallel to Euhemerus' story," ben Abuyah continued slowly, "in the history of Jesus." *A few more steps and they'd be at the marker. Why didn't Mesha stop? Didn't he know it was there?* "Polidorus—you remember that bookseller I used to frequent in Caesarea?—has brought me a new scroll of the 'Apocalypse of Baruch,' but the work is not nearly so fine as your hand. You really are a copyist of the very first class." Only another step and the young man would be beyond the marker. Yet how steadfastly he walked, how sure and calm.

Only another step. Just one more step. . . .

Ben Abuyah reined in his horse, causing it to halt and at the same time forcing Mesha to step back. "You must turn back now," ben Abuyah said, pointing to the Sabbath marker. "Turn back," he repeated.

Mesha did not even bother to look at the sign. Instead he looked up at ben Abuyah and smiled. "You too, rabban," he said softly. "You too."

Ben Abuyah opened his mouth, closed it. His eyes filled with tears. "No," he said hoarsely, shaking his head. "It is too late for me." And with that he rode away.

BEN ABUYAH RODE in silence. Not a soul was on the road; all had returned home to greet the Sabbath with light, feasting, and song. He rode proudly, his bearing still reflecting the arrogance of the youthful aristocrat who had pursued mortal knowledge as diligently as he had sought to master a more spiritual world. His thoughts turned to Beruria, a fitting Sabbath Queen with her dark eyes and hair and beautiful complexion. It surprised him that in the midst of all these terrible fears and visions concerning the fate of Akiva and Beruria's own father, Rabbi Teradyon, he should find himself aroused by a woman. It was something he'd thought he'd put away, lost, or forgotten under the jumble of books and other tools for unlocking the secrets of existence that made up his life. Yet in his youth hardly a day had gone by that did not have its hour warmed by a woman's smile and touch. There were no women in his life now. Only a daughter who cried whenever she saw him and who prayed for him, to his amusement.

There had been another child. A girl, like the first, but hidden from the world. He'd seen her once, as struck then by her beauty as he'd been by her mother's. *Rehab* . . .

She was the daughter of an innkeeper. And he, he was the son of Abuyah of Jerusalem, one of the most promising pupils at the academy in Jabneh, heir to an estate that had miraculously survived the ravishment of war. Besides, he was already married.

I didn't know . . . I didn't know. . . .

Couldn't he have guessed? The manner in which she simply disappeared . . .

And then one day she was back. And there was a child. A daughter. His daughter.

He sent money, and when he learned of Rehab's death, he arranged for the girl she'd borne to come to him, but she simply disappeared from sight. The servant he'd sent to fetch her was discovered murdered on the road; the girl nowhere to be found. She had vanished from his life as suddenly as she'd come into it. He'd never know what happened to her, whether she was still alive or dead. It was another torment.

The road was dark; the way ahead held no light; and still he went forward, memories of youth blazing behind his eyes like the Sabbath lights he would not kindle but which burned despite everything.

JARA WAITED. A rustling sound, a snap of brush, and Andreas entered the ruined house they'd taken refuge in. "The game's up," he said.

"What did you hear?"

"Enough to know they've figured out we're not taking them where they want to go. We've got to get out now."

She nodded and moved wearily to take up the cloak spread on the dirt floor.

"You're tired," he said softly.

"I'm all right."

He said nothing more, but he took the cloak from her and led her gently to where the horses were tethered. "Let me help you," he said, lifting her onto one of the animals.

"I said I'm all right," she snapped.

Again he did not answer, and in the dark she could not be sure of the expression on his face as they rode off, following a path only he knew.

Jara sighed, as much with annoyance as fatigue, but what she was really angry about would have been hard to say.

They'd been on the road for three days. During this time Andreas treated her in new, comradely fashion, without teasing or his usual innuendo. This straightforward attitude, although much more suitable to the situation in which they found themselves, for some inexplicable reason did not make Jara as happy as she had originally thought it would. The fact was, the more time spent with him found her experiencing cer-

tain feelings she would never have dreamed possible with
Andreas—sensations that, even more astonishing, seemed
brought about simply by his presence: a heightened awareness
of her own body whenever he came close, and the glowings of
that secret fire which Simeon's embrace had once kindled. It
was hard now to remember what love with Simeon had been
like, or what she'd felt other than the need to be with him, part
of him. She didn't want to be with Andreas—she hated him!
—and yet he aroused her.

The morning breeze stole beneath her veil while she pon-
dered this confusion, startling her with its intimate touch. She
stared accusingly at the rider alongside, as if somehow he were
to blame for this tender disturbance. The horse rubbing
against her legs seemed Andreas' work too, and the sweat
trickling under her arm as the sun grew high, and the swollen,
ticklish sensation in her lips that only some hard pressure
could abate—all this seemed his doing with nary a touch or
word. Innocent, he rode ahead, taking the lead as the road
narrowed and turned. Furious with herself for feeling as she
did, Jara became angrier than ever with him.

THEY'D GONE several hours without water or the sight of a tree
or anything human or even alive, when suddenly the green expanse of Ein Gedi, oasis in the midst of the Judean Desert,
broke upon them. Gardens, fields of wheat, orchards
stretched before them, culminating in a white beach and the
blue water of the Dead Sea. The air was filled with the scent of
herb and flower; they could hear the rush and fall nearby of
the life-giving spring for which Ein Gedi was named.

Jara turned to Andreas in open admiration. Having succeeded in misleading the Romans, he had then set a course by
which they had managed to lose their pursuers and, after a
very long and hard ride through difficult terrain, brought
them to what was surely paradise. Despite her antipathy—
which at this point was rather forced—she couldn't help being
impressed by the surety and resourcefulness he'd shown
throughout the ordeal; she wondered how he knew his way
about so well.

"I spent some time in Judea when I was a child," he told
her. "My father wanted me to come under Akiva's influence.

But I was always running away for a bit of exploring, as boys will do."

"But you couldn't have come this far. We are nowhere near B'nei Berak."

"That's true," he admitted. "For many years my guide was Josephus. I would read his works and see it all as clearly as if I were here. The Galilee, the wilderness . . . places like Herodium and Masada. . . ."

"Josephus again!"

"Yes," he said calmly. "The 'traitor' Josephus. But as you can see, he's done some good."

"Time will tell," she replied grimly.

"You still don't trust me." He was amused. "Why?"

She did not reply; instead she asked, "Why have we come to Ein Gedi?"

"There's something I want to check out for myself. And I thought it would be a pleasant place to leave you."

"You're not leaving me anywhere!"

"I didn't know you'd grown so attached to my company." A smile played around his lips. "Should I be flattered?"

"You know that's not it." He was teasing again. For some reason she didn't mind. Besides, it was a good sign; it meant they were out of danger.

"Let me guess, then." His tone was still light. "You 'don't trust' me."

She didn't know whether to smile or be stern. She pressed her lips together to hide her confusion.

"Don't do that," he murmured.

"What?"

He put his finger to her mouth, which had fallen slightly open. "That."

It might have been a brand; her cheeks flamed. Disturbed, she looked away.

"I don't think we'll approach the town directly," he said, changing the subject. "Look—over there—you'll find the spring of Ein Gedi. It's a very pleasant place, full of terraced grottoes and pools. You might want to take a swim. In any case, I'm going to leave you there." There was a slight pause. "If I'm not back by nightfall, make your way into the settlement. Say anything you like, but do not admit to knowing me or being involved in any intrigue."

"I don't understand. Ein Gedi is ours. What are you afraid of? I want to go with you."

"Those instincts of yours—well, mine are working now, and they're saying Masbelah bar Shimon might like to pretend he's never set eyes on me."

"Why?"

"Simeon needs help. Men, food, weapons. He's been having trouble from this quarter for some time. Wheat shipments mysteriously disappearing, orders sluggishly followed, collusion among certain individuals who seem to be more interested in becoming wealthy landowners than staying free Jews."

"You don't know what you're saying. Masbelah and Simeon are old friends. They've been together for years."

"Power does things to people. Believe me. Masbelah is in a very comfortable position now. He may not want to lose it by putting his life on the line again."

"But if Rome—"

"Rome could be persuaded to leave Ein Gedi in the hands of an administrator who kept things running smoothly. This is an important piece of property, Jara. There's the port by which supplies are brought in, and there is balsam."

What was it Simeon had once said? *A Jew may be worthless as far as the world is concerned, but balsam is not. Whatever the market calls for is always worth more than blood.*

"But what does this have to do with us?"

"I know what Simeon's orders are to Masbelah. If I disappear, there is one less witness to those orders. You see, everything depends on following Simeon's plan exactly. Even a delay could be disastrous."

"The plan . . . what is it, Andreas?"

"Simeon's determined to hold Severus back. He's planning a large-scale confrontation. Severus has been avoiding this, so Simeon has to draw him into it."

"When is this to happen?"

"Soon. Very soon."

She shook her head. "I can't believe Masbelah would do anything to jeopardize this."

"Neither can Simeon. But I can. Maybe it's only the workings of my own insidious character—whose frailties you've always been so kind to point out—but when it comes to people, I can believe almost anything. And that's what we've got here, Jara. Just people, not a bunch of legendary Joshuas and Maccabees.''

She looked up, startled. He seemed to be saying something more, but she was not sure what.

"Well, will you do as I ask?"

"No. I want to come with you."

"Believe me, Jara, if what I suspect is true, you will be in as much danger as you were in the Roman camp."

"I don't believe you. I don't believe Masbelah could be so false, not after all that's happened. But if he is, then we'll find a way together to deal with him. I'm not helpless, you know," she added, touching the pouch tied to the sash around her waist, wherein, secured by a loop, her treasured *sica* was anchored.

"No," he said admiringly, "you're not. I can't imagine any other female withstanding so well all we've been through. You're a brave girl"—he grinned—"for all your faults. But you must do what I say now. Trust me one more time. Give me at least until the sun begins to fall. Then you can make your way down, and we'll take it from there."

She hesitated.

He tipped her chin back, smiling, his eyes steady. She wondered if he was going to kiss her. "Please," he said.

She sighed. "All right."

THE SOUND of rushing water intermixed with the song of birds as she made her way up the mountain whence the "Spring of the Kid" descended in a series of falls. David had sought shelter from Saul here in the "strongholds" atop the cliff. At the very top there stood the remains of an ancient Chalcolithic temple. Clusters of camphire whose pale yellow flowers gave off fragrance brightened the gladelike setting. The leaves of the plant would be dried and crushed and made into the henna paste which brightened the hair of the daughters of Israel. Jara needed no such cosmetic. The sun that spread its fingers through the trees lit on her uncovered head like a veil of gold and fell upon her shoulders in a mantle of lacy shadows.

Each plateau had its own delight: sun-dappled grassy banks, pools of clear water, shady nooks and caves carpeted with rush, often hidden behind a cascade of water. Near the top of the mountain there was a great wide pool continually replenished by a large waterfall; she descended, however, to a lower, more intimate area nearly hidden from view.

The climb made her hot; it had been days since she'd washed properly. In a matter of moments she was out of her clothes and splashing about. She swam to a small, beckoning waterfall and put her head back, drinking in the fresh, sweet liquid that fell into her open mouth.

" 'Hold him happiest who before going whence he came hath looked ungrieving on these majesties. . . .' " Andreas' voice came softly to her. " '. . . The sun, the stars, water, clouds, fire . . .' And thee.''

She turned and saw him on the bank. She said nothing. She could feel herself begin to tremble, shaken, stripped not only of garments but skin as well, every nerve and muscle played upon by all the elements of nature, the sun and the soft wind and the water around her waist—and the sight of him again. And all that she felt she saw in his eyes.

They stared at one another as the first man and woman perhaps had gazed upon each other in like setting, as though seeing each for the first and most important time in their lives.

And then he was in the water, wading toward her. He hadn't even bothered to remove his tunic.

"No," she whispered, helpless to move. "No . . ."

His hands were on her shoulders now, warm on her wet skin, drawing her close . . . closer to him. . . .

"No," she started to say again, but the word was lost in a sigh as his mouth at last touched hers . . . gently, softly, and then with a hunger that seemed to shoot up from the center of his being, only to be answered by the passion she could no longer deny. "I knew you'd feel like this," she heard him breathe, and then there were no more words for either of them.

THE AFTERNOON PASSED, the green-gold hours catching them finally in a mesh of lengthening shadows as they lay entwined on the bank of the hidden pool.

"Why did you come back?" she asked.

"I decided you were probably right, that I had no cause to think Masbelah would do us harm. It's all these twists and

turns I'm forced to take. When you play the kind of game I
do, you become suspicious of everyone. Anyway," he smiled,
touching her lips with his finger as he had earlier, "I think I
missed you."

Content, she lay her head on his shoulder.

"It's beautiful here," he said, looking up to where the sky
slid through the trees in small patches of blue. "These little
grottoes remind me of places near our villa outside Rome. Do
you see that little cavern behind the waterfall? All it needs is a
statue of Neptune at the entrance. And over there, one of
Pan...."

"Do you worship the Gentile gods?" She sat up, suddenly
aware of how different his background was from hers.

"No!" He laughed. "But I like to look at their images. I
like pretty things"—he reached up, twisted his hands in her
hair, and drew her down to him—"even more so when they're
made of flesh, not stone," he added huskily.

She pulled away from his kiss. "You miss your home, don't
you?"

"Yes, I do."

"But that's . . . Rome!"

"Yes, Rome. Ah, Jara, you don't know how beautiful the
city is, or all that can be found there. Cruelty, yes. But also art
and wit. . . . And outside Rome, in the Tiburtine hills where
we live—where Hadrian is building a new residence—it's incredibly beautiful. By the gods, it is beautiful!"

"You swear like a Gentile," she wondered again.

He laughed again. "It means nothing, just words one picks
up."

"If you love Rome so much, why did you come here?"

He was silent a moment, merriment gone. Then he said
lightly, " 'Change your place, change your luck.' But in listening to the poets I ought to have remembered the words of
Horace. 'He changes his clime, not his disposition, who flees
beyond the sea.' " Another laugh. "As for luck, I'm not sure
what one would call falling straightaway into a war!"

"Beruria said you had many loves in Rome."

"Not 'love,' Jara. Never love." He grinned. "I suppose one
of the reasons I left was to escape the seemingly endless parade
of the Jewish community's eligible daughters. Even my
mother was becoming a nuisance. What happens to otherwise

sensible women when their children are grown, that they make their sons' lives a misery in quest of a grandchild?'' He shrugged. "I suppose I should have married, if only to please her. Little enough to ask, and it wouldn't have changed my life so much. But I have too much pity for the frail thing a woman's heart is to subject its owner to a lifetime of my temperament. Poor Miri . . . I can yet see those sweet, trusting eyes of hers. She's probably still waiting for me to return.''

"Who's . . . Miri?''

"I've known her since she was a child. We're not betrothed, but it's always been more or less understood. . . .'' He broke off, looked at Jara. "Well, have I satisfied your woman's curiosity?'' The devil was dancing in his eyes again. "Do you think you know enough about me now?''

"Maybe too much,'' she replied evenly.

He laughed, rolled on top of her, and after a passionate kiss said, "Don't you yet realize how right we are for each other? The same restless, seeking nature, the same need to touch, to feel, to know everything there is to know . . .''

"I'm not like that—''

"You are! I see it in every step you take, every move, every gesture, every kiss. . . .''

And again a tide engulfed them, he lost to everything but the need to possess her, she wanting his hands, his mouth, his body as much as he wanted hers.

"Do whatever you want to do," she heard him whisper. "Nothing is wrong. Everything is right.'' And it was as if a hammer had come crashing through stone, sending bits and pieces flying and the air breaking through so pure it took her breath away. All the energy dormant in her being for so long rushed to escape, as full of some wild unspeakable rage as tenderness and longing. He accepted it all, feeding it and on it, now leading, now following, until finally there was no way of knowing where either of them began or left off.

And so it went. Until at last they drew apart, devoured and stunned by what they had experienced. Still their fingers touched as they slept. And the sun lay across them like filigree.

SHE WAS in her forties, a small woman who took great care with her appearance, of good figure despite a limp. Her skin was dark, the pores and lines made graphic by age further heightened by the effects of living in the desert atmosphere. Her eyes with their sharp gaze were carefully outlined in the black kohl that was not only cosmetic but protection against the sun. Her mouth was a slash of vermilion, her braided coronet carefully hennaed. A variety of necklaces and bracelets jingled as she moved; Jara had never seen so much jewelry on one person.

"Babata." Andreas planted a kiss on the cheek offered for that purpose.

"Well, if it isn't the devil's own son." Babata ran her hand down Andreas' arm and smiled fondly. "How goes it with you?"

"Better than could be expected."

She raised her eyebrows, then, seeing Jara, gave her a quick glance and looked again at Andreas.

"I must see Jonathan. I'm leaving this girl in your care. I'll be back and explain everything. Her name is Jara," he added, exiting.

Babata remained where she was, mouth open. Finally, she turned and said, "If he'd waited a moment I could have told him Jonathan bar Be'ayan is in Tekoa. Well, I suppose Masbelah will serve his purpose." She shook her head. "Moves like the wind, that one. But from the look in your eye I can see you find nothing wrong with him."

"Who?" Jara was confused.

"Elisha, of course."

"Elisha?" She blinked. "Yes, Elisha," she echoed hurriedly.

"Yes. Elisha." Babata studied the girl, eyes narrowing in suspicion. Then, suddenly, she let out a low, throaty laugh, and nodded as if they two shared some secret kinship. "Yes," she said nodding and smiling. "Ah, yes indeed. . . ." Her eyebrows arched. "Elisha!"

HIS HAND on her shoulder woke her. "It's as I feared," he said in a low voice. "Masbelah claims he's heard nothing from Simeon. Yet I know word was sent to him. And Babata says a man she recognized as one of Simeon's aides rode into Ein Gedi three days ago but was never seen leaving or anywhere about."

"What about bar Be'ayan?"

"He's in Tekoa. I don't know when he'll be back or where he stands on this. He may be honest, but I don't know if we can afford to wait and take that chance. And if he isn't in agreement with Masbelah, then Masbelah may try to see to it that we're not around when Jonathan returns."

"What does Babata say? She seems to be a keen observer."

He grinned. "Well, she's rather prejudiced. Her second husband, Judah, was previously married to Jonathan's sister, Miriam, and the family has been giving her trouble for some time. Something to do with land inheritance. According to Babata, everyone in Ein Gedi is a thief." Another grin. "But I wouldn't worry about her. Babata is one lady who can take care of herself. She's already informed me that she's looking for another husband. A young one, this time. Evidently, old Judah departed this world rather quickly after the wedding."

"You seem to know her very well."

"She's an interesting woman." He was taking off his clothes. "Move over."

"But what about Masbelah?"

"Masbelah. Unusual name. There was a priest once named Hanan ben Masbelah who was killed during the previous war with Rome. Simeon bar Gioras, who led the Jewish fighters, suspected him of treason. I wonder if it's the same family. Mmmm . . . You feel wonderful. . . ."

"Andreas . . . I mean, Elisha . . . shouldn't we be getting out of here?"

"Probably." His lips were traveling the length of her throat.

"Well, then?" she asked weakly.

He sighed. "Jara . . . Do you really want to get up now and put on your clothes and go riding off into the night as we've been doing for nearly a week?"

"No." Despite herself she had to kiss him. "But I don't want to be murdered in bed."

"Don't worry." The crooked smile. "If anybody gets killed, it will be me, not you."

"What does that mean?"

"Well, for one thing, Masbelah doesn't know you're here."

She thought that over. "Oh."

"Feel better?"

"Mmmm." She was under him now. She wrapped her legs around his and sighed happily. "Yes."

"You little bitch," he said, grinning. "You don't care if I live or die."

She put her arms around his neck, her fingers finding their way through the black curly hair. "I care," she said softly. "And anyway, you won't die."

"How do you know?"

Jara smiled. "Trust me," she said.

SHE WOKE LANGUIDLY, stretching contentedly. Sun streamed into the room Babata had given them. She rolled over, basking in its warmth, then sat up with a start. Andreas was gone.

Remembering what he had said about Masbelah, Jara dressed quickly, trepidation beginning to gnaw. Babata, too, seemed to have disappeared. She ran outside.

There were men and horses everywhere. She started to run, forgetting Andreas' admonition to keep out of sight, when suddenly a voice stopped her.

"Jara!"

She stopped dead in her tracks and turned.

It was Simeon.

He swept her up in his arms. "You're all right—say you're all right. . . ."

"I'm . . . fine."

He set her down again, kissed her head, caressed her hair. "If anything had happened to you . . ."

"No, I'm—I'm all right. . . ." He looked so strange, his eyes so wild and desperate.

"If anything had happened to you . . ." he said again, and again did not finish. "It's going to be all right." He drew her to him as he had before. "It's different now. You'll see. I'll make it up to you. Everything will be fine." His lips crushed hers for a brief, hard moment. "I'm sending an escort with you to Betar. Wait for me there. All will be well." And he was gone.

Jara remained where she was, totally stunned. As if in answer to her confusion, Obodas now appeared.

"The little one from Parthia is dead," the Nabatean said. "The child she brought forth also did not live."

She could do nothing but stare at him.

"It was a boy," Obodas said. "Another son. And still he has none."

"I'm sorry," she whispered. "I'm so sorry."

Obodas nodded. "Now we go to war. It is good Simeon has seen you. It is good that he knows you are alive. If he had lost you also . . ."

She did not reply.

"Be well," the Nabatean said and moved off to join the others.

"Be well," Jara whispered, repeating the familiar farewell of Bar Kokhba's Brothers.

"I hate unfinished business."

She turned to the opposite direction to stare dumbly at Andreas.

"There's an armed escort waiting to take you to Betar," he said.

Still she did not reply.

"He has but to beckon." No bitterness, only the crooked, wry smile. "Bar Kokhba has only to crook that little finger he's supposed to have chopped off—"

"Stop it!" She closed her eyes, opened them. "You don't understand. . . ."

"Don't I?" He shook his head. "I must have been mad to imagine you could ever forget him. What were you doing when you closed your eyes, thinking of him? Pretending it was him?"

"No! No!" She covered her face with her hands. "Don't do this to me," she whispered. "Don't make me tell you how it was with us—you and me—when you know . . . you must know. . . ."

"Jara . . ." And suddenly she was in his arms, clinging to him while he covered her face with kisses. "Don't go to him," he begged. "Don't go back to him." He took her face in his hands, searching her eyes for a response, but all he saw were tears. He gripped her shoulders. "What about us?"

It was more than she could take. She pulled away now and said angrily, "What about us? *What about us?*"

He took a step back, startled by the sudden vehemence.

"You're quiet now, aren't you?" she said with some bitterness. "What right have you to torment me? You got what you want! What you've been after from the first moment we met!"

His face went white. "Is that what you believe . . . ?"

"What else am I to think? You made it very clear what you think of women. Oh, go away, Andreas!" she cried in desperation. "Go back to Rome and your little . . . whatever her name is! No, I'll go away," she said suddenly. "Yes, that's it. I must go away! From both of you!"

BOOK IV

1

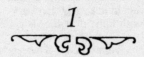

A HOT WIND swept across the Valley of Rimmon. Utter quiet prevailed, broken only by the flapping of some torn fabric or the clatter of a broken lance falling against rock, pushed from a precipice by the dervish wind.

Jara turned at the sound, but there was no one, Jew or Roman, still locked in battle. And yet the place seemed alive with all who had fallen, numbers so vast that the wadis had run red with rivers of blood. Here, brave Samson who had forged the swords put in the hands of Bar Kokhba's Brothers, had died. There, his horse killed beneath him, Rami, son of the *Resh ha-Galut*, was slain. And others, how many others. . . .

In the very spot where Joshua ben Hananiah had counseled peace and compromise, where Simeon ben Kosiba had wrested a promise from Akiva that was to unite the whole of Judea, the man called Bar Kokhba had stood and addressed his gathered troops. "You are to understand," he'd said, "that within a day the Roman general will be here. He had twelve legions at his disposal . . . horses, skirmishers, at least ten thousand archers. Your part is neither to think about that nor to ask questions. I tell you the truth, and you must prepare for it. If you are newly married, then, according to the laws of our people you may go home. If you are frightened, leave now."

But they'd stayed—all of them.

In the end, victory was no one's. After two days' fighting, Bar Kokhba's troops were forced to retreat under the onslaught of a newly arrived contingent of legionaries. Severus stayed to count the dead and to claim the stony valley as

Caesar's prize. When the Romans had moved on, the Jews came back and claimed the lifeless bodies of their sons and brothers, and took them away and buried them. Only remnants of broken armor remained, here and there a solitary sandal lying amid the wildflowers newly sprung from the earth or a silver denarius caught in a rocky crevice.

The smell of death hung over the valley; the hot wind was pungent with it.

"Come away," Obodas said. "There is nothing here for anyone."

Silently Jara followed him away.

Rimmon had not been the end. Despite stunning losses, Severus had pursued the Jewish army, which was forced to fight again and yet again and again. Amazingly, the Jews survived, resisted, met challenge after challenge and even, on occasion, managed to harass their pursuers. It took six months for Severus finally to take back Jerusalem, whereupon the emperor Hadrian was content to leave for Rome, his victory established even though Simeon ben Kosiba and the remnants of his army had not been captured. At least Bar Kokhba had finally been rendered immobile, forced to take refuge in the mountain city of Betar.

A siege wall, not unlike the circumvallation the Romans had used at Masada, had been thrown around the city. Despite this, there was some traffic via a secret, hidden entrance that led to the top of the mountain through a cave in a gorge below. By this means Simeon was able to maintain some contact with the rest of the country: places like Ein Gedi, which was still unoccupied by the Roman forces, and B'nei Berak, which was watched by Rufus but unmolested.

Twice, letters had arrived requesting that Jara come to Betar, but she had remained with Akiva. Finally, Obodas appeared. "You must go to him," the Nabatean said. "He is alone in the midst of all. The Brothers are loyal, the people around him love him still. But Bar Kokhba is alone. He has much pain," Obodas told her. He made a gesture indicating half of one's face. "It comes upon him without warning. He lies alone in the dark until the pain goes away."

Jara nodded. Simeon was prone to headaches.

"He said there was a potion you used to give him. . . ."

"Did he send you here?"

"No. I thought . . ."

She looked away. "You love him, don't you, Obodas?"

"As you do, Little Cat."

"I . . . I . . ." Tears came to her eyes and she could not go on.

"You are young," the Nabatean said softly. "Life burns like a flame in you, and flesh longs for flesh. Yet Simeon is part of you and you are part of him, and this is a greater love." He took a step toward her. "Your stars are good, your future long. Look into your heart for this moment."

And so she left B'nei Berak once more and came with Obodas to a place where there stood an almond tree. And the trunk was hollow, and through the hollow they entered a cave and through the cave a subterranean passage that led up to the city of Betar.

HE LOOKED OLDER than she remembered. The auburn head was sanded, his beard nearly all gray. His right eye seemed more prominent than the left, the vein pulsing noticeably in his forehead, a sign of the headaches which plagued him from time to time and which, in these last months, had begun to attack with greater frequency. Still the opalescent eyes, that cloudy blue flecked with gold, were bright as they had ever been and keen and caring.

They embraced like family.

"You shouldn't have come," was what he said.

"Why?" she asked, taken aback and surprised.

"Don't you see what's out there, waiting for us?"

"Twice you sent for me."

"Before. That was before."

"It is no different now."

"Yes. The options are fewer."

"Were there ever options, Simeon?" She shook her head. "Not for us. Not for Israel."

He embraced her again. "You understand," he whispered against her hair. "You always understood."

BETAR WAS NOT as it had been. Business went on as usual, but life was not the same. One look at the ring of Roman camps below was sufficient to explain the tension permeating the mountain air. This was a city under siege.

The fortress was well protected by nature. It stood some seven hundred meters above sea level and was surrounded by deep canyons on the east, west, and north. In the south, a narrow saddle connected the top of the spur on which the city sat to the main ridge of mountains, but this was cut by a fosse, or moat, five meters deep, fifteen meters wide, and eighty meters long.

The main fortified core, or citadel, comprised about twenty-five acres, the surrounding wall with its semicircular bastions and square towers having a circumference of about one thousand meters. The suburb, equal in size, lay northeast of this. When the legions appeared, most of the inhabitants had taken up residence within the city walls.

The entire area had been surrounded by a siege wall with a circumference of over four thousand meters. Two main camps lay in the southwest, housing units of the Fifth Macedonica and Eleventh Claudia legions. Smaller camps were scattered in the vicinity.

"They will come from the south," Simeon said, pointing to the fosse. "It's the only place they can try to set up one of their assault ramps. So we must stop them"—he pointed to the semicircular bastion defended by a square revetment opposite the moat—"there."

But Jara was staring at the camps, with all their companies of men and animals and equipment. Her eyes went to the siege wall with its intervals of guards. "I've never seen so many of them all together," she said in hushed tones. "Like a line of ants. . . ."

"Get used to it. Don't look away. Don't pretend they're not there. Don't think they'll disappear, that you'll wake up one morning and they'll be gone."

"What must we do?" she wondered.

"Fight." His eyes went out to the camps below. "Nothing's changed," he murmured. Suddenly, the truth of that statement struck him. "Nothing we've done has made a damn bit of difference!" He fell silent; Jara could see the vein throbbing in his forehead.

As they walked back, they heard the happy noise of students let out of school. There was a hush as the children recognized Bar Kokhba. Suddenly one of the boys cried out angrily, "There he is! Bar Kosiba! The great Liar! He's not the Messiah! He's a liar! Liar!"

He had no sooner made his accusation than two other lads jumped him and threw him to the ground. Simeon went over to the group and with his large hands separated the battlers. "Enough," he said brusquely. "Enough!"

"Don't listen to him," one of the boys said, indicating the one who had called Simeon *Bar Koziba*, and who now stood shuffling and red-faced, tears streaming down his cheeks. "Don't listen to him, *Nasi*. He is a coward!" He turned to Simeon, and said solemnly, "We will help you, *Nasi*. We will help you fight."

"How will you do so?" Simeon asked softly. "You hold a pen in your hand, not a sword."

The boy held up his stylus. "Then we will stab them with these!"

This idea appealed to the youngsters, who all became very excited and happy, even the one who had caused the trouble. "If the enemy comes against us, we will go out and stab them with our styluses!" they cried, and began to invent elaborate schemes by which to engage and defeat the legionaries. Simeon stood listening and smiling while one plan after another was proposed to him, until suddenly a young rabbi who had been in the school came out and, seeing what was going on, turned bitterly to ben Kosiba and said, "How long will you continue this corruption?"

"What do you mean?" Simeon asked.

"Filling their heads with impossible dreams, turning their thoughts from prayer—making murderers of us! Yes, murderers! And what has it got you?" He turned to the boys. "You think God loves him? Look below the city, all around, and see what awaits him! See what the author of this madness has brought us!"

Jara looked quickly at Simeon, but he remained calm. He was staring at the rabbi with an almost dreamlike expression. "What did you do," he asked, "before the people of Israel rose against Caesar?"

"I lived a life of study and prayer. I taught others to do the same."

"And what will you do when there is no Bar Kokhba?"

"The same as now, as I have always done."

Simeon stared at the rabbi a moment and then, with a barely perceptible nod, turned to leave.

"Is that all the Son of a Star has to say?" the young man

taunted, made bold by Simeon's silence.

Simeon turned back briefly. "What point is there in speaking?" He sounded tired. "You live in another world."

Unable to contain himself, the rabbi rushed forward and caught Simeon by the sleeve. "Yes," he said, triumphant. "My world will survive!"

Bar Kokhba spun around now, and the sight of him with his great wide shoulders and shaggy head lowered was enough to stop a legionary. But the rabbi stood his ground. "I will survive," he repeated.

"As a cockroach survives," ben Kosiba replied, his voice dark with anger. "Like a rat, or a mole hiding from the light!" He swept past the man and went back to the gathered students and took now this one and now that one by the shoulders and gazed deeply into their eyes. Finally he said, "Listen to me. Listen well. All that your teacher has taught you, all that you have read in Torah, is true. And you must live by this, or the actions of men like myself are for nothing. *But what must be done must be done. No man has the right to make himself master of another.*" He paused. "You breathe the air of freedom now. If that is taken from you, then no matter how long you go on living, you are never truly alive." His eyes found Jara, as they had the night Akiva had proclaimed him Bar Kokhba. As though remembering that time, he said quietly, "I never asked for the honors I've received. But I have accepted willingly the responsibility of leading Israel against the forces of Caesar. What will be, will be. Perhaps it will be said that I behaved badly or wrongly or foolishly. But let it be said that I made a stand. And whatever happens, nothing I believe in has changed."

BY THE TIME they reached the inner chambers of the citadel, his face was pale with pain. Jara brewed a tea of herbs and sat with him while he drank it. When he had finished, he let out a sigh and sank back on the narrow pallet that was his bed. "Better," he murmured. "I feel better already." He passed a hand before his eyes and sighed again. "What do you put in that stuff?" he asked suddenly. "Not a doctor in all of Betar can come up with it."

Jara smiled. "It is something the Old One taught me. Long, long ago. . . ."

"The Old One. . . . Well, whatever it is, it helps." He looked at her. "Or maybe it's just seeing you again. . . ."

"It's the drink," she said softly. "Soon you will sleep."

"Sleep . . . would be good."

He closed his eyes now, and after a moment she went to him and brushed the hair from his brow and stroked his temples. His eyes opened. "I wonder," he said, "if Saul felt for David . . . what I feel for you."

Her lips turned up impishly. "I hope not."

He appeared delighted with this response. "Do you?"

She did not answer but returned her hands to her lap and looked down shyly.

"There aren't too many of us left," Simeon mused with another sigh. "Your old friend Samson's gone. You should have seen him at Rimmon. He could not have been better named. Rami's dead, too. Andreas took the body back to Parthia. I'd promised the exilarch . . ."

She nodded. "Obodas told me."

"I'm sorry about what happened, Jara."

She looked up. "What . . . what do you mean?"

"I thought you would be with Obodas. I trust him with my own life. I never thought—"

"It could not be helped," she said somewhat breathlessly. "And as you see, it turned out as well as it could."

"Yes. No harm came to you. Thank God for that."

"You must rest now," she said, still in that breathless tone. She rose. "I will go and let you sleep." With that she hurried from the chamber.

IT WAS SOME HOURS later, as she lay in her own bed, that she saw him standing in the doorway to her room.

"What is it?" she asked, drawing the blanket up under her chin. "What do you want?"

He took a step toward her and then another. "You said . . . one day . . . I would beg . . ." He stood there, stiff, unable to move or say more, the moonlight making sad hollows of his eyes.

She sat up slowly.

"I'm begging, Jara," he whispered. "I'm begging. . . ."

"No . . . no, don't." Her voice broke. "There's no need. No need," she repeated. She held out her arms to him.

"Come," she whispered. "Come . . . and be warm."

And Simeon came to her and knew her, and slept with his head on her breast.

HE WAS BACK. Somehow, some way, he'd made the journey from Parthia and managed to slip inside Betar. "In time, I see, to help stave off the enemy below," he remarked with his usual wry smile.

"And to celebrate a betrothal," Simeon rejoined, slapping Andreas on the shoulder in welcome.

He stared at Jara, who had come up now. The dark eyes flickered but a moment as they exchanged glances. "I see. Congratulations," he added politely. "Circumstances permitting, do you intend to wait the full year?"

Simeon looked startled at this, then laughed and slapped Andreas' back again affectionately.

Her cheeks pink, Jara ran from the place.

IT DID NOT TAKE him long to find her. "So you came back after all," he said softly.

"So did you," she replied, turning.

He let out a short, surprised laugh. "Yes . . . I guess I did."

"Why?"

"Because I'm a fool. Because to my great surprise I discovered I'd rather be with a band of crazy Jews on an isolated mountaintop about to be attacked by scores of Rome's finest than anywhere else in the world. And because . . ." He did not finish. "Akiva told me you were here."

"You've been to B'nei Berak? All is well?"

"All is well. For now."

"I'm glad of that. And I'm glad . . . I'm glad you are well. No, don't. Don't come any nearer. Please . . . you mustn't."

"I want to hold you. I've got to take you in my arms again . . . the way it was. . . ."

"It can never be the way it was, Andreas. It was a dream. It never happened."

"It happened! It wasn't a dream. We flew to the sun, Jara. Together we touched the sun."

"No . . . it was . . ."

"It was the way it will always be with us. I know it just look-

ing at you now. I see it in your eyes. Don't tell me you don't
feel anything.''

"What I feel doesn't matter! I can't believe I'm saying that,
but I am. I must. Andreas, you know what's important now.
Simeon is the only one who can hold it all together."

He gave a small sigh. "There isn't much left, Jara," he said
solemnly, "to hold together."

"Then why did you come back?" she retorted. "You said it
yourself: not because of me. And I'm glad. Truly I'm glad.
Because if you feel that way, then others will. They must! And
then we're not as alone or as few as we seem."

He had a smile. "You never give up, do you?" He shook his
head. "It's over. That was the dream, Jara. That was the
dream."

"How can it be over when we're still here? We're here,
Andreas! Bar Kokhba is here."

"He's only a man, Jara."

"Do you think I don't know that?" Their eyes locked.
"Don't you see? Don't you understand . . . ?"

"You belong with me," he insisted abruptly. "Here,
Parthia, Rome—anywhere in the world! We can make our
own world. Ah, Jara! We're two of a kind! Old Noah couldn't
have done any better. We don't just live life, we devour it!
We'll be happy together. I'll make you happy. I've thought of
nothing else all these months, try as I did to forget you. And
you'll be lying to me," he added fiercely, "if you say you
haven't thought about me."

"Of course I thought about you," she cried angrily. "All
that's happened . . . Rimmon, Jerusalem . . ." She turned
away, upset. "Not knowing if you were alive or dead . . ."

"Jara . . ." Smiling now, he moved to take her in his arms,
but she pulled away.

"No!" Her voice sank to a whisper. "Oh, please
don't. . . ."

"You love me," he said softly. "You know you do."

She turned to stare at him, the pupils of her eyes like bottle
glass. "When you and I . . . were together . . . I felt alive in a
way I'd never known or dreamed possible. It was as if the bars
of a cage had been ripped out, and for the first time in my life
I felt truly, totally free. I've thought about what happened
between us . . . and about you . . . a great deal. I want to feel
the way I did at Ein Gedi, and to go on feeling that way. I

want to be with you. Is that love? I don't know. Perhaps it is." She closed her eyes. "Before, with Simeon, all I ever knew was that I was safe. I was safe in his arms. Nothing, no one could hurt me. I wasn't alone. Simeon blocked out the whole world for me. And he did something more. He tried to change the world. Whatever I may feel for you, I can't turn away from him now."

Andreas was silent. At last he said with a sigh, "I wish I could say something horrible about the man. I'd like to. But I can't. The fact is, I came back as much for him as for you. And so I know—despite all I've said—there really isn't much point in asking you to let me at least get you out of here. Obviously, we've both made up our minds to stay."

She nodded.

"Well!" He drew in his breath a moment. "This is rather difficult, don't you think? For both of us." He smiled crookedly. "All this . . . nobility! I can't help wondering if it suits us."

"Don't joke," she whispered. "I can't bear it."

"What else can I do when I want you so badly—"

She fled before he could finish.

Andreas stood there, alone, a thoughtful look in his eyes. Then, slowly, the crooked smile returned as he remembered the proverb: Whosoever can restrain woman can hold the wind, and with one hand grasp oil. Never were words more apt, he thought.

THERE WAS some activity in the field. Bands of rebels who had thus far managed to evade capture suddenly appeared and began to harass the camps and divert the guards at the siege wall with the hope of giving those who wished to escape the chance to do so. Their presence cheered the residents of the city, but few chose to leave, the rest placing their faith in the superb strategic position of Betar and the presence of the man who many still believed was the catalyst for God's justice.

But Severus was not about to be defeated by the natural strength of the place or by any daring raids. As Simeon had predicted, he set about building a platform across the fosse against the southern, most approachable section of Betar's fortress.

Once again, as they had suffered some sixty years earlier during Titus' advance on Jerusalem, the heights roundabout were stripped of their trees, and along with the timber a mountain of stones was piled up. Then, as a shelter from the rain of missiles Bar Kokhba ordered sent down, a line of hurdles supported by uprights was erected, under which an assault ramp was constructed. While this was going on, another group tore up the hillocks nearby and kept up a constant supply of earth to the builders. Meanwhile, the Jews launched great rocks from the walls together with every kind of missile, to hinder the work.

Severus countered by setting up his own projectile-throwers, which, in a synchronized barrage, bombarded the men on the wall with stones and lances, together with firebrands and a dense shower of arrows from a host of Arab bowmen who let fly at the same time as the artillery, driving the Jews not only from the bastion and revetment but also from the area immediately inside their wall.

Unable to retaliate from the ramparts, Simeon embarked on a new strategy. Every device of guerrilla war was brought into play; daring night sorties destroyed what had been built during the day until, exasperated both by the failure to complete the ramp and by the fearlessness of the defenders, Severus withdrew his troops, determining to blockade the town until starvation and thirst forced its inhabitants to surrender. And if it still came to a final battle, how much easier it would be to overwhelm Bar Kokhba and the desperate remnants of his army when they were exhausted from lack of food and drink.

Severus withdrew. It was summer; there would be no rain to collect on rooftops and in barrels set out for this purpose. The only other source of water was a spring that flowed from a rock southeast of the spur. The flow of the spring to Betar could be stopped. There would be no rain.

Severus withdrew, and waited.

THE ROOM WAS sparsely furnished but not uncomfortable. There was a small urn with a single flower; the petals had begun to turn dry and droop. There were no bars on the window, no guards at the door. Marcellus Quintus turned and saw the girl staring at him.

He knew her, not her name, but he knew her. Those pale, enigmatic eyes, that long neck, and the slender shoulders with their bounty of nymph's locks. . . .

In Severus' tent her hair had been drawn severely back, all but hidden beneath the veil all Jewish women wore. Now, soft tendrils escaped that head covering, framing the face he had first seen above the road to Galilee. Later, he'd come upon her again, in a small village that was no more, and in the palace at Tiberias, where unknowingly she set in motion the raking of his very soul. How many times since had he followed some female in a marketplace or turned the shoulder of some girl in some town, only to find it was not she? He had sought her, at first with murder in his heart and then driven by something else for which he had no name and did not understand. And though he found her nowhere, he saw her everywhere, in every village where a woman cried over her slain husband, in the shrieks of the girls claimed by Rome's army, in the eyes of children who had ceased being children.

And then, one day, there she was again. He knew in Severus' tent she was not what she said she was, nor what the Christian claimed her to be, although perhaps she was something of a witch. Certainly she had changed him. And yet he'd agreed to the escape, knowing she would slip through his hands no matter what.

"What is your name?" he asked.

At that moment a man entered the room, and the girl, like a recurring dream, disappeared. Quintus stared at the newcomer.

"My name is Simeon ben Kosiba," the man said. "I am *Nasi* of Israel," he added matter-of-factly. He moved to a chair and sat down, motioning for Quintus to do the same. His movements were quick and strong, though he was not much taller than the centurion, who was himself of good height; his whole being seemed to exude a kind of fierce power that made him seem giantlike. "You are Marcellus Quintus," he said when the other was seated. "Though you serve as a centurion, you are of the equestrian order. Rome respects you, the men of your army love you, and the emperor is your friend."

Quintus let out his breath slowly. The band of Jews that had descended on the camp during the night had been sent to do more than wreak damage on the siege platform. Their finding him was no accident. They'd knocked him out before he could draw his sword; next thing he knew, he was in this room, in Betar. They must have carried him the whole way.

"Taking me prisoner won't do you much good," he told Simeon. "No one is going to bargain for my life."

Simeon seemed to smile. "Can't count on your friends, eh?"

Quintus was taken aback. He never could get used to what he perceived as the Jews' strange predisposition for joking. It always came at odd times, when it was least expected, always incongruous under the circumstances. It was something more than gallows humor, although it would be safe to say their experiences had made the Jews expert at that. He responded straightforwardly. "What do you want of me?"

"Answers."

"I don't think there's anything I can say that you don't already know."

Ben Kosiba stared at him a moment and then got up and began to pace. There was nothing restless in his movements, but again Quintus had the feeling of enormous power held at bay, of strength contained while the wheels of the mind turned. It suddenly occurred to him that here was a man who probably, like himself, enjoyed long walks in solitude when he had problems to solve. Where did he walk now, this cornered commander? Quintus wondered. On the ramparts of Betar's wall while others slept?

"All activity below," ben Kosiba was saying, "indicates to me that your general has decided to pull back and wait. For what? For us to make a break from the city? For us to surrender?"

"Will you do either of those things?"

"No." A pause. "He knows that. Your general knows that." Another pause. "Or does he? What would make us desperate enough to break and run, or just give up?" The blue eyes with their sparks of gold studied the silent centurion. "In Jerusalem," Simeon said suddenly, "Titus crucified Jews in plain sight of the city walls in order to strike terror into the hearts of those who saw it. At Masada, your people used my people like animals to construct the ramp that brought your victory. Whatever the people of Masada did against your soldiers, you did to the Jews you'd enslaved, so that Eleazar ben Ya'ir could do nothing lest he murder his own kind. Well,

I am not Eleazar ben Ya'ir. If your general sets a thousand Jews to working on his ramp, I'll let fly a thousand stones and arrows and weep later.''

"Is that what you want me to tell him?"

A pause. "Perhaps."

Quintus hesitated. Then he said, "As far as I know, there are no plans to import more Judean labor."

"Israelite," ben Kosiba corrected him. "We are Israel, not Judea."

"You are whatever the Imperial Empire of Rome and Caesar declare you to be," Quintus snapped. "The whole of your land with the exception of a few minor outposts and this city is under our protection again. But for you, the Pax Romana is complete."

"Don't speak to me of peace, Roman. Your emperor plans no peace for us. And that is what I want to know. What does he plan?"

"I am only a soldier. I am not privy to that information."

"You are Hadrian's friend and confidant. And, according to my source, one of the few honest men left in the world. Don't spoil your reputation."

Again there was that sense of wry intelligence at work. Did the Jews accept a messiah who joked? Or would it be impossible for them to accept one who did not? Despite himself, Quintus found himself beginning to enjoy this encounter. It would probably end with his dying, but why lie about it? He'd been intrigued by this man—yes, even admired him—long before now. And he felt, he wished, they could just sit down together and talk not as Jew and Roman but simply as men.

As though sensing this longing, Simeon said brusquely, "Don't think we can be friends, Roman. Don't think that but for this or that we could share a bottle of wine and speak of what it feels like to send a hundred men into a place they may never come out of alive. There is nothing between us but a drawn sword. You are Hadrian's friend. You can never be mine."

"The emperor is no longer in Ju—Israel," Quintus offered.

Simeon nodded. "I am aware of that. I presume he is on his way to regale your Senate with news of his victory. Tell me, was Jerusalem all he wanted? If so, then he may claim himself master of that ruined city—for the moment. It is not over yet," he added ominously.

"Isn't it?" Quintus felt suddenly weary.

"It took three years after Titus burned the Temple for Masada to fall. Three years, centurion. While your Caesar marched through Rome in triumph, the people he claimed to have conquered were still making the lives of your legionaries a misery. Three years more! Tell me, are you prepared to wait again so long?"

"In the end, Masada did fall," Quintus reminded him.

"And then there was Alexandria. And Cyprus. And Cyrene. And here we are again, back where it all started. And we on Betar, let me assure you, are not the people of Masada."

"What does that mean?"

"Think about it. The victory your emperor claims—prematurely—has not been without loss. Have you ever stopped to count how many men you've left with us—permanently? The bodies of your legionaries lay end to end in Bab el-Wad, and in the valley of Rimmon—" He stopped. "How is it life is so cheap to you? What are we to you that you are willing to make so many widows and orphans of your women and children? What is Jerusalem to you? You have a hundred cities, each of which you claim to be more beautiful than the next. You have built your gods a thousand temples. For us there is only one. Where is it written, Roman, that you must have a hundred and one cities, a thousand and one temples, and we none?" He shook his head. "I can understand the need to possess our land—not for its abundance of foodstuffs and gold, for we are a poor neighbor—but to secure your borders and to keep a powerful nation like Parthia at safe distance. I understand that. You want rewards for your soldiers. They give you twenty years of their life, and in the end, if they are still walking, you give them a farm, a plot of land—somebody else's land, someone here or in Britain or in Gaul. But all right, I understand that too. But why, why, Roman, do you stand between us and our God? Don't you know, doesn't your wise and wonderful Hadrian understand, that we could never abide that? You might have gone on as you were for another hundred years, raping this land, if you had only kept on killing people and not tried to run your sword through Torah."

Once again Quintus sensed a note of mockery beneath Bar Kokhba's anger. Before he realized it, he was answering stiffly, "And what do you suppose will happen to your Torah now? However determined Caesar may have been to ensure the homogeneity of the Empire before, you can be certain that your actions have only increased this desire.''

"You talk like a politician, not a soldier. What are you saying? I've made things worse for my people? Congratulations. You've just become a rabbi."

"It's true in any case."

"You mean being partly dead is better than totally dead."

"I mean you might want to think about what's to come."

"That's why you are here, centurion. *I want to know what is to come.*"

"Your water supply has been cut off." The words came in a rush. "Unless your God makes a miracle and gives you rain in a season where there has never been rain, you will perish from thirst. You will eat whatever food you have and there will be no more. Oh, you may be able to smuggle a messenger in and out from time to time, but a single goatskin of water or bag of flour won't take care of a whole city. Meanwhile, we'll be looking for that secret door and building our ramp. And when the stink of death is in the air, when the bodies of the very old and the very young lie rotting in the streets of Betar and your sword hangs heavy from your weakened hand—then, then we'll make our way up and finish the job."

Simeon was silent a moment. Then he said with such unexpected objectivity that, again, Quintus was caught off balance, "Makes sense. I'd do it myself—if Torah allowed it," he added wryly. "You see, even in war, the Jew is forbidden to despoil his enemy's land, to cut down his trees or divert his water or lay siege to the very old and the very young. No doubt these barbaric notions are indeed a disruption of the homogeneity Hadrian desires. War, after all, is war. There can be no niceties."

Quintus did not reply, but his face had turned a dark shade of red.

"Still, you're not telling me what I need to know. The water . . . I'd surmised as much. We've been on rations—food and drink—ever since your siege wall was completed. No one likes it, but there it is. We can hold out."

"Until the rains come? That's months away."

Simeon turned away. "We can do whatever we have to do," he replied brusquely. He went to the window and looked out. "I don't enjoy the idea of people rotting in the streets, as you put it. Or turning on one another for a crumb or a mouthful of water. They still tell stories of what went on in Jerusalem when your legions lay siege to it. People ate straw, dogs, rats. They boiled the bones of their dead babies and made broth from their own flesh. I have heard the tales. . . ." He turned back to Quintus. "I need an honest answer. Not a promise. Not a vow. An honest answer." Before Quintus could ask what the question was, Simeon went on, "One of the reasons the people on the Masada refused to surrender was because they knew what had happened at Machaerus."

"Machaerus . . ."

"A fortress similar to Masada, also on the Dead Sea. Its defenders agreed to give up on the understanding that those who had not fought at Jerusalem would be free to go away. Once the men had come out, however, your legions massacred them and enslaved every woman and child."

The expression on the centurion's face was unreadable.

"Now the thing I find interesting," Simeon went on, "is that the whole pattern of this war is dissimilar to the earlier one that resulted in the events at Machaerus and Masada. First, since the day your general Severus arrived, there have been no requests for surrender. No demands in any of the towns or places you've taken for the Brothers to give themselves up in return for whatever leniency or degree of compassion you were prepared to offer, or to spare the other inhabitants. You haven't even cared to spare yourself; you've allowed yourself no easy victories. Second, there's been little concerted effort to get at me alone. No bribes, no bounty on my head. Another man might be insulted. But what I perceive in all this is something more ominous than I could ever have imagined. Your Hadrian does not merely want to put down what he considers—despite his losses and the effect generated throughout the world—a provincial rebellion. Your legions are beyond what you call punitive expeditions, the aim of which is to destroy insurgents, discourage further rebellion, and restore the status quo."

"You are wrong. We have every intention of destroying you and your army and seeing to it that no Brothers, as you call them—Sicarii, Zealots, whatever—raise their heads in the future."

"No, centurion, I did not say you have no desire to do what you have just described. I said you are willing to go beyond that. And I take note that in answering me you say nothing about a status quo or return to what you would perceive as normality."

Quintus felt his chest tighten. Was it possible the man before him knew what he himself dared not think?

"We're probably the only people in the world who have no desire to rush your borders and take from you what is yours. The Gauls, the Thracians would as soon blink as do to you all that you've done to them. We want no more than the land God has given us. Yet your desire to be rid of us exceeds anything you feel for any other nation." He shrugged slightly. "I'll tell you what I think. I think your emperor is determined to destroy the Jews completely and forever. I think he just plain wants to wipe us out."

"If so, haven't you brought that on yourself?"

"I may have brought it out," Simeon conceded. "I did not bring it on. It was always there. So," he went on briskly, "with all this to consider, I still must ask you . . . if . . . I and my men give ourselves over to your general, will it be over?"

Quintus stared at him, uncertain as to whether the man was truly offering to surrender or merely posing an academic question. As if in answer, Simeon said, more to himself than to the Roman, "I must know all the options." Still, Quintus was silent.

"I have to know. You must tell me, centurion—*Roman*—as honestly as you can, what will happen to my country if Bar Kokhba is no more? Will Israel become Judea again and be as it was? Will Betar be spared?"

Quintus took a deep breath and slowly expelled it. There was bound to be a battle no matter how long this man and his followers held out. Weakened as they might be from weeks, perhaps months, of deprivation, they would fight as fiercely as the defenders of Jerusalem had after Titus' long siege. Whatever the outcome, scores of boys whom Quintus had trained and men he'd fought alongside would join the dead and the dying of Betar. A word now, and that would not come to pass. Simeon ben Kosiba and the remnants of his troops would pass quietly into the hands of Rome. And Rome's soldiers—all those men and boys out there—would remain alive.

And then he thought of Hadrian, whom he had once loved, and the dispassionate plans of the emperor and his general,

Severus, as they'd walked the plowed field that had been the site of Jerusalem's Temple, regarding the fate of the Jews. He thought of all Bar Kokhba had said, and felt the heat of those opalescent eyes as he struggled with what he knew and what he felt. And there was the voice of the man now, this man the Jews called *ha-mashi'ah*, saying in a strangely gentle and compassionate voice, "Let me make it easier for you. Answer only this: If I come out now, will Betar be spared?"

Quintus sighed. "No."

"HADRIAN WANTS the ultimate example," Andreas said when informed of Quintus' answer. "Also, he wants to downplay what has really occurred. A victory march through the streets of Rome, with Bar Kokhba in chains, would elevate the events that have taken place to the status of the war he has so far denied. Another man might risk that for the sake of the glory contained. But Hadrian does not view himself as a mighty conqueror and has no wish, I think, to foster that image in the eyes of the world. He sees himself as a man of peace and culture and wants to be known as such."

"And to that end he will destroy us," Rabbi Eleazar of Modi'in said, his voice hushed at the thought.

"Is that what you think, Uncle?" Simeon demanded. "Do you think Caesar can destroy us?"

The rabbi sighed. "We did not fulfill the promise of Jerusalem. You never made the city your own, Simeon. And in the end, you abandoned it. I think God is angry."

"I think God understands I had to keep my forces mobile. Even now, we've still got people outside. In Ein Gedi and Tekoa . . ." He exchanged glances with Andreas, but the look on the other's face indicated he expected no further help from that quarter.

"We must pray for guidance," Rabbi Eleazar said. "As the star lights up the darkness of night, so you, Simeon—Bar Kokhba, Son of a Star—have been a beacon for Israel. That light must not diminish. For if what you say is true, if Hadrian is determined to destroy all the Jewish people, then what happens now in Betar is of the greatest consequence."

THE EFFECTS of the rationing soon began to be manifest. In

some quarters, stoic calm prevailed and inner nobility surfaced as parents sacrificed for children, children for parents,
those who were well for those who were ill, and those who felt
themselves beyond recovery for those who would be better
able to defend the rest. In other quarters, all the worst traits of
human character were starkly illuminated: Water was bartered
for gold, fights broke out, accusations were hurled in every
direction, and hoarding, stealing, scavenging became the
occupations of the day. It was then that the discipline of the
Brothers stood firm, and Bar Kokhba's men took complete
control of Betar. An armed man stood watch as the daily dole
of precious water was administered; in his presence the recipient was required to drink one mouthful. A list of the sick and
feeble was drawn up, and food and water were brought to
them. The council of rabbis sat in judgment on those who attempted to make profit from the situation or deprive others of
the sustenance of life, these matters being defined by Torah
and that oral tradition which, since the time of Johanan ben
Zakkai, found expression in the Talmud.

And as sometimes happens at such times, one man more
than any other appeared almost a saint, a very angel of God.
This was Eleazar of Modi'in, uncle of Bar Kokhba, and by
birthright a priest. His presence seemed to take the edge off
hunger, to dispel the horrible knowledge that all within Betar
were subject at any moment to death by sword or by thirst.
Surely, with this pious man in their midst, God would send
down a miracle or two. What was a rainstorm to the Almighty, who had parted the sea and dropped manna from the
heavens? What were a dozen legions to the Eternal One,
Blessed be His Name, who had slain Pharaoh's thousands,
who had destroyed the whole earth but for Noah and his ark?
Was not Betar an ark of sorts, filled with those who had
striven only to defend the Law? What if Simeon ben Kosiba
was only a mortal man? What was wrong with being that, a
man "little less than the angels" who had stood when all
others had cowered in fear and in shame?

Where was the justice of it?

Where was God's mercy?

But wait, wait. There would be a miracle. Only wait, and
God would provide the answer.

Meanwhile, minds were working to alleviate the situation.
Its mountainous position provided Betar, like Jerusalem, with

a heavy accumulation of dew during the night and early morning hours. With Obodas' guidance, the people devised every possible means to trap that moisture. Grapes, which grew plentifully at this time of year, slaked both thirst and hunger. In the dark of night, men made daring sorties not to harass the enemy but to gather as much fruit and produce as they could from the exposed garden suburbs outside the fortress wall. Still, supplies were short, with tempers to match.

"It's the waiting," Simeon said. He brushed a hand before his eyes, which were weary and smarting from staring so long at the Roman positions. His head was pounding again. Here, on the rampart of Betar's wall, the sun seemed harsher and more relentless than it had in the desert. The Roman camp was becoming a blur, the voice of his uncle Eleazar an annoying buzz.

"How long, how long will it continue?" the soft-spoken rabbi was asking. "Men are beginning to drop in the streets—"

"I know, I know," Simeon replied brusquely. Only that morning he'd come upon a crowd gathered about the fallen figure of an old man. The fellow's heart had given out as much from age as anything else. But the daughter wept that he had been giving his water allotment to the children, and as the son began to chant the *Kaddish* for the dead man, Simeon had not been able to restrain his own angry voice. " 'Blessed and praised, glorified and exalted, extolled and honored, adored and lauded be the name of the Holy One,' " he had recited with unmistakable bitterness. " 'Blessed be He, whose glory is beyond all the blessings and hymns, praises and consolations that are ever spoken in the world'—and who has condemned His people, His chosen people to everlasting torment and despair and struggle without end!"

He should not have said what he did. He must allow these souls their prayers and hopes and faith. No one had the right to take that away. But another voice in his head kept shouting. *Tell them the truth! Tell them it makes no difference who goes down to Hadrian's general willingly and who resists to the very end.* The end for all would be the same. In Betar and everywhere else.

No, he could not tell them that. It was better for them to believe as they did, that Bar Kokhba or God would deliver them—or even that Bar Kokhba was to blame for their present misery, that, if not for the presence of the Brothers who had taken refuge in Betar, they would all be safe.

As though divining his thoughts, Eleazar of Modi'in said now, "The Israelites spoke words of complaint against Moses and also against Aaron, saying, 'Would that we had died in the land of Egypt when we sat by the flesh pots, for you have brought us forth into this wilderness to kill this whole assembly with hunger.'"

Simeon smiled wearily. He had not always gotten along with his uncle, but the last few months had brought them exceedingly close—or as close as they could ever be. Of all who might have heaped recriminations upon the *Nasi's* head, Eleazar had shown the most forbearance. He had even admonished complainers, saying to them, "He who has enough to eat for today and says, 'What will I eat tomorrow?'—behold, he is of little faith."

Well, but the priest-rabbi was as much a part of what had happened as Akiva and Simeon himself.

Akiva. What would be his fate? Jara had thought he would be safer in Betar. How ironic that seemed now.

Jara . . .

She was changed, all that molten sap turned gentle, a deep-flowing stream, sweet and somehow sad. . . .

He could not let her fall into the hands of Rome again. It was a vow he'd made long ago, yet nothing seemed so clear as the need to keep that promise.

Where was she now? He needed her medicine. His head would split; a thousand suns burst in his brain every time he blinked. There was a sour taste in his mouth. He closed his eyes, pressing his fingers against the lids, but the suns kept on exploding.

"The manna was created on the eve of the Sabbath at twilight," the rabbi was musing. "Also the rainbow, the rod, the writing, and the tables of stone."

What was the man going on about now? Rainbows, manna . . . A bolt of lightning would be more in order, one that would stab the hearts of those men below. It felt as if there was lightning now inside his brow, cracking open his skull. . . .

"Elijah has yet to restore the bottle of manna which Moses gave unto Aaron to lay up before the Lord, to be kept for the generations."

I am going mad, Simeon thought. *I am going mad, or he is.*

Aloud he asked wearily, "Why this talk now of manna, Uncle?"

"It is a sign, Simeon. That, and the bottle of sprinkling water, and the bottle of anointing oil."

I never asked to be anointed. I never wanted it.

"Seven things are hidden from man," Eleazar of Modi'in said softly, "and they are these: the day of death, the day of comfort, and the depths of judgment. No man knows by what he can make profit, nor what is in the heart of his fellow man. No one knows when the kingdom of David will be restored. And no one knows when this wicked kingdom will be uprooted. But this is certain: the day of Gog must come. Great suffering must precede the time of beauty."

Talk plainly! Why can't you speak in simple words? Tell me, tell me now. . . .

"There is a way out of what lies before us. We are born to die. No one can dispute that. But in dying we can yet serve the Lord, as men have done before us, to sanctify His Name."

The Kiddush ha-Shem. *He wants the* Kiddush ha-Shem.

"The ultimate act, Simeon. Not done from fear or vainglory, but in service to the Almighty."

Masada . . . He wants another Masada. He wants us to kill ourselves.

Simeon swallowed the bile that leaped into his mouth. "Hadn't you heard, Uncle?" he murmured. "The Lord has commanded us to live by His Law, not die because of it."

"Then what have these last three years been about?" the rabbi responded quietly. "We are not the first to fight, Simeon. And whatever the Roman says, I do not believe we will be the last. Those who went before us, men like Eleazar ben Ya'ir, left a legacy to our people. Now it is our turn."

Simeon closed his eyes again, racked by pain that went even deeper than the blood coursing angrily to his head. His hand went to his brow, to his eyes, as though he were searching like a blind man for some image in the darkness. But there was nothing, only the darkness and a thousand faceless suns, and a cry shot up from his bowels and his heart and his throat: "No! No Masada! *There will be no more Masadas!*"

The words hung in the air. As they left his tongue, he'd flung his hand away from his face in a gesture of anger and anguish, felt the side of his palm strike something soft, and startled, opened his eyes.

Eleazar of Modi'in lay at Simeon's feet. Knocked sideways by that glancing blow, the rabbi had struck his head upon the rampart wall and been killed instantly.

Horrified, Simeon stared at the crumpled, lifeless figure. Slowly he knelt down beside him. There was no blood. The pale face was as peaceful in death as it had been in life and throughout all adversity. It was as if the man's soul had simply been snatched away.

Simeon drew in his breath, the sound like a great, shuddering sob. "What have I done?" he murmured dully. "What have I done?"

HE HAD ALWAYS been moody. From the beginning, as a boy, he obviously was a maverick, restless, proud, impatient, and easily bored with others. He'd always made his own rules. After his marriage he had been a dedicated farmer, throwing himself totally into the work. Not sparing himself, he spared not others, and years and fame magnified these traits. Even before Akiva's pronouncement, Simeon had become a law unto himself.

He brooded over his uncle's death. And yet, considering what was to come, perhaps it was a blessing.

It wasn't death that Simeon feared, not the act of dying—he didn't mind that and never had. Not that he wanted to die; he just didn't give a damn so long as it was quick and final. But the thought of going in pieces, slowly, agonizingly, as he had seen his mother die, racked by illness, was enough to make him shudder. And there was the way they had died at Jerusalem, even before Titus broke through the gates. It took days before people succumbed to starvation and thirst. Days, weeks . . .

On Masada, the Jews had taken their own lives; men had killed their wives and children. He'd always hated that. Even now, he hated it.

But the *Kiddush ha-Shem* was quick and final; merciful, some might say.

"No . . ." It was the growl of a trapped animal.

"No!"

Jara hurried into the darkened room, only to be met by a blank stare. Without a word she opened the windows, letting in air and light. Simeon did not move. She sighed. He had been like this since the accidental death of his uncle, too brusque or too silent, retreating into his chamber where it was always night, and where she would find him sitting and staring, his head in his hands.

"Give me something," he mumbled.

"I have no potion for what ails you."

"I have a headache!" he shouted.

"In that case I'm sorry. But I have no herbs—"

"Damn you! Get me a doctor, then! Where are all the doctors?"

"Administering to those who have real need of them."

With an oath he sprang up now and grabbed her, tearing at the pouch tied to her waistcord. Suddenly the *sica* was in his hands. He stared at the Sicarii knife and then started to laugh. "There it is! There it is. . . ." He held it before his eyes, translating the symbols inscribed on blade and hilt: *Death is nothing. Freedom is everything. Only God shall be our King.* Slowly he brought the blade to her throat. "I can't," he whispered hoarsely. Tears came to his eyes. "I can't. . . ." He dropped the knife and took her in his arms. He was crying.

"Well," he said at last, clearing his throat and turning away from her. "Now you have seen Bar Kokhba weep. Like a woman."

"Like a man," she said softly.

He shook his head. "I'm numb, Jara. I can't think anymore. They're out there waiting for me to spread my cloak like some heavenly raiment, to shelter them and protect them or . . . I have this dream. Everyone in Betar is holding on to me. They've got hold of my arms and my legs and my hair. Every finger and toe is clutched by a child, and each child has another child holding on to him and another and another. . . . And I'm trying to fly. Everyone is praying and singing and waiting for me to fly with them all holding on. Only I can't move. In the dream I can't move. I can't fly. I can't even walk. And they're all holding on. . . .

"It's done, finished. I can do no more. There's no help from any quarter, not even our own people out there. And everyone looks at me. . . . I don't want to see all those eyes anymore! I don't know what to tell them! I don't know what to do!" He sat down heavily. "Bar Kokhba. I'm not what they thought I was. I'm not what they want me to be."

"You mean the Messiah of God?" she asked coolly.

"The Messiah. . . ." He laughed sadly. "Do you know what Johanan ben Zakkai used to say when they came to him and said this one or that one was the true Redeemer? He would say, 'If you happen to be holding a sapling in your hand when someone tells you the Messiah has arrived, first plant the sapling and then go out to greet him.' " He laughed again, sadly, wearily. "There was one rabbi who had the right idea. A thousand trees will take root and grow and die before this world ever sees true justice. The Messiah . . . I wish I were he, Jara. Not for the God of Israel, but for those boys in their schoolrooms and the girls in their white dresses. . . . And for you." He sighed. "But I am not. I am not he."

"Whoever said you were?" she retorted. "Not I!"

He appeared startled.

"I never—not for one moment—ever thought or hoped or dreamed that a band of angels would do for Israel what we must do for ourselves. And I thought you felt the same. You were the only one who said, 'This can be done—if we think and plan and work together and stay together!' Not 'if we sacrifice bullocks on an altar, or close our eyes tight and trust to heaven.' And we did it! You did it, Simeon! You brought a nation back to life! You took back Jerusalem! You held the world's mightiest army at bay for over three years! You destroyed an entire legion!"

"For nothing. It's all come to nothing."

"I don't believe that! I never will! It's not over! We're still here, aren't we? I'm here! The plague couldn't kill me, and I'll be damned if the Romans will! I don't know about you, but I intend to die in bed, a very old lady, surrounded by grandchildren and . . . and . . ." Desperate, she threw her arms around him. "If it must end," she whispered brokenly, "let it not be that way." She nodded in the direction of the *sica*, its blade gleaming on the floor where he had dropped it. "When we first met, you said to me you could never act as the people of Masada had acted. 'What would you do?' I asked. 'Fight,' you said. 'To the last man. To the last child.' "

With a groan he drew her even closer, and they clung to each other, melded in anguish and fear and a rage to live. The fire was stronger in her, and slowly he allowed himself to be nurtured by it, feeding on that undiminished will as a babe takes life from its mother's milk. His flesh, which had been cold and damp, grew warm. He let out a great sigh, then pulled back to look at her. His gaze was steady, calm. There was so much love in his smile that she felt shy.

"You mustn't give in," she pleaded. "Not to Hadrian, and not to the rabbis."

He was still smiling. "The *minim* call me Anti-Christ," he said. "What do you think the men of the Sanhedrin will call me now?"

"*Nasi*," she said firmly. "Prince of Israel. That," she added softly, "ought to be enough for any man."

THE AIR on the parapet was cool. Jara wrapped her cloak around her, shivering slightly, yet grateful for the wind. The dark was thick with moisture, the dew that fell each night. She tilted her head back tiredly, not to wish upon the moon or to wonder what future the heavens held in store, but to bathe her face in the fine, wet mist, succor against the dry, dusty day that would follow.

"How is he?"

She turned slightly, saw now the figure against the wall. "I . . . I didn't realize anyone was here."

Andreas came forward out of the shadows. "I come here often. Most every night. Just as you do."

"I . . . I never knew. . . ." She tried to compose herself. "Why didn't you ever speak?"

"You would have run away if I had. Just as you do whenever you see me," he pointed out gently. "Just as you want to now. Don't. Please."

She hesitated, then gave a slight nod to show she would remain.

"You come from Simeon." It was a plainly stated fact.

"Yes."

"How is he?" Andreas asked again.

"Better, I think." She sighed. "You don't know how he suffers. All the killing that's been done, what lies ahead . . . and now with people saying he murdered Rabbi Eleazar. . . ."

"It was an accident."

"Oh, I'm so glad you believe that! It was. It was, Andreas!"

"I'm sure it was. The point is not what you and I believe or even what people say, but what Simeon thinks."

She sighed again. "I don't know. . . . Anyway . . ." She

brightened. "He seems in better spirits. He fairly shooed me out the door, he was so eager to go over the plans of the city again, saying so many men must be positioned here, so many there. . . ."

"He is feeling better," Andreas agreed. "That's good news, Jara. You've done your 'healing' well." He paused. "If only," he could not resist saying, "you would work your powers on me. You fixed my shoulder once," he reminded her. "The problem lies now with my heart, I think."

She lowered her eyes.

"Can it be, sweet physician, you are in need of healing too?" He took her hands in his.

The warmth of his touch made her tremble even as the wind had. "Kiss me, Jara." His voice was like the wind, touching her. "Heal us both. One kiss . . ."

"No. . . ."

"I won't move, I promise. I'll stand here still as stone. One kiss, that's all. I've come such a long way to be here . . . and we have so little time, all of us. I'm not asking you to leave Simeon, or to betray him. . . ."

"Aren't you?" she whispered.

"If one kiss with me betrays Simeon, then you're lying every time you lie with him."

"No." She looked up. "I love Simeon, Andreas." She tried to make him understand. "What I feel with him is not what I feel with you. But it's real. And I won't betray him. That, as you put it, *would* be betraying myself."

He was silent.

She waited, studying his face in the moonlight, wanting even now to run her fingers through the dark curly hair, to press her lips against the finely chiseled mouth turning up now in the funny little half-smile she had grown to know so well.

"The damnable part of the whole thing," he admitted at last, "is that I love you all the more for saying so."

"I love you too, Andreas."

"Do you?"

"Yes. I do."

The dark eyes seemed at peace now; anger, at least was gone. He took her face in his hands. "Then kiss me," he said softly. "One last time, Jara. To last forever. . . ."

There was no escaping now, nor did she want to. His face drew close, his mouth at last touched hers—gently, tenderly, lingering, speaking to her without any words. She closed her eyes, sinking into his embrace, unable to resist, unwilling to let the moment end.

He could not keep his promise. His hands left her face, went under her cloak and around her waist, pulling her body to his, holding her tight against him. She let out a small gasp; she felt as if she were going up in flame. "I want you," she found herself whispering. "I want you more than anything. . . ."

"Jara . . ."

"And I daren't . . . I daren't. . . ." She wrenched herself free, stood there a moment, her eyes filled with longing and despair, and then fled from the place as she had once before.

THERE WERE SIGNS that the miracle long prayed for was about to occur. Several new sources of water were found, indicating the presence of underground springs other than the one the Romans had dammed up. The flow was not abundant, but it was enough to raise everybody's spirits. In addition, Bar Kokhba was his old self again, moving among the people with confidence and words of encouragement. The rumors that he had killed his uncle became less strident, while others claimed the *Nasi* had done so only because he'd discovered the rabbi was a spy. Meanwhile, to everyone's surprise rations were doubled, and despite the continued presence of Severus' troops and the siege wall surrounding the entire area, a holiday air—somewhat desperate, perhaps—suddenly prevailed. A great show was made of tossing a small amount of garbage over the side of the fortress wall to indicate that all inside were feasting like kings. Someone wanted to empty a waterskin as well, but wiser souls prevented this display.

"Your Bar Kokhba is not acting with much sense," Quintus remarked to Andreas. "Severus will realize there's been a change of fortune and move to seek out and stop the water that's coming in."

Andreas nodded thoughtfully. At the rate both food and water were being given out, the stores would be depleted in a week, never mind what Severus might do. What was Simeon thinking of?

"I don't care what tricks your Son of a Star may be playing," Quintus said suddenly. "You're not going to get out of this alive. None of you are."

"You may as well include yourself in that statement, centurion."

Quintus nodded. "I suppose so. Frankly, I'm surprised I'm still around. A trial and public execution of a legionary would be wonderful tonic for the people here. We do it all the time. Good for morale."

Andreas grinned. "Thanks for the suggestion."

Quintus allowed himself a wry smile. "I was right about you all along. The thing is, I don't really understand why. I know your family, your background, the home you come from, the people you move among in Rome. They were never to my taste," he added of the latter, "but hardly a preparation for this. You had nothing at all to gain by involving yourself in these events, and everything to lose. For what, then? Freedom? You had that in Rome. For your God? The synagogues of Rome are there for you, inviolate—subject to acts of vandalism from time to time, I admit, but not forbidden to you. What do you have in common with these rough people? Why did you leave Rome?"

"Why did you? You are no ordinary centurion, Marcellus Quintus. That old Sabine stock which spawned you is the same root which gave the likes of Vespasian to Rome. You have an exquisite villa in the country, a library of books—very few statues on your grounds. You are said to prefer the beauty of nature to works of marble. It is well known that you would rather prune a tree than cut down a man, yet immediately your wife died, you returned to service. Because of your honesty and compassion for all men, you are known among the Jews of Rome as a 'righteous Gentile,' a sometime champion of my people. And yet here you are, waging war against us."

"I did not mean it to be so," Quintus admitted tiredly. "I thought I could be of service—I wanted to be of service—to my emperor . . . and to a people I believed misunderstood. . . ."

"Service? How, centurion? By leveling a small village in the Galilee and murdering all its inhabitants because a girl stuck a knife in the Roman commander who raped her?"

Quintus turned white.

Andreas smiled crookedly. "You say you always saw through me. Well, I saw through you as well. Even in Rome, when the people of our synagogue were praying for your wife's recovery because you were a 'good man,' I knew what you were. Just as I know what I am. No matter how I look, what tongue I speak, inside, I am a Jew. And you, no matter what you say, are a *goy*."

"I have heard that word. . . ."

"*Goyim*," Andreas said pleasantly. "Gentiles. It means simply, the 'others.' "

"Yes," Quintus said now, eagerly. "Yes, don't you see? That was what it was all about! A world without 'others'! A world where we are all one! That was the dream. That was always the dream. You are no stranger to Hadrian. Surely you know that is what is in his heart."

"We all know what the emperor of Rome wants and is planning to do," Simeon said, coming into the room. "Spare us, centurion. Spare us the 'good intentions,' the 'inner sensitivities' and 'love of all mankind.' I do not think I care to learn that the man who intends to destroy me has his heart in the right place."

"It could have been different," the Roman insisted. "But you people are unbending, unwilling ever to compromise or to change."

"One does not compromise with God. We are the Lord's people because we have kept the covenant Abraham made. You are right: There can be no compromise on that matter."

"The edict against circumcision was not directed solely against the Jews," Quintus said impatiently. "The ban against bodily mutilation is a universal one. You've got to understand how far-reaching the frontiers of the Empire are now. There are many barbaric tribes that must be brought to the level of our civilization in order to ensure world peace. But all that was explained to you long ago."

"The equality of the law. . . ." Andreas spoke again. "Yes, I've always been impressed by how impartial civil justice can be. Both the rich and the poor are forbidden to steal food."

Simeon waved the arguments of both men aside. "I'm not one for long talk on what was, or for debating what might have been or could be. The situation is what it is. The man you serve," he told Quintus, "exists only in your own mind. To me he is a fantasy. There are no 'champions of civilization' except for those who need to justify the dirty work they do. Your Hadrain speaks of 'culture' and 'beauty' and 'art' and 'universal brotherhood'—and my people get cut down. Our beliefs, our way of life differ from what Caesar deems acceptable, and so we must give up our beliefs and change our way of life, or die. That's the real gist of it. And if you were truly honest you would say so—like your emperor Julius Caesar, who spoke the plain truth: 'I came, I saw, I conquered.' "

Quintus' surprise at hearing Julius Caesar quoted was compounded as the evening went on. Of a sudden Bar Kokhba became an ingratiating host, the hostility that had been so manifest earlier replaced by an air of cordiality almost approaching camaraderie. The man had a kind of rough charm that no doubt endeared him to the masses. But there was evidence also of sharp intelligence, a brilliantly functioning mind, the results of which Quintus had learned well on the battlefield. The centurion had no doubt that he was being probed now; the question, as always, was why.

The girl helped to serve them. Bar Kokhba saw Quintus follow her with his eyes, and when she left the room said, "Her name is Jara. Her grandmother died on the Masada. Her mother was kidnapped by your soldiers and sold to a brothel. The pouches tied to her waistcord hold a number of herbs which she has learned to administer medicinally. One pouch holds a knife. It is a very old knife, a Sicarii blade. She likes to think it belonged to her grandfather. She used it to kill a Roman commander."

"I know," Quintus said softly.

"She is my betrothed."

Quintus raised his glass of wine in tribute. "She is very beautiful."

"And young. Too young to be cut off from all that is life. But there are many in Betar who are young. Children. What will you do with them, Roman, in the name of 'civilization' and 'art' and a 'world where all are one'? What will happen to the girl you just saw in this room and others like her? Don't bother to answer. Drink," he said pleasantly. "Drink your wine."

Later he took up a handful of nuts from the bowl that had been placed before him and began playing with them. "You know," Bar Kokhba said, "when I was a boy I used to play with another boy named Yoni ben Reuven. Now, this Yoni was a very clever fellow. Every Passover he would take up a fistful of nuts and hold his hand over the table. If you wanted to gamble with him you had to place one nut on the table for guessing odd, two nuts for guessing even. And then the nuts would be counted. If Yoni won, he kept them all. If he lost, you got the entire fistful. Well, every year Yoni played that game. And he never lost a fistful of nuts. It drove me crazy. How did he do it? No one knew. Well, more years went by . . . this and that happened . . . and one day I found myself close to death, bitten by a snake. For a number of days I hovered—trembled—between light and darkness. And suddenly I had a vision of Yoni ben Reuven, and everything made sense to me. I started to laugh. Obodas, who was with me at the time, thought I was still delirious. But in fact it was the sanest moment of my life. Because I knew how Yoni had done it! You see, he always put an odd number of nuts in his hand. When you guessed odd and paid one nut for guessing he added that nut to the odd number, making it even. When you guessed even and paid two nuts for guessing, he added the two nuts to the odd number in his hand, leaving it odd." He grinned. "Sounds simple now, but when you're six years old . . . well, that's the story of Yoni. You're probably wondering why I tell it now. I don't know. Crazy . . . the things that come to you when you're close to death. But I remember, in the desert, when it came to me, there was something else. . . . Something about God . . ." He shrugged, letting the nuts he'd been playing with fall from his hand. "What do you think, Roman? Do you think it's a fixed game?"

SHE WAS WAITING for him in the chamber. There were flowers in the room; she'd used the extra water to fill a small glass vial with a few stray blooms she'd found pushing up against the fortress wall. They were wildflowers, weeds; they wouldn't last the night.

"Why didn't you sup with us?" he asked. "You were welcome."

She turned away. "I don't sit with our enemy."

"Our prisoner," he pointed out. "And you helped to serve him."

"No, I didn't. I served only you."

That was true. She had avoided Andreas as carefully as she had the centurion. Too carefully. . . .

"I have sent for some food and drink for us now," Simeon

said. "I thought it would be pleasant."

"It would, but . . . Simeon, is there really enough to go round? Everyone has been feasting. Is there enough—"

He put his finger to her lips. "We must be strong to fight. And no one has really been feasting. It only seems so because we have done with so little for so long."

"You said 'fight.' You have a plan."

He smiled. "Yes."

"I knew it!" She sighed happily. "What is it? Please tell me."

"In time. In time you will know everything." He went to a chest now and drew something forth from it. "Here, this is for you." He held up a white robe of fine linen. A pattern of leaves had been skillfully woven around the hem. There was a braided sash of many colors.

Wonderingly, Jara stared at the garment.

"For our wedding. It was to be a surprise. But I can't wait. I want to see you in it now. Put it on for me."

Delighted, she obeyed. When she was dressed in the white gown, he took the flowers from the vial and placed them in her hair. Then he took her face in his hands and kissed her.

There was a knock at the door, and a tray was brought in. Simeon filled her goblet.

"I feel like a queen," Jara said shyly. "It is all so grand."

Simeon smiled. "A handful of grapes, some nuts, a cup of wine. . . . You are easy to please, my love."

" 'My love' . . . You never called me that before."

"I'm not good with words like that . . . and they never seemed necessary with us."

"Then why do you say them now?"

He waited until she had taken another sip of the wine and then said, "Because I wanted you to know I love you."

"I know, Simeon." She yawned slightly. "I always knew. . . ."

He smiled. "Drink some more wine."

"I'm sorry. . . . I don't know why I feel so sleepy. . . . Is it very late?"

"Yes. . . ."

She took another sip of the wine and then slowly lowered the goblet. "I can hardly keep my eyes open. . . ."

He caught her as she fell and carried her to the bed. He

smoothed her hair, kissed her eyes, her lips, her cold hands.

The door to the chamber opened, and Obodas entered the room. Simeon looked at the Nabatean and nodded. Then he looked again at Jara and said softly, "You see, my love, you are not the only one who understands potions and such." He kissed her hands again. "So to sleep . . . and dream no more of a man called Bar Kokhba."

ANDREAS AND the centurion were waiting at the entrance to the underground passage. A piece of cloth had been tied over the Roman's eyes. Simeon undid the blindfold; immediately Quintus looked around, trying to place the setting deep in his mind. Simeon smiled slightly. "I'm sending you back to your people," he told the man.

"If you do, I have no choice but to return."

"Yes, I'm aware of that. I expect it." *Long for it . . . long for it. . . .*

Quintus hesitated. "You'd better bind my eyes again," he said finally.

"No need of that."

"I am duty bound—"

"Yes, I know. Very well. In a moment." Obodas came out of the shadows now. There was a body in his arms. "You will see to it that she is safe," Simeon said. "You will see that she and Andreas get through your own lines. After that, I don't care what you do. Give me your word."

Quintus nodded. "You have my word."

"Good. Farewell, then." He moved to tie the cloth around Quintus' eyes once more, then stopped and said gently, "Don't look so forlorn, Roman. We both know what we have to do. But I will tell you this: Your general may take Betar. Your emperor may enslave or kill everyone of us in this land, obliterate Jerusalem—even the name Israel—and he will still not destroy us. Somewhere in a desert cave or in the hills of Galilee . . . in Parthia, Egypt, or Rome itself—when Caesar is saying to himself, 'I have destroyed all the Jews and all they hold dear'—even then, a woman will be kindling the Sabbath lights. A man will be teaching his son Torah. And the moment those candles take fire, be it the smallest spark—the moment that child says, be it the smallest whisper, 'Hear, O Israel, the

Lord our God, the Lord is One'—in that moment I am alive,
and all here live again. Betar, Masada, Jerusalem, all Israel is
alive. And Caesar has lost.''

SIMEON WENT with them nearly half the way, carrying Jara in
his arms as though loath to give her up. Feeling her begin to
stir, he stopped the others and said, ''I must go back now.''
Tenderly he put the girl down, keenly observing how quickly
Andreas set down his torch and went to her. He put his hand
on the younger man's shoulder. ''Be well.'' And then he was
gone.

Still under the effects of the drug Simeon had given her,
Jara opened her eyes dazedly. Seeing Andreas' face in this
dark underground setting, she believed what was happening to
be a dream and allowed herself to be led the rest of the way
through the tunnel. By the time they reached the gorge far
below Betar, light was breaking, the last star all but faded
away. Somewhere in the haze of morning, her mind still not
wholly awake, she perceived that Andreas was speaking with
another man. Then the man was gone, and Andreas was
leading her away again, she knew not where. It might have
been a dream: Was she running from Tiberias, or going to
Rimmon with Simeon's men? Were she and Andreas still
leading the Romans in false pursuit? If so, Ein Gedi was
waiting, and the pool there, and the cave of rushes. . . .

But the sound in her ears was not the water falling from Ein
Gedi's spring. Like the sun slicing through the gray mist, the
noises of the Roman camp came crashing into her con-
sciousness. And suddenly it was all clear to her, and with that
realization a cry of anguish and denial spilled out of her
mouth, only to be drowned by the sound of wheels rolling over
rock and the clang and hammer of flint and stone against
wood as the men on the ridge above worked on the assault
ramp.

Andreas had rolled on top of her, stifling her cries with his
hands and body. She fought him, and they rolled over and
over in the dust until stopped by the presence of a large
boulder. He dragged her behind the rock, covered her mouth
again with his hands. She was sobbing. ''Shut up, Jara,'' he
whispered in her ear. ''You've got to be quiet, or I'll have to
knock you out.''

She nodded, tears meanwhile streaming down her face, lips tightly pressed to contain her weeping.

He studied her a moment, then, content that her will to live was stronger than any other feelings she might have, removed his hand from her mouth and turned his attention back to the men in the camp. "We'll have to wait until dark," Andreas whispered. "Quintus will give the signal."

She swallowed. Her tongue felt swollen. "I want to go back," she said dully. "Let me go back to Betar."

He looked at her. "I can't do that," he said finally. "I gave my word."

She closed her eyes and turned her head away from him and wept silently against the rock.

2

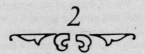

ELISHA BEN ABUYAH stood before Tinneus Rufus in the governor's palace in Caesarea. "These works are well known to Caesar," he said, indicating the books Rufus was detachedly perusing. "There is nothing inflammatory. . . ."

" 'Arts of Carpocrates,' 'Writings of Simon Magus' . . ." Rufus looked up and shook his head, bemused. "Ah! Now, this . . . this looks familiar!" He pointed to a papyrus he'd unrolled. "But what's this? Another paper tucked inside . . ."

"Yes, yes." Ben Abuyah hastened to explain. "The first is only lines gathered from Homer—"

"There are numbers beside the verses."

"Each is a sort of lucky message or oracle. You select the one meant for you by throwing dice. The numbers refer to the appropriate throw. The other papyrus reveals the same principle. However, it is used by the Christians, employing texts from their gospels. I find the parallel amusing."

"Yes, I'm sure you do," Rufus murmured, studying the papyruses again. He smiled. "So, it's only games, is it?"

"There are those who take such endeavors seriously," ben Abuyah replied carefully. "If one believes in oracles, then the pattern on a leaf can have significance, or even a shadow cast by the sun."

"And you . . . what do you believe?"

Ben Abuyah spread his hands. "I believe I am in the governor's palace in Caesarea, brought here by your guards from the bookseller I have frequented for many years. For what reason I have not been told."

Rufus smiled again. "I don't need a reason."

Ben Abuyah sighed inwardly. Exercises in power were rarely interesting and almost always dangerous. Now he must stand at attention, being careful to appear neither servile nor arrogant, while this pompous imbecile rescued from disgrace by the efficiency and intelligence of another man, Julius Severus, played at being Caesar. At times like this he wished there was real magic. A word, a gesture, and this brainless insect would dissolve in a puff of smoke while he, Elisha ben Abuyah, would be transported back to the musty comfort of his own study. "May I sit down?" he asked politely.

Surprised, Rufus nevertheless nodded acquiescence, and ben Abuyah took a seat.

"You are not unknown to us," Rufus said after a pause. "You were born a Jew, but the Jews disclaim you. They will not even speak your name. We both know why. You are an apostate. You have forsaken the faith of Moses. Would that your countrymen were so wise."

Ben Abuyah remained silent.

"Obviously you are a man of intellect. I know through your friend Polidorus, the bookseller, that your interests are many. Science, mathematics, astronomy, magical arts . . . but most of all, you pursue philosophy, the thinking of the Greeks, which is in fact the best love of Hadrian Caesar. You are a man of reason. And it is to that reason I now appeal. Yes. Appeal."

Bewildered, ben Abuyah asked, "What is it that you want of me?"

"The war of Bar Kokhba is over. But for Betar and a few scattered outposts in the desert, the province is once more blessed with peace. Pax Romana. And even as I speak, the soldiers of Rome are preparing to make a final end of the author of these three years' folly. Much damage has been done on both sides. What has occurred must never occur again."

Ben Abuyah gave a slight shrug. "You said yourself, it is over. With Simeon ben Kosiba and his followers dead, there is an end to it."

"You don't believe that, and neither do I. When Titus burned Jerusalem, we said it was over, and it was not. When Masada fell, we said it was over, and it was not. When the Jews of Alexandria were destroyed and the Jews of Cyprus and Cyrene put to death by Trajan, we said, at last, it is over. And still, it was not."

Ben Abuyah did not reply.

"The emperor is convinced that the rebellious spirit of the Jews cannot be broken unless their superstitious idolatry of an invisible God is also broken."

Ben Abuyah's face remained impassive, giving no sign of the sudden blanket of cold enveloping him, the bitter chill of all his nightmare landscapes becoming reality. A shrug masked the shudder. "Jerusalem is no more," he said. "Bar Kokhba's vain attempt to restore the Temple of the Jews has come to nothing as a result of your most efficient forces."

Rufus shook his head. "No," he said, wagging a finger in denial. "No, we shall not make that mistake again. Caesar is well aware that while your temple and holy city may go up in flames, the study of the laws which bind your people can go on anywhere—outside Jerusalem, outside Judea. It is that which keeps the memory of your cult alive and the prayer for restoration—not only of your temple and holy city but of a Jewish nation—strong. So long as that impossible dream is nurtured, your people will continue to cause trouble, to hold themselves apart from the rest of mankind, and hence to suffer grievously. Logic, the very reason you hold dear, compels you to agree with me."

"Yes," ben Abuyah responded quietly. "You are quite correct."

"The edict against circumcision remains in effect. Additionally the following is prohibited: observance of the Sabbath, adherence to any calendar but that of the Roman Empire, practice of any and all customs solely in accordance with the Law of the Jews, the teaching of that Law, and the study of same. All these things shall be punishable by death. Well, what do you think?"

The bright blue eyes glittered; there was no other response.

"You can be of service now to your emperor, Elisha ben Abuyah, and though some may not see it so, to your people. The very reason—that genius which caused a lesser group to shun you—can work for their good. And your own, of course. Believe me, you will be doing all concerned the greatest benefit."

"What do you want?" ben Abuyah asked hoarsely.

"Help us seek out the teachers of your Law, the schools where all the seeds of disaster are continually sown. You were a pupil of the sages. You know the laws, the customs, the words that must henceforth never be spoken again. Instruct the soldiers of Caesar so they will know what to look for, so they will not be tricked. Work with us. Be Rome's friend and we will be yours." Rufus paused. "I am not going to make any ugly statements in regard to a decision on your part not to cooperate. You realize, I feel sure, what lies ahead. Any benevolence shown in the past will not be forthcoming. The emperor Hadrian is surely the most just and compassionate man in all the world. I tell you frankly he has not one shred of tolerance left in his being for the Jews. And as far as I'm concerned, if it means killing every man, woman, and child among you to keep this province peaceable, I am fully prepared to do so."

AKIVA WAS WAITING anxiously. From the window he saw Mesha hurriedly entering the courtyard, and quickly went to the door.

"I couldn't get through," Mesha announced, breathing heavily. "They've moved in tighter around Betar. They're massing on all fronts. The roads are full of soldiers. Severus must have called for reinforcements. I managed to slip through their ring, but there was too heavy a concentration of men in the vicinity of the secret passage." He paused nervously. "I think they know where it is. Either they found it themselves or someone's given it away. If so, Severus will try to divert Simeon by means of the ramp in the south, while another group sneaks in through the underground tunnel. And there's no way we can warn them!"

"Simeon is clever in battle," Akiva said slowly. "In any event the passage is surely watched at all times."

"No. Not in number anyway. If its location were obvious, every fool in Betar would be rushing to escape, thereby jeopardizing the rest. Anyway . . ." He shook his head, troubled. "Why is Severus moving to break the siege now? The stir in the camp makes me believe the decision was sudden."

"It may be for the best." Rabbi Tarfon, who was also present, came forward now. "Many days without water or food. . . . One's strength is sapped, the mind wanders. It is not the same as a fast," he, who had known many, added. He sighed. "May God be with them."

"There's more, rabban." The young man hesitated. "I heard the soldiers talking." He turned back to Akiva. "You are in great danger. We all are."

"If Rufus wished to arrest me for my part in all this, he could have done so long ago," Akiva replied.

"The danger does not lie in helping Bar Kokhba," Mesha declared. "The crime of which we all will be accused is . . . teaching Torah."

Now, at last, all was clear to them. Tarfon sat down again. Slowly he raised a finger to his lips in contemplation. Then a spark of anger leaped into his eyes, the finger curled back into his hand, and the hand became a fist crashing down onto the table. The moment passed. The fist opened, fingers spread wide on wood. Tarfon's eyes became the eyes once more of a rabbi lost in thought or prayer.

Akiva had the look of a man dealt a mortal blow.

"The soldiers say . . . as soon as they've finished with the rebels, they're going to start exterminating every rabbi and student of the Law. Hadrian has declared it a capital offense to be a Jew."

Akiva remained silent. Then he said, "This is only hearsay. Soldiers' talk. Hadrian is no Antiochus. He is angry, yes, but to do such a thing—"

"Why not?" Tarfon broke in brusquely. "Why wouldn't he do such a thing? Because he is a man of 'culture' and 'reason'? Because he is so tolerant of other men's gods that he builds a great Pantheon? Because he deigns to sup with the humblest peasant in the humblest province—comes and sits at your own table, Akiva, and engages you in long philosophical discussion!" He made a disgusted gesture. "Why should we be shocked? This is the man who made no secret of the fact that he wanted to build a temple to Jupiter on Mount Moriah, our most sacred site. This is the man who paraded his male paramour like a prince before the world, who would turn a dead, womanized boy into a god and force all to worship the emperor's whore! No . . . no. . . ." The anger that had surfaced briefly earlier could not be contained now. "I am not shocked, and I do not doubt it. My heart was never in this war because I knew, I felt—I feared!—it would only lead to this. But I tell you now I'm glad we fought. I'm glad! And if it be my last prayer to God, I pray Simeon ben Kosiba takes as many Romans with him to eternity as he is able!''

ANDREAS REACHED OUT and caught Jara's hand. It was not a moment too soon, as her foot slipped on the narrow ledge below. She clung to him and to the side of the cliff, clawing at the rock face until, her balance recovered, she managed to regain her footing on the precipice. Another step, and he had hold of both her hands and was guiding her up and into a cave that opened on the side of the steep mount, rising over a deep winding defile. Exhausted, she stumbled a few feet forward into the cavern and then sank to the floor. Her white robe was dirty and torn; the strip of ragged fabric at the hem had nearly been her undoing. She tried to rip the piece off now, numb to anything but the present task.

"Here," Andreas said. "Use this." He placed a small dagger in her lap.

She stared at the familiar blade. "Simeon said you were to have it." His eyes searched hers.

She nodded, still staring at the knife. Then, without a word or sound, she covered her face with her hands.

MESHA LAY STILL as stone in bed, his eyes open, staring, his brain racing.

Beruria snuggled against him, her body warm and soft. She put her hand on his chest. "You can't sleep."

"No."

"Is it Simeon? Is it Betar?"

He hadn't told her all he'd heard. There was no need to just yet. Besides, as Akiva had said, it might only be soldiers talking.

"Yes," he replied. "I'm thinking of Simeon."

"I thought so." She sighed. "It always ends this way. I don't mean to be cruel, but it's true. Violence leads to more violence. Look what happened to Jerusalem when men tried to fight Caesar before."

He turned to look at her. "Are you saying we shouldn't have fought?"

"I don't know. Men killing other men, for whatever reason

. . . I don't know," she said again. "I don't really know if that's what God wants. Did you . . ." she began hesitantly.

"Did I what?"

"When you were with Simeon and the others, did you . . . did you . . . kill . . . anyone?"

"I don't know. I don't think so. I mean I just—I just tried to keep from getting killed myself."

"You had no business being there. You never belonged with them."

"I'm not a coward, Beruria."

"Of course not. Why, did you think you were?" She raised her head, surprised. "Oh, Mesha," she said at last, sinking back again, "why do men believe everything must be proved with swords?"

"I don't know," he answered, smiling a little. "I do know one thing, though. I'm no general. Even Simeon had to admit that. He said I could never be a commander because I thought too much about what had to be done. He said I'd had too much training as a rabbi. I can hear him now: 'There are no ifs or buts in battle, Mesha. You can show no doubt. At night, when you are alone, you can look at it and wonder if you were wrong. But you never show it.' Do you know what else he said? He told me he always knew when he went into the field that he would win and come out safely. He said you had to feel that way or you'd never come out of it. I wonder what he's feeling now, what he's thinking. . . ."

" 'They who live by the sword shall die by the sword,' " she quoted softly.

"Perhaps." He turned his head away.

"You're angry with me. I can't help it. That's the way I feel."

"No, I'm not angry." He slipped his hand under her head, caressed her shoulder. "But there is a gulf between us, a chasm that even love cannot ignore. I suppose no matter how close they come, man and woman never fully comprehend each other. The gulf remains."

"What can we do about it?"

"Understand that it exists. Bridge it if we can. Respect it." He kissed her forehead. "Go to sleep."

"No, I don't want to be away from you now." She paused. "Do you want to pray for Simeon? Shall we pray together?"

"I don't know how," he confessed. "I don't know what to say." He thought of all she'd said, and of Bar Kokhba's Brothers caught in Betar, and of the scholars in that city, and all who'd fought and all who'd prayed and how, finally, they would come to the same end. "I don't know what God wants," Rabbi Meir said. "I don't know what God wants of us."

ANDREAS STOOD in the entrance to the cave, his back to her, one hand touching the arch above his head. He'd remained like that, motionless, silhouetted against a red sky that had turned to ink. The cold light of the moon illuminated the canyon outside, scarcely lighting the cavern in which they'd found shelter.

Jara huddled on the ground, knees drawn tight against her chest. From someplace deeper in the recess came the sound of water dripping; the accumulation of moisture from the roof and walls of the cave had formed a small pool in the rear. There were traces of goat dung, pieces of broken pottery around the pool, the remains of an ax, evidence of shepherds, prophets, other refugees who had found their way here.

She felt weightless, light-headed, all cried out, and too tired to sort the bits and pieces swirling behind her eyes.

"I can see the lights of the Roman camps."

She looked up, startled. *Andreas*. It was Andreas speaking.

He turned around. "How are you feeling?"

"I don't know. Numb, I think." She sighed. "Why did he do it? Did he think I would be afraid at the end?"

"No . . . I don't think so."

"Then why?" She looked around helplessly. "I shouldn't be here. I should be there!"

"No, Jara, this is where you belong. Simeon knew that."

"You talk as if he were dead. He's not dead! Simeon is not dead!"

He did not answer.

"That man," she said suddenly. "There was a man with you in the ravine. I saw him!" She closed her eyes tightly. "It was the Roman. Yes, it was! Tell me it was not!"

"You saw Marcellus Quintus. Simeon wanted him to—"

"Liar!" She sprang at him before he could finish. "You

helped the Roman to escape! You drugged me! It wasn't
Simeon! It wasn't!''

He grabbed her wrists before she could strike him and
swung her around so that her back was against the wall, her
body held prisoner by his own. ''It was Simeon! Simeon! He
wants it over, can't you see? Now! While they've strength
enough to fight!'' He let out his breath. ''Quintus has seen the
secret passage. He won't hesitate to use it. He's a loyal
Roman. He'll do what he has to do. If I know Simeon, he's
counting on that. As for you . . . he wants you to live. It's as
simple as that. He loves you and wants you to live.''

She swallowed. ''Does he know about us?''

''I think so. I never said a word, I swear it. But how could
he not know? It was obvious every time I looked at you.''

She turned her head away, unwilling even now to confront
those dark eyes that reached so deep inside her, yet feeling his
body warm against hers, warm and warming. . . .

''It was in your face as well. You couldn't hide it. That's
why you went out of your way to avoid me. Do you think
Simeon couldn't see how you avoided me?''

''Never! I hate you! I've always hated you!''

''You hate yourself for being like me, for wanting all that
life has to offer, not just the world of a Jew! You reached out
and grabbed for Simeon because he's something special, Jara.
Even I would be a fool to deny that. I could never compete
with what he is, and I don't want to. You may not believe this,
but I hope to God he comes out of this. And if he does and
you go back to him, I won't say a word, because I know now
how much he loves you. But now, tonight, you're mine.''

He brought her roughly to him, but even as his mouth took
possession, her arms went around him. Just as quickly,
though, she drew back, confused. ''No,'' she said tearfully.
''No, not now. It's wrong. . . .''

''Wrong?'' His lips brushed her hair. ''Can you tell me
what's wrong, Jara? Or what's right? I've always believed the
world was insane, but never more so than now. The only thing
I know to be true is what I feel for you.'' Tenderly, he took
her face in his hands. ''I've been in synagogues and temples to
every god there is all over the world. I've fought for Jerusalem
and Israel. Yet this cave and this moment seem more holy to
me than anything I've ever known. I want to pray,'' he said.
''I want to pray in you.''

There was a sweetness to his kiss now that she had never before experienced, and a tenderness coupled with such deep urgency that it took her breath away. But his talk of temples and Israel brought back the faces of all in Betar who at this moment might be fighting for their very lives. And so she said sadly, "But now . . . why now?"

"Because we're here," he answered fiercely. "Because we're alive! And because I love you, and I don't know what tomorrow will bring. All we may have is now, this moment. . . ." Even in the dark she could feel his eyes burning hers, and then suddenly he was saying, "No, not this moment. Forever! Damn it, forever! Whatever comes . . . forever. . . ." He grabbed her hands in his. "According to the Law of Moses and Israel thou art consecrated unto me from this time forth. By all that is holy, I take thee Jara, to be my wife, now and forever, in heaven and on earth. And I do pledge thee—" He stopped, then continued softly, "I do pledge thee my undying love."

He kissed her mouth again and the tears on her cheeks and her throat and her trembling lips once more.

And in a cave like that of Adullam or the Wandering Shepherd, in a place where some early family of man had built a hearth, where prophets of a later age saw visions of Zion, in a canyon niche not unlike the recesses where fleeing Essenes had buried their scrolls or the hunted Brothers of Bar Kokhba would take refuge, one man and one woman came together in the eternal promise of love and the everlasting covenant of life.

THE HOURS OF NIGHT passed. Morning came, and still rabbis Tarfon and Akiva talked. If what Mesha said was true, then the demise of the war signaled the start of another, subtler one in which every man, woman, and child who called himself a Jew would be forced to participate.

Together the two aged men went over the names of their peers and students—sages and scholars who might soon be hunted as the Brothers of Bar Kokhba were. With growing shock and grief they realized how many religious leaders would be lost if only those in Betar were slain. The school alone there had upward of four hundred students. Moreover, many members of the Council of Judges had been caught in the besieged city and were likely to die. An accounting was made of those who could take their place and of the students currently being taught by themselves and by Hanina ben Teradyon, Judah ben Bava, and Rabbi Yossi the Galilean, who might be ready for ordination. Escape to Parthia was mentioned, and all manner of deceptive practices by which the study and teaching of Torah might continue were calmly laid forth in hushed but practical tones.

At last Rabbi Tarfon rose and made to leave. Akiva walked with him until they reached the fig tree under whose broad leaves scores of scholars had sat listening to the words of their beloved sage. As though remembering now the time when they sat together, themselves students in the orchard of Jabneh, recalling all the years of friendship and debate—often heated—that they'd shared, Tarfon said with a nostalgic smile, "I always thought you heaped together a lot of words to make a simple point, Akiva. But your points were always well taken."

Akiva took into his own the hands of the man he called "the father of all Israel," and said, "Tarry awhile."

"My teacher and master," Tarfon replied, "anyone who is separated from you is as if separated from life. But a class awaits me in Lod. Also, there is a monetary dispute upon which I have promised to make judgment. I am already late."

Akiva nodded, but he was still loath to see the man depart and so walked with him until the road. From a distance came a sound like muffled thunder, and both men shuddered, for they knew it was the sound of men at war, that no rain would fall this hot summer day.

The time had come to part. The two rabbis embraced, Akiva silent but with a thousand fond words shining in his eyes. Tarfon nodded as if he'd heard every thought spoken. "I must go," he said again. "The day is short and the work is great . . . and the laborers are sluggish," he added. Both men smiled. "But the reward is much," Rabbi Tarfon went on, "and the Master is urgent. It may not be for us to finish the work. But neither can we shirk it."

BABATA CAST a worried glance around the room. Had she packed everything? No, not everything, but enough, please God, to see her through this present horror. She checked the basket sitting atop the table. It was filled to the brim; it would not hold another object. She went over in her mind the basket's contents: her best wooden bowls, her kitchen knives, her mirror and jewelry box, the flat iron frying pan she'd used since she was a young bride.

Another basket, woven of willow, unlike the first, which was made of palm fronds, sat on the floor. This too was full. Having made up her mind, Babata managed to slip a pair of sandals into the basket on the table just as a man appeared at her door.

"Will you hurry, woman?" Jonathan bar Be'ayan growled. "It's past noon. The legions were sighted hours ago. We must get to the caves before dark—and, more important, before the Romans spot us."

"A moment, a moment. I want to be sure I have everything."

"Crazy woman . . . do you think you are going on holiday? Take whatever you want and can carry, but go with the others now!"

"Yes, yes, I am coming. I am coming. Not that I expect any help for a poor lame female such as myself, alone and husbandless. . . ."

With a curse and a sigh, bar Be'ayan swept the basket off the table and made a gesture to show he would carry it for her. "Now, come. Quickly!"

Babata smiled sweetly and followed him out the door. In her arms she carried a leather pouch, wrapped in sacking and tied together with rope.

"What have you got there?" bar Be'ayan asked as they joined the stream of people fleeing Ein Gedi.

"Letters . . . things of a personal nature," the woman responded evasively. She limped behind the Jewish commander. "I am a sentimental woman."

"You are a crazy woman," bar Be'ayan responded testily. "A lot of good those things will do you where we're going."

Babata smiled but did not reply. Jonathan bar Be'ayan could not know that the package she carried so protectively contained every deed and document she needed to pursue her claim against his family and to protect her own interests. This war would not last forever, and when it was done, she, Babata, would have her day in court.

*   *   *

THE HOVERING TWILIGHT seemed like a canopy held aloft by the wings of the birds swooping across the iridescent sky, their gay chatter somehow misplaced. They lit on the tree under which Akiva sat, strutted confidently at his feet, and perched on his knees and shoulder. But Akiva, deep in thought, was oblivious to their play. Suddenly a figure coming down the road caught his eye, and he stood up to see who approached. It was a young woman or girl, the hem of her gown jagged and torn, the fabric soiled as by grim endeavor. She walked tiredly, as though at any moment she might fall. The setting sun cast a halo of fire round her hair.

Seeing the rabbi, Jara's spirit was renewed, and her pace quickened. She hurried forward now, as though fearing if she but stopped a moment she would sink exhausted to the ground, or worse, Akiva would disappear. He was all that remained. At dawn Andreas had led her from the cave and set out with her in this direction. Sometime in the afternoon, when she could walk no further, they'd rested. She fell asleep in his arms. When she awoke, he was gone.

The sky was the color of fire now. All the birds were still. Akiva held out his hand, and Jara took it and walked with him into the house at B'nei Berak.

IT IS WRITTEN that Betar fell on the ninth of Av, the very day in which the Temple was destroyed first by Nebuchadnezzar and then by Titus. Its demise marked an end to the war that had lasted three and a half years, although there continued to be skirmishes and sieges in the Judean Desert where many rebels had escaped. None of the Brothers with Simeon ben Kosiba in Betar, however, escaped from that doomed place. Virtually the entire population of the city was killed.

Having taken possession of Betar, Severus ordered a general massacre. In time-honored tradition, the Roman soldiery roamed the streets, cutting down anybody they saw. They broke open houses and slaughtered whole families, searching out hiding places and cutting down their terrified occupants. The streets became slippery with blood; mutilated corpses lay everywhere. The schoolboys who'd vowed to fight were wrapped in their study scrolls and burned alive. Scores of children were picked up by their heels and swung against a rock, their brains dashed upon the stone. The *Midrash* would lament that the blood from Betar streamed down to the valleys below, carrying large boulders with it, and ran into the sea four miles out.

Severus' action was deliberate, intended to create terror in every city, town, and village of the Empire. If any other province entertained thoughts of emulating the Jews in defying Caesar and the Roman army, Betar would serve as the ultimate example of the consequences.

But there was more perhaps to the zeal that attended the absolute destruction of Bar Kokhba's last stronghold.

It would be said later that there were two brooks in the Valley of Yadaim, each going in a different direction. After the fighting, they were filled with the blood of the slain and ran with two parts of water to one of blood. That much of that blood was Roman, history would not deny. As the historian Dio Cassius would be compelled to write, so many Romans perished that for the first time a Roman emperor, Hadrian, reporting to the senate on the outcome of the war, was forced to omit the customary opening phrase, *Mihi et legionibus bene*: "I and my troops are well."

Bodies lay everywhere—in the city, on the ramparts, outside the fortress wall. As night fell, the soldiers withdrew, unwilling to remain in the dark with all the dead. In the morning, when they returned to collect their own and to continue the general looting, they found the body of one Marcellus Quintus, a much loved centurion, killed in the fighting.

Jews were denied access to the area; no burial was permitted, in deliberate violation of Torah. On the sixteenth day of the month, when the Jews were at last permitted to gather what was left of their countrymen to be interred in a decent manner, the sight that greeted them was past bearing. There were scores of nude, decomposed bodies; heaps of charred remains of youngsters who had met their death outside the school where they had been taught to love God, the putrid matter festering on a giant bloodstained stone, which had served as a gory altar for the small victims whose crushed skulls lay nearby. And there was the stench, the smell not just of death under the hot sun but of murder, carnage, massacre.

"Where was God?" someone asked, stunned by the ghastly scene.

Where was man? the angels replied.

THE BODY of Simeon ben Kosiba was never found. The stories of his prowess and superhuman valor that had attended him in life followed him in death. Some claimed that at the end he rose up to heaven in a chariot of fire. Others said that the pile of soldiers he slew was so great it caused the earth to open and swallow him up. Many believed that he was still alive, hiding in the hills or the desert, from which he would one day emerge to renew the struggle for freedom. Talmudic legend would have it that a Samaritan brought the hero's head to Hadrian. But when they went to bring the body, they found a snake circling its neck, and Hadrian exclaimed, "If his God had not slain him, who could have overcome such a man?"

There were many curious tales told of the fall of Betar, even among the Romans. One young legionary claimed he'd seen a giant figure of a man emerge from the dead, blood gushing from a score of wounds, half-crazed from all that was around him as well as all he'd endured. He stumbled about, going from one lifeless form to another, oblivious to any danger to himself. He'd take in his arms now one body, now another, and then another, and over each he would murmur the same words. What those words were, the young soldier could not say, for they were spoken in the tongue of the Jews, but they seemed to be some kind of prayer. Finally the legionary came up behind the man and delivered the final blow that killed him.

3

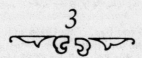

IT WAS a moonless night, but with brilliant stars. The only sounds came from the ship as oars were dipped and withdrawn in perfect time, the water dripping from them as they were raised aloft. Waves washed against the galley's side. Otherwise all was still.

The man on deck stood looking out to sea, nothing before him but a vast silver and jet expanse, yet his expression seemed to reflect a full display of sight and sound. In his eyes a world revolved.

The planks of the deck creaked with approaching footsteps. Slowly but deliberately, the man turned, his dark eyes wary, his reverie gone.

"Can't sleep." It was the passenger from Salonika. The man moved to the rail and stared across the water as the other had been doing. He took a deep breath of the clear, cold air. "Shouldn't do that," he commented. "Like to fill myself full of demons and such. But it looks so peaceful. . . ."

"Yes," the dark-eyed man murmured.

"Expect we'll be seeing the coast of Palestine soon. Can't say as I'm really eager. It's a hard country, they say. Don't doubt it. Always figured if the Jews had a nice, cushy place to live they wouldn't have turned out to be such a surly bunch, always going on about other people's pleasures, if you know what I mean. What with the war and all, don't suppose their disposition's gotten any better. Not that they're likely to cause any trouble now. Still," he went on, "I don't expect to have an easy time of it."

Dark eyes surveyed him briefly, came to a conclusion. "You've bought land."

"Yes! Guessed that, have you? Couple of vineyards and such outside . . . ah, what's it called? Beth—Beth—"

"Bethlehem? Bethel?"

"Bethlehem. Yes, that's it. Ever been there?"

A nod.

"Hear it's not too bad. Flat. Good soil. Plenty of grapes and olives. Balsam too, that's the best of it. Fellow who sold me the place said there's a fortune to be made if it's handled properly. Well, I'm no farmer. But I expect I know how to organize things. That's all it takes. Of course, there's plenty of labor. Slaves cheap as dirt since the war. No market in bones anymore, even in Salonika. Just Jews and more Jews since they got rid of that Bar Cochebas fellow. Pick them up penny a piece. Personally I prefer the Germans. Big and dumb, that's how I like them. Give you your money's worth. The Jews are always thinking too much, if you know what I mean."

"Why is he selling?"

"Eh?"

"The man who sold you this estate—"

"Oh, he's just the broker. Place belonged to a soldier who served with the Tenth. Fellow's homesick, wants to go back to Firenze or wherever. Can't say as I blame him. Once I'm rich, I'll be on my way as well." He cast a quick glance at the somewhat exotic garb of his fellow passenger. "Don't suppose money's a worry to you. They say you Parthians are stuffed with gold."

A slight turn revealed the gleam of a dagger beneath the man's fine woolen cloak.

"I mean," the fellow said, laughing nervously and backing away a trifle. "That's what they say. Everyone in Parthia is rich."

There was a trace of a crooked smile. "And everyone in Salonika is a clever businessman."

More laughter tinged with relief. "Well, yes, I expect that's so." Silence. The look in the Parthian's eyes made one's blood run cold; it was the look of Asmodeus, no doubting it. The Prince of Night. "Well, ah, I'd better be getting some sleep. Night air's bad for you, they say. Full of demons and such. . . ." He backed away.

The dark-eyed man turned to the sea and let his thoughts fly across the waves once more.

NEARLY FOUR YEARS had passed since the fall of Betar. The victory brought Hadrian his second acclamation as *Imperator*. Julius Severus was granted the *ornamenta triumphalia* and made governor of the entire Syrian province. Tinneus Rufus retained his office, but the name of the area he administered was changed. It had been the province of Judea that fell to Vespasian. Under Simeon ben Kosiba the country chose to revert to the name of Israel, as it had been called during the kingdom of David. Now Hadrian decreed that the land of the Jews would be known as *Palestine*, meaning the Land of the Philistines. It was a calculated Roman insult, meant to convey the idea that the children of Abraham had never had a homeland at all, a curse that would endure long after the tread of the legionary could be heard no more.

In Jerusalem the plan Hadrian had conceived before the war was immediately put into effect. The city was turned into a Roman colony with the name Aelia Capitolina. No Jew was permitted to live there or even to enter the city under penalty of death. Even the Christians, who were allowed to resume their colony in the paganized city, were forbidden to have among them there any coreligionists of Jewish birth. From that time on their bishop would be of Gentile origin.

A temple to Jupiter had been erected on the Temple Mount. Where the altar had stood, a statue of Hadrian on horseback was placed. The image of a pig or wild boar, symbol of the Tenth Legion, was carved on the southern gate of the city, facing Bethlehem. A shrine to a Roman god stood on the grave of Jesus, and a sanctuary to Venus on the place of crucifixion.

THE FIRST YEAR after Bar Kokhba's defeat had been the worst —perhaps worse than anything the Jews had ever known under Roman occupation. In the desert, in the area of Herodium, Masada, and Qumran, scenes of earlier destruction, the last rebels were flushed out from their hiding places or besieged there—women and children among them—until they starved to death. So too did the refugees from Ein Gedi

meet their end, leaving their belongings buried deep in the
caves that became their tombs.

The most stringent regulations since the time of Antiochus
forbidding the study and practice of the Jewish faith were immediately put into effect. For the first time men began to pray
that their wives would be delivered of girls; many forswore
marriage. Those who did marry during this era did so cir-
cumspectly, refraining from open celebration, while the birth
of a male child was kept secret for fear of the *boleshim*, the
dreaded Roman military patrols engaged in search and intelligence. The *boleshet* was prone to predatory behavior; its
commander had the right of the first night with any Jewish
bride and would order slain any baby boy found to be circumcised, and the father as well. Candles or oil lamps found
to have been lighted on the Sabbath and positioned to indicate
observance of the holy day meant death for all the inhabitants
of the house, as did a scroll of Torah discovered in any residence.

Innumerable men, women, and children were sold as slaves.
So many were offered for sale at the market of the Terebinth
in Hebron that Jewish flesh sold for the same price as a horse.
Those who could not be disposed of were taken to Gaza and
sold there or sent to Egypt and elsewhere, many of them dying
on the way of hunger or shipwreck. After the war, virtually
the entire population of the southern part of the country,
which had been most active in the rebellion, was dead, enslaved, or in flight either to the north—the Galilee—or out of
Hadrian's Palestine entirely.

And so it was that Jara found herself once more living in the
place where she had been born.

THE TREE was still there. Guardian of the mount. Sentry of the
road below, where as a child she'd watched for Romans. She
watched for them now.

"Jara. . . ."

She turned. It was Beruria. The woman was holding a small
boy by the hand. Jara took the child in her arms and kissed
him. "How did it go?"

"As well as it could, considering there is no daily instruction. But they remembered all I'd taught them on my last visit.
One or two are too frightened, I think, to learn properly. But

the others . . ." She sighed. "They sit there like little Zealots. Warriors. It's strange in a school. . . ."

Jara smiled. "It's because they know this is how they must fight—for now."

Beruria regarded her solemnly a moment, started to say something, then changed her mind and shook her head. "We are not commanded to pray for our enemy's death," she said at last, "but that he repent of his sins and change his ways."

"Our enemy, as you put it, is not going to change his ways," Jara said flatly. "Nothing changes. Nothing."

"Not even you?"

"I don't give up, if that's what you mean." She kissed the child again. "We don't give up, do we, Beni?"

"Oh, Jara," Beruria began softly, then stopped. "You ought to hear your little one recite Torah," she said with a smile. "He's very quick, Jara. Very bright. You really ought to come with me to Tiberias."

"Next year, perhaps."

"Things are much better now. They don't search out the children so much anymore. Only the newborns, really. And Benjamin is tall. You could say he was born before Betar."

"As if they'd believe me."

"You could dress him as a girl. Many do that. With those curls it wouldn't be hard."

They both laughed. "No," Jara said, still smiling. "It's easier here in the hills. There are many places to hide."

"In Tiberias, too. How else do you think we manage to get on?"

"Next year, perhaps." They walked on a ways. "Have you heard anything from Mesha?"

"No. Nothing. Not for almost a year. But there is a ship due from Parthia. Perhaps . . ."

Jara squeezed her hand. "Perhaps."

Beruria nodded.

"Any news of Akiva?"

"Joshua ha-Garsi should get back from Caesarea soon. We are awaiting a judgment. Why don't you come too? I would so love to have you visit. It is lonely. I am busy with the work, but . . ."

"All right," Jara said. "But I shall have to leave Beni here. And I won't be able to stay for more than a day."

"Can't you bring him? I'll guard him with my life, Jara.

And I wouldn't even suggest it if I thought—"

"All right. We'll see. Perhaps." The hunger in Beruria's eyes was too much. "All right."

Beruria's face glowed. She bent down now and kissed the child. "Goodbye, Benjamin Ami. Will you remember all that I taught you?"

The boy nodded.

Beruria smiled. She straightened and kissed Jara goodbye. "I envy you," she whispered.

Jara hugged her. "He'll be back. I know it. Be well. And be careful."

Beruria nodded and with a wave of farewell set off for Tiberias.

Jara watched her go, wondering at her strength. Despite all that had happened to them, Beruria's devotion to God and Torah remained unfaltering. She continued to teach, without thought for her own safety—not to defy Rome, which was Jara's attitude, but to fulfill the biblical commandment. So too had her father done.

Despite the edicts, Rabbi Hanina ben Teradyon had continued to teach openly after the war. He was finally arrested, tortured, and then wrapped in the parchment of the Torah scroll he had been reading when captured and thrown into a pyre of moist twigs, tufts of wool soaked in water placed on his chest so that he would burn slowly. He was not the only rabbi to be martyred during this period. Rabbi Tarfon was also killed; Judah ben Bava met his end defying the prohibition against the granting of *semikhah*. Leading a group of scholars into a secluded valley in Galilee—for Rome had declared that "whoever performed an ordination . . . and whoever received an ordination should be put to death, the city in which the ordination took place demolished, and the boundaries wherein it had been performed uprooted"—ben Bava ordained six disciples in the no-man's land between Usha and Shefaram. Catching sight of the approaching soldiers, he exclaimed, "Children, run for your lives!" Then, turning back with arms outstretched, he took the full brunt of attack, his body pierced by dozens of spears.

One of the young men who escaped from that valley was Rabbi Meir, who, in a symbolic act, had received a second ordination. He was forced to hide now. Beruria came to him in the cave where he had taken refuge with Simon bar Yohai, also under sentence of death. She had witnessed the execution of her father and seen Akiva carried off to Caesarea, where he was imprisoned, his fate uncertain.

"You must leave the country," she told the fugitive men. "You are as dangerous now to Rome as Bar Kokhba was." And she told them of the plan that had been worked out for their escape. In the end, though, Mesha went alone. Bar Yohai refused to leave the cave, saying he believed it was God's will that he should remain there, but that it was also meant for Mesha to go to Parthia. Beruria too remained behind, despite her husband's entreaties. "Everyone knows it is forbidden for a woman to receive *semikhah*," she'd explained. "And nobody believes any woman knows Torah well enough to teach. But I do, Mesha! I can do what it is forbidden to do, and they'll never suspect me. Besides," she'd added with a tremulous smile, "Rufus will be too busy hunting you even to think about me."

As she walked along the road leading to Tiberias and the small house she lived in, with its narrow bed, empty now, and the underground room filled with the children she taught, none of them her own, she could see Mesha's face before her, feel his hand touching her cheek. . . .

"Will you be like Rachel after all?" he'd wondered. "It may be years before I'm able to return."

"I know," she'd whispered. "I know."

"But we will be together again," he'd promised, drawing her close and kissing her. "I'll come back to you, Beruria. As you believe in God, believe it!"

Beruria entered the quiet, empty house. It would soon be night, time for evening prayers. She closed her eyes. "I believe it," she whispered. "I believe. . . ."

JARA RETURNED with her son to the hovel that was their home in the small community that had sprung up once more atop the ashes of Kefar Katan. Compared with the way she'd been forced to live since her escape from Betar, it seemed reasonably comfortable. Rabbis and scholars weren't the only ones who'd taken to caves; many young girls hid themselves for fear of being sold into the Roman brothels. And many, like Jara, took to the hills and cliffs in order to hide their pregnancies, in case they gave birth to males. For more than a year,

she'd lived like a nomad in places more used to wild goats than
humans, alone for the most part, her belly growing bigger,
never getting used to the smell of bat droppings, watching the
wadis fill with rain, a torrent of water gushing over the side of
a nearby cliff a thousand times greater than the fall at Ein
Gedi . . . making pictures of the stars overhead in the cold
winter nights . . . finding a wild melon where the hot summer
earth had cracked apart, the root trailing long and deep from a
hidden reservoir of water deposited by winter storms.

Alone, she brought forth the child, and wept to see him so
strong and beautiful. Because she could not be sure who had
fathered him, she named him Benjamin Ami, after her own
father and for all her countrymen, the name meaning "Son of
My People." But it soon became clear to her that the child,
with his black curly hair and cleft chin, was Andreas' issue.
His eyes, once they lost the blue of infancy, were a greenish-
brown or hazel color.

He had become her only joy in the years following Betar.
And in a way, he'd saved her life, for had she remained at
B'nei Berak it was certain she would have been taken as a slave
or killed when the soldiers came for Akiva.

She stood watching over the child, napping now on his little
mat. He was strong and beautiful—and quick, as Beruria had
noted, quick to stand and to speak—with an eager, merry
nature despite their hard life. But what was hard to a child?
Jara reflected, remembering her own youth. So long as there
was food and birds and bright flowers peeping from the rocks
and a mother's arms to hold him during the cold nights, a little
boy could be happy. He didn't know yet, didn't understand
what it meant to be a Jew in a world of others, how his life
could be forfeit at any moment for that simple fact. He knew
"the soldiers did bad things" and that he must run and hide
whenever he saw one, but it would be a while before the sleeping boy would truly comprehend what made his existence so
perilous, or why. It would be a while before he understood.
Perhaps he never would.

Jara stretched out a hand and lightly touched the boy's soft
curls. He was her son, and there was nothing she would not do
to keep him well and safe. She had gone without eating to feed
him, even stolen food in order that he should not go hungry,
yet without the slightest hesitation she had taken him when he
was eight days old to the cave of Simon bar Yohai to be cir-

cumcised, seeing that he received the mark by which his identity and perhaps his doom would be sealed.

There were many in this period who behaved otherwise and obeyed the Roman edicts; but while these Jews fell away from observance of their own laws and customs, they did not necessarily fall into the worship of idols and the gods of the Greco-Roman world. Moreover, they were not the first to "assimilate" and might well have done so in any event, by choice and not out of fear; certainly, a life that did not run against the grain of common culture was easier to bear. For others, though, the war went on, a war fought not by bands of armed "Brothers" but mostly by women and children and old men. For some of these, what they did came from love of God. For others, like Jara, promulgating the word of Torah and sustaining its laws was a means of rebellion, a matter of *dafka*, a Hebrew word meaning, in essence, "because" or "in spite of."

So the secret army carried on, mobilizing its young in the hidden rooms and underground chambers where no swords and lances were hidden now, but weapons of another sort: books and slates and styluses. The men and women who brought their children to these outlawed schools may well have perceived the subtler intent behind Hadrian's decrees: to reduce future generations to a state of universal illiteracy more in keeping with their status as slaves. Hadrian, in turn, may have realized that the study of Torah was not only a mode for the worship of the God of Israel but a contributing factor in the democratic tendencies of the Jew. For if Torah study was an obligation incumbent upon everyone, its availability could not be restricted to only a portion of the community. Indeed, as the Church Father Clement of Alexandria noted, every Jewish child went to school.

So now another group joined those who faced death in their devotion to God or in simple defiance of the foreign authority: those who refused to let their children be denied the ability to learn; to think. Deprived of liberty and homeland, the Jew of this new Palestine turned inward for the strength to survive and to preserve his sacred Torah, setting in motion a pattern of study and prayer that for countless generations would be his sole comfort.

*   *   *

ALTHOUGH IT WAS hardly past noon, a lighted lamp could be seen in the entrance of an open door, left ajar perhaps inadvertently but more likely to signal the celebration inside. A candle by day meant a Jewish wedding was taking place. The noise of grindstones meant a circumcision was being performed. The words of Jeremiah had become a secret code by which the commandments were fulfilled: "The voice of mirth and the voice of gladness, the voice of the bridegroom and voice of the bride, the sound of millstones, and the light of the lamp."

Jara walked past the house, being careful not to show any awareness of what she knew was taking place there. Beni, however, would have peeped inside had she not caught him and, swinging him off the ground, carried him squealing happily to Beruria's residence.

Joshua ha-Garsi had arrived from Caesarea. He was close to tears. "He will die," he kept saying. "My master will die."

"Has Akiva been sentenced to death?" Jara asked.

"No," Beruria replied. She gave Beni a wafer dipped in honey. "But he is sure to fare even worse now than before. Rufina Livia, Rufus' wife, was a believer in the One God and had many discussions with Akiva even before the war," Beruria explained. "Some say she practiced the faith of Moses secretly. I don't know about that. But it is certain she had great love for Akiva. After his imprisonment in Caesarea, she took great care to see that all his needs were met, bringing him clean water, food he would not have to deny, blankets, and so forth—sometimes in open defiance of her husband. It may be that Akiva would have been condemned to death long ago were it not for the wife of Tinneus Rufus. But she has been in poor health since the end of the war, and now, Joshua says, she is dead. He says she was no sooner buried than Rufus ordered Akiva's rations cut. And now no one is even allowed to see him."

Jara stared thoughtfully at the grieving disciple. He was all that was left of the household at B'nei Berak. Tobita had died shortly after Akiva's arrest. The defeat of Bar Kokhba and the imprisonment of her master seemed to have stunned her into finally succumbing to old age. She never got over either, but she remained resolute in her faith to the end. Her last words were: "God, You have done a great deal to make me stop believing. But in spite of all, a Jew I am and a Jew I shall remain, and all that You have brought will not avail You."

"I managed at least to get the judgment we were waiting for," ha-Garsi said to Beruria. "I posed as a peddler again and stood outside his cell window hawking my wares. Between calls I put the question to him, and he answered. So you may tell the father who inquired to come forward." He put his head in his hands. "What will become of him?" he mourned. "What will become of us all?" He looked at Jara. "Every day I was allowed to bring him water, a small quantity; yet only half of that would he drink, and use the other half to wash. Now I am not allowed to see him, the lady is dead, and I know for certain the Rabban will not touch food unless he is given sufficient water to wash his hands. He will die. I tell you he will die."

"He won't die," Jara said flatly. "When he gets good and hungry he'll eat. Anything. Without washing. And he'll drink anything."

Ha-Garsi stared at her, amazed.

Beruria shook her head. "You still don't understand. . . . You don't give up the ways of a lifetime. Not when the ways are God's commandments. And not when you are Akiva."

It was Jara's turn to stare. "All right," she said finally. "I see what has to be done. Beruria, you'll have to look after Beni for a few days. If anything happens to him while I'm gone—"

"No, no!" Her face held both astonishment and delight. "I swear I'll guard him with my life. But where are you going? What do you plan to do?"

"I plan to see Akiva."

"But you can't!" Joshua ha-Garsi exclaimed. "They won't let you! Besides, it's dangerous. A woman . . ."

"Well, then, you'd better pray for me, hadn't you?" Jara said. She looked at Beruria. "Both of you."

THE CITY, with its bustle, its fine houses, its plethora of ships, excited her, as cities always did, and for a moment Jara's eyes sparkled. Then she remembered that the avenues of Caesarea were closed to her; for a Jew, the town held only the promise of the brothel or the slave market. The blood that had leaped with spontaneous delight at the sight of Caesarea's spires and towers, its graceful columns and neatly laid out streets, now coursed angrily to her cheeks; even the honey smell of the hot pistachio-crusted cakes sold by the street vendors became bitter to her.

Joshua ha-Garsi, who had accompanied her to Caesarea, mistook the look on Jara's face for determination. "You always were fearless," he said, admiration tempered by the feeling that she was an unorthodox sort of female. Still, Akiva had always been fond of her, loved her even as a daughter. "It is a blessing to have such faith."

Jara turned to him. She was about to say that what she was had nothing to do with faith when the sight of a great white building with many steps and columns caught her eye.

Joshua ha-Garsi had seen it too. "The Praetorium," he said. "That is the place of Tinneus Rufus." He stopped. "What you wish to do is a great *mitzvah*, a deed of great goodness, but I am afraid for you. I know the guards. They are a coarse, brutal lot." He sighed. "Rufus is no better, for all his fine clothes and position. You are a beautiful woman. I saw, in B'nei Berak, how the scholars looked at you. But for their love of God and devotion to the commandments of the Almighty, the Evil Impulse would surely have taken control of their actions. How then shall these animals who have no God restrain themselves? And knowing this, how can I bring you here? For surely, if evil were to fall upon you, the shame would be mine."

"Don't you believe the Lord protects those who do good deeds?"

"I used to," he admitted sadly. "Now I cannot say. I've seen too much. But the ways of the Lord are not for me to judge or even question. Though I am too ignorant to understand God's purpose, it does not mean there is none."

"You believe that? You believe there is a purpose to all of this? To Betar—all those babies slaughtered? To Akiva—locked up in jail, starving to death for all we know? You believe that?"

"I know it."

Jara sighed. "Well, as you said, it is a blessing to have such faith." She touched the man's arm lightly. "Stay here. I'll go in myself."

"I cannot let you—"

"I don't want you with me. Be at peace," she said more kindly. "Whatever happens, you are not accountable. I want to see Akiva." She thought of the Christian soldier in Severus' camp. "It may not be so bad as you think," Jara said. "Those who have no God, or who believe in other gods, may still be kind and generous. If I believe in anything, Joshua ha-Garsi, I believe in that."

"May it be so," the man replied. "God be with you."

THE JAILER was having lunch. An onion, some salted olives, and a round, flat piece of bread shared a wooden plate. The cup in the man's hand was filled with a vinegary mix of wine and water: the *posca* so dearly loved by the soldiers of Rome. The man himself was a native of Caesarea, of mixed Greek and Syrian blood. He barely looked up at the female who approached.

"I want to see the prisoner Akiva ben Joseph."

He bit into the onion as if it were an apple, tore off a piece of bread, wiped that in the oil of the olives, and stuffed it in his mouth.

Jara waited.

He drank from the cup, wiped his mouth with his hand, and then shook his head.

"I said—"

"I heard what you said." He looked at her now. "Orders are the prisoner gets no visitors."

"I'm not a visitor. I just want to bring him some water."

"Is that so?" He turned his attention back to the food on his plate. "No."

"Just let me bring him water. What harm is there in that?"

He did not answer. He took the cup in his hand once more and studied the female before him. There wasn't much to see, the way she was all covered wih that veil, just her face exposed. She had eyes like a cat. "What's the old Jew to you anyway?"

"Nothing. I promised—"

"Promised?" Good mouth. "Who? Who did you promise?"

"My mistress. The wife of Tinneus Rufus. Surely you knew

her. Before she died, I promised I would look after the Jew as she had done. He is nothing to me. But I gave my word to my mistress, a dying woman. . . ."

He had gotten up from the table now and began to circle her slowly. "Liar," he said calmly.

She did not move.

With a sudden, quick gesture, he pulled the mantle back from her head, noting with satisfaction the leonine fall of hair. Still she did not move. "I said you're a liar."

"No—"

He tore away the mantle, laughed. "You think a serving girl in the governor's palace would wear those rags? Even the slaves have better clothes." He ripped her robe down off her shoulders, exposing the white flesh. "A maid to the governor's wife wouldn't have arms and face one color and the rest of her body another." He ran his tongue over his mouth. "She'd be all perfumed—I know those girls—her hair braided and oiled, bracelets jingling on her arms. . . ." His fingers were kneading her shoulders now. "You never served Rufina Livia," he said softly. "Dead or alive. You're a Jew."

She did not answer.

"And if you're not, then you're one of those Christians, covering yourself up the way you did. But I doubt it. And if you're thinking of lying again," he said, whispering in her ear, "you may as well know I have about as much love for that kind as I do for any of your sort. They worship a Jew, you know. Some filthy bastard Caesar had the good sense to crucify. Good riddance, I say." His breathing had become heavy. "What do you say?"

"What do you want?"

"You know what I want. And I know what you want. What say we strike a bargain. I can make a lot of trouble for you. And I can make trouble for myself if I do what you ask. But it seems harmless enough to me, if it's only water you want to give the old man. Still, I'm taking a chance. But I'm a good-natured sort, as you can see. I have a generous heart. I'm willing to lend a helping hand now and again to those not as fortunate as myself, so long as I'm not made a fool for my trouble, so long as I get something in return. . . ."

She was silent.

"Good," he said, as if the matter were settled. He slid the

torn robe down her arms. He ran his hands over her breasts. "You're a clever girl. You understand how things work. You pay me, I pay you. That's the world, isn't it? That's the whole world for you."

And still she was silent. The man touching her, rubbing his body against hers, pressing his mouth to her flesh, could not know that in the space of a moment's breath she had weighed killing him.

It would be easy. The little knife was in the pouch tied to the cord around her waist. She could withdraw it, plunge it into him. . . .

Joshua ha-Garsi waited outside. Akiva . . . Akiva was in one of the cells. Could she free him, escape with him? No . . . no, it was the stuff of dreams. If she killed this man now, ha-Garsi and Akiva would pay for it, no matter what happened to her. And how many others, as had happened long ago to Arnon and Batya and all the rest?

She had come here only to see Akiva and to do what she could for him. That was why she was here, that was what she must do. Nothing else.

The man was tugging at her now, pulling her down with him, hands and mouth working at a hot pitch. She turned her face aside, feeling his spit on her neck. Every nerve and muscle, every sense rebelled, but she willed her body to be placid, neither participating nor resisting but enduring.

If the man had bothered to look into her eyes, he would have seen that she was far, far away.

AKIVA BEN JOSEPH sat motionless in the dimly lit cell; only the slight movement of his lips as he prayed showed that he was alive. A shaft of light from the single, high-placed window fell upon the table that held an empty bowl and a cup. There was a stool, a sleeping mat, and a blanket. A small scroll and implements with which to write lay under the blanket, hidden not so much from his jailers but from Akiva himself.

He was forbidden to receive books. The ban against the study of Torah, however, did not preclude writing materials, which were brought regularly to him by Joshua ha-Garsi. But ha-Garsi was no longer permitted to visit, and Rufina Livia was dead. Therefore Akiva must be careful with what re-

mained to him, using it sparingly and well. How to transmit
what he wrote was another problem. Still, he believed a way
would be found.

Though denied the presence of Scripture, he was not without the Word. Memory, cultivated by years of study, brought
all the books of Moses to him as well as the proverbs, psalms,
and prophetic writings that he loved and knew as intimately as
the moments of his own life. Closing his eyes, he saw the vineyards of Solomon glow green and lush, radiant with dew,
while all the desert wilderness howled about him, his dark cell
ablaze with the sun of Amos and Isaiah. He saw too the
friends of his youth, the people of his family, the companions
of his old age. Gentle ben Azzai was in the shadows, smiling
when asked why he did not marry, murmuring, "What can I
do? I love to study. The world will have to be carried on by
others." And there was Simeon ben Zoma, so deep in reflection, saying, "I was observing Creation, and do you know,
there is nothing between the waters above and the waters
below but the breadth of two, maybe three fingers. . . ."

And Rachel.

She was always with him now. How keenly he felt her presence. She, who had been born to wealth and ease and had
chosen to live in a shepherd's hut, toiling while he, born to
ignorance and poverty, sat like a rich man's son in the school
at Jabneh. . . . If the Almighty had blessed him with anything,
it was Rachel and the ability finally to make up to her what she
had lost and endured for his sake. "My queen," Akiva whispered, young again. "My adorable queen. . . . The work is
almost done. I've kept my promise to you."

He could feel her with him, almost see her in this poor
place, which in his reveries took on the dimensions of earlier
abodes. It was therefore with no surprise that he viewed the
female figure who suddenly appeared, and rose dreamily to
greet her. It was only as he drew closer that he realized it was
not Rachel and remembered where he was.

"Jara," he said, wonderingly. "Child . . . is it you?"

The guard with her withdrew. There was the sound of the
door being bolted again.

"Jara . . ."

"There is water for you, rabban," she said, pointing awk-
wardly to the jug that had been carried into the cell. "Enough
to wash and to drink. Later I will bring you food."

"What is food and drink to me now when I can see you, know that you are well?" He came toward her, hands upraised to hold her face between his palms and bestow a kiss of greeting. But she had backed away.

"You must drink, rabban," she said somewhat breathlessly. "The room is full of dust. Your throat must be dry. And you must eat to keep up your strength. Let me go now to bring you food."

"Not yet. You must talk to me. It's been so long. Come. . . ." Again she backed away.

"No, really, I should go. Please, no, don't touch me . . . please." Her voice sank almost to a whisper. "It is not right that you should touch me." Again she shied away. "No, don't! Please . . . I . . . I am unclean."

His eyes, full of puzzlement at her behavior, now took in the averted gaze and trembling lip, the mantle clutched so desperately to her breast. Then he saw the water jug which had been set on the floor, twice the size of any that had previously been given to him. Then he knew.

Before she could move away again or speak, he had drawn her into his arms, and held her close until he felt a shudder go through her body and heard her weep. And still Akiva did not let her go, but wept with her and for all the rest.

"I'M TIRED," she said. "I'm so tired, rabban. Sometimes I feel as though I'll never be able to take another step or even lift my hand. If it weren't for the child . . ."

Akiva nodded. He stroked her hair as she knelt beside him, her head in his lap. "I know. But you must go on. You must not give up."

"I tell myself that. But I don't know why or what for. They've taken everything from us. We live worse than before. I don't mind it so much for myself—I've grown used to it— but I want a better world for my son. He must have better than this!"

Again Akiva nodded. What could he say?

"We were right to fight!" she said suddenly, fiercely. "We were right to do what we did! If only . . ." She sighed. "Now we must begin all over."

"No."

"Yes! It's the only way!"

"No . . ."

"Yes!" She had risen now and was moving about the room excitedly. "You'll see, rabban! We did it once and we can do it again. Simeon will come—"

"Simeon is dead, my child."

"You don't know that. No one knows. His body was never found. He could still be alive. For all we know he is . . . hiding in some cave, or in Parthia gathering together a new army of brave brothers. . . ."

"He's dead, Jara, Simeon is dead. Bar Kokhba is no more."

She stared at him, eyes wild, uncomprehending.

Akiva rose, went to her, took her hands in his. "He's dead," he said gently.

The look vanished from her eyes. She nodded. "Yes," she said with a sigh. "Yes."

"But I believe as you do, that we were right to do what we did. I suppose I should grieve for all that has befallen us—and I do—but not without the firm conviction that we acted in accordance with God's will. And that this too is God's will."

"If you believe that, then how can you believe that God is good?"

The question did not shock him. "How can I doubt it? We see God's wisdom all the time. It is all around us. When we look up to the sky and see the stars . . . or here, on earth, when we look at the order of things—the seasons, the bounty of fruit and flower, hills rising from valleys, sand slipping away to sea . . . and life everywhere. On bough and branch, in the depths of the ocean, growing inside us. . . . Think of it, Jara. Tell me you did not look at your baby and marvel at the perfection there. Ten fingers curling and uncurling, ready to grasp the world! Ten tiny toes, a mouth, eyes, ears, nose—all of it working, a wondrous thing whose devising is past comprehension. Who could imagine a human being but God? Or the clouds, the sea, the sun . . . ? His wisdom is everywhere. When it comes to God's mercy, however . . . we don't see as much perhaps. He shows us not enough. But I myself cannot believe that so much wisdom goes completely without mercy."

"If God is merciful, why do we suffer so? We are taught that the Gentiles will be punished for the sins of idolatry and injustice, but what shield do we find in goodness, what protection is righteousness? Whichever way we turn, we are cut down. Time and time again. And you expect me to believe in a merciful God, a just God, a loving God?"

"Then why are you here? Why did you come to this place with all that it holds?"

"For you! I did it for you, not God!"

"And why did you go to Betar when you knew it was only a matter of time before it would be destroyed?"

"For Simeon. Not for God but for Simeon."

"And your son—he is circumcised, is he not? You told me yourself you have helped to organize schools for the children. You carry food to bar Yohai and the others hiding from the authorities—at the risk of your own life. Why, if not for God?"

"For Israel," she corrected him firmly. "For Israel."

"And what is Israel?" Akiva asked. "What is Simeon— what am I—but creatures of God's devising? You say you do not love God. But you love me, you loved Simeon, you love your child—and how many others in your life? That is love of God, Jara. If we but love one other human being—if we but love ourselves!—then we love God."

She stared at him, then turned away, confusion in her eyes.

"I know the doubts you have," Akiva said, "the questions. . . . Do you think you are the only one to have such questions? Let me tell you something," he went on lightly. "I was not always a rabbi, you know. Or an old man. When I was a boy, I was a shepherd, first in the Lowlands and then near Jerusalem. We were so poor that in all our family there was but a single outer garment which we had to share. Yet we served those who had a hundred cloaks and mantles, who paid poorly for the services that enabled them to feast, and who, if they were priests, were still entitled to a portion of what little was ours. I hated them, Jara. Even more so the sages who sat in the Court of Justice and interpreted the laws in their own favor, against the poor and unschooled. If anyone had told me then that I would one day find myself sitting at the feet of the likes of Johanan ben Zakkai and Joshua ben Hananiah and grow to love them and wish to be as they were, I would have said that person was a madman!

"My father used to take me with him to Jerusalem when we brought the lambs to the Temple, where they would be slaughtered for guilt offerings. I stood with my father in the Court of the Israelite and saw the priests cut the throats of those gentle animals, those soft and innocent creatures who were my friends, my children, in the hills away from the city. And I would look at all the people in the Temple courtyards and in the Seven Markets, thronging the narrow streets, going up to the Temple Mount, congregating at the walls and gates; rich and poor, sturdy and lame; the beggars with their outstretched hands, the daughters of the great houses with their long earrings and heavy necklaces, whose walk produced the sound of bells. . . .

"All the way home and for days thereafter I would question my father: 'Why do we take the lambs and kill them and eat them? Why do some people grow fat and others starve? Why is one woman beautiful, one man strong, while others are born without hearing or sight, or the use of an arm, or a crooked leg?' Why and why and why?

"My father would tell me, 'This is the way God wants it.' Sometimes he would say, 'If we were good or better to each other, then God might be better to us.' And sometimes he would say, 'This boy is making me crazy with his questions!'

"All of us ponder those questions. We are all bewildered and frightened. We look at the world and ask, 'What is going on here?' But we still hope. We hope. . . .

"And hope is faith."

THE SUN was falling into the sea again. Jara walked along the shore, the noise of the city growing fainter, fading behind the cries of the birds that swooped down to the sand at day's end and the murmur of a gentle tide. Joshua ha-Garsi had remained in Caesarea, hoping still to serve his master.

She would never see Akiva again.

"As you love me, do not come here," he'd said. "I cannot allow it." But even without his prohibition she felt somehow this time together was the last.

The rocks jutting out to sea barred her path. Climbing over them, Jara discovered a small sheltered cove, a place to swim, to sleep, to dream. The sun was nestling on her shoulders, the scent of the sea a tantalizing lure. Almost before she knew it, her clothes were in a heap, anchored by a rock, and she was in the water.

She was no swimmer or she would have judged the tide better, been aware of the whirlpools and treacherous tugs beneath the soft rolling surface. As it was, she gave no thought to the deep before her or how far she'd come from shore. The waves were rocking her as a mother rocks a child, lulling her with their whisper, cleansing her. . . .

Suddenly some force snaked around her submerged form, pulling her further out to sea. She began to fight it, only to find herself pulled under the waves, swallowing water, struggling to break through the whirling darkness, reaching desperately for sun and air.

She fought with all the strength she possessed, and still the tide controlled her; she was like a doll in some monster hand, tossed up and down, gasping for breath in the too-brief respites when she managed to lift her head above water. But it was too strong for her, too much; neither will nor muscle would save her now. She was under again, her chest bursting, her ears ringing, darkness everywhere. . . .

And then, just as suddenly as the sea had swallowed her, it spit her up, tossed her back, sent her to shore on a great pillow of a wave.

She lay exhausted in the ripples of the surf, dazed, stunned by what had happened. After a while she managed to crawl back to where she'd left her clothes, dressed, and then rested, her back warmed by the rock while the day turned to night.

She slept on the beach, her dreams all of women, some of whom she recognized, others unknown to her. They were good dreams. As she had felt the terrible force of the sea, so now, waking, she felt herself possessed of new strength, freed somehow of ugliness—not only the ugliness of what she had seen and experienced in her lifetime, but also the ugliness of despair and hatred, of life lived only for revenge.

The morning world was like a newborn child: fresh, innocent, clean. Jara watched the birds circling in the air, their white wings held in graceful arcs. Some flew out to sea. How did they know where to find the shore, she wondered, or where to seek food? On what did they alight when no land could be seen? Could they fly without rest across all the Great Sea? How did they fly? What made them so?

Who but God could imagine a human being, Akiva had said. Or a bird. Or the sea.

It was time to return home. If she wanted life to be better for her son, then she must make it so, not by war but by some other way . . . some other place, perhaps. The sea did not go on forever; there were worlds on the other side. There had to be some place where they could be free.

SHORTLY AFTER Jara left Akiva, the rabbi received yet another visitor: Elisha ben Abuyah.

The two men stood across from one another, ben Abuyah hardly able to withstand the welcome in Akiva's eyes. He made an abrupt gesture to indicate their surroundings. "You see," he said gruffly, "what it has come to."

"A temporary arrangement."

"What makes you say so?"

"You've come to see me, Elisha. It makes me believe I am going to die."

"I didn't think I would be welcome. You've heard, no doubt, how I've helped the authorities."

Akiva nodded. "I also know that many who found their way to Parthia, such as Rabbi Meir, would not have been able to do so without, shall we say, a helping hand."

Ben Abuyah turned away. "I can do nothing for you," he said after a while in a low voice.

"You have done much just by coming here."

"Maybe I only want to point out to you and to myself the consequences of being a fool."

"Don't be perverse, Elisha," Akiva responded with a smile. "Say what is in your heart."

"That is the second time you've called me by my given name. No one has called me that for years. Not even my . . ." He hesitated. "My new acquaintances."

"Well," Akiva noted, still smiling, "at least you don't call them friends."

"I don't have friends, Akiva. I never did, but for you. And despite all I did."

"Never against me. Against yourself."

"How little you see, even now. I hated you, Akiva," he said matter-of-factly. "You had everything."

"I?" He was truly amazed. "What are you talking about? You were rich, handsome. . . . Learning came so easily to you. When you spoke it was like music."

"But Rachel loved you. It was you she loved. Tall and thin

as the shepherd's rod you carried, with the accents of a peasant, the stink of sheep and garlic. . . . And she loved you. When she came into the house, there was grass in her hair. She ran away when our fathers spoke of a betrothal. She ran to you."

"But . . ." Akiva shook his head. "I didn't know." He appeared stunned by this revelation. "I never guessed. You were the first to befriend me at Jabneh," he wondered.

"I hoped to ruin you. The books I obtained for us—the works of the Greeks, scrolls of the ancients, even the writings of the *minim*—all those forbidden words I held out like the fruit offered by the serpent in Eden. I thought you would become confused, that your faith would be shaken. I thought you would lose your way and be forever damned." He sighed. "But all that is in the past. I am the one who is damned. Ah, Akiva! Do you remember what it was like to be young? The orchards at Jabneh, the circle of sages with their hoary beards, their keen eyes. . . . I used to wonder what made ben Zakkai so revered—apart from the fact that he'd managed to live so long. He hadn't one original thought in his head. He bored me to tears. . . ."

"His task was not to be original," Akiva pointed out, "but to transmit what otherwise would have been lost. An original mind at that moment—such as yours, my friend—would have done more harm than good."

"His task," ben Abuyah echoed. "You believe Johanan ben Zakkai was chosen by God, don't you? Well, maybe the Almighty did choose him. Maybe he chooses all of us . . . for something. Your Bar Kokhba certainly didn't play his part right. But then, God did not choose him to be the Messiah. You did." Tears started up in the bright blue eyes. "Fool . . ."

"No," Akiva said firmly. "It was not without purpose. None of it. I see that now. Our losses, catastrophic as they are, are also our gain. Listen to me, Elisha," he said excitedly. "In Jerusalem, when Simeon ben Kosiba drove the Romans out and we took back our city, I watched the descendants of the priest gathering together on the Temple Mount. I saw them prepare to build an altar and all the chambers of a Sanctuary. And I remembered the way it had been: the tithing, the burnt offerings, the rich paying for their sins with pigeons and lambs! I alone, of all who stood in Jerusalem giving thanks for its return and the renewal of the Temple rites, felt no joy and wondered why. It is only now, when all that has been snatched away from us again, that I realize what has been given to us, what in winning we came so perilously close to losing."

Elisha ben Abuyah could only stare, amazed.

"When the Eternal One, blessed be He in His wisdom, found us, we were children. And he spoke to us as a father speaks to a child, and He gave us a way of understanding such as a teacher gives to his youngest pupil and the tasks also that are appropriate to one of limited knowledge. And the scattered seed became a tribe and grew. We grew not only in number but in understanding. And again the Lord made His will known to us, and the tribes became a nation with a Law and land. Now, I believe, the Almighty is directing us once more. It is this belief, Elisha, which causes me to rejoice and to be at peace and to love God with all my heart."

Elisha ben Abuyah sat quietly for a moment; then he said, "What divine direction do you speak of, Akiva? What is the God of Israel revealing to His chosen people but the way to annihilation?"

"We will survive these events," Akiva said calmly. "Israel is the sword dipped in flame. Again and yet again we are bathed in fire, only to emerge each time stronger than before. We will survive," he repeated. "And we will grow."

WHEN JARA RETURNED to Tiberias, she was met by a heart-warming sight. There, with his arm around a radiant Beruria, was Rabbi Meir.

"Mesha!" She embraced him warmly. "Is it really you? How wonderful! But is it safe—"

"Yes. Yes, I believe so. I bring good news. Hadrian is dead."

Jara looked from one to the other. "What does this mean?"

"Not much yet. But the new emperor doesn't appear to be so interested in pursuing Hadrian's policies against us. In time he may even rescind them altogether."

Beruria's eyes widened. "Can that really be possible?"

Mesha laughed. "Anything is possible when Rome gets a new Caesar. They say it was a painful death," he noted with some satisfaction. "I have heard that Hadrian was never the same from the moment he returned to Rome, that he was like a haunted man; unfriendly, withdrawn, morose."

"Who killed him?" Jara wanted to know.

"No one. That is, he didn't die from any human hand. He suffered for more than a year from dysentery and dropsy. They say he died every day without dying."

All three fell silent now, as though recalling how each of the emperors who had defiled the land of Israel had met an untimely and painful end.

"I've brought you something," Jara said. She handed Mesha a scroll. "Akiva gave it to me, and Joshua ha-Garsi said I must bring it here immediately."

"It's the calendar," Mesha announced, studying the parchment excitedly. "He's managed to bring the calendar into order—it's been neglected for nearly a decade. Look! Look, Beruria! He's fixed the date for the Passover! Blessed be the Name of the Lord for giving us men such as thee, rabban," he uttered breathlessly. "Do either of you know what it took to do this?" he asked the women, his eyes shining. He shook his head, overwhelmed.

"We must look to the future," Beruria said. "And pray that things will be better." She nodded at Mesha. "We have much to hope for."

"Yes," he agreed, his eyes lighting on the little boy who had awakened from his nap and run to greet Jara. He kissed his wife. "Yes."

But their mood of optimism was soon shattered. Within a week, Joshua ha-Garsi had returned with the news of Akiva's death. Freed perhaps from a promise made to his wife or an order from Hadrian, Tinneus Rufus had finally ordered the execution of the rabbi. It was accomplished by a process of refined cruelty: the flesh was torn from Akiva's body with iron combs. He bore his sufferings with such fortitude that at last one of the Romans present was moved to ask how he could endure so much pain, to which Akiva managed to reply that he had always wondered whether he could fulfill the precept "Thou shalt love the Lord thy God with all thy heart and with all thy soul . . . even if you must pay for it with your life," and now he knew that he could.

He prayed to the end, his last words being "Hear, O Israel, the Lord our God, the Lord is One."

So died the man who had proclaimed, "Thou shalt love thy neighbor as thyself," and who taught, "Beloved is a man in that he was created in the image of God."

TIME TOOK ON a new meaning for Jara. Beruria had said they must look to the future, and that was what she began to do—not for her country but, for the first time, for herself and, overriding all, for her son. Simeon was dead, and she was no longer a child dreaming of a hero who would rescue Israel. Nor could she pray, as so many Jews did with even greater fervor than before, for "the true Messiah" to appear. The human, blessed by God, who would champion the people's freedom and lead the way to "the just kingdom," was becoming more and more a supernatural figure, an angel-being whose presence would herald the very end of the world. Jara wondered what Akiva would say to this. He had chided her gently for nurturing the hope that Simeon, despite Betar, would somehow appear again. "The strength of a people cannot lie in one man," he had said, "just as the faith of a people cannot depend on one *rabban*. Everyone who seeks justice and freedom is the Messiah. And everyone who loves God and lives by His commandments brings God's mercy upon the world."

"Jara. . . . Have you given any thought to my proposal?"

She looked up from the patch of herbs she was tending. It was Boaz. He was about thirty, a weaver by trade, from Sepphoris. "Have you closed your shop today?" she asked, evading his question. "Is it a holiday?"

"It will be if you say yes," he replied.

"I thought we agreed that when I visit Beruria next week—"

"I couldn't wait. I think of nothing but you," he confessed. "It's been that way ever since I saw you in Tiberias." He swallowed. "I'm not a scholar, but I make a good living, Jara. My work is known for its quality, and I give an honest account. Most of my customers are Gentiles, and they don't care that I am a Jew. They are very friendly to me. What I mean is, we don't have to worry."

She did not reply.

"I can take care of you and the boy. You shouldn't be living like this, selling herbs and potions and such. You never know when people might start to say you are . . . you are . . ."

"What? What do they say?"

"A woman alone, without a man to look after her. . . . People say things. I wouldn't want any harm to come to you."

"I can look after myself."

"It isn't that. I'm going about this all wrong," he muttered.

"No," she said. "I'm making it difficult for you." She sighed. "Don't ask me why. I know you're right."

"Then marry me," he said eagerly. "We've both suffered. I've lost one family, Jara. I want another. I want you and the boy. And we can have children, more children. . . ."

She hesitated. "Beni's father . . ."

"He's dead. Or as good as dead. What other answer is there? But if you're worried about it, we can speak to Rabbi Meir. Many have lost husbands and wives, not knowing who's dead or alive—it's certain the rabbis have come to a conclusion."

She nodded. "I suppose so."

"I must get back to my shop. I have a large order to fill. Business is very good. I mean it," he said fervently, "you would want for nothing. And the boy will be as my own son."

But he isn't your son, she thought when he had gone. *He is Andreas' son.*

Andreas.

She tried never to think about him; she'd forbidden herself to think about him. But it was hard when she saw his face every day, the curly black hair, the dimpled chin, that merry, mischievous expression. Was ever a child so quick to run when walking would have done just as well, so inquisitive, so beguiling? Through the son she had come to know the father more fully than she had ever known the man, come to love him more than she dreamed possible.

They'd had so little time together, yet each moment they had shared was etched indelibly in her mind. Even before Ein Gedi, where their love had blossomed like a flower of the oasis, there were images of him scratched on her heart.

The first time she laid eyes on him in B'nei Berak, at the dinner for Hadrian, she'd thought he was the emperor's boy: He was so handsome. It had made her angry, he was so handsome; and later, it made her angry to think he was a Jew and so friendly to Rome.

She'd thought him soft, spoiled, interested in nothing but

his own pleasure and the pursuit of wealth. Even when she'd seen him in Bar Kokhba's camp, she had mistrusted him. Meeting him in Severus' tent confirmed the suspicions she had briefly put to rest in Jerusalem. Only, then, he had surprised her again by arranging their escape. And then that too seemed a ruse until—

Oh, but he was a mysterious creature! Andreas. Elisha. Who was he really? What was he? Did it matter . . . ? He was dead now. Or perhaps, after all, fled to Rome. He'd simply vanished, leaving her to wonder sometimes if their escape from Betar, the cave, all he'd said to her and the vows they'd shared had ever happened at all.

But of course it had happened. There was Benjamin Ami to prove it had happened.

And it was Beni she must think of now. She didn't love Boaz, but he seemed decent and kind. No doubt he would want Beni to follow in his craft. Well, worse things could happen. "Though a famine lasts seven years," went the saying, "it does not pass through the gates of an artisan."

She therefore made up her mind to accept Boaz, thinking also that in time she could persuade the weaver to resettle in Parthia, which was not under Roman rule. Despite what seemed to be a relaxation of persecution, Jews were continuing to flee their lost homeland in great number, not trusting the sudden shift in the imperial attitude.

Jara walked slowly back to the small one-room dwelling she had managed to make out of the ruined structure that had been her father's and then her half brother's house. It was a sorry, lopsided affair, but it kept out the rain. She thought with satisfaction of the house she would have in Sepphoris: a real house, a real table and beds, instead of mats on the floor. She smiled at the thought, and in the back of her mind she seemed to hear the sound of hoofbeats.

When she was a child she'd dreamed of someone like Judah the Maccabee, like her own grandfather Eleazar ben Ya'ir, or like Simeon carrying her out of this dreary village, slaying dozens of legionaries on the way. But when the horses did come to Kefar Katan, they'd carried Romans who had taken first Sharona and then herself.

Hoofbeats.

Memories didn't die, just people. Sharona had died; she'd

become someone else. Simeon was dead. Akiva. Andreas, for all she knew . . .

There was Samson's house. Rabbi Kawzbeel, Arnon, Batya . . .

Hoofbeats . . .

And in the end a weaver had come to rescue her. A weaver who walked around with a small distaff behind his ear.

The hoofbeats were getting louder. Then, suddenly, they stopped. Strange. . . . The sound had been so real.

"Jara . . ."

She turned around slowly.

The man on horseback was richly dressed. The cloak spread over the back of his mount was red like a legionary's but embellished with some foreign design. He was clean-shaven, and his dark, curly hair was cut in the Roman style. His eyes devoured her.

She watched him dismount and walk toward her, thinking it was a dream, a vision like the ones she'd seen sometimes in the darkness of the caves in which she'd hidden; faces, figures outlined against the stone and air, vanishing whenever she reached out to them.

He took only a few steps before he stopped, as though afraid to come nearer, as though fearing that she too might be a fantasy that would disappear. Then he asked, "Do you know who I am? Do you know me?"

And now she could say the name she had not uttered for more than three years, had not allowed herself to say: "Andreas." But even before his name had left her lips, his arms were around her, and he was holding her, kissing her, touching her face, her hair, all the while murmuring, "I've found you . . . I've found you."

"WHILE YOU SLEPT I went off to check our position and to see if the road was clear. I was captured by a patrol. The leader recognized me and brought me back to camp, where I was held prisoner for some time and then taken to Caesarea. By then I knew about Betar. I tried to find out if you'd made it back to Akiva, to get word to B'nei Berak, but it was impossible. I was kept under heavy guard and isolated for long periods. The only thing that saved my life was being a Roman citizen. I had the right of trial in Rome. Severus agreed to it, and I was put on a ship filled with prisoners. I won't try to tell you what it was like. Men died every day. But we outnumbered the sailors, and after a few weeks at sea managed to get the better of our captors and take over the ship. It was madness. None of us knew much about running a galley. But it would have been worse madness to remain as we were. Fortunately, we had a number of clever heads among us and one or two who had some knowledge of sailing. The important thing was we were free.

"After a number of adventures—and misadventures—I managed to get to Parthia. I confess I was torn between wanting to find you and trying to get word of my family in Rome. I was afraid they'd suffer for my actions, and I didn't know whether Hadrian's edicts had been applied to the Jews of Rome.

"Before I could do much of anything, I fell ill of a fever I'd caught at sea. I was housed in the exilarch's own residence and every attention was given to me, but I remained weak, in and out of delirium for some months. When I finally regained my strength, I learned to my relief that my family had not been penalized, but that they were constantly watched and suffered some restriction, as did all our community in Rome. The exilarch, at my request, had arranged to trace your whereabouts. He could discover nothing at all, only that you'd disappeared from B'nei Berak about the time Akiva was taken to prison. He believed you were dead and counseled me to accept it.

"All my contacts here came up with nothing. I went back to Rome. I thought that if you had been captured, in all likelihood you would have been taken to a brothel or sold to some rich man, possibly one of Severus' officers. There were plenty of girls there, spoils of war, but not you. It never even occurred to me to look for you in the Galilee. I'd forgotten you were born here. And, of course, these hills are a perfect haven."

"What made you come here, then?" she wondered.

"After Hadrian's death the new emperor, Antonius Pius, was gradually persuaded to relax the ordinances against us. I don't mind telling you that the Jews of Rome did all they could to help bring this about. History may make no note of it, but you can take my word for it. Anyway, with things easing up a bit, I was determined to come back and scour every inch of this land before giving you up for good. I found Mesha and Beruria—they told me where to find you. And they told me about the boy."

She nodded.

"He's beautiful, Jara. I can't believe I'm so blessed. Finding you both . . ." He brushed her hair with his lips.

"He's very clever," she said shyly, proudly. She felt awkward in his arms. It had been so long; so much had happened in the years they'd been apart. He was dressed so fine, like a prince, as he'd been the first time she'd seen him, sitting beside Hadrian. For all the dreams in which she'd conjured up his image, all her memories, he was a stranger. A stranger . . .

"What is it?" he asked, sensing her confusion.

"Nothing. I . . . I guess I'm just not used to miracles."

"It's no miracle, Jara. I'm as stubborn as you are. After finding the one female in the world that I wanted by my side, I wasn't about to give you up again. I never stopped believing, and I never stopped searching."

"What about Miri?"

"Miri? How do you know about—" He stopped, shook his head in wonder. "You women are amazing! After all this time and all we've been through. . . ." He started to laugh. "Miri's been married to my cousin for the last seven years! She has three children, and from the looks of her when I left, another is on the way." Smiling, he drew her back into his arms. "I'm sure you'll find her to be a good friend when we return to Rome."

"Rome! No . . . I . . . I can't. I . . . Rome, you say?"

"You don't suppose I'd allow you and my son to go on living like this, do you? Besides, it isn't safe. Everyone is so crazy here, another rebellion could very well break out."

"What if it did?" She was defiant.

"It would be less than hopeless, it would be pathetic. It's over, Jara. Here, it's over. Do you think Simeon's going to rise up from the dead and lead an army of corpses—" He stopped. The expression on his face changed. "That's it, isn't it?" he said slowly. "Simeon. Bar Kokhba. All these years. . . . It wasn't me you waited for," he exploded angrily, "but Simeon! You think he's still alive. . . . Just as I never gave up hope about you. How disappointing it must be," he said with bitter civility, "seeing me again, and not him."

"Stop it!"

"Well, it doesn't matter, because I'm getting you and the boy out of here whether you like it or not! And by the way, thank you for not naming him Simeon."

"Stop . . . Andreas, stop. . . . I love you! Oh, please, you must see that! I love you!"

He caught her to him fiercely now, but it was she who covered his face with kisses, who sought his mouth hungrily as all the feelings he aroused, all the emotion and longing she had checked for so long, at last broke free. "I love you," she whispered. "I've never stopped thinking of you, wanting you, and praying, yes, praying, that you were alive."

"And Simeon?"

"You know why. This land—what we are as a people, what we've been—is part of me. I can't just let it go. I can't forget. I can go on, but I can't forget. Simeon will always be part of that."

He was silent a moment. Finally, he nodded as though to say he understood, the look in his eyes indicating he shared her feelings more than he dared give voice.

She lay her head on his shoulder. "I do love you, Andreas. And I've borne your child. There's a bond between us now stronger and deeper than anything. I want to be with you and live with you . . . but not in Rome. Not there!"

"Then we'll go to Parthia. We'll get a villa in Nehardea— everything the best, dozens of servants! You'll have a different gown for every hour of the day, jewels. . . ." He kissed her again. "I'm going to spoil you rotten!" He grinned. "Wait until the *Resh ha-Galut* sees you. And they think Sassanid women are beautiful! What is it? What's wrong?" She'd broken away again.

"I . . . I'm afraid. . . ."

"You? I don't believe it. Anyway, there's nothing to fear. The Jews in Parthia are free—"

"Not that. I . . . I don't belong in the world you know. All those people with their beautiful gowns and jewels. I . . . I don't know if I could be with them."

"You'd be with me," he said firmly. "Jara, I don't believe

I'm hearing this from you. It doesn't make sense after all you've been through—"

"Yes! After all I've been through! I've lived like an animal! Alone, barefoot, a baby at my breast . . . running, and hiding at the sound of leaves blown by the wind! I've stolen food from people who barely had enough for themselves. I've killed a man, Andreas. But you already know about that. And I—" She broke off, swallowed. "And you expect me to dress like one of your fancy ladies and sit politely among all those rich, fat friends of yours who were drinking wine and licking their fingers while we were fighting and dying here!"

"In the first place," he replied coldly, "I was here, too. Remember? And you will find many in Parthia whose stories rival your own, even some who fought with Simeon. As for my 'rich, fat friends,' well . . . one of the things I'm going to have to teach you, my darling, is that there are ways of fighting for what you want that have nothing to do with swords and lances." He took her hands in his. "If it makes you feel any better, know that there's still work to be done. Refugees arrive in Parthia every day. They need help. And there are thousands of slaves to be ransomed. All this while trying to see that what happened to our people here doesn't happen elsewhere. It will be hard for you," he admitted. "You don't know what it's like to be a citizen of a country that will never be your homeland. It takes a certain kind of alertness, a certain courage that is different from that shown by men like Bar Kokhba, but every bit as demanding." He kissed her hands. "If that's what worries you, I understand. As for the other, manners and such . . . well, there's something you ought to know.

"I am a wealthy man by any standards in the world. My family has survived six emperors and two wars, during which time our assets have not only remained undiminished, but expanded to a very large degree. That alone can buy freedom, Jara, and, I'm sorry to say, a certain respect. All that I possess is yours. No one has more right to it, not only because you are my wife and the mother of my son, but because the very foundation of all that I am heir to rests upon the house of Harsom from which you are descended.

"My grandfather," he went on quietly, "was the man called Josephus. Alexandra of the house of Harsom was brought to him in Caesarea and given to him a wife by the emperor Vespasian, who at that time," he added wryly, "was merely a general. Josef ben Matthias, as he was known in Jerusalem, was himself a prisoner of Rome. He was eventually released and, the story goes, held in high esteem by Vespasian for prophesying his ascension to the throne. Alexandra—your grandmother, Jara—left him. All her family's property was given to my grandfather, who now called himself Flavius Josephus, along with other rewards. By the way, most of the villages in the King's Mountain were the possession of one of your forebears, Eleazar ben Harsom, who served as a high priest for eleven years. That land became Josephus' land, and eventually mine. I'm sorry I can't give it back to you, but unfortunately it's out of my hands now. And, by the way, my father was not unaware of the rebel activity there.

"Josephus settled in Rome, in style, I might add. He married again—twice. But he never forgot Alexandra. For years he made inquiry of slave dealers, slaves—anyone from Judea. Finally, a woman was brought to him who had survived the Masada. Knowing that my grandfather was writing a history of the war, Vespasian had given orders that all extraordinary captives were to be given to him to be interviewed. The female in question had the name Miriam. She remained with the family, becoming a member of the household and helping to care for the children. My father loved her, I think, more than his own mother. I never knew her. She died before I was born. But I knew about Alexandra of the house of Harsom. Before he died, Flavius Josephus told my father all about her, and much more. That knowledge was passed on to me. I found it an odd, interesting tale, but never gave it further thought until we found that old gate in Jerusalem. I almost told you then . . . who I was . . . but I thought if I did, you would hate me even more than you already did."

"Did I hate you?" she wondered.

He laughed. "You certainly did! And the way you carried on so about 'the traitor Josephus,' I thought for certain you'd stick that funny little knife of yours in my gut first chance you got."

"I used to think that knife belonged to my grandfather," she mused, still caught up in what he'd told her. *Eleazar ben Ya'ir. Josephus. Alexandra of the house of Harsom.* The ancient visage of the Old One suddenly loomed before her, and

Jara could hear as she had when she was a child the woman's dry, cracked voice with its alien accent making a strange music as she spun out the past, those glittering threads of love and deceit and rebellion that had been emblazoned on the girl's mind and heart for so many years.

The Old One had chosen Jara, of all the others, to remember. She had chosen well. Nothing was forgotten, and it was perhaps that finely tuned memory combined with the special awareness which Jacob of Kefar Sakanya had sensed kindred to his own powers that had caused such immediate and violent antipathy to the young man she had first seen sitting at Hadrian's table. It was more than the fact she had believed him to be a Roman, more even than, later, she resented his bold and teasing manner. She suddenly realized that from the first moment she had ever set eyes on Andreas, she had thought that he looked exactly as she had always imagined Josef ben Matthias—Josephus—must have looked, and all that Andreas had confessed to her now, somehow she had always known—just as she'd known Florus Valerens would come for her, that Simeon ben Kosiba would become the man Bar Kokhba, that Jacob would be murdered and Sharona had not been killed, and that Akiva would meet his end soon after she saw him.

Just as she had known, always, that Andreas was not dead. And that Simeon was.

All of this came to her now, and the images too that had swirled about the ruined courtyard of the priest Shammai in the city of Jerusalem. Then the faces of the dead disappeared, and before her stood the man who had traveled half the earth to find her, who had made her his wife, set his seed inside her, and who loved her as she loved him.

"The Sicarii knife," she said dreamily. "I still have it. You brought it out of Betar, do you remember?"

"It's time to put away those weapons, Jara. Time to put aside the bloodied past, the ghosts," he confessed, "that haunt us both. I don't need to run anymore from what I am, to prove to the world and to myself that I'm not Josephus. And you, my darling . . . it's time for you to go out into the world, to live as other people live, without war and isolation."

To go out into the world . . . far beyond the boats of Tiberias. . . .

He had touched something she'd kept buried for so long,

forbidden herself even to dream of as she had forbidden
herself to speak his name during the years they'd been apart.
Now the white wings of the dove fluttered, longing yet hardly
daring to fly free, and the sound inside her head was like
someone singing.

She sighed. "If that were only possible."

He gripped her arms tightly, the look in his eyes not daring
and devilish but steady and sure; strength flowed from his
hands, warm and certain. "It is possible. I promise. Our lives
are just beginning."

THEY SET OUT FROM the Galilee the next day. The ship—
Andreas' ship—which was named the *Star* lay anchored in
Jaffa. They would leave it at Antioch and then make their way
east, across land.

Although certain localities were utterly devastated, the
countryside was beginning to show signs of recovery, as it had
after the earlier war with Rome. But the new settlements were
not built for Jews, not even as tenant workers. The Jewish
farmer had been displaced in the South and would soon disappear from the North of the country as well. The exodus from
village to city, abetted by the rabbis, who now encouraged
employment in trade and crafts, was part of the larger
Diaspora from Palestine to other lands that had now begun.
Jaffa was filled with families seeking passage on its ships; the
roads teemed with travelers hoping for a better life. Within
another century, the once-thriving fields and orchards of the
Land of Milk and Honey would be abandoned or turned into
pastures, as its new owners appeared neither to feel an attach-
ment to the land nor to possess the skills of their predecessors.
Forest and desert would encroach upon the deserted farms,
most of the coastal plain would become swamp and
wasteland, and the Jew's talent for agriculture would fade
even from his own memory.

AS THEY WERE PREPARING to board ship, Jara felt a slight
touch on her shoulder and turned around to find herself staring into the smiling eyes of the young woman she had known
as Sharona. Surprise and delight written in her expression, she

immediately embraced the new Christian, who responded shyly but eagerly.

"I wasn't sure you'd remember me."

Taken aback momentarily, Jara responded heartily, "How could I forget? Your name is . . . Suzannah."

"Yes." Was there something unspoken behind the serene gaze? "Yes." She smiled. "Suzannah."

"And do you remember my name?"

Again, there seemed to be more in her eyes than the words she spoke. "How could I forget?" she echoed softly. "Jara. . . ."

Kin, they stood there a moment, each holding the other's hands, saying nothing and everything.

"Are you sailing?" Jara asked at last.

"No, we are come to Jaffa to visit with friends on the holy day of Resurrection. And you?"

"We will be going to Parthia, by way of Antioch. That is my husband you see aboard ship. That is my son in his arms."

"They are both very handsome." She smiled. "As we used to imagine . . ."

Jara looked at her, but there was nothing further. "Goodbye," she said at last.

Sharona leaned forward and kissed her. "Go with God," she said softly. "My sister."

"And you. *Shalom*. Be well."

Jara made her way up the gangplank now, a young woman of remarkable beauty and grace. No one looking at her would suspect what she had gone through: war, pestilence, and poverty. But for all she had seen and done, her life, as Andreas had said, was just beginning. When she set foot in the magnificent villa of which she would be mistress for many, many years, she would be only twenty-two years old.

THE SHIP WAS SAILING. As Jara stood at the rail, looking back, a host of memories seemed to rise from the sea and dance on the waves. Once more she found herself recalling the boats of the fishermen bobbing on the Sea of Galilee, saw herself as she had been then . . . standing on the shore, licking salty oil from her fingers, hearing the vendor ask if she wanted another fish, she seemed so hungry, when what it was she'd wanted, her heart near bursting with longing for, was . . . what?

They'd fought. And died. For something that now seemed to have no more substance than a passing cloud in the sky, or a shadow looming large, then gone. Or a dream. . . .

Even the land was fading from view, receding in the mist of spray and sun, soon to be lost in the falling night.

"Bidding goodbye to Palestine, miss?" It was one of the sailors. He'd meant to be friendly, but the look in her eyes as she whirled around at the sound of that hated name was enough to freeze the smile on his face. Before she could reply, however, someone else cried, "Look! Look!"

Lights like small stars were twinkling from the dark hills behind. Bonfires had been kindled on all the mountain crests.

"What can that be?" the sailor wondered. "What does it mean?"

"When the Sanhedrin met, it determined the calendar by reckoning the moon," Andreas said thoughtfully. "The people were informed by means of such signals. But there is no Sanhedrin now." He looked up at the sky. "As for the moon, there does not seem to be . . . Wait. Fires after sunset . . . A holy day, perhaps. Yes, it must be that. This time of year . . . Passover! Of course! It's the Passover! But how—"

"Akiva's calendar," Jara said. "It was the last thing he did." She gripped the rail hard now, her eyes fixed on the spots of light illuminating the darkness. And suddenly she saw the face of Simeon ben Kosiba, as clearly as if he were standing before her, and heard his voice like a voice in her sleep.

You may say you have destroyed us, and even then a woman will be kindling the Sabbath lights and a child will be learning Torah. And the moment those candles flame, I and all who have died live again.

She caught her breath. The fires on the hills were growing smaller with each dip of the galley's oars. She leaned forward, as loath to give them up as the land whose presence they marked. Smaller and smaller they seemed, yet never out of sight. . . .

I'll be back.

I'll be back, this I vow.

Someday I'll come back.

And if not I, then my children. And if not my sons and daughters, then their sons and daughters.

We'll be back.

Someday, we'll be back.
And you will be ours again.

There was the sound of singing. A group of passengers had gathered at the rail, and now they began to chant the age-old refrain, "*David, melekh Yisrael! Hai! Hai! Vi-ki-yom.* . . ."

Benjamin Ami was not asleep on his father's shoulder after all; he suddenly raised his curly head and began to sing with the others, to Andreas' great amusement. Jara smiled too, realizing it was the first song she had taught the boy, just as it was the first one she had ever learned. She touched the child's cheek. "*Am Yisrael hai,*" she murmured.

"What?" Andreas asked, glad to see her smiling. A moment before, as she stared out to sea, the look in her eyes had been the same look he'd come to know as Bar Kokhba's, seen in Simeon's eyes so many times.

Simeon was still with them. He'd always be with them, but in a way, Andreas knew, he could accept.

Yet now, he thought, seeing Jara smile at the child reminded him of Akiva, and he wondered why that should be so, although he welcomed it.

He smiled too. "What did you say just now?"

Jara looked up at him. Her eyes, so bright in the dark, glowed like the lights on the faraway hills, a fire that would never die, a light that would never go out.

"*Am Yisrael hai,*" she said again. "Israel lives."

Author's Note

I GATHERED MUCH of the historical background for this novel in the course of research for *The Tenth Measure*, which was the story of the first Judeo-Roman war, ending with the fall of Masada in 73 C.E. Many times during my work on *If I Forget Thee*, I found myself wishing that "the revolt of Bar Kokhba," like the earlier war, had had a Flavius Josephus to record it. Instead, I have relied on those few historical accounts of the conflict that have come down to us, on the conclusions of such modern scholars as Shimon Applebaum and Mordecai Gichon, and most of all on the discoveries made by Israeli archeologists in 1960–1961 that are wonderfully recorded by Yigael Yadin and have served as my primary source of information and inspiration. I am also grateful to my good friend Dr. Emanuel Tov of Hebrew University for taking the time to help me coordinate my studies and field work.

For centuries, Bar Kokhba was legend among the displaced Jews, a national hero much like King Arthur. His existence was documented by contemporary historians during Hadrian's reign, by writings of the early Church fathers like Eusebius and Jerome, and by descriptions in the Talmud and the Midrash. But all this information put together was so scanty, albeit intriguing, that everything about Bar Kokhba was, until recently, seriously debated. Then, in 1951–1952, Bedouins of the same Ta'amirah tribe that had discovered the Dead Sea Scrolls offered for sale some documents they had found in a cave in the Judean Desert. Among these was a papyrus that began with the following words: "From Simeon ben Kosiba to Yeshua ben Galgola and the people of the fort, *Shalom.*"

Nearly ten more years would pass before Israeli archeologists would be able to make a thorough search of the area, but the finds at Wadi Murabba'at were to yield rich treasure. Letters, utensils, and articles of clothing—items hidden by the rebels and their families fleeing the Roman legions—were unearthed after long centuries of darkness, along with the names of Yehonatan (Jonathan), Masabala, Yehuda (Judah) bar Menasha, Ben Galgoula, a mysterious courier known only as Elisha, and even a woman named Babata, whose entire life could be reconstructed from the documents neatly stored in a willow basket.

But for all the new information, very little is known to this day about the actual course of the war—and absolutely nothing about the personal life of Simeon ben Kosiba, the man called "Bar Kokhba," who signed his letters "*Nasi* of Israel."

The letters reveal a terse, plainspoken, no-nonsense commander. Simeon's victories, however temporary, are evidence of military acumen, and the messianic overtones of the revolt suggest a charismatic personality. Historical descriptions tell us that he was extremely courageous and possessed of enormous physical strength. The camaraderie that must have existed among "the Brothers" is seen again and again in the Murabba'at letters, which invariably end with the words, "Be well." (One packet of letters must have been written at the very end of the war. Only poignant fragments survive: "till the end," "they have no hope," "my brothers in the south," "of these were lost by the sword," "these my brothers.")

Perhaps the real clue, however, to the kind of man Simeon ben Kosiba was lies not in what we know about him but in what we know of his mentor Akiva, who remains one of the most beloved figures in Jewish history. The scene of his death, indelibly impressed on the eyes of Joshua ha-Garsi, gave rise to a particular Jewish tradition: the recitation of the *Shema* as a deathbed affirmation of faith.

All of the rabbinic figures in *If I Forget Thee*, with the exception of Kawzbeel, are real, as opposed to fictional, characters. They are a fascinating crew, from Elisha ben Abuyah, sometimes called "the Faust of Judaism," to Joshua ben Hananiah, who developed such skill as an astronomer (selftaught) that he was able to predict the phenomenon later known as Halley's comet.

While the character called Obodas in this novel is fictitious, his name is that of a real Nabatean king (alternate spelling: Avdat)—in fact, three of them. The last Nabatean monarch was Rabel II (70–106 C.E.), who would ostensibly have been the father of ben Kosiba's friend. (Friendship between the Jews and Nabateans of this period is documented in the Bar Kokhba finds; for example, Babata's son had a Nabatean guardian.)

Jacob of Kefar Haruba is a real figure of the period, a Judeo-Christian who seems to have conversed with rabbis and was known to "utter charms over wounds" in the name of "Jesus son of Pantira." The Ebionites are described by the Church Father Irenaeus (125–202 C.E.), Justin Martyr, and Eusebius. There appear to be only two major original texts that reveal the sect's beliefs, one of which is *Kerygmata Petri*, and I am indebted to *Christian Centuries: First Six Hundred Years*, by Jean Danielou and Henri Marrou, for an overview of the period. Once the teachings of Paul became Church doctrine, the Judeo-Christian groups began to be excluded as heretical, and sects such as the Nazarenes, Elchasites, and the Ebionites ultimately disappeared.

The Roman characters Quintus, Andreas, and Valerens are creatures of my imagination. Or are they? Long after this novel was begun, I stumbled across an old book in the University of Pennsylvania Library: *Proceedings of the Society of Biblical Archaeology*, 1898. With visions straight out of Jules Verne of well-fed Englishmen sitting in the large leather chairs of a London club, I picked up the fragile volume and began to turn the pages gently, when I came upon a report of the "Meeting, held on the 11th January, 1898," during which a Mr. Joseph Offord read a paper entitled, "Roman Inscriptions relating to Hadrian's Jewish War." And there, in Mr. Offord's account of the numbers of Roman legionaries and auxiliaries employed in "the suppression of this Jewish revolt," demonstrating "how serious a menace the revolt of Bar Cochba was to the Roman power," appeared a reference to a document "found in the Hauran" that listed a centurion named—Quintus Flavius.

Hadrian, of course, is real, as is the Bithynian slave boy Antinous, of whom there are a great many sculptures. While Hadrian has generally been regarded as a competent, civilized ruler, a man of exquisite taste and humanistic philosophy, he remains an anathema to the Jews. After Betar, the most strin-

gent regulations forbidding the study and practice of the
Jewish faith since the time of Antiochus were put into effect,
remaining law until Hadrian's death. (The war and Antinous'
death, however, seem to have destroyed Hadrian. There is no
doubt that his charm, outgoing personality, and intellectual
curiosity were jolted, and upon his return to Rome he appeared disillusioned, misanthropic, suddenly old. He died of a
painful illness three years later.)

Beruria is one of the few women mentioned in the Talmud.
By all accounts she was remarkable. While I have fictionalized
her romance with Rabbi Meir, she was indeed married to him,
and the traits of her personality are strongly suggested in the
Talmud (which is the source of the story, among others, in
which Rabbi Yossi asks directions to Lod). I want to make this
latter point clear because I am sometimes charged with creat-
ing heroines who are too enlightened for their time, implying
that any intelligent, adventuresome, and courageous woman
character found in a setting prior to the last ten years must be
anachronistic. I refer such skeptics to the historical passages
concerning Beruria. No doubt they will find interesting a later
legend to the effect that, in retribution for her pretensions to
being above "feminine weakness," she was led astray by one
of her students and ultimately committed suicide. Most
modern scholars, I might add, discount this story.

Unlike Beruria, Jara is fictitious; the only historical basis
for her character is the inspiration provided by such biblical
heroines as Devorah and Judith and by the long line of
courageous women who have fulfilled one of Judaism's most
dearly held tenets, found in Proverbs:

> A woman of valor who can find?
> For her price is far above rubies. . . .
> Strength and dignity are her clothing;
> She laugheth at the time to come.

But to return to the enigma of Simeon ben Kosiba. Embit-
tered by persecution and terrified that any resurgence of
militarism would provoke out-and-out genocide, the rabbis
who came after him apparently did all they could to tarnish, if
not to eradicate completely, his memory. The Talmud speaks
of him briefly, calling him "Bar Koziba"—a deceiver—and
remains silent regarding the triumphs that, ironically, were

fully recorded by Roman historians.

Nevertheless, the legend lingered. In the centuries that followed the events of this book, "Bar Kokhba," as well as "Bar Daroma" and "the Brothers of Kefar Haruba," would become cherished names to Jewish children who, to this day, play "Bar Kokhba and the Romans" with makeshift bows and arrows at the yearly festival of Lag Ba'omer. Down through the ages, the stories, like a fleeting dream, cast a glimmer, a spark, a small light that would become a flame in the darkness of the Warsaw Ghetto and, finally, the blaze that would reclaim the land of Israel.

—Brenda Lesley Segal
January 1983

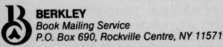